EIGHT DAYS TO LIVE

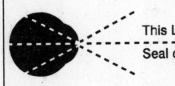

This Large Print Book carries the
Seal of Approval of N.A.V.H.

EIGHT DAYS TO LIVE

IRIS JOHANSEN

THORNDIKE PRESS
A part of Gale, Cengage Learning

GALE
CENGAGE Learning™

Detroit • New York • San Francisco • New Haven, Conn • Waterville, Maine • London

GALE
CENGAGE Learning

Thorndike Press® Large Print Basic.
The text of this Large Print edition is unabridged.
Other aspects of the book may vary from the original edition.
Set in 16 pt. Plantin.

LIBRARY OF CONGRESS CATALOGING-IN-PUBLICATION DATA

Johansen, Iris.
  Eight days to live / by Iris Johansen.
    p. cm. — (Thorndike Press large print basic)
  ISBN-13: 978-1-4104-2524-9 (alk. paper)
  ISBN-10: 1-4104-2524-X (alk. paper)
    1. Duncan, Eve (Fictitious character)—Fiction. 2. Artists—Fiction. 3. Paintings—Fiction. 4. Cults—Fiction. 5. Human sacrifice—Fiction. 6. Large type books. I. Title.
  PS3560.O275E44 2010b
  813'.54—dc22   2009053872

Published in 2010 by arrangement with St. Martin's Press, LLC

Printed in the United States of America
1 2 3 4 5 6 7 14 13 12 11 10

Eight Days to Live

ONE

Paris
Day One
7:35 p.m.

She was laughing, Jack Millet thought, enraged. Even as Jane MacGuire had left the sidewalk café, a lingering smile had remained on her lips.

He had to smother the anger, remind himself that she would not be laughing for very long.

Eight days, bitch. Just eight more days, and I'll send you to rot in hell.

He had watched her sitting there in the café, staring out at the Seine, and the seething anger had been building steadily within him. She had no right to look that serene and content.

Liar.

Blasphemer.

He started after her, careful not to get close enough for her to know she was being followed. He knew where she was going. The Denarve Art Gallery was only two blocks away and tonight they were exhibiting Jane MacGuire's paintings and would probably be heaping praise on her.

Blind. They couldn't see the ugliness of the atrocity she had committed.

She moved lithely, gracefully, her red-brown hair shining as the sunlight burnished it. Everything about her shouted that she was young and vibrantly alive.

And that enraged him, too.

Dead. You should be dead. You should be burning in Hell.

Eight days. But he wanted it to happen now. It was a deep hunger that wouldn't go away.

But if he could hurt her, it would help him to wait for that final glory. If he could rip and tear at her and destroy everything she valued and loved, he might be able to keep himself under control.

Take her, torture her, and make her scream with agony.

But he had to do it himself. He could order help in the taking, perhaps Folard, but after that, he couldn't trust his brothers to be able to stop themselves from killing her before her time. Their souls weren't as strong as his had become through all the years of service to the Offering.

She was quickening her steps as she approached the gallery. The sun was going down, and the rays of the setting sun were causing her hair to blaze with fiery highlights.

Blaze. Scald. Burn. Suffer.

Yes, fire is an exquisite weapon. Knives. Scalpels. Whips. There are so many ways to hurt you, Jane MacGuire.

I know them all.

Malevolence.

Overwhelming malice.

Jane stopped, stiffening, as her hand reached out to open the carved oak door of the Denarve Gallery.

For an instant she couldn't breathe, and she instinctively glanced back over her shoulder at the street behind her.

Nothing. A peaceful Parisian street on a beautiful spring day. No threat.

Imagination. A trick of the mind. Maybe a little nervous reaction because of the show tonight?

But she didn't usually have nerves.

She glanced over her shoulder again.

Nothing.

Imagination.

She pulled open the carved oak door and

went into the gallery.

"There you are." Celine Denarve turned to Jane and frowned with mock indignation. "I thought I was going to have to send the bloodhounds after you. Marie and I have been slaving with the preparations to make this exhibit the finest I've ever given for any artist, and you go strolling off as if it has no importance. It's an insult."

Jane grinned. "You know that you would have whisked me out of here if I'd offered to stay and help." Celine was reacting with her usual sense of Gallic drama, and it always amused Jane. High drama was so far removed from her own practical character. She had flashes of intensity and recklessness, and that might be why she and Celine had so quickly become friends, but it was Celine's basic shrewdness and kindness that had cemented that friendship. "How many times have you told me that an artist should paint and stay out of the business of selling her work?"

"Many times." Celine turned to her assistant, Marie Ressault, who had come out of the office carrying an ice bucket. "Put it at the bar, Marie. If I give everyone enough champagne, they will forget that Jane's not really the Rembrandt I've been hyping for the past month."

10

"I believe those art critics may already be a little skeptical," Jane said dryly. "Though if anyone could convince them, you could."

"You're right. I'm splendid." She smiled brilliantly at Jane. In her late thirties, Celine was sleek and dark-haired and as attractive as she was shrewd. She might know every trick in the book about pushing a young-and-coming artist up the next rung of the ladder, but she did it with honesty and a bubbly exuberance. "That's what it takes to make a starving artist an icon."

"I hate to tell you, but I'm not a starving artist. I did have a few successful shows before you appeared in my life."

"Yes, but those other gallery owners didn't make you focus on the important things. They should have made you do publicity to make you a household name."

"Not my cup of tea."

Celine made a face. "That's why you make my life so difficult. I have to work twice as hard just to make you show up for an interview. I've begun to tell everyone that they have to forgive you because, after all, you're just an artist with a shy and sensitive soul."

"What?"

"It works," Celine said cheerfully. "They don't know you."

11

"That's obvious." Sensitive soul? she thought with amusement. She couldn't think of any term that would be less applicable. She hoped she was kind and caring and could see beneath the surface, but she was neither fragile nor temperamental. She was only a street kid who had been lucky enough to have been born with a certain talent and the drive to make that talent come alive.

She smiled as she thought about what Joe Quinn would have said about her sensitive soul. She had been a tough ten-year-old when she had come to live with Joe and Eve Duncan, and they had accepted her and made sure that she knew how to handle herself in any situation. He was a detective with the Atlanta Police Department, and his teaching had been both thorough and intense. Karate, Choi Kwang Do, and, when she grew older, training in weaponry. Those lessons had forged a bond that had helped draw them closer, and it was her very good fortune that she hadn't been a prissy kid who would have forced Joe to treat her delicately. No, he would have laughed himself silly at anyone thinking she was overly sensitive.

"You're smiling." Celine was studying her face. "What are you thinking?"

"That you must be very persuasive to make them believe that bullshit."

"Yes, I am extraordinary." She took a step back and tilted her head as she gazed at the paintings beyond the velvet ropes. "The lighting is perfect. That's essential, you know."

Jane's lips quirked. "Yes, it makes even my humble paintings look good."

"That's what I thought." She glanced away from the paintings to Jane. "But perhaps they're not completely humble. I didn't totally lie when I told those critics you were the next Rembrandt."

"Crap."

"No, you're exceptional. You're young, only a few years out of college. In another five years, you'll rock the art world. If you'll let me help you." She shrugged and changed the subject. "Lighting may help your paintings, but no amount of lighting is going to help you if you're dressed in those jeans and shirt. Not here in Paris. Hurry. Go upstairs and change. The first guests should be here in forty-five minutes."

"I'll be ready." Jane headed for the elevator. Celine maintained an apartment above her gallery, and she had insisted that Jane stay with her before the exhibit. "I promise."

"You cut it very close," Celine called after

her. "Where did you go?"

"Just for a walk, then to the café to have a glass of wine. I thought I'd relax before the hullabaloo tonight."

"It will be a very elegant hullabaloo. Did it work? Did it relax you?"

"Yes." She had a sudden memory of that moment just before she had entered the gallery and that feeling of malevolence so intense that it had shaken her. Imagination. It had to be imagination. "For the most part." She got into the elevator and firmly dismissed that chilling moment from her mind. "Yes, I guess it worked."

10:45 p.m.

"A wonderful show." Celine Denarve locked the door of the gallery after her assistant, Marie, had left. "A *magnificent* exhibit. We've sold everything but the three paintings you've put a hold on." She smiled over her shoulder at Jane. "How can I convince you to let me sell those, too? How am I to become a rich woman if you persist in being selfish with the best of the lot?"

"They're not the best of the lot. I just have a personal attachment to them," Jane said. "The technique is much cleaner in some of the others." Lord, she was tired. She hated these art shows. The critics who dissected

14

her work, the reporters probing how she felt when she was painting a certain canvas, the people who bought art because it went with their furniture. But she supposed she should be grateful that she'd met with such success so early in her career.

She *was* grateful. And she couldn't have asked for a gallery owner more enthusiastic and devoted than Celine. This was her second show at Celine's gallery and their warm relationship made all the bullshit bearable.

"You look exhausted. You need a glass of champagne." Celine moved toward the small bar against the wall. "Though you shouldn't need any stimulation at all. You should be walking on air. Like I am."

"And so you should. Tonight is as much your triumph as it is mine."

"That is true. I did well." She turned and smiled at Jane. "And you did well, too. You did not look bored. You were actually charming to that art critic from the *London Times*. I think I'm getting through to you."

"Don't count on it. I'm glad it's over. You're right, I am tired." It's only that it has been a very exhausting month, Jane thought. She was ready to go home and close herself away and just paint.

"This will wake you up." Celine poured

them both a glass of champagne, and her gaze went back to the three paintings about which she had been previously talking. "You may not see it, but those paintings are very special." Celine crossed the room and handed the glass to her. "Technique is important, but when there's so much passion, one can overlook a few mistakes."

She frowned. "What mistakes?"

Celine chuckled. "See, you may criticize yourself, but I may not. You have an ego like all artists."

"I never said I didn't." Jane grinned. "I'm no Rembrandt, but I'm pretty good. In spite of what your French critics say. They don't agree that passion is more important. But I do get better all the time."

"The proof is in the pocketbook," Celine said. "And name me a great artist who didn't suffer for their art." She strolled up to the two paintings at the end of the row. "Me, I prefer to sell your paintings and not suffer at all. My commission will buy me a fine house on the Riviera." She tapped the frame of the painting of the castle that towered on a steep cliff that overlooked the sea. "Not like this one. It's much too forbidding. I don't like Scotland. Not enough sun." She tilted her head. "But you must like it. That castle has substance and power.

It's very . . . strong."

"I don't know much about Scotland. I've only visited MacDuff's Run a few times."

"But it had great impact on you."

"Yes." She took a sip of her champagne. "You could call it impact."

"I've met John MacDuff. He was here for a charity ball several years ago. I was dazzled. Earl of Cranought, Lord of MacDuff's Run . . . It's hard to ignore all that intensity and Rob Roy mystique."

"I assure you that he's no Rob Roy." Though the people on his property looked upon him as something of a folk hero and kowtowed to the Laird. MacDuff had won a gold medal for archery several years ago at the Olympics, then joined the 45th Commando Unit of the Royal Marines and earned a chestful of medals for bravery. "And he's arrogant as hell."

"But he's sexy enough to get away with it," Celine said. "I tried to throw myself into his bed, but he would have none of me."

"Then he was a fool."

Celine nodded. "I think so, too. He doesn't know what he missed." She glanced slyly at Jane. "Tell me, did you make it into his bed? I'll forgive you if you let me sell this painting."

Jane shook her head. "Our relationship

17

was a little more complicated."

"Nothing is more complicated than sex," Celine said. "Nor anything so beautifully simple."

Jane chuckled. "You're just trying to live up to your image as a Parisienne."

"I don't need to live up to it. I live and breathe it." She added teasingly, "Come now, tell me the truth. If you visited that cold castle more than once, he must have offered you a warm bed to lure you. Why else would you go there?"

Celine clearly wasn't going to give up. Just give her the bare bones and make her happy. "Actually, it had to do with a chest of gold coins, a lost ancient family treasure belonging to one of MacDuff's ancestors. I'd become involved with tracing that chest from its origin in Herculaneum."

"Ah, a lost treasure." Celine's eyes were wide and shining. "Tell me more."

"There's not much more to tell. You wouldn't be interested."

"Which means you're closing up and don't want to share." She was obviously disappointed. "I would be interested, you know. I'm not just being inquisitive. I consider you my friend as well as my client. It's natural to want to know about people you care about." She shrugged, but her

18

expression was wistful. "But I will try to understand."

Jane stared helplessly at her. Celine was an irresistible force who was all the more appealing because she was sincere. "It's no big deal." Though those weeks at MacDuff's Run had shaken her entire life at the time. "It was years ago, when I was a student in college. I was an art major with a minor in archaeology. I became interested in stories of a young actress, Cira, who was the toast of ancient Herculaneum. She fascinated me. It was rumored that she had escaped the eruption of Vesuvius and fled to Scotland, carrying with her a chest of gold coins that would be worth a fortune today."

"But you said it was a long-lost MacDuff treasure."

"Cira changed her name and identity and she and her husband, Anthony, founded the MacDuff family in the highlands."

"And you went to Scotland to find the chest and found MacDuff. Now that's a treasure I can appreciate. How romantic."

"Not at all romantic. I wasn't the only one trying to trace that chest. Thomas Reilly, a criminal who would take first place on any scumbag chart, was after it, too. He was interested in some specific coins that were supposed to be included with the others.

19

Before it was over it got very ugly. Good people were hurt."

"But you and MacDuff found the chest and lived happily ever after . . . in bed?"

"No, in the end finding the treasure wasn't worth it to me."

Celine shook her head reprovingly. "Treasure of any kind is always worthwhile. This story is very disappointing to me."

Jane smiled. "Sorry, I'll try to concoct a more interesting tale for you next time."

"Please do that. I'm losing faith in you." She glanced at the portrait next to the one of MacDuff's Run. "You said this was one of the young men who grew up on MacDuff's estate? Jock . . . ?

"Jock Gavin. Yes, his mother was housekeeper at the estate, and he grew up running in and out of the castle. He was like a younger brother to MacDuff."

"He's quite beautiful, almost an Adonis with that fair hair and those silver-gray eyes. But he's too young for you."

"There wasn't anything like that between us. I painted that portrait years ago. He was nineteen when I did that first sketch. I was only a couple years older and we . . . bonded. Jock was going through a rough time, and I was able to help him through it."

"Nineteen. He looks younger." She frowned. "And older. I can't quite put my finger on it. There's a kind of an explosive breakability. Intriguing. What kind of a rough time?"

Jane was silent a moment, then said reluctantly, "He was close to a breakdown."

"Why?"

Jane didn't answer.

Celine's gaze narrowed on her face. "You don't want to talk about it. You were willing to tell me all about MacDuff and that silly treasure but not about this beautiful boy. That's even more intriguing."

I don't have the right to talk about it, Jane thought. Celine might be a good friend, but Jane was still fiercely protective of Jock. What was she going to say about him? That boy you think so beautiful had been chemically brainwashed and trained as an assassin by Thomas Reilly? That gentle kid was one of the good people who had been twisted and hurt? Jock, who had already killed over twenty people before that portrait had been painted? Jock, the boy who had tried to commit suicide three times before she and John MacDuff were able to break through to him and bring him back to sanity?

No, that was just between her and Jock Gavin and would remain that way. "He's

my friend. I don't gossip about my friends."
She added teasingly, "Which should make
you happy. I could have a field day if I
decided to gossip about all your affairs."

"I wouldn't care. It would only make me
seem more fascinating. But it's good to
know that I could trust you." She smiled.
"More champagne?"

"No, I haven't finished this one."

"Too bad. I'm trying to get you a little
mellow."

"So that I'll let you sell the painting of
MacDuff's Run?"

"No, I'll let you keep that one. And the
portrait of the beautiful boy." She sipped
her champagne. "I was only leading into my
big pitch."

Jane gazed at her warily. "Celine?"

Celine moved to the next painting. "Now
this is a painting that I feel it is my duty to
take off your hands. True, it also has impact.
But who would want to keep it with them
all the time? It's depressing. Even the title.
Guilt. What is that supposed to mean?"

Jane stared at the man's face in the portrait. He was bearded, his cheeks sunken,
his dark eyes burning. She had painted that
face years ago. It was one of her works that
had been a compulsive obsession until she
had finished it. And, once created, she

hadn't been able to let it go. "I have no idea. He doesn't exist except in my imagination."

And in those dreams that had occurred over and over until she had completed the painting.

Dreams . . .

No, she wasn't going to mention those dreams, not even to Celine. "*Guilt* seemed right at the time."

"You don't know him? He's not your favorite uncle or your brother?"

"No."

"Then there's no attachment." She beamed at Jane. "And you can give him up to make us both rich."

"Celine, I told you that —"

"No, no. Wait until I tempt you." Celine pulled a card out of her evening purse. "Donald Sarnoff. Computers. San Francisco. He came to me when the show first started and made an offer on *Guilt*. Very nice. I regretfully refused."

"Good."

"But then he came back fifteen minutes before the show was over. He said that he had to have the painting."

"Too bad. He can't have it."

"Jane, he offered seven hundred thousand dollars for it."

"What?"

Celine nodded. "My darling Jane, you're very successful, but you've not reached that particular pinnacle yet. We'd be foolish to refuse an offer like that. Money is important."

"Yes, it is." Jane glanced back at the canvas. Celine was right about its being an uncomfortable painting. Yet she had never been able to give it up. It owned her as much as she owned it.

But she didn't like to be owned. She had fought it all her life. From the time she was a street kid just trying to survive in the slums of Atlanta.

"Jane?" Celine was softly nudging, wheedling. "I could give a release to the papers, and it would increase your status enormously. It would be a great career move."

Everything Celine was saying was true. But, dammit, she didn't like the idea of her career depending on how much money her painting was worth.

For heaven's sake, that was life. Forget the idealistic bullshit.

"May I sell it?" Celine asked. "Make me rich and yourself famous. What do you say?"

Jane looked back at the tormented face in the portrait. She didn't speak for a long moment. "I say that I may be crazy, but I'm not giving it up." She finished her champagne. "And that I'm tired and want to go to bed."

Celine shook her head. "You are crazy." She shrugged. "But I will keep at you. Maybe I can get this California billionaire to go even higher. You hesitated for a moment." She made a shooing motion. "Go on upstairs and get to bed. I have to make a few phone calls, then I'll set the alarm." She filled her champagne glass again. "Though how you can sleep after such a victory is a mystery to me. I want to go out and celebrate."

Jane smiled. "Then do it. You deserve a celebration. This is the best show I've ever had, and it's all due to you. You're a brilliant woman, Celine."

"Yes, I am." She tilted her head, considering. "And I believe I will go out. *Sacré Bleu,* one of us should do it. I don't know why I like you so much. You're very boring."

"True. But I had a rough week at home before I came back here to your Never-Never Land. I could use a little peace and quiet."

Celine nodded. "You should stay here in Paris. I know you told me how much you love your adopted parents, but they have to be very grim people. Your Joe Quinn is a police detective. And I've read about Eve

Duncan and how famous she is for her forensic sculpting." She gave a mock shudder. "But dealing with all those skulls? Very depressing."

For Celine it would be depressing, Jane thought, so she wouldn't attempt to explain how Eve's work brought final closure to many parents of children who had been lost for years. "They're not grim. They just live in the real world." She looked around the gleaming marble floors and crystal chandeliers of the gallery. "And this is Cinderella's ballroom."

"The real world is what you make it," Celine said. "And I prefer my world beautiful and full of wonderful toys. When I was a child growing up wearing my sister's hand-me-downs, I swore I'd surround myself with nothing but things that were new and fresh and unique." She added, "Like you."

"My work?"

"Yes, yes. But they only reflect what you are. You're like me. You grew up tough, but you didn't let it poison you. You're still full of curiosity and willing to take risks." She nodded at the painting. "But refusing that offer is a very big risk. I'll have to concentrate on showing you the error of your ways."

Jane smiled. "You don't feel like concentrating on anything but celebrating tonight. Go party." She headed for the elevator that would take her to Celine's elegant suite. It was a charming apartment, beautifully decorated and totally private. Celine might be a social butterfly, but she clearly liked to divorce herself from the gallery when she got on the elevator and went to her apartment. As Jane punched the button, she glanced back over her shoulder.

Butterfly indeed. Celine was wearing a black Valentino dress that was the height of sophistication, but she was pulling on a red silk cape that made a brilliant splash of color and caused the ebony darkness beneath it to shimmer. "You look beautiful. Have a good time." She added quietly, "Thank you for everything, Celine. You're right, it was a wonderful show."

"Yes, it was. I did splendidly, didn't I? I can't talk you into coming with me?"

"Not tonight. But I'd love to have dinner with you tomorrow if you don't have plans."

"Then we'll have another celebration tomorrow. We'll go shopping and buy you a midnight blue dress with many sequins, I think. It will be dazzling with that wonderful red-brown hair."

"Sequins aren't my style. And I don't dazzle."

"No, maybe not usually. But you're beautiful and people stare at you and remember your face after they've forgotten all the dazzle around them. But I still think we need a *little* dazzle to set my Paris whirling." She swept toward the door, with the red silk cape flowing behind her like a banner. "Go to bed, you boring person. I'll set the alarm to keep someone from stealing you, but don't expect me in before dawn."

Jane was smiling as she got on the elevator. Celine might not be in before dawn, but she'd be up and working in her gallery by nine. As for Jane, she'd be packing and perhaps spending a few hours walking around Paris before she met Celine for dinner. She loved this city though she never felt totally at home here. It was too sparkling and effervescent. She had been much more at home in Scotland at MacDuff's Run though the castle's grandeur should have intimidated her. Particularly since her time there had been filled with the overwhelming threat engendered by that bastard, Reilly, and his hunt for MacDuff's lost treasure.

Why had she suddenly thought of MacDuff's Run? Why not the lake cottage back in Atlanta?

It must have been Celine talking about the painting and her lust for MacDuff. He

28

had obviously impressed her. Why not? MacDuff was an impressive man, and the force of his personality was pure magnetism. She wasn't sure that Celine had believed her when she'd told her that she hadn't gone to bed with MacDuff. Their relationship had consisted of part ally, part adversary in the past few years. Whenever they were together, he ignited a response in her that always put her on the defensive. She didn't need MacDuff in her life.

The elevator opened, and she stepped out into Celine's apartment. All blues and creams and Louis XV furniture and gorgeous bronze mirrors. Restful, but exquisite. All Celine. Not at all Jane. She'd be glad to get back to the U.S. and the simplicity and comfort of her own apartment.

Day after tomorrow. She'd already made her flight reservations.

For now, shower, crawl into the bed that looked like Marie Antoinette had probably slept in it.

In a few minutes Celine would probably be at a club, flitting from table to table like the butterfly to which Jane had mentally compared her.

Jane didn't envy her at all.

Jane's cell phone was ringing.

She reached out sleepily for the phone on the nightstand.

"Whore."

She was jerked wide-awake at the hoarse male voice.

"Bitch."

"Who is this?"

"Blasphemer."

An obscene caller. She was about to hang up when something occurred to her. "How did you get my cell number, you creep?"

"Liar."

"I'm going to hang up. And then I'm going to call the police and see if they can trace you."

"They won't be able to do it. I have all the angels of paradise on my side."

"I don't believe angels would have anything to do with a slimeball like you. You'd better check your information."

"You sit there spitting foulness at me in your little cocoon above the gallery of sin, Jane MacGuire. You think you're safe."

A chill went through her. Gallery. This was no random obscene call. He was speaking in English. He knew where she was. Who she was. "I am safe."

"Not from me. Not from us."

"Who are you?"

"I've left a calling card at the front door.

Come and get it."

"No way."

"Never mind. I see a taxi coming down the street. It may be the whore who runs this gallery. I'll give my card to her."

He hung up.

Celine.

She jumped out of bed and ran to the window overlooking the street. There was a taxi drawing to the curb across the street.

Damn. Damn. Damn.

She'd be stupid if she went down and opened that door.

But if she didn't, then that bastard who had called her might attack Celine when she finished paying the driver and came into the vestibule of the gallery.

She dialed Celine's number.

No answer.

Dammit, she wished she had a gun. But it was just too difficult traveling with even licensed firearms through airport security. So compromise. Call the police and tell them she suspected an intruder, then go downstairs and talk to that son of a bitch through the door and try to distract him.

She ran to the kitchen, grabbed a butcher knife, and ran toward the elevator. What the hell was the French version of 911?

The gallery was dark. Celine must have turned out the lights when she had put on the alarm before she left.

Jane froze for a second as she stepped out of the elevator.

The carved oak door of the front entrance was directly across the room from where she was standing.

She could see the headlights of the taxi through the plate-glass window to the right of the door.

Stay where you are, Celine. Don't get out of the taxi.

She ran across the room.

Distract him. Quick.

When she was close enough to be heard, she stopped, and called, "I'm here. Are you out there, scum?"

Nothing.

"You're brave on the telephone. Talk to me, bastard."

Silence.

Had he gone away, or was he waiting for Celine to come toward the door?

And then the front door began to slowly open.

She froze.

But it couldn't be opening. The door was locked, and the alarm would have gone off.

She took a step back, her grasp tightening on the butcher knife.

Someone was there.

A dark form was silhouetted against the dim glow of the streetlight.

Her heart was pounding. Where the hell were the police?

"Blasphemer." He stepped forward. "He told me to wait for you. I'm trying to wait, but it's an agony. Come to me." He had something in his hand, something dark and pointed. "Surely the angels will forgive me."

"I've called the police. They'll be here any minute." Dear God, he was big. But she had the knife, knew karate, and if that wasn't a gun in his hand, she might be able to —

He sprang toward her.

She sidestepped, then sprang forward, and the edge of her hand came down on the side of his neck. It was only a glancing blow, but he staggered and almost fell. She ran past him and out into the street.

The taxi. Warn Celine.

"Celine! Stay where you are. Don't come —"

A hand grasped her shoulder, spun her around. "Bitch." That bastard had followed her from the gallery. He was raising his hand with the odd-shaped weapon. Her foot lashed out and connected between his legs.

He screamed but didn't release her.

She'd have to use the knife.

He suddenly arched violently backward and cried out.

What was hap— ?

Then she saw the gleam of metal as a dagger exited his chest.

Someone was behind him. In the darkness, she could only make out a man, tall, lean, powerful.

"Jane."

He knew her name, but so had the bastard on the phone. Her hand tightened on the butcher knife. She stiffened, waiting.

The man who had attacked her was falling to the street.

"Don't make me take the knife away from you, Jane. You'd fight, and I might hurt you."

She knew that voice and that faint Scottish accent. Relief poured through her as her gaze flew to his face. "Jock?" She stared at him in bewilderment as she lowered the knife. "What are you doing here?"

"At the moment, cleaning up Venable's mistakes." Jock Gavin was bending over the man lying before them, going through his pockets. "And trying to get a step ahead of the police I hear a few blocks away. You called them?"

"Yes." She could hear the sirens, too, now. Relief was surging through her. The police were coming. Jock was here, everything would be all right. She could trust Jock. At times she felt as if they had been closer than brother and sister.

He flipped open the man's wallet. "Henri Folard."

She was suddenly jarred out of her shock. "Oh God, you killed him, Jock."

"Yes."

"You'll get in trouble. I could only report an obscene caller. I don't even know if we can even prove he was trying to attack me. I know you were only trying to help me, but you have to get out of here."

"No. Tell them I was up there in the suite already, and I came down to protect you until the police got here."

"But we can't prove he was any threat to me. It was only an obscene —"

"We can prove it, Jane," Jock said gently. "Look at the door."

"Door? What are you talking about?" Jock's hands were on her shoulders, gently turning her to face the gallery, to face the huge oak door that had slowly swung open to reveal the man who had attacked her. "What has —"

She lifted her head and looked at the door, which had swung back closed from the weight of the burden it carried. The burden that was now illuminated by the streetlight.

"*No!* Oh, God in heaven, no!"

Celine Denarve, still dressed in her flamboyant red cloak, stared back at Jane, her face frozen and contorted with pain and horror. She had been nailed to a cross that had been fixed to the oak door by a huge crucifix nail. There were nails in her palms and feet.

There was another nail piercing her chest.

Jane screamed.

Two

"Easy." Jock turned Jane around, and his hand pressed her head to his shoulder. "You were going to see her anyway, and I wanted you to get it over with before the police got here. Now don't look at her again."

"He . . . killed . . . her." She still couldn't understand it. "But she was in the taxi. I ran down from the apartment to distract him. He wouldn't have had time to —" She buried her head in Jock's shoulder. "She was in the taxi."

"No. It was a trick to get you down here. There were two of them. Someone else was driving the taxi. I saw him pulling away after I killed Folard."

She couldn't comprehend it. "It was a trick?"

"What he did to her had to take a while. He had to have her keys and the alarm code. He probably grabbed her earlier in the evening. If he hadn't been able to lure you down, he would have run the risk of going upstairs after you."

She had a memory of Celine going out the door with her red silk cape flying behind her. "He was waiting for her, stalking her?"

"Yes, it's likely. You were the big game, but they wanted you to see what they had done to her before they took you. I'd bet he'd been given his orders not to kill you tonight. But when you fought him, you were just an irresistible temptation." He tilted his head, listening. "I think that's the police just down the block. They should be here any minute."

"Venable," she said suddenly. "You mentioned Venable. He's CIA." She'd dealt with Venable and the CIA years ago when she'd been trying to keep him from taking Jock into custody after he'd been hospitalized. The experience had not given her any overwhelming sense of trust in the agency. But his appearance in her life at this time and place made everything even more bizarre. "What's he got to do with this?"

"I'm working for him right now."

"The CIA? You? Why would you be —"

"Later."

Yes, later. She couldn't think through this veil of horror surrounding her anyway.

38

Celine was dead. Celine had been butchered.

She dazedly tried to fight her way through the fog. "Why did this happen? I don't understand any of this, Jock."

"I know you don't. It's going to be okay, Jane." He turned her to face the police car that was pulling up to the curb across the street. "I'll give Venable a call and see if he can pull strings to make it any easier for you. But it should be pretty clear to the local gendarmes that this was self-defense. Folard even has the spike he was thinking of using on you in his hand."

She had noticed something dark and pointed, but in the dimness she hadn't recognized it as a spike. She felt sick as she remembered the spike in Celine's chest. Was Foulard going to drive the one clutched in his hand into Jane's heart? "She was such a good person. I liked her, Jock. We were friends."

He nodded. "I know it's difficult for you. I'll try to get you through this as quickly as possible."

Get her through it? He was worried about Jane. What about Celine, who had been full of joy and life only hours before?

Don't look at her. Think of her as she'd been before she'd walked out of the gallery, laughing, joking.

Not the brilliant, helpless butterfly pinned to that door.

Dammit to hell.

Millet's hands tightened on the steering wheel of the taxi as fury tore through him. He should have grabbed the bitch himself instead of relying on Folard. He hadn't thought there would be a problem, and it was smart to let his men have a small part in this taking.

But Folard had failed. He had let her triumph. He had let Jock Gavin triumph. That son of a bitch had appeared out of nowhere.

Jock Gavin. Millet had last seen him yesterday in Rome, but here he was in Paris, interfering, putting himself between Millet and Jane MacGuire. He should have known better than to think that Gavin could be trusted when he'd accepted him into the Sang Noir. Betrayal.

He drew a deep breath and tried to control himself. It would still go well. He would continue with the grand plan and find a way to take Jane MacGuire as soon as possible. She was not only his revenge, she was to be his salvation.

But his stomach was clenching at the

thought of the delay. Celine Denarve's agony had only whetted his appetite.

He wanted Jane MacGuire.

He needed her *now*.

Venable answered Jock Gavin's call on the fourth ring.

"You screwed up, Venable," Jock said. "You promised me that you'd have someone near the gallery to protect Jane until I could get here."

"I did my best. Presnell was supposed to be there. What happened?"

"Celine Denarve was murdered, and Millet almost got his hands on Jane. Your best sucks."

"Shit. Is she okay?"

"No, but she's alive. I had to kill Folard, one of Millet's errand boys. Get busy and pull strings to keep the police from taking us in for questioning. Jane's been through enough tonight."

"It may take a while."

"It had better not," Jock said softly. "I'm very angry with you, Venable."

Venable felt a chill go through him. He shook it off. It was difficult not to feel a little intimidated by Jock Gavin. His history alone was enough to make a man think twice. He had been an assassin without equal, and that lethal coldness lingered like a shadow that refused to leave him. But Venable had been a CIA agent for too many years to let the intimidation be more than temporary. It was his job to deal with men like Gavin, and he'd do his job and do it well. "I'll call you back if I have any trouble." He hung up.

Trouble? There was nothing but trouble popping up all over the place. Dammit, everything was going to hell.

Presnell, the agent he'd sent to protect Jane MacGuire, was almost certainly dead. He was too good a man to screw up like this.

Find out. Then send another man to watch Jane MacGuire. Though with Jock Gavin on the scene, it would probably be extreme excess.

His phone rang, and he glanced down at the ID.

John MacDuff.

Oh, shit. He should have known MacDuff would be hovering over Jock Gavin like a protective hawk. He considered Gavin his responsibility since Gavin had grown up on his estate, MacDuff's Run, in Scotland. Though, God knows, Venable had hoped that the two might have lost contact since Gavin had moved to the U.S. He wasn't looking forward to dealing with MacDuff.

He punched the cell. "I was just going to call you."

"The hell you were." MacDuff's voice was silky. "What are you trying to do, Venable?"

"Gavin called you?"

"Yes, he didn't want to involve me, but he thought Jane MacGuire might need help since you're screwing up. You son of a bitch, you're trying to drag Jock back into that same hellhole he pulled himself out of."

"I needed him." He paused. "I'd do it again, MacDuff. There was a leak among my team. I needed someone good who had no connection with the Company. It's not as if Gavin was an innocent. He was lucky I didn't lock him up and throw away the key. After all, he was probably one of the most accomplished assassins either one of us have ever seen."

"We made a deal. I helped you get your hands on that bastard, Thomas Reilly, who had brainwashed Jock and all those other kids he'd kidnapped, and you gave me custody of him."

"I needed him to do a job for me. Don't expect me to feel guilty for using Gavin." He repeated, "He was an assassin."

"He was a young kid who was medicated and brainwashed. Do you know how many times he tried to kill himself after he started to come off that medication?" His voice turned savage. "I should turn him loose on you, Venable."

"Go ahead. But that wouldn't keep him from going right back to Jane MacGuire afterward. I'd just be a minor bump in the road. And you might need me. This is a very ugly business."

"And you used Jane to draw Jock into doing your damn job."

"She was in the middle of it anyway. She just didn't know it. But, yes, I gambled that he'd do anything to keep her safe."

"Since Jane was the one who brought Jock back to the land of the living. Sure, why not send him out to kill a few scumbags to show how grateful he is?"

"What do you want me to say? I did it. I'd do it again. Dammit, I may have lost a man tonight while he was protecting Jane MacGuire." He paused. "And the situation in Paris may be awkward. It's too late for me to do a cleanup. We need damage control."

"If Jock is roped into your damage control, I'll come after you myself."

And he'd do it, Venable thought sourly. MacDuff was a throwback to the Lairds who first ruled MacDuff's Run. He was possessive of every person on his property and protected them with passion and ferocity. Jock Gavin had not only grown up in the village at MacDuff's Run, but MacDuff treated him as a younger brother. "Actually, I was going to rope you into doing that for all of us. They love you in Paris. You're a big hero to them. As I recall, one of the medals you won was a Croix de Guerre. Do you know the prime minister?"

"I've met him several times."

"Then it shouldn't be difficult to convince him that it would serve no purpose to victimize a young woman who has suffered enough already. The media doesn't need to know anything about Jane MacGuire." He paused. "Or Jock Gavin. They're both obviously innocent of the crime that took the life of an outstanding French citizen, Celine Denarve. And that scum that Gavin put down was clearly no loss. Can you convince the prime minister that for you to remove both Gavin and Jane from the public eye would permit the police to focus on what's important in the case?"

MacDuff was silent. "It's possible I can get him to go along."

"More than possible. I'll do my part behind the scenes to help it along."

"Very well. Hang up, and I'll call him. I'll

have to work fast. He won't like being roused at this hour of the night."

But Venable had seen MacDuff when he was moving toward a goal with a confidence and charisma that was truly awe-inspiring. He was as good at negotiating his way through social and diplomatic circles as he had been searching out the enemies in the jungle as a commando. Hell, maybe there was something to all that Laird bullshit. "I knew you'd be willing to cooperate when you realized that we all have to do what we can to make sure that —"

"Listen, Venable. I'm not willing to co-operate with you on any level. I'm pissed off, and I can't see that changing in the foreseeable future. I'll call the prime minister because I don't want to have to run the gauntlet when I get to Paris. I should be there within two hours. I have a plane standing by." His voice lowered to velvet softness. "And after I finish the call, I'm going to phone you back, and you're going to tell me everything you know or guess or even vaguely speculate. Is that understood?"

"Of course."

"I mean it, Venable," MacDuff said. "I don't like the idea of your manipulating one of my people. It's not going to happen again." He hung up.

"I made you coffee." Jock crossed to where Jane was sitting on the brocade Louis XV couch and handed her the tiny flowered cup and saucer. "But this is all I could find to put it in. It's hardly worth bothering."

"Celine loved dainty cups. She said she felt like a princess when she —" Jane drew a deep, shaky breath. "I argued with her. I was used to cups that were more like pitchers. Eve never liked to run to the kitchen for a refill while she was working on her reconstructions, and she always started out with a big cup. When I'm painting, I do the same thing. But Celine said that coffee should be an experience and should be savored and — I'm babbling, aren't I?" She took a sip of the coffee. "Thanks, Jock. Thanks for everything." The hot coffee tasted good and some of the chill that she was feeling ebbed away. It would be back, she knew. Every time she thought of Celine, it attacked like an enemy in hiding.

But for this moment Jock had managed to lessen that terrible hollowness. He was smiling gently at her, and it warmed her. Gentleness, strength, and yet that sense of underlying loneliness.

Strength. Yes, she always thought of him as the boy she had first met, but he was older now, in his early twenties. Just as stunningly handsome, with those silver-gray eyes and wonderful features, just as quietly contained, but the years had taken away that almost breakable quality and replaced it with a sort of subtle power.

"I'm sorry your friend was killed." He sat down in the chair across from her. "She was a beautiful woman."

"How could you tell?" She shivered. "That expression was —"

"Entirely natural considering the circumstances," he said gently. "But I could still tell she had a flair for living."

"Yes." She moistened her lips. "I'm sorry that you — I didn't want you to kill again, Jock. Particularly not for me."

He smiled. "You're suffering more than I am. You and MacDuff are always worrying about my immortal soul. Since I'm virtually sure that it's lost already, I don't let it trouble me."

"It wasn't your fault. You were sick. You didn't know what you were doing."

"Shh." He lifted his cup. "Drink your coffee. It's not important right now."

"It's important. You're important." She rubbed her temple. "What happened, Jock?

48

Why was she killed? Celine didn't have an enemy in the world. Was he crazy?"

"In a way, I suppose."

"And why were you here?" Though heaven knows she had been grateful to have him. Not only because he had probably saved her life but for staying with her during those two excruciating hours of police questioning. The inspector had at first been brusque, then had turned amazingly kind and respectful. He had not even made them go down to the police station to give their statements.

But perhaps leaving the gallery would have been better. She would not have been so aware of what the police forensic team had been doing to Celine. She quickly veered away from that memory.

Now that the first shock was over, she had to fight her way through the horror and try to make some kind of sense out of that act, which had no resemblance to reason. "Why are you here? I haven't seen you for a long time, Jock. You didn't just drop in out of the blue and —"

"No." He shook his head. "My timing's not that good. I thought there might be a problem."

She sat up straighter on the sofa. "What kind of problem? Venable. You mentioned

Venable. You said you were working for him? The CIA? That doesn't make any sense. We were all walking a tightrope just to keep Venable from taking you into custody. If MacDuff hadn't been able to make a deal with him, he'd have thrown you into prison."

"But it seems he had something else in mind." His lips twisted. "A man of my talents can be a valuable commodity in Venable's line of work."

"He's using you?" Anger flared through her. "Dammit, get him on the phone. I want to talk to him."

He smiled faintly. "Only you would want to jump in and take on Venable when you've just had a knockout punch of your own. You don't need to protect me. I'm not a kid any longer, Jane."

She knew that with her mind but she couldn't stop seeing him as that beautiful, broken boy he had been. "I still want to talk to Venable. Yes, I'll give him hell, but maybe I can squeeze some information out of him."

"You won't have to squeeze. Not him. Not me. But give yourself a little time. Drink your coffee." He leaned back in the chair. "You'd only get upset if I dove in and tried to explain now. You're very protective, Jane." He smiled. "No one should know that better than I do."

"Dammit, I *am* upset. My friend was murdered and nailed to a door. I wasn't very protective of her, was I?" She leaned forward. "Now you tell me what's happening, Jock."

"Wait for MacDuff," he said quietly. "He should be here anytime now."

"MacDuff? He's coming, too? I don't want to wait for MacDuff. I want you to —"

"Leave the lad alone, Jane." MacDuff was standing in the open elevator. "I know you've been through a great deal, but so has Jock." He smiled. "You mustn't intimidate the poor boy."

She stiffened as MacDuff stepped out of the elevator. Presence. Charisma. Force. She was always aware of those three aspects of MacDuff's personality when he came into a room.

"Intimidate?" She shook her head. "I've never been able to intimidate Jock."

"That's not true," Jock said. "You're a truly fearsome woman, Jane. From the first time you sketched me in the garden at the castle, I knew that I'd never be free of you." He got to his feet. "So I'll leave and let MacDuff handle you. He likes to think he can call the birds from the trees."

"Then you should have given me the chance to talk you out of letting Venable use you," MacDuff said curtly. "I'm not pleased with you, Jock."

"I quake. I quiver." Jock moved toward the kitchen. "I have to make decisions for myself now, MacDuff. Venable used me because I made the choice."

"Stop it," Jane said. "I won't have this."

MacDuff turned back to her. "You're right. Jock and I are both a little on edge, but we should contain it. You have a right to be upset with us." He smiled. "But then we wouldn't be so frank in front of you if we didn't regard you as family."

"Is that supposed to flatter me? I've no desire to be a part of you or that crumbling estate. Go to hell."

Jock glanced back over his shoulder. "Now it's time for you to quake and quiver, MacDuff." He disappeared into the kitchen.

"Is that what you want?" MacDuff asked her quietly. "I'll work on it if it will please you."

"Bullshit."

"Aye." His lips indented at the corners. "But it's bullshit that put a little color in your cheeks. I don't like to see you pale and strained. Has it been a bad time for you tonight?"

52

"Bad time? You might say that. That bastard crucified my friend. He pinned her to that door like a —" She broke off. "And I don't know why. But I'm going to find out."

"Yes, you are." He moved across the room toward her. He looked different, she thought. He was wearing a gray tweed suit, and she was accustomed to seeing him in casual slacks and sweaters. No matter what he wore, it was difficult to take your eyes away from him. He was tall, muscular, in his mid to late thirties with dark hair pulled away from his face. His light blue eyes were a striking contrast in his olive face. It was no wonder that Celine had been drawn to him. He was forceful, magnetic — all the things that would have attracted Celine.

He said, "May I sit down?"

She nodded impatiently. "Venable has something to do with this."

"Yes." He dropped down on the seat Jock had vacated. "I'd like to say the bastard had everything to do with it, but that would be giving him too much credit. He was only a cog." He frowned. "But Venable should have come to me. I would have taken care of you. He had no business bringing Jock back here to do his work."

"Taken care of me? What are you talking about?"

"I told you I regard you as family. Naturally, I'll take care of what is mine."

Arrogant, possessive bastard. Don't argue. "Just tell me why anyone should have to take care of me," she said through set teeth. "Why did Jock show up tonight?"

"He thought you were in danger. He'd received some information earlier today, and he had to make a move. He didn't trust Venable's men to protect you."

"But why me? Why would anyone be targeting me?" Jane lifted her hand to her eyes. "Don't start in the middle. The beginning, MacDuff."

"I'm not certain where the beginning is yet," he said grimly. "But I'll tell you what Venable told me. Though I'm not sure that he told me everything." He reached in his pocket and brought out a folded newspaper. "Do you recognize this?"

She took the newspaper. *Le Monde.* Feature section. "Yes, it's an article that appeared two weeks ago. Celine was over the moon that she managed to wangle an article about the show." A photo of herself looked up at Jane. Beside it were five of her paintings that were to appear at the exhibit. "It was taken before I left to go home on a visit to Atlanta." She frowned. "Why?"

"One of Venable's informants, Ted Weismann, sent him a copy of this article. Your photo was circled. And a date was inserted beneath your picture."

"What date?"

"April 1."

"So?"

"According to Venable's informant, it was the date that you had to die."

Shock. No time for shock. She had to recover quickly and go on, "But April 1 is eight, no seven, days away. And it's Celine who died." She shook her head. "It's all crazy."

"Venable didn't think it was crazy. He respected this particular informant. He'd been working with him and trying to round up a group of killers for hire called the Sang Noir, who specialized in murdering political figures. He hadn't been very successful. No proof. They're careful and seemed to have enough money for bribes to skirt the law. It's headed by Jack Millet. Very lethal. Very nasty. The group is responsible for at least two assassinations of world leaders in the last year. Jorge Ralez, President of Colombia. Kim Thai of South Korea, Head of the Parliament."

She shook her head. "According to the

media, Ralez's death was drug-cartel related."

"And Kim Thai was supposedly targeted by North Korean secret police. Neither of their killers was caught. High-profile cases and still no one brought to justice. Very strange."

"Yes, but it has nothing to do with me."

"It didn't until Venable's informant, Weismann, sent him this newspaper with your photo. He'd copied it from one that Millet had in his possession." He paused. "He also said that Millet had been sent the photo by a businessman who was closely involved with Millet and the Sang Noir."

"What kind of involvement?"

He shrugged. "Weismann wasn't sure. It wasn't unusual for Millet to negotiate hits with anyone who had the money. Murder is murder. The payout would have had to be spectacular to get him to agree to any deal." He paused. "But he was on the phone ranting and raving with the man who sent him that clipping the moment he received it."

"And who is this businessman?"

MacDuff shook his head. "Millet kept his arrangement with him very hush-hush. Only a few people knew about it. It took a lot of digging before Venable's informant, Weismann, could tell him the little he found out.”

Jane impatiently shook her head. “Look, none of this has anything to do with me. Even if Millet had a copy of this article, it couldn't be considered very high priority. I've no connection with any of those people. Which could mean that the whole idea of my involvement was a fluke.” A horrible mistake, a dreadful fluke. “For God's sake, I'm an artist. I stay as far away from politics as I can get.”

“I don't think that it was a mistake. They went to a great deal of trouble to zero in on your location here. And your friend, Celine, was murdered. Crucified.”

She flinched. *Crucified.* The word was as ugly as the act itself. It took a moment for her to regain control.

Then she shook her head wearily. “I don't know. All I know is that it doesn't make sense.”

“It has to make sense. We just have to find out how. Because it's not only you on the line now. Jock killed one of their men tonight. I told you, Millet is very nasty. He's not going to forgive and forget.”

“Jock shouldn't have even been here,” she said bitterly. “Damn Venable.”

“He justified it by saying there had been

several leaks, and he couldn't afford another one in a sensitive operation. He went after Jock because he knew that he could trust him to get rid of any threat to you. He sent him to Rome, where the main branch of the Sang Noir is located, and told him to see what he could find out. There wasn't any question of his completely infiltrating the group. They're very tight. But he was able to cruise along in the shallows and be on hand to pick up information as it became available." He smiled sardonically. "They weren't suspicious of him. Venable got Weismann to spread the stories about Jock's background. After all, he had excellent credentials in their field of expertise. Word does get around."

Their field of expertise. Death.

Yes, no one could say Jock wasn't a prime expert in that field. And he'd added another body to that reputation tonight, and it had been for her sake.

MacDuff shrugged. "Anyway, Jock had been aware of something stirring about you for the last few days. But he only found out late yesterday afternoon that Millet had left Rome for Paris. He called Venable and told him to make sure you were protected, then headed for the airport. It appears he got here just in time."

"Not for Celine," she said dully. "Such savagery. Why?"

"I don't know." He shrugged. "But Jock is no fool, and he thinks that Venable is right and April 1 is your death date."

She tried to smile. "April Fool."

"I don't regard it as a joke."

"I know you don't. Because Jock killed a man tonight because of me."

"Yes." He met her eyes. "And because you're family, and no one threatens my family."

She pulled her gaze away from him. She had told him several times that she had no connection to his blasted family. But he had gotten the idea into his head and wouldn't let go of it. "I'm no MacDuff. I'm an illegitimate street kid, and I like it just fine that way. Joe Quinn and Eve Duncan are the only family I need or want. And I'll take care of my own threats, MacDuff."

"Whatever you say." He smiled. "Cousin. But the portrait of Great-aunt Fiona MacDuff on my wall at home makes me wonder. There's no discounting the resemblance."

"She lived during the late eighteen hundreds and everyone looks like someone. We're a homogenized race."

"You don't believe that, and neither do I.

We both have egos that tell us we're unique." His smile disappeared. "And someone has put you on a list that definitely makes you stand out."

"Not that you didn't stand out before." Jock stood in the kitchen doorway with a huge cup in his hand. "I found a souvenir mug on one of the top shelves." He came toward her. "Much better than those little cups." He gave her the mug and took the other cup away from her. "Now drink that down. I'm sure MacDuff has told you enough to make you need another jolt of caffeine."

"You should have come to me, told me." She shook her head. "MacDuff says there's no mistake, but I still can't see any connection that would make sense."

"There was a connection. No one mentioned your name, but I saw that newspaper article in the possession of at least three of the members." He made a face. "It was pretty frustrating not to be able to learn more. They welcomed me on a very tentative basis. I wasn't privy to any crucial information, and they watched me as much as I watched them. But they definitely thought I might be useful to them at some point." His lips lifted in a sardonic smile. "Why not?"

"Did you know anything about Folard, the man you killed?"

"No, he was never in Rome. But if he was sent after you, then he was probably one of the core eight."

"What?"

He shrugged. "I gathered that there are eight who are considered the core or most important members. They're the only ones that Millet trusts and allows to travel with him."

"How many people belong to this Sang Noir?"

Jock hesitated. "I'm not sure. The Sang Noir has twenty or thirty members in Rome. But I understand he gets phone calls from all over the world. Of course, they could be clients."

"But you don't believe that?" MacDuff asked.

"I don't know what I believe. I was only concentrating on getting information that pertained to Jane." He paused. "I didn't give a damn about anything else. Let Venable track down all Millet's dirty business. If I'd run across something about this deal Venable's so concerned about, I'd have told him, but it wasn't a priority. I knew he was using me." He added, "In fact, he suggested rather bluntly that he wouldn't be opposed

61

if I took out Millet."

"Son of a bitch," MacDuff said.

"It wasn't totally unreasonable. It could have solved Venable's problem. I might have done it, but I couldn't be sure that would have stopped the plans for killing Jane from going forward. I decided to let him live."

The words were said with an off hand coolness, and Jane felt a ripple of shock. She knew that Jock still wrestled with the numbness that had been instilled in him during that period when he had been brainwashed. Yet the Jock that he showed to her was so gentle and caring that those glimpses always caught her off guard. But Jock wouldn't have been put in the position of making decisions like that if he hadn't been trying to help her.

"Tell me about Millet and this Sang Noir," she said. "They have to be crazy, or they couldn't have done what they did tonight. But I'm lost; there has to be something that I can grab and hold on to."

"I'll tell you what I know," Jock said. "Most of it is what Venable filled me in on when he tapped me for his little job. As I said, the group is very tight and they don't talk much. Millet supposedly grew up in Syria. His mother was Syrian and his father, Jim Millet, an American from Miami. His father was a smuggler and had a record a mile long before he settled in a village in Syria. He was under suspicion for beating his first wife to death before he left Miami. His second wife disappeared when Jack Millet was sixteen."

"Disappeared?"

"Her son and husband claimed she had run away. There wasn't much of an investigation. In spite of the strides Syria has made, a wife is still often thought of as property. Millet's father died a year later, and Jack Millet dropped out of sight for a number of years. Then he showed up in Rome and Venable began to hear rumors of the Sang Noir."

"He didn't have a record?" MacDuff asked.

"He was under suspicion for killing a thirteen-year-old girl in a brothel in Barcelona." He added grimly, "He toyed with her for three days. The kid was cut to pieces."

"Nothing else?"

"Only rumors. Very ugly rumors. His favorite sport is inflicting pain. But by that time Millet had formed his group of killers for hire, and no one would testify against him." He looked at MacDuff. "One thing Venable told me that was a little unusual. I'm sure Millet charged a small fortune for his hits, but even when he'd had no work for a long time, he seemed to have plenty of money and was able to maintain his killing squad."

"So we look for the money."

He shook his head. "Venable can look for the money. We just take care of Jane."

"I don't care about the damn money," Jane said. Jock's summary of Millet's background had not yielded anything of value except that he was a sadistic monster, and she already knew that. She felt helpless, frustrated. "I don't know enough about him. I don't even know what he looks like. I didn't pay any attention to him in that taxi."

"I can help there," Jock said as he took his phone out of his pocket. "I took shots of all the Sang Noir while I was hobnobbing." He flipped through the photos and handed her the phone.

Millet appeared to be in his thirties, with thick brown hair, a hook nose, and a burly neck. Not handsome but not a terrible-looking man, she thought, sick. He didn't look like a monster who would crucify —

She quickly handed the phone back to Jock. "At least I'll recognize him if I see him." She tried to search through her memory for anything else that might help. Dammit, her contact with Folard and Millet had been only a few minutes. How could she —

A thought occurred to her.

"How did those members of the Sang Noir speak? What kind of phrases did they use?" Jane asked suddenly. "Were they religious?"

Jock's brows rose. "Not unless they kept it very private. They weren't the churchgoing types. Priests very seldom give absolution for cold-blooded murder." He gazed at her inquiringly. "Why?"

"That man Folard . . . When I was on the phone with him." Her forehead knitted. "He was accusing me of all kinds of things. Whore. Bitch. I didn't think much of it. Obscene callers usually use terms like those. But he called me Blasphemer. That wasn't the same. The word sounds almost biblical. It means sacrilege, doesn't it?"

"Or wickedness, profanity . . ." MacDuff said. "But it does sound a bit odd."

She was remembering something else. "And when he attacked me, he said something about the angels of paradise having to forgive him for his impatience."

"If he was on the side of the angels, it must be one hell of a weird heaven," MacDuff said dryly.

"But it sounds as if he believed he was

65

doing something he thought was right." She reached up and ran her fingers through her hair. "I don't know why I'm trying to take his motives apart. He had to be crazy to have done that horrible thing to Celine. What difference does it make if he thought all the angels in heaven would cheer if he crucified me as he did Celine?"

"It might make a difference. It's certainly unusual."

"But knowing it's unusual and being able to decipher it are two separate things. Which leaves me as much in the dark as when I started." She got to her feet. "I can't think right now. I'm going to take a shower and call Eve, then go to bed."

"Call Eve?" MacDuff said. "You're going to tell her? It will only make her concerned. I've arranged to keep your name out of the media."

"Joe's a cop. We can't be sure he wouldn't stumble on it somehow. I can't take a chance they'll find out and be worried." But she'd probably try to downplay the threat to herself. Though how to do that was a mystery. Eve was too sharp and would see through her. "And that police inspector said it would be okay if I left here tomorrow. I'm going to be on a plane by tomorrow night."

"You're going back to Atlanta?" MacDuff

asked. "To visit your Eve and Joe?"

The lake cottage. Joe. Eve. It all beckoned with irresistible allure. "Yes, for a little while."

"Do you think that's wise?"

"Why not?"

He didn't answer.

Celine pinned to the door, her face contorted with pain.

Her hands closed into fists. "Damn you. No, it's not wise. It's not safe for me to be around anyone until I find out what's going on. I'll go to my apartment in New York instead."

"You could come home with me," MacDuff said. "You like it at the Run."

She shook her head.

"Why not?" Jock asked. "MacDuff will take care of you. I'll be there, too, if you'll have me. I haven't been home in a long time."

"I don't want MacDuff to take —" She broke off. Jock would never really understand. He was accustomed to the Laird caring for him, his family, and half the county. He had changed, become much more independent, but old ways died hard. "I'm going back to the U.S." She started for the bedroom. "And, please, stay away from Venable, Jock. Don't let him talk you into doing anything like this again."

He didn't answer, and she glanced back over her shoulder.

He smiled, that beautiful, gentle smile that had first drawn her to him when he was a boy scarcely out of his teens. "Things aren't good for you, Jane. I have to make them better."

She shook her head helplessly. In his way, he was an implacable force on the same scale as MacDuff. "Good night."

She closed the bedroom door firmly behind her.

THREE

"You have to make sure that she goes to the Run," Jock said, as the door closed behind Jane. "We can protect her there."

"*I* have to do it," MacDuff repeated. "You're the one Jane's always tried to care for. You persuade her."

"But you wouldn't like it," Jock said. "You always have to run things. It's your nature. It would bother you." He smiled slyly. "I wouldn't want to bother the Laird. It's not my place."

"You bastard," MacDuff said. "It wasn't your place to pull us all into this mire, either."

"No, it was my duty." Jock's smile faded. "I think a lot about duty these days. It gives me a kind of structure to hold on to. I have a duty to you, a duty to my friends, and a duty to my country."

And Jock needs structure after all he went through, MacDuff thought. "Duty is a hell of a reason to hit one of Venable's targets for him."

"It's as good a reason as any." He looked back at the door. "It was all about Jane. Try to take her home with you."

"And if I don't, you'll be hovering over her and doing God knows what."

"Yes," Jock said. "And so will you. Neither of us wants to see Jane nailed to a door like that poor woman."

MacDuff was silent a moment. "This Jack Millet who's head of the Sang Noir. You said that you only knew what Venable had told you about him. But you were with the group long enough to take a measure of the man. What was your impression?"

"Ugly," Jock said. "He's smart. Or maybe cunning is the word. He's definitely into power. He handpicked the men in the group, and he keeps them under his thumb. They're afraid to step out of line." He nodded. "And dirty. You can't imagine how dirty. Or maybe you can after what I told you about that kid in the brothel. And a little crazy. You can tell, he burns with it. We have to keep that filth from touching Jane." He turned away. "Now I'm going outside and take a stroll around and make sure that the area is secure."

"It's not necessary. The police will probably still be outside."

"I know. But I can't trust them." He got on the elevator. "Duty . . ."

Even MacDuff couldn't understand why he was being so overcareful, Jock thought, as the elevator doors closed. The Laird knew him better than anyone in the world, but he hadn't been in that room years ago when Jane had risked her life to pull him out of almost catatonic darkness into the light. Thomas Reilly had kidnapped and brainwashed him to become the assassin he could use to do his killings. When he had broken free, the posthypnotic suicide suggestion had kicked in and almost destroyed him. He had disobeyed and, therefore, had to put an end to himself. Jane had not been able to fight the suggestion with sympathy and understanding, so she had circled and gone at it with an aggression that could have been fatal.

At that moment, he'd been swirling down, locked in silence, trying to fight against that bastard Reilly's mental conditioning, but he'd probably never been more volatile or lethal. Before Jane had left the room that night his hands had tightened on her throat, and he'd come close to choking her before he'd realized what he was doing. She'd had to cover her neck for days to hide the bruises so that no one could see what he'd done to her.

Later, when he'd fought back to normalcy, he'd realized that Jane might have been his savior, but she was no saint. She was honest and passionately caring, but she was mule-stubborn. She was smart, but she didn't suffer fools gladly. Because of her street upbringing, she was cynical and had trouble trusting in any relationship.

But none of that mattered.

She was his friend.

And no one was ever going to hurt her.

"Come home," Eve urged Jane. "Get on the next plane. I'll meet you at the airport."

"I'm leaving here, but I'm going back to New York." Jane paused. "It will be okay, Eve. Stop worrying."

"I will worry. So will Joe. Come home so that we can take care of you," Eve said. "This is incredibly ugly. We'll get through it together."

"I'll keep in touch."

"That's not good enough." Eve didn't speak for a minute. "I'm feeling helpless. I don't like to feel helpless. If you don't come to us, I'm going to come to you."

"No," Jane said sharply. All she needed was to have Eve involved in this nightmare.

"I'll work it out."

Eve hesitated. "You say MacDuff is there?"

"And Jock. Venable is giving me protection. I don't need you, Eve."

"You mean you don't want me involved. I believe I've said that to you on occasion. It didn't do me any good, did it?" She didn't wait for an answer. "At least, you're safe while MacDuff and Jock are with you. We'll talk tomorrow." She was silent a moment. "I'm sorry about your friend, Celine. You told me you liked her very much."

"I did," Jane said. "You would have liked her, too, Eve."

"Does she have a family?"

"Only a sister, Yvette, who lives in Lyon. I had to call her a few hours ago and tell her about Celine. She was almost hysterical. She's coming to Paris tomorrow morning. I have to stay until tomorrow night and see if I can help her deal with things at the gallery. There are all those paintings of mine that Celine sold tonight. At least, I know where she keeps the records. She has a part-time assistant, Marie, who may be able to help Yvette with the rest of the final details."

Final. When several hours before Celine had all her life before her and had thought death was somewhere far in the distant future.

That realization had returned and was hitting hard. She had to get off the phone before she broke down. "I'm going to bed now, Eve. I'll be fine. I'll let you know if there are any problems."

"We'll talk tomorrow," Eve repeated. "Good night, Jane."

That last sentence had sounded very firm and held all the determination she was familiar with in Eve, Jane thought as she hung up. She had known that would be Eve's reaction. Their relationship had been more as best friends than mother and daughter all these years, but Eve could display a tigerish maternal protectiveness when the people she cared about were threatened.

Jane had tried to downplay that threat, but how could she do that when Celine's ugly death loomed over her like a poised guillotine?

She would have to think of something to keep Eve away from her. That guillotine must never threaten Eve. But right now, her mind wasn't functioning very well. She turned toward the bathroom. Take a shower. Get to bed and try to sleep. Heaven knows, she was exhausted. Maybe when she woke, everything would become clear to her.

Or at least a little less clouded.

■ ■ ■ ■

She might be exhausted but there was no way that she was going to sleep, Jane realized.

She had been lying here in this bed for fifteen minutes, and neither her muscles nor her mind would release their tension.

The darkness is overpowering, Jane thought, as she stared up at the ceiling. This guest room had seemed friendly, soothing, all the other nights she had spent in Celine's apartment.

Or maybe it was the memory of what had happened downstairs that was overpowering. She couldn't get away from the picture of Celine on that door.

Hideous.

She closed her eyes and tried to block it out, once more remember Celine as she had been earlier in the evening. So full of vitality. So full of joy.

The tears were suddenly running down her cheeks. She had felt numb before, unable to comprehend anything beyond the horror. But now the horror was fading, and the sheer tragedy of that vibrant woman whose life had been taken was with her.

Damn that bastard.

And if MacDuff and Jock were right, then Celine had died because she had been connected to Jane. Why? It didn't make any more sense to her now than it had when MacDuff had first told her.

She huddled down in the bed and closed her eyes as sobs shook her body. Celine . . .

What was she doing? she thought with sudden self-disgust. Next she'd be covering her head with the covers. She had lost a friend, but Celine had lost her life. She wiped her eyes and struggled to sit up in bed. Okay, stop whimpering and start thinking. Figure it out. She wasn't going to be sleeping anyway.

First step.

Find out why she had been targeted.

Blasphemer. Very flimsy. But, if it had meaning at all, what sacrilege had she supposedly committed?

She shook her head in frustration. Who knew what small infraction might be interpreted as sacrilege to a fanatic?

All right, then go to step two.

The newspaper story that Venable had gotten from his informant and the identical copies that Jock had said other members of the Sang Noir been given. Since Jane had no previous contact with the group, was there something in the article that might have triggered that crazy act? What had she said to the reporter? Was there some quote from her that had started the nightmare? She couldn't even remember any of the questions the journalist had asked her. She was never very patient with interviews. She knew that publicity was necessary, but she always thought that her work should speak for itself. There was no telling if that impatience might have translated into a less-than-diplomatic answer.

She turned on the light and threw the covers aside. There was no use wondering when she had the article itself. She had tossed the newspaper on the chest by the door when she had come into the bedroom.

Her own photo smiled up at her from the page. She actually looked friendly and approachable. She vaguely remembered Celine's joking with the photographer and making faces at Jane.

Celine, again.

She drew a shaky breath and started scanning the text. Nothing controversial, actually pretty boring. How long had she been painting? She had a mixture of portraits and landscapes in the show. Which did she prefer doing? Why had she painted MacDuff's Run? Did she have an intimate relationship with the earl? That one had almost made her lose her temper. She was always getting that question, and she'd almost stopped putting the painting on exhibit to avoid it. But Celine had begged her to bring the painting to Paris because the speculation alone would help the show. Good business, she had said. It had been Celine's wheedling that had made MacDuff's Run a part of the twenty paintings in the gallery downstairs.

No, there was nothing that she could see in the article itself that would offend anyone. She glanced at the photos of the paintings that marched vertically down the page. That was the only part of the article she'd been happy with. All in color, all a decent-enough size to show detail. *Storm Morning.* A landscape she'd done in southern France. *MacDuff's Run.*

Silhouette at the Lake. A shadow picture of Eve framed against a blazing sunset on the lake. *Child at the Circus.* A little boy with cotton candy and huge dark eyes wide with wonder. *Guilt,* the portrait that Celine had tried to persuade her to —

Guilt.

She stiffened. She was looking for unusual, and the offer tonight had definitely been out of the ordinary. Even Celine had thought that the amount of money the computer executive had offered was mind-blowing.

What had he seen in the painting that had made him so determined to have it?

She grabbed her robe and headed for the door. She turned on the gallery lights as she got out of the elevator. The first thing that jumped out at her was the oak door, now taken from its hinges and propped against the wall. They'd had to take the door down to remove Celine, and the opening was now only veiled in plastic. The police forensic team had taken the actual cross on which Celine had been nailed with them and said they'd pick up the heavy door on the next trip to check it for any additional evidence.

She found herself looking to see if she could see traces of blood on the wood.

She quickly averted her eyes and moved past the velvet ropes toward the painting.

Guilt.

Burning dark eyes, a bearded face twisted with torment. A painting of which she was very proud, but perhaps not one for which an art collector might pay an exorbitant sum.

"What are you doing down here?"

She turned to see MacDuff coming toward her. "I could ask the same of you. Where did you come from?"

"I was outside with Jock. I saw the lights

go on." He glanced beyond her at the painting. "It's very good. Powerful." He smiled. "But I prefer the one of MacDuff's Run. You're sure you won't sell it to me?"

"Yes, I'm sure." She took a step closer to the painting. "Now that you're here, you might as well help me. That frame is heavy. Will you take the painting down for me?"

"It would be my pleasure." He lifted the painting off the wall. "May I ask why?"

"I want to look at the frame and see if it's been tampered with. Set it against the wall." She knelt to examine it. "Someone offered Celine much too much money for *Guilt* this evening. Some computer billionaire. She said he was very persistent. I'm wondering why."

"Tastes in art can become obsessive. Maybe he thought it was worth it to him."

"Or maybe someone managed to insert something into the frame that he wanted to retrieve. It seems more likely."

MacDuff knelt beside her. "Where was the painting framed?"

"New York. I chose the frame." She was running her hand over the decorative scrollwork. "But that doesn't mean that after I got here it might not have been tampered with. You look at the other side."

"I'm flattered you trust me."

She didn't answer. Everything seemed okay, but what did she know? Maybe she'd get lucky. She went carefully over the other sides of the frame.

"Nothing," MacDuff said.

She sat back on her heels. "Call Venable. We need an expert to go over the painting and frame. In this world of microdots and all that other technical crap, nothing is what it seems."

"You're thinking that the attack had something to do with this painting?"

"How do I know? I'm grabbing at straws. There are holes in every theory I come up with. They had the keys to the gallery. Why not just come in and steal the painting if they wanted it? Or maybe those scumbags were going to take the painting after they killed me. All I know is that they had no reason to murder me so I have to search for some other cause. This is the only common thread I can find. The painting was in the article. And even Celine didn't think that the offer for the painting was reasonable." She determinedly blinked back sudden tears. "She didn't care. She was just happy. Will you call Venable or shall I?"

"I'll do it." He reached for his phone. "And while I'm at it, I should probably probe a little into the man who offered for the painting. What was his name?"

"Donald Sarnoff. San Francisco."

"Right." He glanced down at her feet as he dialed the number. "You're barefoot. Go get on some slippers." Before she could tell him to mind his own business, he turned away and was talking on the phone to Venable.

Later.

She dropped down on the granite bench a few feet away. The stone was cold against her bare thighs. She was suddenly cold all over. The lights seemed glaringly bright, and the face of the man in the portrait of *Guilt* appeared threatening.

Crazy. She had painted that face. She had not used a model, and the creation had been born entirely from her imagination.

No, not entirely imagination.

There had been the dreams.

Dreams that had come every night. Dreams that would not go away until she had finished the painting.

She didn't want to think about the dreams.

But she had never felt any sense of threat before. It had to be the stress of this terrible night that was playing tricks on her.

MacDuff turned away from the phone. "Venable will have an expert here within the hour."

"I won't let him take the painting. He'll have to do the work here at the gallery."

"I didn't think you'd let it out of your sight. That's what I told Venable. Didn't you hear me?"

She shook her head.

He studied her. "No, I believe you're holding on by a hair at the moment." He took off his tweed jacket as he crossed the short distance separating them. "You're shaking. Why couldn't you just go to sleep and face all this tomorrow?" He knelt beside her and put the jacket around her shoulders. "Would it have been too much to ask? You're a great deal of trouble to me, Jane MacGuire."

The jacket was warm from his body, smelled faintly of spice and the outdoors and felt deliciously comforting. And, in spite of his words, his tone was also oddly comforting. Yet comfort wasn't a word that she had ever thought of in connection with MacDuff. Forceful, domineering, charismatic, sometimes even amusing, were all apt descriptions. Never comforting.

No, that wasn't right; years ago, she had watched him comforting Jock during one of the bad times for the boy. But then Jock was one of his people and therefore an exception to every rule. For anyone else, there could be a price to pay for any softness MacDuff showed them. "I couldn't sleep. How could I? I started to go over in my mind all the possible reasons why I should have a gigantic target painted on my back."

"And you came up with that less-than-cheerful painting."

She nodded. "*Guilt.* It was in the newspaper story. Someone wanted it very badly at the show. Maybe it's not really me. Perhaps those crazies think I have something that belongs to them." She shook her head. "But I could very well be wrong. I know it's pretty flimsy but it was the only thing I could think of."

"It's not all that flimsy. I'd say it was very canny reasoning."

"Guessing."

He smiled. "Then we'll just have to see if it pays off." He sat down beside her, put his arm around her shoulders, and pulled her close. He felt her stiffen and gave her a little shake. "You're cold, and it makes me very frustrated not to be able to help you in some way. Could you not give in and forget your independence to make me feel better? Cousin to cousin?"

"I'm not your —" She stopped. She didn't want to be independent right now. Independent meant alone, and she didn't want to be alone. MacDuff's arm around her shoulders felt strong and good. Let him call her cousin, sister, Great-aunt Fiona, or anything else he wanted. It didn't matter.

Venable's expert would be here soon. She would gather her stamina and be ready to face everything again by then. She relaxed against MacDuff and tried not to look at either the oak door where Celine had died or the face of *Guilt* before her.

"That's better," MacDuff said.

"Heaven forbid I make you frustrated, MacDuff."

"Aye." He smiled. "Heaven forbid."

"I just heard from Venable," MacDuff said as he walked out of the storage room where Venable's art expert was working. "No computer billionaire named Donald Sarnoff from San Francisco. No entry records into this country for a Donald Sarnoff."

"A phony," Jane said. Excitement was beginning to pierce the veil of exhaustion that was surrounding her. "Why would he lie to Celine? Why would he offer that much money for the painting?"

"Maybe we'll know soon. I think Cardot is almost finished with his examination."

"It's about time." Paul Cardot had been in that back storage room of the gallery for over two hours. And every hour had seemed an eternity to Jane. "Did he give you any hint about —"

"Nothing," Cardot said as he came out of the storage room. "The frame is a fine mahogany and has no microdots or any other devices embedded in it. The portrait itself appears to be just what it seems." He nodded at Jane. "A very fine painting. Unless you, the artist, encoded something in the color or design that I wouldn't be able to determine without extensive cryptographic analysis, then there's no reason to believe *Guilt* is anything but a work of art."

Jane gazed at him with disappointment. When Cardot had unloaded all of his equipment, X-ray machines, special lights, and an entire box of chemicals, she had been encouraged. Then when MacDuff had told her that Sarnoff was a phony, she had hoped they were at last getting to the bottom of this nightmare puzzle. "You're sure?"

He nodded. "Venable doesn't send careless professionals to do this kind of examination. He's going to go over my report with a microscope. Particularly since he knows I'm going to take him to the cleaners for dragging me out of bed in the middle of the night and making me lug all my equipment across town." He started packing up his bottles into his case. "I'll be out of your gallery in fifteen minutes, Ms. MacGuire."

"It's not my gallery," Jane said. "I hoped you'd be able to give me some —" She turned away. "Thank you for coming."

"I'll see him out, Jane," MacDuff said. "If you won't go to bed, will you go upstairs and rest?"

"Yes." She glanced at the faint light streaming through the plate-glass window at the front of the gallery. "It's after eight. Yvette Denarve should be here soon."

"And you're in fine shape to deal with her, aren't you?"

"Good enough." She turned toward the elevator. "Stop nagging me, MacDuff. I have to do this for Celine."

"I don't nag. Nagging is for shrews and —"

"Lairds who want their own way in everything." She got on the elevator. "Go check on Jock. He hasn't come inside since that expert showed up."

He smiled. "Jock can take care of himself now, Jane. No one could do it better. You were never able to grasp the concept that he's not the brittle lad he was when you first met him."

She could grasp it. She just could never quite believe it. The memory of that breakable boy struggling to keep his sanity was always with her. She knew with her mind how deadly he could be, but not with her heart. That struggle had made her ache with sympathy, then and it still did now. "Go check on him."

"As you like." His smile disappeared, and his expression became thoughtful as the elevator door closed between them.

Jane rubbed her temple as the elevator started to move. Okay, there wasn't anything secret hidden in the painting or frame. But the man who wanted *Guilt* was very much a mystery. Sarnoff was not his name, and computers were not his game. Who the hell was he?

She got off the elevator and headed for the bedroom. She'd wash up, get dressed, then pack. She supposed she should eat something before this day started. It was promising to be a hell of a rough day once Yvette Denarve showed up on the scene. Or perhaps she wouldn't bother to eat. It seemed too much effort at the moment and she was —

There was a note pinned to her bedroom door.

Jane,
There's fresh coffee made in the kitchen,

and I washed your enormous cup. I noticed there was orange juice and milk in the refrigerator, and I put a box of cereal on the table.

Jock

She could feel the moisture sting her eyes. Stupid to be touched by such a simple thing. When had he slipped by them to come up and get all of this in readiness? No pushing, no nudging, just Jock doing what he thought best for her.

Hell, it wouldn't take that long to eat a little, and she could definitely use the coffee. She turned and headed for the kitchen.

FOUR

Paris

Day Two

Venable called MacDuff just after noon that day. "I need to talk to Jock Gavin."

"Then why are you calling me?"

"Because if I didn't, you'd accuse me of going around you and trying to victimize the poor boy."

"He's a man, not a boy."

"Then let him protect himself," Venable said sourly. "That's what I'm trying to tell you. I gave him the option of saying no."

"After you set up a scenario that made it impossible for him to refuse." He added impatiently, "So why do you want to talk to him?" He glanced at Jock, who was sitting in a chair a few feet away. "I'm turning up the volume and putting you on speaker. Don't say anything to me that you don't want him to hear. Or do you want me to hang up, Jock?"

90

Jock shook his head. "I have no secrets from you."

"Not today. Yesterday was a different matter," MacDuff said dryly. "Talk, Venable."

"I want to know about Ted Weismann."

"You should know all there is to know about him," Jock said. "He's your informant. You paid him to introduce me into Sang Noir."

"I know he's greedy, and his information always panned out. You were around him for over two weeks before you took off for Paris."

"That doesn't mean that I know much about him. I wasn't concentrating on Weismann while I was there. What's the problem?"

"The problem is that the minute you took down Folard, Weismann had to go on the run or end up like Celine Denarve. Millet was there and recognized you, and he made the connection. I knew it would happen. One way or another, I was preparing to lose my informant."

"And?"

"Weismann contacted me and wants to make a deal. No more dribbling bits of information. He's prepared to spill his guts for a large enough sum that would permit him to find a hiding place that would be luxurious enough to make it worth the risk."

"And what's your question to me?"

"Just how much does he know? Would I be wasting money?"

Jock thought about it. "It's possible. I got the impression he wasn't as deeply into the group's confidence as the core eight. But he's very personable, and Millet did send him out a couple times to scope out possible jobs. A man who regards information as cash and loves money would make it his business to find out all he could. And why would he have been willing to introduce me to his fine friends when he knew I'd possibly have to blow them away? He might have acquired enough information to be ready to step away from them and go into retirement."

"So that he could make me pay through the nose."

"It's all supposition, of course." Jock paused. "I don't know if Weismann is a good bet for you. I do know he's clever and self-serving. He was probably keeping an eye on me to see when I was going to make my move." He was silent a moment. "Clever enough to dangle something out there to tempt you. What was it, Venable?"

For a moment MacDuff thought Venable wasn't going to answer.

"He said that he knew why Jane MacGuire was targeted." He paused. "And who sent Millet that article and hired him for a possible future kill."

"Then pay it," MacDuff said harshly. "If he's lying, then take the hit. You owe it to her. You screwed up."

"I'll consider it. If she agrees to cooperate. If you agree to cooperate."

"A deal?" MacDuff asked. "Forget it. You're not going to use me. You're not going to use Jock. And you're sure as hell not going to use Jane."

"Why don't you take that up with her? Weismann sent me a bit of information to prove his good faith. He said to tell Jane MacGuire that the order had gone out for a total on her."

"Total?" MacDuff repeated. "What the hell does that mean?"

"Total extermination," Jock said slowly. "Family, friends, coworkers. Wipe every trace of the target from the face of the earth."

MacDuff glanced at him. "You're familiar with the term?"

"Yes, the Sang Noir wasn't shy about talking about total extermination while I was with them. They were very proud of the concept. But it was a punishment levied only against special enemies. I heard they'd actually only used it once."

"Who?"

"Juan Parillo, a police chief in Nardez, Venezuela. It's a small city outside Caracas. He supposedly tortured and killed one of the Sang Noir group three years ago. They wanted to make an example of him."

"And what did that mean?"

"They killed Parillo, his wife, his brother, and his three children. Then they systematically went down the list and murdered two of his officers and their families. They even took out his next-door neighbors because they were reputed to be his best friends."

"Wiped from the face of the earth," MacDuff repeated. "Everyone close to him . . ."

"I told you the Sang Noir was ugly," Venable said. "And crazy as hell."

"Celine Denarve," Jock said. "She was Jane's friend and coworker. A double reason for them to kill her if Jane had been targeted for a total." He suddenly straightened. "But that wouldn't be good enough for them. It would only be a token." He looked at MacDuff. "Celine Denarve has a sister. She was supposed to meet with Jane today."

"No, Yvette's not here yet," Jane said when

MacDuff phoned her. "She called me at nine and said she was on the road." She paused. "Why do you ask?"

"She was driving from Lyon?"

"Yes, I told her I'd meet her if she decided to take the train instead. She's really too upset to be driving. I've been a little worried. She said she'd be here by eleven."

"Do you have a number to call her back?"

"Yes." She frowned. "What's happening, MacDuff?"

"I hope nothing is happening. Call her back and make sure she's okay. Get back to me." He hung up.

Jane pressed the disconnect. She'd been a little worried, but now she was afraid. MacDuff didn't cry wolf unless the wolf was leaping in for the kill. She quickly checked Yvette's number and dialed.

Nothing.

She tried again.

Voice mail. Yvette's voice, cheerful, casual. So different than the shock and near hysteria that had shaded her voice when Jane had talked to her.

She hung up and called MacDuff back. "I can't get hold of Yvette. Now, dammit, tell me why you're worried about her."

"It appears that you've become a special case to the Sang Noir. Let me call Venable back and have him check on the logical route she would take and the car she should be driving. Jock and I will start looking for her."

"What do you mean 'special' —" She stopped. "Another one? You're saying that Yvette may be another victim?"

"I don't know. I just don't think we can take the chance. I don't have time to go into it now with you. I've got to call Venable. I may be wrong. She may walk in the door of the gallery in the next five minutes."

"If she doesn't, I'm going with you." She hung up. Dear God, it was too horrible to be true.

Let it not be true.

Please walk in that door, Yvette.

Forty minutes later Jock, MacDuff, and Jane were on the A6 leaving Paris.

"It's a black 2005 Volvo," Jock said as he hung up the phone from talking to Venable. "And Yvette Denarve stopped at a gas station on A6 and used her credit card over three hours ago."

"I'm going to call her again," Jane said. "Maybe she just had a flat tire. It's possible."

"Yes, it's possible," MacDuff said. "Look sharp, Jock. See if you see any sign of the car in trees or at the side of the road."

"We don't have any cliffs or sharp inclines around here," Jock said. "Even if she had brake trouble, there wouldn't be too much danger."

He's right, Jane thought. Level ground and plateaus. But it wasn't the terrain they were concerned about.

A black Volvo.

MacDuff was driving slowly so that they could keep an eye out for the car.

Two miles.

Five.

Seven.

"There it is!" Jock pointed to a stand of trees up ahead. "But I don't see anyone in the car."

The black Volvo was a good hundred yards off the highway, Jane noticed. Not good. How could Yvette have driven that far into the woods if she'd had car trouble?

"I don't like this." MacDuff parked by the side of the highway. "Jock and I will scope it out. You stay here."

But Jane was already out of the car and heading for the Volvo.

"Or not," MacDuff said as he got out of the driver's seat. "Have it your own way."

"I will. It's broad daylight and those pines are too thin for anyone to be hiding behind.

I just hope that Yvette is in —" She had reached the car and saw that the entire driver's side was smashed as if sideswiped. She felt a rush of panic. Her gaze flew to the interior of the Volvo. "No one's in the car."

"Then we'd better fan out and see if we can find any trace." Jock glanced inside the car. "No blood. That's good."

"Yes." She glanced around the area. Tall scraggy pines were scattered over the entire plateau. It was broad daylight but the trees were casting dark shadows. It was terrible to have to think that an absence of blood was a good thing. "I hope."

"But the car wouldn't have been pushed this far by a glancing hit." Jock was heading toward the deeper woods. "It would have had to be driven."

Jane didn't want to hear her own thoughts put into words. She moved toward the trees to the left of the car, her gaze raking the shrubs, then the ground.

"Jock!"

It was MacDuff calling from the other side of the stand of trees.

She stopped. "MacDuff?"

"Stay where you are, Jane," MacDuff said. "You don't want to see this."

She closed her eyes for an instant. No, she

didn't want to see it. She didn't want it to be true. Her lids flicked open. Face it. She started in the direction from where she'd heard MacDuff's voice.

MacDuff's and Jock's backs were to her as she pushed through the shrubbery. They were looking down at a woman in black slacks and a green-striped blouse.

Dear God.

It was true and there was no running away from it.

"She's dead?" Jane whispered.

Jock looked over his shoulder. "Oh, yes. It's not pretty, Jane."

"I told you not to come. Do you ever pay attention to what I ask?" MacDuff said.

"No." She took a step closer, her gaze fixed on the body of the woman. "What did they —" She inhaled sharply. "My God." Her stomach lurched. "What happened to her head?"

"We haven't discovered that yet," MacDuff said. "But it was taken off cleanly, probably by a blow with an axe."

"Decapitated," she said numbly. She couldn't take her gaze from the headless woman.

Blood.

Jagged flesh, bone.

Lord, she felt sick.

"Seen enough?" MacDuff asked roughly. He stepped closer and spun her around to face the road. "Go back to the car. Lock the doors. We'll keep an eye on you until you reach it. Jock and I will do a search of the woods to see if we can find her —" He stopped. "If you want to do something, call Venable and tell him to get his people out here. I'm not having you wait for the police."

"We shouldn't leave her like —"

"No," MacDuff said. "You're out of here." He turned back to Jock. "Let's do it."

Jane hesitated, then slowly started toward the car. Just put one foot in front of the other and don't look back. She had no desire to stay here with that headless corpse who had once been Yvette Denarve. Somehow, that act robbed death of all dignity. No one should be allowed to do that to a human being. Life had meaning. The end of life should also have meaning.

Then do all the things that would show respect and make Yvette's death important.

She got in the car, locked the doors, then leaned back and closed her eyes.

Blood. Headless. Horror.

Her eyes flicked open again. Would she ever be able to close her eyes without seeing Yvette's mutilated body?

Dammit, don't think of yourself. Think

about that poor woman. Try to do something for her.

She reached for her phone to call Venable.

MacDuff and Jock didn't come back to the car for another thirty minutes.

"No luck," MacDuff said briefly as he got into the driver's seat. "They must have taken her head with them. Unless they buried it. And I didn't see any turned earth."

Jane had thought that Yvette's death couldn't be any more horrible, but she was wrong. The idea of someone's carrying that poor woman's head around like a trophy was beyond atrocious. "Why?" she whispered. "Why would they do that? It's like something from the time of the barbarians."

"We have quite a few barbarians strolling around right now," Jock said. "What did Venable say?"

"He told me he'd have a team out here within the hour." She paused. "He said that maybe we should believe that Weismann had the goods."

MacDuff started the car. "Weismann is a self-serving son of a bitch. But he may be able to tell us what we need to know."

"Like why Yvette Denarve had to die?"

"I think we have to assume that Weismann may have been right about the reason she

101

was targeted."

Total extermination. On the way here, MacDuff had told her about Weismann's message, and she had found it as incredible as everything else connected to this nightmare. She shook her head. "I can't believe that."

"Because you're in shock. Let it sink in, then we'll talk about it."

She didn't want to talk about it. She didn't want to think about it. She wanted everything to do with this horror to just go away.

And that horrible vision of Yvette Denarve's headless corpse to fade from her memory.

At the gallery, they had to show identification to an officer at the entrance and cross the yellow crime-scene tape.

Marie Ressault, Celine's assistant, came out of the office in the back. She was pale, her eyes red and swollen from weeping. "I was wondering where you were," she said to Jane. "I thought that you'd be through talking to Yvette, and I could go over the funeral arrangements with her. Celine wanted to be cremated, you know."

What should I say? Jane wondered. Sorry, there would be no discussions because

Yvette had been murdered with as much shocking cruelty as her sister? "Yvette didn't show up here. Maybe you should just go home, Marie."

"I don't know . . ." Marie shook her head. "I want to do the right thing."

"Go home," Jane said gently. "Celine would want you to rest. You can handle everything tomorrow."

Marie nodded jerkily. "It's so hard. I loved her, you know. Everyone loved her." She straightened. "You're right. Tell Yvette to call me when she gets here, and we'll talk." She headed for the front door. "There are cards of congratulations and boxes of flowers for you in the office. They're on the table beside the door. They've been arriving all morning. They must have been sent last night before anyone heard about Celine . . ." Her voice broke, and she hurried out of the gallery.

"She obviously cared very much for Celine." Jock was looking after her. "You can see how difficult it is for her. It's right that you didn't tell her about Celine's sister."

"She'll have to know soon. I just wanted to give her a little recovery time." The recovery time that Jane had been denied. Death upon death, shock after shock. "Like Marie, I want to do the right thing, but I'm not sure what that is. Everything's a blur right now." She started to turn toward the elevator. "I've got to finish with my suitcases, then come down and pack up those three paintings. At least, it will keep me busy until I can start thinking again. I seem to be having trouble with that —"

MacDuff muttered a curse.

She turned to look at him, but he was staring at something on the floor. "What's wrong?" She followed his gaze. "Why did —"

A thin trickle of blood was running under the door of the office.

She stared at it, stunned.

Then she slowly moved toward the door.

"No," MacDuff said sharply. He stepped in front of her.

"Don't tell me no." She pushed him aside and opened the door.

The blood was running slowly down the side of the table by the door. It was coming from a huge cardboard floral box on the table.

She slowly crossed the few feet to stand before the table.

"Don't touch it." Jock was there beside her, his hand on her arm. "Don't open it. Please, Jane."

"I have to open it."

"No way," MacDuff said. "Get her upstairs, Jock. Carry her if you have to do it."

"No." Jane jerked her arm away from Jock. She glanced at MacDuff, and said fiercely, "I'm not going to hide away from this. Keep your hands off me. I know what you're thinking. I'm thinking the same thing. But I have to *know*."

"Then let me do it," Jock said.

"It's not addressed to you," she said bitterly. "It's addressed to me, aimed at me." She reached out with a shaking hand and untied the silver ribbon. She took a deep breath and then lifted the lid of the box.

Blasphemer.

The single word on the card nested in the green tissue paper.

The tissue paper now soaked in blood.

She stared down at the paper.

Do it.

She pushed aside the paper.

Dark eyes staring up at her, dark hair drenched in blood.

She flinched back.

"Jane."

Her stomach was heaving.

"It shouldn't have happened," she whispered. She couldn't stop staring down into Yvette Denarve's eyes. "I didn't know her, MacDuff. I hadn't even met her."

MacDuff pulled her back and stepped between her and that box on the table. "No, it shouldn't have happened. And you shouldn't have opened that damn box." He took out his handkerchief and was wiping her hand. "Now get out of here and go upstairs."

Why was he wiping her hand? She wondered dazedly. She looked down at the pristine white handkerchief and saw streaks of blood on it. Oh, yes, she'd gotten blood on her hand when she'd pushed the green tissue paper aside.

Yvette Denarve's blood on her hands. Celine's blood on her hands.

"Go upstairs," MacDuff repeated. "Jock and I will call Venable and take care of this."

She wasn't going to argue with him. It was one shock too many. She had to pull herself together before she could cope with any more.

And she *would* cope with it. Monstrosities like these couldn't be allowed to happen.

"Yes. Take care of it." Take care of the remains of an innocent woman who had done nothing to deserve this butchery. She wheeled and half staggered toward the elevator. "And then come and talk to me."

It was over three hours later that MacDuff

and Jock stepped out of the elevator.

MacDuff gazed at Jane searchingly. "Are you okay?"

"No," Jane said. "I'm not okay. I threw up twice, and I couldn't stop shaking for over an hour. I'm still sick and I'm angry and I'm scared to death." She got up from the couch and headed for the kitchen. "I just made coffee. First, I had to take a shower. Though I was tempted to leave those traces of blood on my hands to remind me what they did to her." She glanced at him as she poured coffee into the cups. "But I didn't need any reminders. This is going to be with me for the rest of my life. And that's why I'm so angry that every other emotion I'm feeling is fading into the background."

"None of this is your fault, Jane," Jock said.

She knew that was true, but it was difficult getting over that first feeling when she had looked down and seen the blood on her hands. "Not directly. But I have to have been the trigger," she said. "Even if it was those monsters that actually did the killing." She handed MacDuff the cup, making an effort to keep her hands from shaking. She couldn't give in to weakness. The time was past when she could allow herself that luxury. "How did that flower box get here?

It couldn't have been more than a few hours from the time that they killed her. They had to work very quickly."

"The box was delivered by a man in a postal uniform together with a few other boxes and a bunch of cards. The box was heavy cardboard, and there was no blood on it when it was delivered. There were even a few utility bills for Celine in the mix. They had it all planned in advance."

"Like they did Yvette's death. They knew her sister would come to Paris when she heard that Celine was murdered."

Jock nodded. "They were probably watching her to see if she would drive or take the train from Lyon."

And Yvette had driven that highway, and they had brutally taken her life, taken her head, and thrown her body into the woods. The memory was causing her to shake again. She had to keep control.

"Was there any problem with — Did Venable take care of everything?"

He nodded. "He had someone here right away. He'll arrange for her death to look like a traffic accident, and he won't let anyone know the gory details." His lips twisted. "That may piss Millet off. I'm sure the bloody bastard likes to take credit."

"Good." She handed a cup to Jock.

"Yvette wasn't married, but did she have anyone close to her besides Celine?"

"Not as far as Venable can find out. Why?"

"Because we can't be sure who would be safe. The ugliness is spreading out like ripples from the center of a whirlpool. I wanted to be sure to protect anyone who needed to be protected." She took a sip of her coffee. "And it seems as if anyone who even nodded at me on the street might fill that criteria. I want you to tell Venable that Marie Dessault has to be protected." She looked at MacDuff. "And Joe and Eve will be close to the top of the list. I have to make sure to keep them safe. Will you help me?"

"Of course. How?"

"I'm going to bring them to MacDuff's Run. The people in your villages and the estate are almost slavishly loyal to you. I can't imagine anywhere they'd be safer."

"Neither can I." He paused. "That's why I wanted you to come home with me."

"I'll have to come for a little while. Eve and Joe wouldn't consent to go if I didn't. I may have trouble getting them there anyway." She had another thought. "Eve's mother lives in Atlanta. It shouldn't be as much of a threat for her, but I'll have to make sure Joe arranges security for her at her condo." She turned back to Jock. "And you'll come to the Run, too. When you killed Folard, the chances are that you set yourself up for the same kind of retribution they're dealing out to me. Isn't that right?"

He nodded. "But I knew that was a possibility. I made the choice."

"Well, you didn't give me the choice. I won't have your blood on my hands, too. And what about all the people who are close to you? How are you going to keep them from being hurt?"

"My mother is dead now," Jock said. "I have no one close to me they can hurt." He glanced at MacDuff. "Except the Laird, and he can take care of himself." He smiled. "Unless you'd like me to stand over you and shoo all the wicked villains away? It would be my pleasure."

"I believe I can handle my own protection," MacDuff said. "I've managed a number of years without your help, Jock."

"Aye," Jock said solemnly. "But those years may be telling on you, and I'm just going into my prime."

"You'll go with us, Jock," Jane said. "You said you would before."

"Again, it will be my pleasure. That's what I want to do." His gaze narrowed on her face. "You're functioning at high efficiency.

I didn't expect it after seeing you down-stairs."

"I was in shock when we found Yvette's . . ." She had to stop before she could go on. "Head. I couldn't believe that anyone could be that savage. I've been in a state of denial since I saw Celine nailed to that door. But I have to believe it now. I have to assume that they'll do anything and everything that they feel like doing. It doesn't matter if it makes sense to me." Her lips tightened. "But they're not going to hurt anyone else in my name. And I'm not going to stand by and let them kill one more person if I can stop it." She put her cup down on the counter. "And I will stop them. It will just take a little time."

"They don't want to give you that time," MacDuff said.

"That's right." She said. "Eight days till doomsday, didn't you say?"

"Seven days now," Jock said.

"And they're killing everyone around me to prepare the way." She frowned. "Why are they waiting? Why not kill me now? Even Folard thought he was committing some kind of a transgression by trying to kill me before April 1." She glanced at Jock. "You got no hint about that when you were with them?"

111

He shook his head. "I was an outsider. They didn't talk to me."

"But this Ted Weismann says that he knows."

"Yes."

"Damn, there's so much that we have to find out. Who's the man who sent Millet that newspaper article? And to what kind of job is that article about me connected? We have to make Weismann tell us. Venable has to pay him."

"I've told him that," MacDuff said. "After Yvette Denarve's death, I can't imagine him not doing it."

"We have to be sure. Shall I call him back or will you?"

His brows lifted. "I'll do it."

"And then make arrangements for us to go to MacDuff's Run. Oh, and make sure Venable has men protecting Eve and Joe until I can get them there."

"Whatever you say." He tilted his head. "What a bossy bit of goods you are, Jane."

"You bet I am." She looked him in the eye. "Not too eager to claim me as a member of the family now?"

"On the contrary. You're displaying all kinds of MacDuff characteristics. No one ever said we were a tame lot." He turned to Jock. "We'd better get moving and pack up those three paintings for Jane. I want to have her out of here and at the Run within the next several hours."

"Call Venable now," Jane said. "I'll pack my own paintings."

"I can do both."

"Venable first. Weismann is the key to all of this." She turned away. "I have to know why it's happening before I can stop it."

FIVE

Jane's phone rang as she was heading for the elevator to go down to the gallery. Joe Quinn.

She braced herself as she pressed the button. "I was just going to call you. I need you and Eve to go to MacDuff's Run. There are some problems that may involve —"

"You mean a headless corpse and a danger that Eve might follow in her footsteps?" Joe asked bluntly. "Yes, I can see that would be a problem."

"How did —" She stopped. "MacDuff phoned you."

"Hell, yes," Joe said. "He wanted to assure me that he'd be able to keep Eve safe if we came to him. He said he wasn't only going to rely on his people on the estate. He's hiring some of his buddies he served with in the Royal Marines to guard the castle. A very tough bunch."

"So will you come?" She paused. "Will

Eve come?"

"She's in the middle of a reconstruction, but I had a hard time keeping her at the cottage after you called her the night of Celine Denarve's death." He was silent a moment. "She'll come if she thinks you need her. I'd say that this latest murder constitutes a very real need."

"And you'll come with her?"

"I'll come and check out MacDuff's security arrangements."

"Joe."

"No, Jane. I'm not going to be walled up in that castle like a scared rabbit. As soon as I make sure the two of you are safe, I'm going to meet with Venable and see what I can do about catching those sons of bitches."

"Joe, dammit, you'll be a target, too."

"Then let them try to take me down. They won't find it easy going. I face scum like them every day of my life." He paused. "I think you understand. You're probably angry as hell by now. I'd say they've pushed you a little too far."

Joe knew her too well. "I do understand," she said. "But will Eve?"

"If it means keeping you safe. She's lived with a cop too long not to know that I have to do what I have to do." His voice became brusque. "When are you going to MacDuff's Run?"

"Tonight."

"Then we'll see you there tomorrow afternoon. If we can tear through the red tape and get the skull Eve's reconstructing through Security and Customs. Homeland Security is a little difficult these days about things like that."

"You'll breeze right through. I have faith in you."

"And we have faith in you," he said quietly. "We've always been a great team. Hold on until we can get there and give you backup." He hung up.

She felt a surge of warmth as she pressed the disconnect. No sappy sentiment, just those final words of faith and support. Tough yet understanding. Joe. Her friend who had given her that same support and understanding during all those years since she'd come to live with him and Eve.

She should have known he'd choose to team up with Venable. Another thing for her to worry about. Well, Venable would just have to take care of him or she'd —

What was she thinking? Joe wasn't only a detective, he was a former SEAL. No one took care of Joe but Joe. Unless she could find a way of doing it without infringing on his independence. That sounded familiar. Joe and she were a lot alike.

MacDuff was just hanging up the phone when she got off the elevator in the gallery. "You got around to calling Venable?" she asked. "But you called Joe first. Why?"

"I wanted to pave the way for you. And it's the duty of the host to offer the invitation. I learned that at my mother's knee."

"And what did you learn from Venable?"

"Nothing good," he said grimly. "Weismann's running scared. He said he can't trust Venable right now. One of his contacts with the agency set up a trap for him. He barely got away with his skin intact. He's going underground until he decides it's safe for him."

"No!" Jane said. "He can't do that. Who knows how many people could die before he surfaces again. Venable has got to find him."

"He's trying," MacDuff said. "But Weismann has probably been preparing for his vanishing act for years. It's not going to be easy trying to track him."

"I don't care about easy. He's *got* to do it."

"Weismann's ended all communication with Venable. He told him not to come after him, not to try to reach him."

"The hell we won't go after him."

"My thought exactly," MacDuff said. "As soon as I get you to MacDuff's Run, I'll see what I can do. Jock may have some idea how we can trace him."

"But Jock's already said that he didn't know that much about Weismann."

"Jane, we have to systematically go down every path until we find the right one."

"Systematically?"

"Not the word you want me to use, is it? I'd like to jump over all the hurdles, too. But we don't have that option. We'll just have to be patient." He took her suitcases. "Jock is waiting outside in the car. Let's get going."

She didn't move. He was talking about going to MacDuff's Run and hiding away from those bastards. It had been a tolerable solution when she had thought that Venable could make strides in discovering what was happening. It was not tolerable now. "There has to be some way to —"

He shook his head. "No jump starts, Jane."

"I heard you." She headed toward the door.

Systematic. No jump starts. Be patient.

She stopped short as a thought suddenly occurred to her.

"What is it?" MacDuff's gaze was fixed on

her face.

"Probably nothing." That was true. It was only a wild wisp of an idea that had occurred to her.

Or was it?

All it might take would be a phone call . . .

She went out the door and past the crime-scene tape to the car by the curb. Jock got out of the car and held open the passenger seat door for her. "Ready to go?"

She nodded and got into the car.

She was vaguely aware of MacDuff getting into the backseat.

Think.

Was it such a bizarre idea?

Bizarre, yes. But did it have a chance of working?

Consider all the choices. By the time they got to the airport she had to have an answer.

MacDuff had shifted over on the seat so that he could see her face, and she could feel his gaze studying her. He had caught her instant of hesitation, and his every sense was alert and trying to process it.

"We should be at the airport in about twenty minutes," Jock said as he pulled away from the curb. "And we'll be home by midnight." He glanced at MacDuff. "I've missed the Run. It's strange. No matter

119

where you go, you wish to go back to your roots."

"You could have come back anytime. It was your decision to stay away."

"I leaned too heavily on you. I had to learn to stand alone." He looked at Jane. "And Jane wasn't there to protect me from your domineering ways."

"I've noticed you do very well on your own these days," Jane said. She fell silent again. Time was passing.

Think. Concentrate.

That wisp of an idea was taking on form and texture. But would it work?

And how to go about it if she decided that it had a chance?

"You and MacDuff get on the plane," Jock said as he pulled up in front of the hangar. "I'll turn in the rental car."

"Okay," MacDuff said as he got out of the car. "Don't waste any time. I want to get out of here." He reached out to open Jane's car door. "Come on. Let's go."

She braced herself. "No."

He stiffened. "What?"

She didn't move. "I'm not going. You get on that plane and go to MacDuff's Run. I have something to do here."

"No way," he said with great precision.

"You stay, I stay."

"You can't stay," she said. "Eve and Joe will be there tomorrow. I promised them they'd be safe. You made the same promise. The Laird's promise. You have to make arrangements."

"Then you go, too."

"I can't do it. I have to find Weismann."

"I told you that we'd find him. It will just take —"

"Time? Patience? I don't have either one, MacDuff. I'm going to get my jump start."

"How?"

"In a way you'd probably not believe and certainly not approve. But I've got to try it."

"Try what, Jane?" Jock asked.

"I think I know a way I can find Weismann." She gazed directly at MacDuff. "But it's going to be a very delicate process, and I can't have you getting in the way. So you get on that plane, and I'll call you when I find him." She turned to Jock. "Will you go with me? I know MacDuff's not going to let me go alone, and I have to have him at the Run to keep Eve safe."

"You're taking Jock and leaving me out in the cold?" MacDuff asked roughly.

"You'd want to run things. Jock is more reasonable." She asked Jock again, "Will you

121

go with me?"

Jock glanced at MacDuff, then back at Jane. He was silent for a moment. "How could I resist? It's not often that I'm chosen over the MacDuff."

"This isn't smart," MacDuff said harshly. "Jock, tell her that as long as she stays out in the open, she'll be a target. She's obviously not listening to me."

"She knows that she'll be in danger," Jock said. "But it's worth it to her. She's going to do it, MacDuff. We have to make adjustments to the situation." He put the car in gear. "I'll keep her safe. We'll call you every now and then to keep you informed."

"Every now and then?" MacDuff repeated in disbelief. "Damn you, Jock, you'll call me every day, or I'll break your head."

"I can see why Jane chose me," Jock said. "She's right, you're not at all reasonable." He drove off before MacDuff could answer.

"You didn't have to goad him like that." Jane's gaze was on the rearview mirror. MacDuff hadn't moved, and his expression was forbidding. "He's positively fuming."

"It will be good for him," Jock said cheerfully. "He gets his way far too often." He glanced at her. "And you're the one who started it. I didn't initiate this particular rebellion. MacDuff doesn't like to be left out of anything."

"He's not being left out. He's going to take care of the people I love."

"He would regard that as less than challenging."

"It will be challenging enough. I told Joe and Eve I'd be at the Run. They're not going to be pleased when they find out I'm not there."

"And why aren't you there? What is this all about?"

"I told you, I know a way to find Weismann."

"What way?"

"Actually, I think I know someone who can find him."

"With practically no information?"

"I think it's possible."

"Interesting. Who?"

"His name is Seth Caleb."

"CIA? FBI?"

"No."

"A private detective?"

"No."

He looked at her inquiringly.

How to explain Seth Caleb? She had known it was going to be difficult. That was why she had not wanted MacDuff on the scene. Even with Jock, it was better not to go into great depth now. "He's a hunter."

"What kind of hunter? Animal? Big game?"

"Oh, yes. Very big game. He's . . . unusual."

"And how did you come to meet this . . . hunter?"

"Several weeks before I came to Paris, Eve and Joe were trying to capture a serial killer, Jelak. They thought he might have been the one who murdered her daughter, Bonnie, years ago. Caleb was after the same man. We formed a sort of uneasy alliance until they caught Jelak. Caleb was extraordinary."

"*Extraordinary. Unusual.* Not common descriptions, are they?" His gaze narrowed on her face. "But you don't want to tell me why this hunter is capable of finding Weismann."

"Not until I'm sure that Caleb will help me."

"Money?"

"No, Caleb has plenty of money." She shook her head. "Just let me call him and talk to him. I don't want to keep anything from you, Jock. Caleb is hard to explain, and I don't want to waste time until I know that he'll come."

"Then I'll try to be patient." He smiled faintly. "One of those words that you don't like again. But I have no quarrel with it."

He pressed the accelerator. "But I'd better lose the man who is following us so that you can make your call."

"Someone is —" Of course she would be followed. She had just been so absorbed she had not thought of the possibility. "Can you lose him?"

"No problem. It will just take a little while. But it would be best if you don't use your phone. The Sang Noir may have the souls of beasts, but they're techno-savvy. We wouldn't want your 'hunter' to be taken down before he could come to your rescue."

"You're telling me that they could be monitoring my cell?"

"They have the right equipment if they're within a hundred yards."

"And they could know that Eve and Joe are on their way to MacDuff's Run?"

"Yes, but MacDuff has already arranged to have them watched until they're safely within the gates."

Relief surged through her. "Then get me away from them. I have to call Caleb."

An hour later Jock pulled into the parking lot of the Bleinart Inn, a small stone hotel some distance south of Paris. "This should be safe enough. We've lost our tail."

"I'd say that you would have managed to

lose anyone following us," she said dryly. "I'm dizzy from all those blasted turns."

"I'm very good at losing anyone after me. It was part of my training." His lips twisted. "What good is an assassin if he can be traced?" He turned off the ignition. "This place looks decent enough. I'll go inside and check us in. That will allow you to have privacy for your call."

"Thank you, Jock."

"The sooner you make the call, the sooner I'll know what this is all about." He got out of the car and grabbed the suitcases. "I'll be back in fifteen minutes."

She hesitated as she pulled out her phone. It wasn't a call that she wanted to make. Seth Caleb had always been an unknown quantity to her. She had known him for only a matter of days while he was on the hunt for a serial killer who had threatened Eve. Yet their time together had been filled with darkness and a disquieting fascination.

Darkness.

Yes, that described Caleb. The darkness of the unknown, of violence, of death, of power. A few weeks ago, when he had left Eve's lake cottage, Jane had been glad to see him go. She had felt as if she had stood on the edge of an active volcano and looked down into the fiery depths. But then she had been permitted to walk away.

Permitted? Why had that word occurred to her? She ruled her own life. Caleb had no control of her.

But if she'd wanted him to go away, why had she kept his cell number in her phone?

Because there was sometimes a use for darkness and the people who dealt in it.

So stop analyzing my motives. I've already made my decision. Call Seth Caleb.

She dialed his number.

He answered the phone on the second ring. "Surprise. Surprise. What's wrong, Jane?"

"Why do you think there's something wrong? You told me you couldn't read minds."

"I can't. But you've always been wary of me. And rightly so. It would take a serious problem to nudge you into calling. Is it Eve?"

"No. Yes. It may be trouble for Eve unless I can get a handle on this."

"And you think I can help you. Why?"

"You're a hunter. I need to find a man. Quickly."

"I assume you want him alive?"

"Of course."

"There's no 'of course' about it. Most of the people I hunt I don't allow to live."

She smothered the tingle of shock at the carelessness of the statement. It wasn't as if she hadn't known that about him. "I need information, not for you to kill the bastard."

He chuckled. "And I was looking forward to giving you a gift of that magnitude. Not his head on a platter? Since the moment I met you, I knew that it would take something extraordinary to impress you. Information is too easy."

"Not this time. I've had enough of decapitated —". She had to stop as memories flooded back to her. She had to steady her voice. "All I want is for you to find Ted Weismann so that I can question him. Will you do it?"

He was silent a moment. "Decapitated . . . You picked up on that too soon. I wonder why? I think that perhaps there may be an opportunity in this to impress you after all."

"No, I don't want you involved in anything but the search. I don't want to be responsible. It's ugly, Caleb."

"I'm used to ugly," he said. "And I'm touched that you're trying to protect me. And you won't be responsible. If I want to do you a favor, then I'll do it. It's always my choice, Jane."

"I don't want a favor," Jane said. "Favors always have to be returned, and I've never been able to trust you not to have a hidden agenda."

"That's because you're so clever. Of course I do."

"Set a price, Caleb."

"I'll think about it," he said. "In the meantime, I think I should get to work and try to find this Weismann. What can you tell me about him that might help?"

"Not much. He belonged to Sang Noir, a murder-for-hire group, but he's now on the run. He was with their cell headquarters in Rome until the past few days. He's manipulative, money-hungry, and doesn't give a damn who dies as long as he can squeeze enough cash out of Venable."

"Venable. CIA?"

"You know him?"

"No, I've heard of him. But our paths have never crossed. Over the years I've dealt with any number of intelligence agencies. They're a rich source to tap for information. I would probably have gotten around to Venable eventually." His tone was thoughtful. "Sang Noir. I did have an encounter with them several years ago. I was forced to remove one of their members. Well, not exactly forced, it was a pleasure."

"Then I'm surprised you're not on their hit list."

"They had no idea I had anything to do with it. I made sure it looked like natural causes. Poor man had a brain hemorrhage."

She shivered. The casualness of his tone was chilling, but no more than the possibility that he could cause those hemorrhages. It shouldn't have bothered her. Knowing what she did about the Sang Noir, she knew the man had probably deserved death.

"Get over it, Jane," Caleb said softly. "You came to me. Accept me for what I am."

"I do. Most of the time. Sometimes it's harder than others." She had to move on. "Where are you? How soon can I expect some word from you?"

"I'm at my house in Switzerland. After I left Eve's lake cottage, I had a desire to go to my villa on Lake Lucerne. In many ways it's probably even more beautiful than your lake in Georgia." He paused. "But it was the company, not the scenery that I found lacking. I missed sitting on that porch with you."

She had a sudden memory of Caleb sitting on the top step of those porch stairs. Dark, intense eyes gazing out at the water, high cheekbones, sensual, beautifully shaped lips, the faintest indentation in his chin. Though only in his late thirties, dark hair slightly threaded with gray at the temples, his body relaxed but still radiating strength and power. Everything about him had always been high-impact. That impact had stunned her when she had first met him and was affecting her right now even though she couldn't see him. She repeated, "When will I hear from you?"

"I'll get to work right away. I'll head for Rome and see what I can find out. I still know where to find a few of the members of the group. As I recall, there was nothing complicated about them. Neanderthals with high-powered weapons. It shouldn't be too difficult. Where are you?"

"I'm at the Bleinart Inn outside Paris, but I don't know how long I can stay here before I have to move on."

He was silent for an instant. "That sounds remarkably as if you're on the run. Are you?"

She ignored the question. "Get back to me as quickly as you can."

"Oh, I will. But I don't like the fact that you're not telling me everything. You know how curious I can be."

"No, I don't know that much about you. Except that you're manipulative and have no compunction about doing exactly what pleases you."

"Not true. I've told you before, I have a

kind of code. If I didn't have some compunction, then I'd be the same kind of monster as the people I hunt." He chuckled. "But since you've chosen to bring me back in your life, it's inevitable that you do get to know me very well indeed. I'm looking forward to it."

"I'm not."

"I know. As I said, you've always been wary of me." His voice lowered to velvet softness. "Do you want me to take away all that wariness and make you look forward to it, too?"

She felt sudden scorching heat move through her. "Hell, no."

He sighed. "I do hope I can keep from breaking my code and going ahead anyway. You've always been a temptation, Jane." He didn't wait for her to reply. "I'll call you when I have something to report. It will be soon. I'm very, very eager." He hung up.

She drew a deep breath as she hung up. It was done. But what had she gotten herself into?

Nothing she couldn't handle.

Caleb was her best bet in this insane situation. If it was inevitable that they get to know each other as he had said, then it would happen.

She had a sudden memory of the searing

instant of heat she'd experienced a moment before. That undercurrent of sensuality had been present every since they'd first met, but she'd tried to ignore it.

Well, she could handle that, too.

"Finished?" Jock was walking toward her across the parking lot. "You weren't long."

"No?" She glanced at the clock on the dashboard. Less than ten minutes. It had seemed a much longer time. "Were you able to get us rooms?"

"Yes, no problem." He opened the car door for her. "I sent your bags up to your room. No room service, but there's a coffee bar in the lobby, and I arranged for a to-go order. I'll pick it up when we get inside. Coffee and a couple sandwiches. Okay?"

She nodded. "I'm not hungry."

"You should eat. When's the last time you had anything but coffee?"

She smiled. "I had that bowl of cold cereal you set out for me at the apartment."

"Good." He took her elbow. "But that was a long time ago. Let's see if you can get down a sandwich. We'll take them up to your room, and you can eat." He paused. "And then satisfy my appetite for information. I hope everything went well with your Seth Caleb?"

Had it gone well? She couldn't be sure.

She was as disturbed as she usually was after speaking to Caleb. "I suppose that it went as well as could be expected. He's going to help me find Weismann."

"Promising. But I want to know a good deal more about your friend, Caleb. MacDuff will cross-examine me without mercy. If I'm to keep him at the Run acting as guardian, I'll have to have answers."

"You'll have them." She entered the Inn. "But I'm warning you, he'll still have problems with my using Caleb. That's why I chose you and not MacDuff to come with me."

"You didn't eat very much," Jock said. "I know the bread tasted like cardboard but it —"

"It was fine," she interrupted. "I had enough." She lifted the paper cup containing the hot coffee to her lips. "This is all I need."

"It's good coffee." Jock stretched out his legs in front of him. "Perhaps to make up for those atrocious sandwiches." He looked around the room. "This is pleasant. I like all those purple and white flowers on the bedspread. Restful."

"It's too pretty." She glanced at the windows draped in sheer white chiffon. "It looks like something from a ten-year-old girl's wish list."

"When you were ten, would it have been on your wish list, Jane?"

"No, I was always suspicious of anything that was too pretty. I was a tough little kid." She braced herself. "And now that you've tried to put me at ease, hadn't you better start the interrogation?"

"Interrogation? You make me sound like a cop."

No, he was nothing like a cop. His gentle persistence was much more insidious. He would just sit there, smiling that beautiful smile and waiting for her to speak.

"You want to know about Seth Caleb."

He nodded. "Will it be easier if I ask you questions?"

"I don't know. Maybe."

"The main thing I want to know is why you think Caleb can find Weismann when Venable is having trouble?"

"It's what Caleb does. He has a passion."

"For hunting. What kind of hunting, Jane?"

"He finds people who can't be found."

"For whom?"

"He works principally for the Devanez family, who are his relations, but he takes other assignments if they interest him. I know he spent years hunting down a cult that was responsible for the death of his sister."

"Ah, vengeance. Good punishing evil?"

"In a way. It's not that simple. Yes, as far as I know, the people he hunts are slimeballs who deserve to be punished. But Caleb doesn't pretend to be the sword of justice. He's not that hypocritical."

"And by what means is your wonderful hunter able to find those people?"

Dammit, she had known that question would come. "He's . . . unusual."

"You said that before and in just that tone. I'm intrigued. Are you going to explain?"

"Yes." She might as well stop stumbling around and just come out with it. "Caleb has certain talents. One of them is an ability to change people's perception."

"You mean he's very persuasive."

"No." She shrugged. "I mean that give him a few minutes alone with anyone, and he can convince them that they want to do anything he wants them to do. He can turn hatred into friendship. If he asks anyone questions, they're going to answer him. Which would help enormously if you're on the hunt for someone."

"I imagine it would," Jock said absently, his gaze studying her face. "Let me understand you. You're talking about a psychic ability?"

"I know that it sounds weird."

"Oh, yes."

"You don't have to believe me. That's why I didn't want MacDuff coming along. I knew I'd have trouble with him thinking I was off my rocker. I wouldn't blame him. I'm not sure I believe it. I'm a realist, and what I ran across with Caleb was out of my comfort zone. But I saw him do it with the grandfather of my friend, Patty. He changed him from a bad-tempered bastard to someone almost pleasant. He didn't promise that it would be permanent, but even Patty could see the difference in her grandfather."

"One case."

"I was skeptical, too." She paused, then said reluctantly, "He gave me a personal demonstration."

"Personal?"

"Don't ask. I was ready to murder him." She added, "But he can do it, Jock. If anyone can find Weismann, it will be Caleb. He's spent most of his life hunting down people."

"And what does he do when he catches them?"

Her grasp tightened on the paper cup. "I imagine his death count may be as high or higher than yours, Jock."

"Really?" He leaned back in his chair. "You do seem to draw us lost souls to you, don't you, Jane?"

"But he's not like you," she said sharply. "It wasn't your fault. You were sick. You had no choice. He decided on the path he was going to travel."

"There's always something that triggers that decision. What was his trigger, Jane?"

"He had . . . other talents. His background is very dark. For hundreds of years those psychic gifts were passed down through his family. Back in the fourteenth century his family used their talents to inspire fear and dominate the small village in Italy where they lived." She moistened her lips. "According to Caleb, they balanced on the edge of becoming monsters."

"What other talents?"

"Blood. I didn't see it, but Eve did. She watched him kill a man without touching him. Most of it has to do with the flow of blood through the body."

"Blood." He chuckled. "Good God, he sounds like a vampire."

"No," she said curtly. "Don't be ridiculous."

"Is it ridiculous?" His smile faded. "Then what or who is he, Jane?"

"I don't know. I think he believes that he's inherited that bad gene that's been passed down through his family. He said he became a hunter to keep himself under control. Maybe he thought if he was going to kill anyway that he might channel it. The hunting provided a sort of release." Jock was asking questions she had asked herself and still had few answers, she realized in frustration. "He said it helps him maintain his code."

"And what is his code?"

"I don't know him well enough to know that," she said impatiently. "For all I know his so-called code could change with every shift of the wind."

"You appear to be saying that you don't know quite a bit in this conversation. But it's not like you to trust anyone without a substantial reason."

"Then this has to be an exception. Do you think I wanted to have to contact Caleb? I told you, I'm not comfortable with him. But I have to find Weismann."

He took a sip of his coffee. "You're right, MacDuff would not have made it easy for you to pull Seth Caleb into the search. He's a practical man, and he'd not appreciate the whimsy of your action. On the other hand, I have no difficulty with dealing with your psychic friend. I embrace whimsy. Reality can often be too cruel."

"He's not my friend."

"Yet he's coming to help you. There must be some connection."

Connection.

Searing sexuality. Heat. Her naked body moving feverishly beneath Caleb's.

No, it hadn't happened. That had been Caleb's damn demonstration of how he could influence her perception. It had been just a second's sensation that had shocked and angered her. She had wanted to murder him then, and the resentment was still white-hot. But so was the memory, and it wouldn't leave her.

"I don't know why he's doing it. He does what he wants to do. He wouldn't tell me what he wanted in return."

"That's always dangerous," Jock added with hushed melodramatic theatricalism. "What if he wants to drink your blood, my beauty?"

"I told you he wasn't —" She stopped. Jock was joking, but she was having trouble responding with any kind of humor. "Caleb isn't dangerous to me."

"No, he won't be a danger," Jock said. "Your blood is safe. I'll be here to watch over you."

"I didn't ask you to watch over me. You've

given up enough to help me." She grimaced. "And now I'm asking you to swallow something that there's no way you can believe."

"It's true that I have trouble with thinking anyone could possess those kinds of psychic abilities. My instinct is that it's pure trickery."

"Me, too," Jane said. "I understand perfectly."

"But when I was under medication and being brainwashed, I believed what I was being told without question. Could that be part of it?"

"No medication."

"Then I'll be interested in meeting Seth Caleb." He smiled slightly. "Since we appear to be members in the same club." He rose to his feet. "I'll let you get to bed now. I'm right next door. Lock your door. Call me if you need me or if you just want to talk."

"Are you going to call MacDuff?"

"Tomorrow. He won't expect a call tonight."

"And are you going to tell him about Caleb?"

He nodded. "The bare bones. No need to tell him that Caleb is a vampire. It would only upset him."

"I told you, Caleb is not —" She saw his

141

indented lips and realized he was joking again. This time she smiled in return. "Tell him what you like. MacDuff will probably tell you to kidnap me so that he can find a pleasant little funny farm to stash me in."

"He wouldn't do that," Jock said. "He never even thought about putting me in an asylum when I was going through my patch of hell. He cared for me himself."

"I know," Jane said gently. "So let's not make him think he's going to have to straighten my thinking out, too. Once is enough."

"Aye." He nodded as he turned toward the door. "More than enough. I swore I'd never cause him trouble like that again. That's why I think I'll forget to mention any details about Seth Caleb."

Six

I knew that Jock would be skeptical, Jane thought as she got to her feet after the door had closed behind him. She didn't know anyone who wouldn't have thought she was either crazy or enormously gullible. At least he had been kind and not openly scornful. But the skepticism had definitely been there.

Oh, well, it didn't matter as long as she had done what she thought was best.

And what was best right now was for her to get in the shower and crawl beneath that too-pretty quilt and go to sleep. The adrenaline that had been driving her was rapidly seeping away, and exhaustion was taking its place.

No wonder. She hadn't really slept more than a few hours for two days.

She locked the door and headed for the bathroom.

"I'm afraid, Mother."

143

"Shh, you mustn't be frightened, Kalim." His mother was hurrying him down the long dark corridor. "You're on your way to paradise."

"Will you be with me?"

"Not for a while. You're the only one who they think worthy."

"I don't want to go alone." The tears were pouring down his cheeks as he stumbled after her, blurring the sight of the glyphs on the walls. "Don't make me, Mother."

"I do not make you. The angels summon you. Now stop weeping. You've reached your eleventh year. You will shame me. We are almost there."

He couldn't stop the tears.

They had rounded the corner.

The stone altar was just ahead of him. He knew that altar. His cousin, Ali, had been chosen last year. Ali had not been afraid. He had been proud.

Kalim wanted to be proud. He wanted the fear to go away.

His mother had stopped and stepped aside. "Go," she whispered. "Go to paradise, Kalim."

He stumbled forward. He was vaguely aware of the two priests who were coming toward him.

Let me not scream. Let me not bring shame to my family.

But the tears would not stop.

As he was lifted on the altar, he saw the mosaic visage on the wall facing him.

Burning dark eyes, a dark beard, and an expression of agonized torment.

Help me, forgive me. His gaze clung to the mosaic face on the wall. Let me die well.

But then he could no longer see the face on the wall as the priest stepped toward him with the knife raised.

He screamed!

Jane jerked upright in bed, tears running down her cheeks.

She was panting as she swung her legs to the floor.

Just a dream. No, a nightmare.

She moved toward the bathroom and threw water on her face.

She was shaking. The dream had been too real, like the ones she'd had years ago. Like the ones she'd had while she was painting *Guilt*. But those dreams had not been about sacrifice and the killing of small children. There had been danger and pursuit and overpowering sadness but not this horror.

Dammit, how long was she to be plagued with these periods when her dreams seemed more real than life itself?

Get over it.

It was natural that she'd been followed

into sleep by nightmares. The last days had been horrible enough to spawn a thousand nightmares.

And there was no question that the mosaic face on the wall had been the face in her painting *Guilt.*

She had been obsessing about the painting, and it shouldn't surprise her that it had popped up in a dream.

But not in that way, not seen through the eyes of an innocent child about to be killed.

But Celine and her sister had been innocent also. There had been no reason to take their lives. Jane could have made some kind of weird connection . . .

Don't think about it. She could analyze her reasons all night and not come up with anything that would mean a damn. Go back to bed and try to get back to sleep.

Not yet. She'd sit down in that chair and try to pull herself together. There would be no going to sleep while that dream was so vivid in her mind. That poor little boy, Kalim, had been so afraid. He was still with her. She could feel his fear as if it were her own.

The last thing she wanted was to go back into that dream, to that altar, and look up and see *Guilt.*

■ ■ ■

"She's gone." Millet's voice was shaking with rage when Alan Roland picked up the phone. "Gavin dropped MacDuff off at the airport and drove off with her. The bastard slipped away from us."

Shit.

"You're telling me that you've lost her?" Roland asked. "How? You've been telling me how closely you've been having her shadowed."

"I did. Monson's usually a good man. But he said that Gavin was like one of those stunt movie drivers."

"You don't usually accept excuses."

"I won't this time either. Monson will be punished," he said. "But this is your fault. She would have been dead if you hadn't demanded we wait."

"You agreed that it would be more fitting for her to die on April 1. Her transgression has to be treated with due ceremony. Besides, you're not a man anyone can persuade into doing something against his wishes." He added a little flattery to pacify him. "You're too strong. Everyone knows that, Millet."

"No one can beat me when I rely on

147

myself. It's only when I depend on fools and weaklings that I have problems."

The fools and weaklings were aimed at him as well as Millet's inefficient underlings, Roland knew. He felt a surge of anger that he quickly subdued. Millet was only a tool even though he didn't realize it. There would be enough time to rid himself of the bastard when he got what he wanted. He ignored the personal inference. "But you'll punish Monson and can start out with a clean slate again."

"When I find the woman. You have to help me. You're the big man. You have contacts everywhere. I found out that Weismann double-crossed me and is working for the CIA. I've put out a kill order on the son of a bitch. He was the one who brought Gavin to us, and that means Gavin is CIA. You've got money to burn. Spend some of it bribing someone in the CIA to tell you where I can get Jock Gavin. If we find Gavin, we'll find Jane MacGuire."

"Good thinking. I'll start trying to tap my sources and get back to you. Don't worry, Millet. It shouldn't take too long to get a line on her."

Millet was silent a moment. "You're treating me as if I were a child. All that soothing bullshit. You're nothing without me, Roland.

I'm the only one who can give you what you want. All that influence and money, and in the end you're just another power-hungry son of a bitch without the right weapon to make it happen. I'm the weapon. Me. My men. The Sang Noir. Remember that."

Roland hadn't expected Millet to be that perceptive. He had known that Millet had the cunning of a wild animal but had thought that he would be easier to manipulate.

But that was before Jock Gavin and MacDuff had appeared on the scene to complicate matters. Jane MacGuire's support group was becoming increasingly annoying. It was difficult enough keeping a schizo like Millet reined in and under control. But he could do it. The only goal Millet had in life was to keep the position he held as Guardian, with all its power and perks. If Roland could deal with top CEOs and presidents, he could handle this fanatic little bastard. He said harshly, "Listen to me, Millet. You know what would happen if anyone but me knew how careless you were with Hadar's Tablet. They'd tear you apart. What good is a Guardian if he can't hold on to our most precious relic? I'm giving you a chance to save your ass and cement your position. The trade is still as good as when we made it. I give you an offering that will send your stock soaring with the members. You get that tablet back and let me keep it a few days to get it translated."

"But you want your time with Jane MacGuire, too. She's mine. You promised me. I don't know if I want to let you have her first."

Roland tried to retain his patience. "She must know something. She painted *Guilt*. It's not as if it's going to take that long to get the information. I'll try drugs first. Later, I may ask you to use your expertise on her if I don't get what I want." He knew that prospect was pleasing the bastard. "I'm sure you'd succeed if I didn't. You'd get everything you want. What I'm asking in return is nothing in comparison."

"I don't think anyone would say that billions of dollars is nothing."

"A *chance* for billions. But you have to give me that chance. I need my time with Jane MacGuire. You can have her later. I've circulated that photo of *Guilt* among the members, and they're salivating. They'll forgive you anything if you can produce her at the Offering." He paused. "I might even be persuaded to give you a share if you find her quickly enough."

Millet was silent. "I don't even know if

150

you can find the damn place. I can't be sure. You may be all talk."

"You know that rumors have been circulating since the time of Hadar. It's there. It *happened.* Jane MacGuire knows it did. Give me my time with her, and I'll find it." Time to use the whip. "Now are you going to cooperate, or should I be prepared to ask to see the sacred tablet on the night of the Offering?"

"You son of a bitch."

"Will you cooperate?"

Millet didn't speak for another moment, and Roland could almost feel his scalding anger. "Someday I'm going to cut your throat, Roland."

"No chance. I always watch my back. Yes or no?"

"I'll go along with you as long as it suits me," he finally said grudgingly.

"It will suit you." Time to shift away from intimidation. "Our partnership is very important to me, Millet. After all, you're the Guardian of the Offering. I have the utmost respect for you." Now throw the bastard a bone that would please his bloodthirsty soul. "I can understand how your Sang Noir feels cheated that they can't have Jane MacGuire yet. But they may feel better if they take an important substitute. I've learned that Eve Duncan and Joe Quinn have left Georgia and have taken a flight to Edinburgh, Scotland. That probably means that they'll be going to MacDuff's Run. I'm sure the MacGuire woman would be heartbroken if anything happened to them." He chuckled as a thought occurred to him. "And Eve Duncan works on skulls; I don't doubt that you could concoct something appropriately shocking that has to do with her career. How long does it take to boil the flesh off a skull? Or, if you choose, you might even be able to use them as hostages."

Millet was silent, thinking. "They were on our list to be next anyway. Yvette Denarve was only convenient."

"Then you can occupy yourself with them while I try to find out where Jock Gavin took Jane MacGuire."

"Yes." His voice became harsh. "But that doesn't let you off the hook. You're trying to distract me. I want to know where MacGuire is, then I'll decide whether I'm going to wait any longer."

"You'll wait. Think how they'll scream and praise you. She's going to be an offering beyond belief." Roland's hand tightened on the phone. "You wouldn't be forgiven if you waste her death, Millet. You'll know where she is as soon as I do."

"See that I do." Millet hung up.

Dammit, the situation was escalating, Roland thought as he hung up. Jane MacGuire's escape tonight had caused Millet to come dangerously close to throwing out the entire case Roland had built for waiting for the execution until April 1.

Screw him. He had to have his time with the MacGuire woman. Nothing was going to stand in his way.

"He's becoming difficult." Sheila Carmody smiled. "He'd be even more difficult if he knew how you've been screwing him. I've never seen anyone so clever at a double cross."

He turned to look at her. Sheila was blond, naked, and with all the appropriate talents. None of them had anything to do with conversation. Usually she was more discreet in her comments. Not that he had any worry about her talking to anyone else. She was a member and knew what the punishment would be if she broke his confidence. That was why he made sure most of his bed partners were of the chosen. "I haven't been screwing him." Roland moved over her on the bed. "Yet. I've just been finessing the bastard. I've only been screwing you. Now close your mouth and open your legs. I'm about to do it again."

Moments later, he was listening to her cries as he plunged deep and hard. This was power. Take and twist and make her come. Much better than Millet's idea of sexual pleasure. You didn't have to rip and tear to make a woman know she was helpless, and that you were the master.

But if Sheila showed other signs of curiosity, he might have to turn her over to Millet for schooling. He'd recently been stung by that bitch, Adah, who hadn't known her place. He wasn't about to have it happen again. But not now. Sheila was entertaining enough, and he was preoccupied with the problem of Jane MacGuire.

And he'd have to find Jane MacGuire if he was going to have a trade for the tablet. He had to hedge all his bets. Either MacGuire or the tablet had the potential to give him what he wanted.

He had to have both. He had to have it all.

He would find MacGuire first, get what he needed from her, then give her to Millet to play with before his frustration built too high. He'd researched her thoroughly and had an idea which way she'd jump.

A few more minutes with Shelia, and he'd get off her and reach for his phone . . .

Mario Sevelli was a good enough prospect, Seth Caleb thought as he studied the squat dark man sitting at the outdoor café on the Via Rimaldi. He had not paid much attention to Sevelli when he'd been targeting another member of the Sang Noir several years ago. It had not been necessary to involve anyone else in the search. He had known who he needed to find and kill.

But he probably wouldn't have to kill Sevelli. It should be a simple Q and A that might lead somewhere promising. After researching Ted Weismann, he doubted if he would have confided in anyone in the group. But he might have dropped a word, a hint, that Sevelli might or might not remember. If he came up zero, then he'd just move on to someone else. There were at least three other members of the Sang Noir who could be possibilities.

But Sevelli was alone at the table and Caleb wouldn't have any interruptions.

He moved across the street and through the crowded, noisy restaurant to Sevelli's table.

"A beautiful day, isn't it? May I sit down?" He smiled at Sevelli. "I'd like to talk to you."

Sevelli stiffened as he glanced up at him.

Caleb kept his smile in place and made his tone ingratiating. "I'd consider it a great favor."

The tension left Sevelli and he looked Caleb up and down. "I'm not having any. Buzz off, fag."

"I'm afraid you're misunderstanding me." Caleb pulled out the chair across from him and sat down. He gestured for the waiter, then gazed earnestly into Sevelli's eyes. "But I'll take care of that. We're going to be the best of friends."

Paris
Bleinart Inn

"Joe said you'd be here at MacDuff's Run," Eve said when Jane answered her call. "Where the hell are you?"

"I'm still in France." She had been bracing herself for this call. "Did MacDuff explain?"

"He explained as much as he could explain. He told me about Yvette Denarve and that you'd ditched him at the airport." She paused. "He said that you were looking for this Ted Weismann and were trying to locate someone who could find him."

"Weismann has all the answers. I have to find him, Eve."

"I can see that you would. MacDuff said that you didn't tell him who you were going to get to help you."

"He wouldn't approve my choice." She added, "And I don't have to tell you who it is, Eve."

"Seth Caleb. He was the first one I thought about when MacDuff was telling us that Weismann would be difficult to hunt down."

"Not for Caleb."

"You've contacted him?"

"Yes. He said he'd help me."

"Out of the goodness of his heart?"

"I don't know how much goodness there is in his heart. I just know that he agreed, and I'm going to accept it."

"You must feel desperate. If I remember, I was more inclined to be lenient with Caleb than you were."

"You didn't see Celine. You didn't see Yvette. Yes, I was feeling desperate. I can't have anyone else killed because I'm stumbling around in the dark. I have to know what's going on." She drew a deep breath. "I didn't trick you into coming to the Run because I was afraid for you. I *am* afraid for you and Joe. I'm terrified. But I intended to join you there."

"But then you thought about Seth Caleb

157

and knew that he was your best shot." She paused. "I know you'd never try to deceive me, Jane."

"I just had to be sure. I'll come to the Run as soon as I find Weismann. Will you stay there with MacDuff? It will make me feel better. If you were with me here, I wouldn't be able to concentrate on anything but keeping you safe."

Eve didn't speak for an instant. "I'll stay here until I think that I can help you more by going after you. Where are you? Or is that a secret from me as well as MacDuff?" Then she added quickly, "No, don't tell me. I don't know how secure MacDuff's communication setup is here."

"I imagine Jock will tell MacDuff anyway. But I don't know how long I'll be here. As soon as Caleb finds Weismann, I'll have to go."

"Let me know when you do."

"I will." She changed the subject. "Are you working?"

"Of course. When don't I? It keeps me functioning. I brought the skull of a little boy with me. I call him Ronald. MacDuff is going to set me up a grand workroom next to my bedroom in one of the towers. I'm sure it will feel very plush after my humble work area at the cottage."

"There's nothing humble about anything you do," Jane said. Eve was reputed to be the world's greatest forensic sculptor. She tried to stay out of the public eye except when it was to help public awareness of the need to find and identify missing children. Since years ago she had lost her little daughter, Bonnie, to a serial killer, it had been her passion. No, that wasn't quite true. She was dedicated to helping those children and their grieving parents. But her passion was the desire to find her Bonnie's killer and bring the body of her daughter home. Everything else paled in comparison. "But I'm glad MacDuff is taking care of you there at the Run. How's Joe?"

"Restless. He's going to join Venable in Rome tomorrow. He said he told you he would."

"Yes, but I thought I was going to be there to take —"

"Care of me?" Eve finished for her. "Then you can't blame me for feeling the same about you. Come as soon as you can." She paused. "You know, I like this place. It's very grand, but there's a kind of ageless comfort about it. Ever since I stepped inside the gates I've been feeling a sense of . . . rightness. As if there was a reason why I should be here. Crazy, huh?"

"No, you should be there so MacDuff can keep you safe."

"That's not what I meant. I just feel . . . it's as if there's something here or something coming. Something . . . unfolding, and I have a part in it. Did you know there's a painting of one of MacDuff's ancestors who looks like you?"

Jane sighed. "Fiona. MacDuff would have to show it to you."

"He didn't. I noticed it myself. Too bad there's not a portrait of his many-times great-great-grandmother Cira. She might look even more like you."

"Don't mention that to MacDuff. He's insistent enough now that I'm part of his blasted family. I can't convince him I'm done with Cira and her treasure chest and everything else connected to MacDuff's Run."

"Evidently not. Considering that I'm here right now. Well, it will be nice to look at the portrait since I can't have you here."

"Then for the first time I'm glad I look like Fiona," Jane said. "But don't let MacDuff try to persuade you that it's anything but a coincidence."

"MacDuff is too busy making phone calls and talking to all these guards he has trip-ping over each other around the estate to

try to convince me of anything." She chuckled. "And he probably realizes I wouldn't
give a damn anyway. It doesn't matter who
you are to him; it's who you are to me that's
important."

"Thank God."

"Yes, I do thank him very frequently for
bringing you into our lives. Call me as often
as you can. Bye, Jane."

"She wasn't angry?" Jock asked, as Jane
hung up.

"No, I didn't really think she would be,
but I had to explain. I never take our
relationship for granted. It means too much
to me." She stood up. "Let's go for a walk. I
need to expend some energy. Eve said Joe
was restless, and I feel a definite empathy."

"I can see that you do." Jock got to his
feet. "You've been prowling this room like a
tiger cub all morning. Your Caleb had better work fast, or you'll be a nervous wreck."

"No, I won't. We'll walk, we'll have dinner
somewhere, then I'll come back and sketch
you. Working always relaxes me, and I
haven't sketched you for years."

"Since the first time you came to
MacDuff's Run," he said quietly. "You gave
me one of those sketches, and I sent it to
my mother. She could never understand the
monster I'd become. I told MacDuff that

he had to tell her what I'd done. She couldn't be allowed to think that there was no reason I couldn't come back to her. But how could she comprehend a son who killed? She had done her best, raised me to believe in hard work, God, and the Ten Commandments. All the things to which a good Scottish lad should adhere. After MacDuff brought me home from the hospital, he kept telling me that she'd understand. That she'd only think of that time as a terrible sickness." He shook his head. "I couldn't go back to her. It would only have hurt her. But I think she liked the sketch."

"I'm sure she did," Jane said gently. "And I'm sure she still loved you."

"Maybe. Mothers are pretty helpless about things like that." He smiled crookedly. "I'll be glad to have you sketch me again, Jane. It will be interesting to see the difference the years have made, won't it?"

Eve slowly put her phone in her pocket after she had hung up. She had been alarmed when she had first learned what Jane was doing, and she was still just as frightened. Caleb might be able to find this Weismann, but he was probably a more ruthless and dangerous man than the man he was hunting.

Blood.

She shuddered as she remembered what she had seen him do to that serial killer, Jelak, only a few weeks ago. Yes, Caleb had saved Joe's life and perhaps her own, but it had still been shocking. The blood running from the killer's eyes, the screams as his brain hemorrhaged. It had been hard to accept that anyone could have the power to do that. She would never have believed it if she hadn't seen it herself.

But she had seen it, and the memory wouldn't leave her. Had she somehow known that Caleb would be back in their lives?

But not like this. Not this horror involving Jane. She had wanted to keep Caleb away from Jane. She had sensed something between them, a sort of bonding, that had made her uneasy. Dammit, she didn't want Jane drawn into the darkness surrounding Caleb. Yet Jane was walking toward him like a moth to a flame.

No, she was insulting Jane. Jane was doing what she thought was right, and she was no helpless moth. Even Eve could see that Caleb could be the answer to finding Weismann. It was Eve who was feeling helpless and wanting to step in and whisk her away. It had taken all her will not to leave this haven Jane had set up for them and go after her.

Not now. Not yet. Jane didn't need her attention diverted because she was worrying about Joe and her.

So she'd do what she could from MacDuff's castle until it was time to make a move. There were a few things here that were making her uneasy, and she had to get clear.

She left her room and strode down the hallway toward the grand staircase.

MacDuff was coming through the massive fourteen-foot front doors.

She paused on the top step and looked down at him. The hall was all stone and rich tapestries, and simple chests. It had none of the dated furniture pieces she'd seen in other old manors. It looked as if it was a place one of MacDuff's wild, robber-baron forbears could have walked into at any moment. And though John MacDuff was dressed in dark trousers and rolled-neck sweater, he fit effortlessly into that ancient setting. Yes, she thought, he belongs to this place in spirit as well as birth.

He looked up as Eve came down the grand staircase. "You've talked to Jane? Did you convince her to come here?"

"I didn't try," Eve said. "There would

have been no use. She's doing what she thinks is right. I'm the one who will have to go to her if I think it's necessary."

"It's not necessary," he said curtly. "If she needs someone, I'll be there for her. I promised to keep you safe."

"Why?" She gazed at him searchingly. "You're turning your life here upside down. All for Jane." She smiled faintly, "And I don't think it's entirely because you have this idea that she's family."

"She helped Jock when he needed her."

"And that's admirable, too. But you've been trying to coax her back here for at least two years. I've been standing in the background looking on, but I've wondered . . ."

His gaze narrowed on her face. "You're a brilliant woman, Eve Duncan. I'd wager that you've done more than wonder."

"Well, I've made a few guesses." She paused. "You're a driven man, MacDuff. You love this property. It represents your roots, your family. Jane told me that you've almost lost this estate several times to taxes and exorbitantly expensive upkeep but managed to save it at the last minute."

He smiled. "Are you thinking I want to make a rich marriage to save it? I'm afraid Jane doesn't qualify. She's only a struggling artist."

"No, marrying for money wouldn't suit you at all. You're too much like your ancestors who preferred to rob and pillage. I'm talking about the chest of gold coins hidden by the first MacDuffs that you've been searching for all these years. At one time you thought Jane could lead you to it."

"She assures me she cannot."

"But do you believe her?"

"I believe she thinks she cannot."

"That's no answer."

"You want an answer?" MacDuff smile was suddenly reckless. "I think there's a chance that someday she'll be able to tell me where to find it. Look, Jane didn't just happen into my life. She came here because of all those dreams she was having about my ancestress, Cira. Yes, she was a student and fascinated by stories of Cira and her escape from Herculaneum during the Vesuvius eruption. But that wasn't what drew her here. It was the dreams. And in those dreams there was a chest of antique gold coins. It figured prominently in them."

"But her dreams didn't tell her where the chest was hidden."

"Because Jane didn't care about the gold. *I* care about the gold. I won't let my family home go to strangers." The passion vibrated in his voice.

166

"But dreams, MacDuff?" Her brows lifted mockingly. "I wouldn't judge you to be one to pay attention to such nonsense."

"Is it nonsense? I don't believe you think that's true. No one knows Jane the way you do, Eve."

She was silent. "I know that sometimes she's had dreams that were . . . strange. Most of them had to do with the past and people she had never met. But she hasn't had any dreams like that for a long time that I know about." She smiled faintly. "And my hard-headed Jane would deny with her last breath that they were any different from the run-of-the-mill dreams you or I have."

"Then I'll deny it for her. You're right; I'm not a man who believes in foolish flights of imagination. But this is different. Those dreams started a chain reaction that not only enabled us to kill that bastard Thomas Reilly but brought Jock home to heal and become whole again. That's good enough for me. There has to be a reason that happened. I *know* that Jane was sent to help me keep MacDuff's Run from going out of the family. Someday she'll understand that, too."

"And in the meantime it suits you to keep her alive," Eve said dryly.

"No, I'll keep her alive because she's

deserving and a part of my family. I have feeling for her," MacDuff said curtly. "The gold is a separate matter." He stared her in the eye. "And I wouldn't have been honest with you if I hadn't intended you to share what I said with Jane. I know how close you are. Tell her what you wish. It's not going to make a difference. I think in her heart she realizes that she'll have to come back and finish our story. Soon. I have a feeling that it's coming around full circle." He was silent, then asked, "Do you wish to know anything else?"

She studied him for a moment. He was full of arrogance and contradictions, but he was being honest with her. He was no threat to Jane even though he might want to lure her here for his own purposes. She had wanted to make sure of this piece of the puzzle. She was already feeling very power-less stuffed away in this castle. "You really believe Jane is your distant cousin?"

"You saw the portrait of Fiona." He smiled. "But I think she resembles the woman she was having dreams about much more."

Eve smiled as she remembered that she'd speculated on that very possibility with Jane earlier. "Cira, who founded your clan?"

He nodded. "Anything else?"

"Yes, one more question."

"What?"

She made a face. "Will you take me to that tower you've given me as my studio? You said it was close to my room? I need to get to work. It's the only way I can keep myself from jumping on a plane and going to Jane."

SEVEN

"Jane."

The call was soft, invading her sleep with a gentle whisper.

"Jane."

More persistent, but still only a quiet summons.

But the summons was there and she reluctantly turned over and opened her eyes.

And was instantly jarred wide-awake.

Seth Caleb was sitting in a chair only a few feet from her bed.

"What the hell!" She reached over and switched on the lamp on the bedside table.

Caleb smiled. "I suppose you had to turn on the lamp, but I really prefer the moonlight streaming in that window. You look wonderful by moonlight, Jane."

"What are you doing here?" She sat up in bed and glared at him. "Dammit, I locked that door."

"And it was a very good lock. Better than

most hotels. It took me longer than I thought it would."

"You could have called me from the lobby. You didn't have to invade my room."

He shrugged. "It seemed easier. I'm a hunter."

"But you're not hunting me."

"Not at the moment." He smiled as he rose to his feet and picked up her terry robe draped over the chair. "Besides, I wanted to see how well protected you were here at the inn. I'm good, but so are some of the men in the Sang Noir." He handed her the robe. "Where's Jock Gavin?"

"Next door." She took the robe and slipped it over her short T-shirt. She immediately felt less vulnerable, and she had an idea that he had known it would have that effect. "And no one knows I'm here at the inn." She frowned. "How did you know about Jock?"

"Since you were so miserly with information I had to take it upon myself to find out what was going on. I just added it to my search-and-probe agenda."

"I told you all you needed to know."

"But not all I wanted to know. There's a huge difference." His gaze wandered around the room. "No coffeemaker. Too bad. I could use a cup. It's been a long day."

She glanced at the clock on the nightstand — 3:40 A.M. "Then you went overtime. It's the middle of the night."

"I don't mind overtime when the adrenaline is flowing."

She could almost see the adrenaline electrifying him. Lord, he was so *alive.* His dark eyes were glittering, and she felt as if she'd get an actual shock if she came near him. Yet that didn't stop her from wanting to reach out and touch him, absorb that shock until it became part of her. She had forgotten that sheer energy and magnetism that was like a living force surrounding him. Perhaps she had wanted to forget it. "And is the adrenaline flowing, Caleb?"

"Oh, yes." He was prowling around the room and stopped at the table by the window. He picked up her sketchbook and gazed down at the sketch she'd been working on last night. "Is this Gavin?"

"Yes."

"Interesting. You have him looking out at the world with a mixture of wonder and cynicism. Complicated. But then considering his background, Gavin would probably be exceptionally complicated."

"He's a good man," she said fiercely. "Complicated? He went through hell and back. He was lucky to survive with his sanity. Yes, he has a right to be complicated."

"You're passionately defensive of him." He gazed at her thoughtfully. "And he risked his life to keep you alive. But he wasn't in your bed tonight, so the relationship must be different than I first suspected." He dropped the sketch back on the table. "Good."

"It's none of your business what our relationship is," she said. "The only thing I asked you to do was to find Weismann. You didn't have to come here. Go find him."

"I've already started. You said you wanted a report. I'm here to give it to you."

"Already?"

"You were in a hurry." He dropped down in the chair again. "And so was I. I didn't like the fact that anyone had you on the run. It felt like a personal offense."

She gestured impatiently. "What did you find out about him?"

"I interviewed two members of the Sang Noir. One of them, Sevelli, was marginally helpful. He wasn't one of the core group, but he was able to fill me in on the situation surrounding you as he knew it."

"Core group?" She nodded as she remembered. "Yes, Jock told me about them. The eight who are sort of in the elite inner circle."

"Actually, seven, now that Gavin took one of them out of the equation. The others are criminals Millet picked up from the criminal underbelly." He shrugged. "It seems that the elite eight couldn't handle everything themselves. Murder, mayhem, and general destruction require a few peasants to do some of the dirty work. That's why they were considering letting your friend Jock Gavin into the group."

"And Weismann?"

"According to Sevelli, Weismann was an outsider, too. He had belonged to the Sang Noir for two years longer than Sevelli, but he was definitely not one of the core. And now the word's gone out that he's a traitor and has to be tracked down . . . along with your Jock Gavin." He shook his head. "But, according to Sevelli, you're the one who has everyone in the Sang Noir in an uproar. What have you been up to, Jane?"

"Nothing. Not a damn thing. But I have to find out what they think I've done. Couldn't you have asked one of this core group questions? Then I wouldn't have had to find Weismann."

"But I wasn't in your confidence to that extent, was I? I had my orders." He nodded. "I explored that possibility after I talked to Sevelli, but I couldn't get any of them alone to have a discussion. They're very close-knit. I didn't have time to arrange another opportunity. But Sevelli did give me one piece of information he thought interesting. Weismann had been flying to Paris frequently to visit a woman. Sevelli saw him twice at the airport with her when he was on jobs for Millet. Tall, beautiful woman. And a very affectionate couple. He was curious and did a little digging to find out who she was. I think he was considering blackmailing Weismann if the opportunity presented itself. But he decided to share the information with me. After all, family is more important than money."

"Family?"

He smiled. "Why, Sevelli thinks of me as a brother."

Why had she even asked the question? But that weird gift he possessed was still too new to her to accept easily. "And what else did your 'brother' tell you?"

"The woman's name is Adah Ziller, age twenty-nine, a citizen of Syria. She's a human resource executive for Med-Coastal Oil."

"And you think she might know where he is?"

"It's worth exploring."

"Then why aren't you doing it? Why waste

time coming here?"

"Because I knew you'd be on edge about having to spin your wheels waiting for me to come through for you. I got to know you very well while we were in Atlanta together. I didn't want you to have to suffer through all that angst unnecessarily."

"What are you talking about?"

"I thought you'd prefer to come with me to see Adah Ziller. She has a house in a subdivision near Versailles. It shouldn't take us more than an hour to get there." His brows lifted. "If you want to go."

Yes.

"Of course, I want to go. Weismann might even be with her."

"There is that possibility."

She jumped to her feet. "Wait here while I shower and dress." She stopped as she reached the bathroom door. "I have to tell Jock." Then she had a very satisfying thought. "No, you knock on his door and tell him."

His gaze narrowed on her face. "Are you throwing me to the lion, Jane?"

"Yes, you're being so condescending about Jock's being so 'complicated.' You deal with him. I think you'll be surprised at how simple and direct he can be when he chooses." Then she looked him in the eye.

"And I don't want you to do anything that's even a little off kilter. Jock is *not* your brother, and I don't want even a hint that he's feeling like 'family.' "

"You won't. That wouldn't be in the least clever on my part. Besides, it's not according to code. I'll just brave Jock Gavin and try to survive until you get out of the shower."

She gazed at him searchingly. Could she believe him?

"Don't worry." He said softly. "I won't let your lion eat me, but he'll be the same lion when you see him again."

She nodded slowly. "Jock was almost destroyed by a bastard who tried to twist his mind to suit himself. I'd never forgive anyone else for doing it."

"I know you wouldn't. That's why you should feel perfectly at ease."

Would she ever feel perfectly at ease with Caleb? Did he really want her to be comfortable with him? It was clear he was accustomed to power, and sometimes you had to give up one for the other. "I don't know you well enough to be at ease with you, Caleb."

"I'm trying to rectify that." He started to turn away. "How long will you be?"

"Not over twenty minutes, tops." She suddenly turned back to him. "But do you think going to see Adah Ziller will really do any good? Just because she had sex with him doesn't necessarily mean Weismann would confide in her."

"No, that's very true."

"Yet you said that you thought she was an avenue worth exploring. Why?"

"Because I'm curious as to why Weismann went to bed with her at all. So was Sevelli. That was why he thought the relationship might have the potential for a cash return for him." He opened the hall door. "When one other interesting fact that I found out from Sevelli was that Weismann is gay."

When Jane came out of the bathroom fifteen minutes later, she found Jock and Caleb both in the bedroom.

Her gaze flew to Jock's face.

Tension. Edginess. Exactly what she should expect to see.

Caleb shook his head as he studied her face. "I told you I'd be good. You have no trust."

"I'm sorry, Jane," Jock said. "I let you down."

"What?"

"He got into your room. That means it could have been someone else. I should have —"

"Oh, for goodness sake. What could you do? Sleep across my threshold? I was safe, Jock." She glanced at Caleb. "From everyone but him. I've been thinking about it, and I don't usually sleep that hard. I should have heard someone coming into the room. You did something to make sure I didn't do that, didn't you?"

"How suspicious you are."

"Didn't you?"

He shrugged. "I didn't want to frighten you. It was just a little stroking."

"Don't you *ever* do that again. I don't want to be stroked by you."

"Now that's a challenge."

She looked back at Jock. "You can see that there was nothing more that you could have done tonight. I don't believe the Sang Noir would be able to produce a cat burglar who was also able to shuffle perceptions around."

He shook his head. "No, I can't see that, Jane. All I see is that I didn't do my duty to you. Because I can't believe that Caleb can really do that."

Of course he can't, she thought helplessly. She had confronted him with a situation that would have been rejected by anyone. To make it worse, she had given him all of fifteen minutes to dress, pull himself together, and come to terms with his guilt about neglecting what he considered his duty. Then she had thrown Caleb into the mix to increase the tension.

"Do you want me to prove it to him?" Caleb asked her.

"No, leave him *alone*."

He held up his hand. "Don't get upset. Just offering." He turned toward the door. "But if you don't want my help, then we'd better get going. I want to be at Versailles before dawn."

She didn't move. "Jock, did he explain everything to you about Adah Ziller?"

"Yes, but there were other ways he could have found out that information. Bribery, intimidation . . ."

"I'm not arguing with you. I just want to make sure we're on the same page. It doesn't matter how we got there."

Jock gave Caleb a cool glance. "It matters." He turned toward the door. "But if he has a lead, let's follow it. It's more than we had before."

"I'll drive," Caleb said, as they reached his BMW. "You two can ride together in the backseat. As I said, it will take nearly an hour to get to Adah Ziller's house. That should give you time to come to terms with my presence in your midst. Pretend I'm not here."

Jane got into the car. "I will." It was a lie. There was no way that Caleb could be totally ignored. But she wasn't about to be less than blunt about anything connected to him when she was talking to Jock. "I suppose you researched Adah Ziller the minute you found out that she was Weismann's bed partner. What do we know about her?"

"Good-looking, intelligent, grew up in Syria, one of seven children. Her father is a merchant and sent her to England to be educated. She's ambitious and has been climbing the ladder in Med-Coast Oil for the last seven years. This move to Paris is a promotion. She's head of the human resource department here."

"Syria," Jane repeated. "Didn't you tell me that's where Millet grew up, Jock?"

He nodded slowly. "Yes. Interesting coincidence."

Caleb started the car. "And the word is that she slept with at least two vice presidents of the company to help herself get ahead."

"As well as Weismann," Jane murmured. "Busy woman."

"Ambitious woman," he said. "With connections."

"And is that why Weismann slept with her? Or did Millet send him to worm himself into her confidence?" She frowned. "But why did she sleep with him? He was a criminal, for God's sake. Did she know he had a connection with Millet? It would have been logical for him to have lied to her, but what could he offer her? Was it purely physical?" She turned to Jock. "Caleb said that Weismann is gay. Do you know if he swings both ways?"

Jock shrugged. "I told you, I didn't have much to do with him once he managed to get me accepted into the group. I suppose most women would think he was very good-looking and his personality was pleasant enough, smooth. As I told you, I know Millet sometimes sent him as an advance man to scope out his jobs. Particularly when there were women involved. But I didn't even know he was gay. He probably didn't advertise it. Millet is a macho bastard, and he wouldn't have accepted it very well."

"Then Weismann could have had sex with her for the usual reasons."

"As far as I know." Jock frowned. "But I think it's more likely that Millet sent him to her because he wanted something and couldn't get it himself. Weismann is a manipulator, and the woman is ambitious.

Put them together, and you don't come up with a grand passion."

"Right," Caleb said. "We'll have to ask the lady. I'm sure she'll be cooperative."

"Is everyone?" Jane asked curiously.

"Almost everyone. One way or the other."

"What do you mean?"

"Sometimes . . . it's difficult."

"Difficult for whom? You or the person who's mind you're manhandling?"

"Both of us. And occasionally I run into someone that I can't push at all. But it's very rare."

Jock was skeptically shaking his head.

"You might be one." Caleb was gazing at him in the rearview mirror. "Jane is being very protective, almost maternal about you, but it might not be necessary. Sometimes when a mind is broken, it grows back ten times stronger."

Jock smiled faintly. "Is that supposed to make me feel more secure? I never felt insecure with you, Caleb."

"I can see that," Caleb said. "You don't feel insecure with anyone, do you? You've gone way beyond that place." He was silent, then said to Jane, "I can work with him. I was concerned, but it will be fine."

"But can I work with you?" Jock asked. "And do I want to? You haven't proved to me that you can do anything but talk. Jane and I can get through this by ourselves."

"But it will take longer. Jane doesn't want to wait or she would never have called me." He asked Jane, "How are Eve and Joe doing?"

The change of subject was definitely pointed and intentional. "Safe at MacDuff's Run."

"So far."

"MacDuff will keep them safe," Jock said. "Stop making her worry."

"She's already worried. That's why we have to work together. I'd prefer not to do it either, but I can't leave you out. She wouldn't permit it."

"Would you please stop talking as if I weren't here?" Jane asked impatiently.

"Yes, soon. This is important," Caleb said. "Gavin?"

He was silent, then slowly nodded. "Conditionally."

"Good enough." Caleb's gaze left the mirror and focused on the street. "Now you can ignore me."

"Not yet," Jane said. "Why do you want to get there before dawn? What difference does it make?"

"Darkness heightens the senses and changes perceptions. Some things are done better in the dark."

"I don't like the sound of that. We don't even know for sure if this woman is anything but an innocent dupe. What things are easier in the dark?"

"Fear, intimidation." He smiled. "I'm not talking about any particularly foul deeds. I just want everything to be on my side if I have to ask her a few questions. That way I can glide on the surface instead of going deep."

"I don't know what you're talking about."

"I know, and I won't explain. You wouldn't like it any more than you would anything else that I do." He added, "But from the moment I met you, I knew that you could sense more about me than most people. You're a little fey, as our Scottish Jock might say."

"Ridiculous." She didn't speak for a moment. "But I'm grateful that you're helping me. And it's partly my fault that I'm finding this difficult. My instinct is to question, not meekly accept. Yet I knew what I was doing when I phoned you. That makes any argument I give hypocritical."

"How extraordinarily honest and clear thinking of you."

"But I'll still argue anyway."

He chuckled. "You should. Because you

185

didn't know exactly what you were doing. I only let you see the tip of the iceberg. It's a form of self-preservation. I'm not like Gavin. I still have moments of insecurity."

"Bullshit," Jock said.

"Ditto," Jane echoed.

"It's a terrible burden not to be understood. Well, perhaps not insecurity. I suppose I just like the idea of feeling that sense of companionship I knew with you and Eve. It was very unusual for me. I was feeling quite wistful after I left the lake cottage."

She wished he'd look back at the mirror so that she could see his expression. Wistful? Caleb?

It had to be mockery.

"You're trying to make up your mind whether I'm telling you the truth or not. I can't recall ever lying to you except by omission. I guess you'll have to decide for yourself."

"Or maybe she'll just decide it doesn't matter," Jock said coolly. "The only thing she cares about is if you can find Weismann. So I can't see her fretting about whether you're mooning wistfully for old times."

Caleb burst out laughing. "Mooning? What a sickly image that brings to mind. You do know how to deflate a man. Gavin, I believe I like you."

186

"Caleb, I don't give a damn."

"I know. And that gives me still another reason."

Jane was tired of their personal interchanges. Even when they weren't edged with tension, the remarks seemed to breed an intimacy that she would rather stop before it took form. "How long before we get to Versailles?"

Caleb glanced down at the GPS. "About forty minutes."

Forty minutes. They might find out absolutely nothing, but they had a chance. There was only a slim possibility that Weismann was with Adah Ziller, but she might be able to lead them to him. She leaned back in the seat. Try to relax.

At least she wasn't back at the inn twiddling her thumbs. She was moving, and any move forward was progress.

EIGHT

The houses in Adah Ziller's subdivision were obviously meant to look like quaint, thatch-roofed farmhouses. To Jane they resembled the small rural homes she'd seen in the English countryside rather than a French village.

"Not exactly grand," Jock murmured. "I was expecting more presence. It's only a few miles from the palace of Versailles."

"I'm sure they found it more economical to mirror Marie Antoinette's fantasy of being a French peasant than the palace of Versailles." She had a vague memory of visiting the village adjoining Versailles that Antoinette had created so that she could play milkmaid with her ladies and gentlemen of the court. "I wonder why Adah Ziller decided to settle here. Why not settle in Paris?"

"It's close enough," Caleb said. "And she'd have to pass Versailles every day as she drove to work. It could be that she liked that tiny connection with royalty." He pulled the car over to the curb. "Her house is down the block. Number 42. It's better if we park here and walk the rest of the way. Surprise is always more effective."

"Then let's go." Jane got out of the car. Excitement was tingling through her. "What do we do? Surely not just knock on the door?"

"Not if there's any possibility that Weismann is in there with her," Jock said. "And, even if he's not here, I don't think Caleb is planning on a civilized chat with the lady."

"I'll be as polite as I can be. Sometimes it's not possible." Caleb was moving ahead of them. "I'll go around the back and see if I can get in the rear door." He glanced over his shoulder. "Stay with her, Gavin. I'll let you both in the front door."

"I should go —" Jane stopped as Caleb disappeared around the side of the house. "Damn him."

"Come on." Jock took her elbow. "I don't like taking orders either, but this isn't the time to argue. I want to get off the street. It's the middle of the night, but that doesn't mean we won't be seen."

No, they needed to get into the house and out of view with as much discretion as possible. "But we'd be a lot less noticeable to any neighbors if we went in the back way, too."

"Yes." Jock's lips twisted. "I'm sure Caleb realized that, too. But that wouldn't allow him the time he wants inside alone."

Her gaze flew to his face as they reached the front door. "You're saying that you think he doesn't want us to know what he's doing in there."

"Judging by what he was saying in the car, I got the impression that he really doesn't want anyone to know what he's doing at any given time. Of course, you know him better than I do." He bent over the lock on the door. "But I don't like the idea of waiting patiently for him to let us in. Does he think he's the only one who can pick a lock?"

"The alarm?"

"Caleb should have any alarm disabled by this time. I'll just open the door and we'll —" The lock clicked, and he slowly swung the door open to reveal a dark foyer. "No alarm. But no Caleb either," he whispered as he closed the door. "He didn't exactly hurry to open the front door for us, did he?"

Jane didn't answer as she followed him into the foyer. What could she say? Dammit, Caleb may have said he was going to give me the opportunity to share in his hunt, but he was obviously playing his own games.

Jock paused, looking around, then glided silently across the hall toward a wide, curved opening. A library or office? The darkness wasn't as intense as Jane had first thought. The two beveled-glass panels on either side of the front door let the lights from the street filter into the hall and dimly lit the desk and bookcases against the far wall of the room. She followed Jock toward the doorway, trying to imitate his silent movements.

Not a sound. So quiet, so deadly. This is the Jock Gavin who had been trained as an assassin all those years ago, she thought bitterly. How quickly he had fallen back into the old skills. Her fault. He was doing all this for her.

It would do no good to feel guilty. She just had to work through this nightmare.

She moved after him toward the opening.

A bullet whistled by her cheek!

"Down!" Jock turned and pushed her to the floor.

Another bullet, this time splintering the spindle of the banister on the stairs beside her.

Someone was running down those stairs.

Male. White shirt, dark pants.

Jock was rising to his knees, pulling a gun from his jacket.

But the man had reached the door and jerked it open. The light from the streetlight illuminated him for the briefest instant.

Tall. Muscular. Red hair.

Then he was gone.

"Damn! That's Weismann." Jock jumped to his feet and started for the door. Then he stopped. "I can't leave you here. I don't know if there's anyone else in the house. Where the hell is Caleb?"

"Here." Caleb came out of the room with the arched doorway. "Get going."

Jock was out the door in two seconds.

Caleb pulled her to her feet. "I told you to wait outside."

"Go to hell." She was shaking. "And if I had waited out there, whoever was shooting at us would have run right into me." She shook her head as she remembered Jock's words. "It was Weismann. Jock must have recognized him."

"Then let's hope he catches the bastard."

Jane glanced at the arched doorway of the room from which he'd run. "What were you doing in there?"

"Just a little advance reconnaissance —"

"Closing us out. That's what Jock said

192

would happen."

"Gavin is a smart man." He gazed at the door Jock had left open when he'd started after Weismann. "I hope he's as fast as he is clever."

"Why don't you go after him?"

"I trust Gavin to catch him if it's possible. I understand he's exceptional." He glanced up the stairs to the second floor. "If there were anyone up there with him, I'd think they'd be barreling down those steps. Of course, if there's only Adah Ziller in the house, she could be hiding."

"Or trying to climb out a window and get away," Jane said dryly. "Maybe Weismann was trying to distract us."

"It would be quite a jump for her." He looked up the stairs again. "I think I'd better go upstairs and take a look around."

"What were you doing in the office?"

"I told you, I thought I'd see if I could find anything interesting in case Adah Ziller proved difficult." He looked up the stairs again. "Where are you, Adah Ziller?" he murmured. "I don't hear a sound . . ."

Neither did Jane, and she didn't like it. "Maybe she's not here. Or maybe she wants us to think she's not here." She drew a deep breath. She was making guesses because she was afraid to face another ugly reality. "I'm tired of maybes." She moved toward the stairs. "Let's have a few certainties."

Caleb was beside her, then ahead of her, moving up the steps. "By all means. I don't suppose you'll let me go ahead and —"

"No." Her gaze was on the room at the top of the steps. "That door is open." It was all the way open, as if jerked wide when someone had run through it. The other two doors on the floor appeared to be closed.

Which could be —

Caleb muttered a curse. He was at the top of the stairs, his gaze on the interior of the bedroom. "Damn. I was afraid of this. I had a feeling. I'm not going to be able to —" He was striding toward the bedroom. "I'm not going to tell you to stay out. It wouldn't do any good. Just don't blame me if you don't like what you see."

"What are you —" Then she saw the woman huddled on the floor, one arm flung out before her, blood that had poured from a wound in her chest.

Death.

Dear God, another death.

She sank back against the doorjamb.

She stood there in the doorway, watching as Caleb knelt beside the woman. It had to be Adah Ziller.

A pretty woman, Jane thought dully.

Elegantly slim in her gold silk nightgown. Café-au-lait skin and black hair cropped fashionably close around her face. But her expression wasn't pretty, it held an incredulous horror.

"She wasn't expecting him to do it," Jane said. "She looks . . . surprised. Was she shot?"

"No, it's a knife wound." He looked up at her. "A fresh kill. I'd say only a few minutes."

"Right before we got here."

"No, probably *when* we got here. He either saw us approach the house or heard us when we came in."

"So he killed her? Because we came here looking for him?"

"He might not have even been sure who we were. He could have thought Millet had found him. Or even Venable's men. Either way, he'd have considered it prudent to silence anyone who might have known anything about him."

"She was trying to help him. She'd taken him into her home."

"Yes." He glanced at the gold nightgown clinging to the woman's slim body. "And probably her bed."

"Why wouldn't he have just taken her with him? Why kill her?"

"Maybe he meant to do it anyway, and he just had to advance his plans a bit." He stood up. "So he stabbed her and came down those steps firing."

Firing at her. Firing at Jock.

The memory jarred her out of the shock that had left her dazed and bewildered. "Jock. He should have come back by now." She turned. "I have to make sure he's all right."

"Jane to the rescue," he murmured. "Nursemaid to a baby tiger."

"Shut up, Caleb." She started down the stairs. "He's my friend."

"I know. I suppose that's what's bothering me." He went on, "I'll go after him. I'm the one who told him to take off after Weismann." He grimaced. "Not that he would have obeyed any order I gave. All he cared about was that I was here to take care of you so he could run him down without feeling guilty. I would have —"

"He got away. Hell, he was fast." Jock stood in the front doorway. "He had a car parked two blocks away. He was already in it and a half a block down the street by the time I caught up with him."

"Damn," Caleb said.

"My sentiments," Jock said.

"It was definitely Weismann?" Jane asked.

"Yes, what about Adah Ziller? Did you find out anything from her?"

"She's dead," Jane said. "Stabbed."

"Dead end," Jock said. "Then we'd better get out of here. As I was coming back, I saw lights popping on in several houses on the block. They must have heard those shots."

"Not yet," Jane said. "I won't have this be a dead end."

"Jane, they've probably called the police."

"Then we'll have to hurry. Ten minutes, and we'll be out of here. Weismann killed that woman because he wanted to make sure she wouldn't tell whatever she knew. I want to see if she can still tell us." She turned to Caleb. "You said you were searching in the office earlier. Did you find anything?"

"I didn't have a chance before you came into the house."

"Then go back and search it again until you do."

"What are we supposed to be looking for?" Caleb asked.

"I have no idea. Anything that might be different or out of place I guess. How do I know? You're the hunter. Jock, pull the car directly in front of the house and try to find some mud to hide the license number." She braced herself. Lord, she didn't want to do this. "I'll go back into her bedroom and search there. Women often keep things that mean something to them close to them. There's nothing closer or more intimate than a bedroom."

"Ten minutes." Caleb was already down the stairs and heading for the library. He added dryly, "Or when we hear the first sirens."

Jock turned and left the house.

Stop hesitating, Jane told herself. There isn't time to give in to emotion. Turn around and go into Adah Ziller's room and search. It wasn't a violation. Whatever Jane found would help to punish that bastard who had betrayed Adah.

She wheeled and flew back up the stairs.

She carefully avoided looking at the woman lying on the floor.

Bedside tables, first.

She opened the drawer. Birth control. Pad, pencil. She went around the bed to the other bedside table. A small, malachite-studded Derringer pistol. Very pretty, like its owner. It was a pity she hadn't had a chance to use it.

Bathroom.

Nothing but the usual products.

Where else?

Luggage.

She opened the closet door and checked the overhead shelf. Zero.

She pulled out the small Louis Vuitton overnight case.

Empty.

No.

Tucked in an elastic pocket on the side was a small but thick leather book.

She grabbed it and shoved the suitcase back in the closet. Jewelry box on the lingerie chest.

Very nice, very expensive costume jewelry. She seemed to be very fond of heavy silver bangles. She lifted the tray. More jewelry.

And a small chamois pouch pushed to the back of the tray. She opened the strings. Not jewelry. Coins.

"Jane! Get down here."

Jock's voice.

She slipped the pouch into her jacket pocket and ran toward the door.

Jock was waiting at the bottom of the stairs. "I think I heard sirens."

Caleb was coming out of the living room. "Get going. Keep watch for them. Start the car."

"Right." Jock was out the door and running down the walk.

Jane started to follow him.

"Wait." Caleb grabbed a silk runner from

the hall table and draped it over her head and shoulders. "Keep your head down. There are probably a dozen neighbors peering out their windows by now."

"It's a little late. Our fingerprints are probably all over this house."

"It's never too late. We had no idea we'd need gloves when we came here but you have to take precautions where you can."

"What about you and Jock?"

"I'm not worried about anyone remembering me. It's too late for Jock."

No, that's right, Caleb could change their perceptions, she thought as she ran down the walk.

But, dammit, Jock was very recognizable. People always remembered that incredibly handsome face.

"Get in." Jock's face was grim as he threw open the passenger seat door for her. "Those sirens aren't more than a few blocks away."

She could hear them herself. Loud, staccato, not like the wailing sirens at home in the U.S.

"Go south two blocks and make a turn and double back on a parallel street to the subdivision entrance," Caleb said as he jumped in the backseat. "And keep your lights off."

"I'm driving. Stop telling me what to do,"

Jock said as he gunned the engine. "Why do you think I haven't got my headlights on now?"

More lights were going on in the houses they were passing, Jane noticed tensely.

The sirens were louder.

Hurry.

As Jock made the turn, a dark police car with red lights flashing came into view. Before Jane lost sight of it, she saw the patrol car pull up before Adah's house.

"We have time, Jane," Caleb said quietly. "They'll have to go inside and verify what's going on and if there's actually a crime. And, even if all those peeping Toms stream out into the street and try to talk to the policemen, it will take a few minutes for them to sort out what's happening."

"And we should be out of the subdivision and miles away before they get it together," Jock added. "I was only worried about getting a little head start."

"Very little," Jane said. But she was relieved to see that they were passing through the stone-framed gates at the entrance of the subdivision. "And it was my fault we cut it so close, so will you both please stop comforting me and get us back to the inn?" She had a sudden thought. "Is the inn still safe?"

"It should be. But we'll move tomorrow," Jock said. "I'll call Venable and see if he can do anything to smooth over what happened tonight. I don't have much hope. It won't be easy for him to come into an ongoing investigation."

An ongoing investigation. He sounded like Joe with that phrase. She was suddenly so homesick for Joe and Eve that she ached with it. She didn't want to be here in this foreign country, where death seemed to be around every corner.

"You could go to Joe and Eve," Caleb said softly. "I can find Weismann for you."

Her gaze flew to his face. How had he known what she was feeling?

He shook his head as he realized what she was thinking. "Just common ordinary insight. I've always been attuned to you. Now I've begun to know you. It's not exactly comfortable for me." He added simply, "I don't like to see you hurting."

She studied his expression. He was telling the truth.

And that truth was having an impact on her that was very disturbing. She tore her gaze away from his. "I'm not going to run back to Joe and Eve. This isn't their fight."

He shrugged. "Well, I tried. It wasn't the way I wanted it anyway. As I said, it made me uncomfortable." He turned to Jock. "You're being very quiet."

"I was hoping you'd convince her to go to the Run," Jock said. "It's what I want, and it doesn't matter to me how it's done. I'll fade into the background and let you do it."

Caleb was silent a moment. "I don't think you'd ever fade into the background, Gavin."

"I'm not going to the Run," Jane said. "Not yet. Did you find anything in the office, Caleb?"

"A couple possibilities. You?"

"I've no idea. A book. A pouch." She leaned wearily back in the seat. She was suddenly feeling exhausted, and the memories of Adah Ziller lying back in that house, memories that she had tried to push away, were here with her again. She had been full of hope and determination earlier that night, and now everything was in confusion and shambles. "They could be worth absolutely nothing. I'll have to go through them when we get to the inn. I don't want to think about it now."

"Or you could come up with a bonanza," Caleb said. "I'd bet on you. I've always said you have great instincts."

Why did those words give her such a sense of pride? In just a few sentences, he'd been able to lighten the depression that was starting to blanket her. It shouldn't have meant that much to her. It indicated a power she didn't want to give him.

"But on the other hand, no one has ever said I'm a particularly good gambler. So you'd better disregard any opinion I might have."

Clever. He'd sensed her rejection of his words and immediately set out to dissipate any damage. "That shouldn't be a problem."

He smiled. "I didn't think so." He looked out the window. "Then you might as well ignore me entirely until we get back to the inn. Try to rest."

When they reached the inn, they went directly to Jane's room.

Jock handed Jane her key after unlocking her door. "I'll go to my room and call Venable. I should be back in five or ten minutes."

Jane nodded. "Whatever it takes." She wearily rubbed the back of her neck. "I think we're going to need him. And ask him if he can trace any Syrian connection between Adah Ziller and Millet. Dammit, I was hoping that we'd get Weismann tonight."

"Almost," Jock said. "Next time."

After he left, Jane went to the window and looked down into the hotel grounds. "It's getting light." She glanced at Caleb, who was sitting in a chair across the room watching her. "Dawn." It seemed a long time ago that they'd talked about dawn and how darkness could be a weapon.

A weapon he hadn't used. Weismann had been the one using weapons and dispensing ugliness and death. "Before tonight I wasn't really thinking about Weismann in the same terms as those other monsters in the group. He was an informer, it seemed to make him better somehow. I wasn't thinking straight. He's a killer. He's just as bad. Maybe worse."

"Certainly as ruthless. Perhaps not quite as bloody."

"Blood." She looked at him over her shoulder. "You know all about blood, don't you?"

"Enough." He met her eyes. "I know how to take it. I know how to use it to kill. Do you really want to delve into my murky past? If you do, I'll oblige you. But it's not a confidence I'd make lightly. There would be a price to pay. Are you prepared to pay it?"

She couldn't tear her gaze from his. Why had she started this? She was tired and on an emotional edge, and the words had just tumbled out. Her curiosity and fascination with Seth Caleb had always been just been beneath the surface, ready to break free whenever she was with him.

"Are you?" he repeated softly.

Heat. That undercurrent of breathless recklessness. The exhilaration of walking too close to the precipice and wanting to plunge off into the unknown.

Yes. Any price. Just make it worth the cost.

Don't say those words. She would regret it.

Or would she?

She forced herself to look away. Clear your head. It was only because she was disappointed and depressed because they'd not intercepted Weismann that she'd felt this compulsion. She wasn't the type of person to indulge in recklessness. "I'm not that interested."

"Liar," he murmured. "You're as curious about knowing everything about me as I am about you." He smiled. "I almost had you, didn't I?"

"No." It wasn't the truth. She had been very close, but to admit it would be a step nearer to that precipice. She changed the subject. "What did you find in the office?"

He reached in his jacket pocket. "Two first-class airline tickets to Syria, for Adah

Ziller and a Harry Norbert."

"Norbert?"

"Weismann wouldn't have booked under his own name. He probably has a few other phony passports." He threw the tickets on the table. "The reservations are for tomorrow. But he won't be using them after what happened tonight."

"Anything else?"

"A couple keys. They were in an envelope with the tickets. They both are to a safety-deposit box at a bank in Zurich, together with account access information for Adah Ziller."

"She had a Swiss account?"

"She had a number of important lovers. Maybe she kept track of letters and valuable memorabilia that might come in handy later."

"Blackmail?"

"Possibly. Or maybe she put something in her deposit box for safekeeping for Weismann. But at least we have a place to start. A Swiss bank. Syria."

"That's a pretty lame start. There are too many holes to fill in."

"Not so many. Maybe whatever you turned up might help to fill them."

"That would be too lucky." She pulled out the leather book she'd stuffed in her pocket.

"This was tucked in a pocket in her suitcase. It looks like a daytimer or a journal." She flipped open the pages. "Dammit, it's not in English."

"She was a Syrian." He stood up and took the leather book and glanced at it. "Arabic."

"Can you read it?"

"No, but I know someone who can. It's not the first time I've had to have her interpret for me. She speaks twelve languages and is very discreet."

"But is she close by?"

"She lives across the border in Switzerland. We'll stop on our way to Zurich."

"We're going to Zurich? You think we can get into that safety-deposit box?"

"That's the least of our problems."

It seemed a huge problem to Jane. But it was clearly a necessity with which they'd have to deal.

"Anything else?" Caleb asked.

She pulled out the chamois pouch. "This was stuffed in the back of her jewelry box. Most of the jewelry in it was costume. She probably kept the good stuff in a safe."

"Or a safety-deposit box."

"Well, this was pushed in the back. I don't believe its jewelry." She opened the strings and emptied the contents on the table.

Two coins.

Small, silver, edges worn and chipped, incredibly old.

Jane frowned. "What are they?"

"I may be able to help a little but not much," Caleb said. "My uncle was a collector, and he left me his collection when he died. But it was never my cup of tea." He picked up one of the coins. "Old. Coined somewhere in the Middle East about A.D. 5. Pretty common. I saw quite a few in my uncle's collection. I wouldn't think it would be worth much."

"Maybe that's why she kept it with her costume jewelry." She frowned. "But why keep it at all? Even her costume pieces looked as if they were good quality and worth something."

He shrugged. "Maybe sentimental value? We'll have to find out."

"If it's worth finding out. Perhaps I just grabbed the wrong items to —"

Jock knocked on the door and entered. "Venable said that it was probably too late for him to do anything, but he'd explore the situation. He wasn't pleased that we hadn't told him we had a lead on Weismann." He glanced at the coins on the table. "What are those?"

"Coins she found in Adah Ziller's room," Caleb said. "Very old. Also, we came up with airline tickets to Syria, a safety-deposit box in Zurich, and a leather book that we can't read because it's in Arabic. Now you're completely caught up."

"Thank you," Jock said dryly. "For what it's worth." He turned to Jane. "We can't be sure the police won't trace us back here. We were a little too visible. I vote for not waiting until later to move. I think we should pack up and get out of here."

"So do I." Jane turned and strode toward the suitcases she'd set against the far wall. "How long will it take us to get to Zurich?"

"Six hours or so," Caleb said. "Perhaps a little longer since we have to stop and have Lina translate that book."

"Lina? She's the one who does your translating?"

"Lina Alsouk. Yes, she's very good."

"But is she fast? Can we get to Zurich before the close of the banking day?"

"Maybe. We'll work something out."

"That sounds a little too casual to me," Jane said. "If you'll recall, I'm on something of a deadline." She shook her head as she realized what she had said. "Deadline. Dead end. There are so many phrases that have to do with death. They couldn't be more descriptive, could they?"

"No," Jock said. "But not ones I like to

use in your case." He headed for the door. "I'll pack and meet you downstairs in the lobby. Which car are we using?"

"The BMW," Caleb said. "It's not a rental and can't be traced."

"What?"

Caleb shrugged. "I'm a hunter. It's convenient for me to keep a car at several cities in Europe. Paris is one of them. The license-plate numbers are phony, and I have an extra set in the boot."

"Then I didn't need to throw mud on those plates at Adah Ziller's place," Jock said dryly.

"No, but I didn't have time to tell you at the time," Caleb said. "We were in a bit of a hurry."

"We're still in a hurry," Jane said. "I don't want to have to hang around and wait until the bank opens tomorrow morning."

"Then you won't have to do it. I told you that we'll work it out," Caleb said. "I'll go down and gas up the car for the trip."

NINE

Day Four

Lina Alsouk lived in a small picture-postcard cottage in the foothills of the Alps. The scenery was spectacular, the house cozy, and the woman kneeling in the vegetable garden was probably the most beautiful woman Jane had ever seen. Though like the scenery, that beauty was entirely natural and owed nothing to artifice. Lina Alsouk was in her late twenties, with short, dark, curly hair and huge brown eyes that glowed in her thin, tanned face. She had perfect features but wore no makeup and her hair was very simply styled. She was dressed in jeans and a navy sweatshirt that were worn and shabby with use.

"It's about time, Caleb," she said as she wiped her dirty hands on the towel she picked up from the ground beside her. "You tell me to make myself ready, then you take hours to get here." Her English was perfect, with only a hint of an accent. "You're taking me for granted. I should have told you to take your business elsewhere."

"But I'm such a good customer," Caleb said as he got out of the car and strolled toward her. "And you never know when you might need a customer like me. How are you, Lina?"

She shrugged. "Well, enough. And you?"

"Better than when I last saw you." He glanced at Jane, who was getting out of the car. "I had a very successful hunt recently."

"The man you were hunting when I first met you?" When he nodded, she smiled brilliantly. "That is good. I'm happy for you." She turned to Jane. "You are Jane MacGuire? Caleb told me about you. I will try to help."

"Lina Alsouk, Jane MacGuire," Caleb waved at Gavin, who was coming toward them. "And this is Jock Gavin."

Lina smiled and nodded. "I am pleased to meet any friend of Caleb's."

"Well, he doesn't exactly consider himself my friend," Caleb said. "But he's definitely Jane's friend."

"Yes." Jock held out his hand to Lina. "May I help you up?"

She shook her head. "I'm dirty."

"So am I." He took her hand and pulled

her to her feet. "It just doesn't show." He smiled. "And I like the feel of earth on my hands. I had a garden of my own until recently. Gardening is very healing, isn't it?" He looked at the rows. "Vegetables. I planted mostly flowers."

"I like to make sure I'm totally independent here. I can eat tomatoes; flowers aren't nearly as digestible." She tore her gaze away from him and turned to Caleb. "Where is this book I'm supposed to translate?"

"I have it." Jane took the leather book out of her purse. "It looks like some kind of journal. I don't know if any of the information will be pertinent. I think I could make out a few of the dates. Some of the earlier entries appear to be over five years old."

"I can't touch it yet. I have to wash my hands." She turned toward the front door. "Come in."

The interior of the cottage was one huge room with an adjoining kitchen. The furniture was sparse, comfortable, but very simple.

Lina went to the stainless-steel sink and began to wash her hands. "I'd offer you a cup of tea, but Caleb said you were going to be in a hurry."

"We are," Jane said. "Thank you." She handed her the towel on the hook by the sink. "I'd appreciate your doing it as quickly as possible."

She nodded as she took the book. "I'll do what I can." She took her laptop and a pad and pencil from the desk and sat down in a chair at the kitchen table. She started to flip through the book. "I usually do a scan first. Just to pull out the main content. Is that all right?"

Jane nodded. "Whatever. Maybe you can tell us enough to know if we can use any of it."

She flipped back to the first page. "Adah Ziller. It is a journal of sorts. But it spans years and is very spotty. It starts when she was a schoolgirl in Syria. It seems to skip several years and continues when she was at the university in England." She flipped more pages. "It's pretty disjointed. It's going to take some time."

"How much time?"

She shrugged. "Six, eight hours minimum." She saw Jane frown, and said, "Do you want accuracy or guesswork? I don't do guesswork."

"Okay." She nodded. "I guess I'm impatient. There are reasons."

"There are reasons for everything. I'll get it done as quickly as I can."

"I know you will," Caleb said. "We can't

wait for it. As it is, we won't be in Zurich before nearly five. We'll come back and pick it up." He turned to Jane. "If you'll trust the book out of your hands?"

Jane hesitated.

"You can trust her," Caleb said. "I guarantee it. No matter what's in that book, she'll forget it as soon as she makes the translation."

"That's not what I was worrying about. I don't even know if this translation is any more than Adah Ziller's bedroom antics." She looked at Lina. "But the woman who wrote this was murdered. There may be people who are interested in it as much as we are."

"We weren't followed, Jane," Caleb said. "I made sure of it."

"I'm glad you're sure. But I'm not sure of anything," Jane said. "Except that she has to be warned."

Lina smiled faintly. "Thank you. Some of my clients haven't been that considerate. But I can take care of myself. After I left Afghanistan, I made very sure of that." She leaned forward and opened the ledger. "Now get out of here and let me work. I want to get through with this so that I can get back to my garden before dark. I need to finish putting in my tomatoes."

"I could help when we come back to pick up the translation," Jock offered.

She shook her head. "I like to do things on my own. I don't need anyone. Go away."

"Whatever you say," Jock said as he turned toward the door. "I'll ask you again when I come back."

She didn't answer. She was already making notes on her pad.

"I'll call you when we start back from Zurich," Caleb said.

She nodded absently.

They weren't even there for her, Jane thought, as she left the cottage. The woman's concentration was so intense that she had closed out everything but that handwriting on the page.

"She'll get it done," Caleb said as he opened the car door for her. "Lina is brilliant. She'll get every phrase right."

"I'm not doubting her ability. You wouldn't deal with anyone who couldn't do the job." She looked around the hillside, then down to the valley. Majestic mountains plunged into the crystal blue lake, and only a few farmhouses dotted the landscape. "It's just that it's so isolated here. She's very vulnerable."

"And you're worried about us coming back and finding her with no head." The words were blunt and brutal.

She flinched. "I'm worried about anyone I come in contact with."

"Well, she's not as vulnerable as you might think. She has an AK-47 in the pantry of that cozy kitchen, and she knows how to use it. She's trained in martial arts, and she's not bad with a knife. You'll notice her cottage is on a hill, approachable only from one direction, and she can see anyone coming. If she hadn't been expecting me, she wouldn't have been in that garden when we drove up."

"She's still isolated."

"She likes it like that," Jock said suddenly. "No one too close."

Caleb glanced back at him as he started the car. "You appear to understand her. Gardener to gardener?"

Jock didn't answer as he gazed back at the cottage. "How did she get that AK-47? You can't buy them on every street corner."

"I gave it to her. That's what she asked me to give her instead of cash for the first job she did for me. The AK-47, a Glock, and lessons on how to use both of them. I didn't teach her martial arts or how to use a knife. She must have made a deal with someone else for that."

"And how long ago was that first job she

did for you?" Jane asked.

"Nine years. She'd just been smuggled out of Afghanistan and was trying to start a new life."

"With an AK-47?" Jane asked dryly.

"She thought it might be necessary. She was probably right. Considering her background, I wasn't going to try to talk her out of it." Caleb lifted his shoulders. "Not that I would have made the attempt anyway. It was her business."

"What was her background?" Jock asked. "Afghanistan?"

"She belonged to a very traditional Afghan family. She was permitted to go to a very good private school when she was a child, and she showed signs of brilliance. But her father took her out of school when she was twelve, and he began to hunt for a husband for her. With those looks, she was a prize. He arranged a marriage for her to a wealthy businessman when she was thirteen. He was old enough to be her grandfather and a sadistic bastard. He wanted a son from her, and she couldn't conceive. He'd fly into tantrums and beat her unmercifully. She had to be taken to the hospital twice." His lips twisted. "But even then her own family wouldn't interfere. She belonged to her husband, and he could do anything he wished to her. She ran away when she was eighteen, but her husband found her and claimed she had been unfaithful. He wanted her stoned."

"Good God. I thought the Afghans were becoming more moderate," Jane said.

"As long as it's not behind closed doors. It could very well have happened. But this time her brother stepped up to the plate and arranged for an ex-CIA friend to smuggle Lina out of the country. That's as far as he'd go because he feared family disapproval."

"So she was totally alone," Jock said.

"John Garrett, the man who smuggled her out of Afghanistan, gave her enough money to go back to school and got her false ID papers to keep her safe."

"Why did she need false ID?"

"Her husband died of a heart attack shortly after she left Kabul. His family blamed his death on her and swore to avenge him."

"She hadn't been through enough?" Jane shook her head. "I think I would have wanted to have an AK-47, too. But I wouldn't have let those bastards drive me into hiding in the mountains."

"She's not hiding. She stopped doing that after she finished her schooling."

"And learned how to fire an AK-47?" Jock added.

"When she left Afghanistan, she had very little formal education but an enormous determination to survive. Now she speaks and writes twelve languages fluently, including Japanese and Arabic. Translating was a career that she could do on her own terms if she became good enough. She's accurate, nonjudgmental, and completely confidential."

"Perfect for you," Jane said.

"Perfect for a lot of people in this wicked world." He slanted her a glance. "Including you at present."

She nodded. "You said she wasn't hiding any longer?"

"When she came here, she bought the property under her own name. If anyone was searching for her, she wanted to make sure that they knew she wasn't afraid and was ready for them."

"And has anyone come searching for her yet?"

"I don't know. It wasn't my business. If you want to know, you'll have to ask her."

"It's not my business either." But she was still curious. Her brief encounter with Lina Alsouk had been as intriguing as it had been frustrating. "If she does her job, that should

221

be all that's important to me."

"She's wounded," Jock said. "You sensed it when you first saw her. That's why you weren't certain you should leave the translation with her. You didn't want her to be hurt any more than she was already. You have trouble ignoring the wounded."

"You make me sound like a do-gooder. If she's wounded, then she's walking wounded, and she's using an AK-47 as a crutch."

"It will still bother you." He smiled. "Your instinct is to heal wounds. You can't help it."

"I just don't want anyone else to be hurt or killed because of me." She turned to Caleb. "You said we'd be at the bank in Zurich by five?"

"Yes, by the skin of our teeth. We have to stop at a drugstore first. And we just have to hope that Henrik Barnard isn't taking a day off."

"Who is Henrik Barnard?"

"Your own private banker."

"What?"

"Well, Adah Ziller's banker. It was the name on the same card that had her bank-account number."

"Then why did you call him my banker?"

"Because the only way we're going to get

into that safety-deposit box is if you're Adah Ziller."

She stared at him in astonishment. "Are you crazy? Adah Ziller was black."

"Actually, to be precise, a beautiful coffee-with-cream brown. A good bronzer makeup on your face and hands should take care of that. We'll have to tuck your hair under a hat."

"And where are we supposed to get that?"

"The drugstore. You can get practically anything at a drugstore these days."

"I'd never get away with it," she said flatly. "Drugstore? This is all too crude. Banks have cameras. Swiss banks are the most sophisticated in the world."

"You're right. And the most private. That's why we have an excellent chance." He glanced at her. "You don't have to worry about being under intense scrutiny. No one is going to get close to you but Henrik Barnard. We only need the dark makeup to make sure that nothing is too obvious."

"Obvious? It's obvious that I'm not black. And I probably weigh ten pounds more than Adah Ziller. She was built like a runway model."

"Trust me. It will all come together," Caleb said.

"If she doesn't get arrested," Jock said.

"There will be guards all over that bank."

Caleb looked directly into her eyes. "Trust me."

It was crazy. A bank full of officers and clerks and guards ready to step in and protect the sanctity of the Swiss banking system. Yet Caleb wasn't crazy, and he thought they could get away with it. They needed to know what was in that safety-deposit box.

Why the hell not try? she thought recklessly. "You'd better not be mistaken, Caleb."

"I won't let you be hurt." His glance shifted back to the road. "I promise."

She looked back at Jock. "You're not arguing with me."

"It wouldn't do any good," Jock said quietly. "I'll just have to go along with him and see if he hurts you." He smiled. "And then I'll kill him."

Caleb burst out laughing. "A good plan."

"Jock, you don't go in that bank with us," Jane said firmly. "I won't have it."

"I won't argue about that either," Jock said. "Someone has to be free to get you out of trouble if this idiocy blows up in your faces. I'll be the getaway man again."

"You said if," Caleb said. "Not when. Interesting."

"Is it?" Jock leaned back in the seat. "Take it apart, analyze it. It will give you something to do on the drive to Zurich."

"That bronzer is pretty good." Caleb was gazing at her critically. "But you need more on your hands."

She took the pad and poured more bronzer on it. "I can't get it dark enough. I just look like I have a deep tan."

"So did Adah Ziller. You're dark enough." He handed her the black straw hat and gold hoop earrings. "Hurry. It's quarter to five."

"Pressure." She tucked every strand of her red-brown hair beneath the wide-brimmed hat and put on the two-inch hoops. She did look exotic, she thought critically, as she looked at the mirror on the dashboard, but nothing like Adah Ziller. "It's not going to work."

"It will work." He got out of the driver's seat and came around to open her passenger door. "All we have to do is make it easy for them. Some of the other bank employees may possibly have seen Adah Ziller, but it's not likely. This is a private bank."

"What does that mean? What's the difference?" Jock asked as he got out of the back and changed to the driver's seat.

"Private banks are often by invitation only,

and that invitation is extended principally to individuals with extremely high assets. Or by recommendation by another current customer in good standing. Since on the surface Adah doesn't appear to have that kind of money, I'd bet that her recommendation must have come from one of her past liaisons. One of the privileges is that she'd be assigned a bank officer to take care of her assets."

"Henrik Barnard," Jane said.

He nodded. "And the chances are that there would have been some personal contact between them or that he would have at least seen a photo of her."

"Then you're screwed," Jock said flatly.

"No," Caleb said. "Not if I go in first and prepare the way. Adah Ziller is probably not particularly high-profile on the bank's charts. Unlike what the movies would lead you to believe, there's no high-tech retina scan or fingerprint analysis. We only have to jump over the barrier of the bank officer. Here's the way it's going to work. Barnard will escort you to the vault and get your safety-deposit box. The box is actually a box within another box. You have a key and so does the bank officer. You both have to use your keys to open the outer box. Then he'll take the inner box and you to an adjoining room and leave you there to go through the contents in privacy. You call him when you're done, and he takes the box back to the vault."

"What if they already know that she's been murdered?" Jane asked as a sudden thought occurred to her. "What if it's in today's newspaper or something?"

"It's a possibility, but that happened in Paris. It's not local news here in Switzerland. We have a good chance of her death not being noticed here so soon. If it is, it won't be front-page news. I'll know before I call you to come into the bank. I'll tell him I'm your attorney, Jason Smythe, and wish to accompany you to the vault." He opened the glass door. "Wait here, Jane. It shouldn't take long." He disappeared into the bank.

"It can't work," Jock told Jane. "It's not too late to change your mind."

"I'll take my chances."

"You really believe he can pull it off." Jock shook his head. "It's not possible. He can't just march in there and convince that bank officer that black is white."

"Actually, he's going to convince him that white is black," she said ruefully. "I hope."

"We'll see." He glanced up and down the busy city street. "I don't like this. I feel . . . uneasy."

So did Jane, but how else could she feel under the circumstances? she thought. Jock was right, this entire scenario was bizarre in the extreme. "It should be over soon." It couldn't be over too soon for her.

"Adah." Caleb had opened the gold-lettered glass entrance door and was smiling at her. "I've already told Mr. Barnard how sorry we are not to have called and made advance arrangements." He turned to a small, plump, gray-haired man in a navy blue pinstriped suit. "I promise we won't keep you too long."

"Nonsense." Barnard was beaming at Jane. "As I told Mr. Smythe, I'm at your disposal twenty-four hours a day. All you'd have to do is call me, and I'd have come back and opened the bank for you, Miss Ziller. Come in. Come in."

"That's very kind." She moved into the bank and was at once enveloped in the aura of hushed murmurs, charcoal-colored granite countertops, rich mahogany executive desks. "I don't want to be a bother. My attorney just told me that he had to have those docu—"

"That's none of my concern," Barnard said. "My only business is to make things as easy for you as possible. Step this way, and we'll get the matter taken care of immediately." He smiled as he led her toward the back of the bank. "And may I say how wonderful you're looking today? I understand you were a trifle ill when that photo I have of you was taken. But now you appear very fit."

"Thank you." She supposed that translated to the more than twenty pounds she had over Adah Ziller. "I'm feeling much better." She glanced at Caleb. "Aren't I, Mr. Smythe?"

"Blooming," he murmured. "Though you couldn't look anything but beautiful. That comes from within." He stepped aside to permit her to precede him into the vault. "I've always known that you have an extraordinary soul. It shines through."

"This way." Barnard was waiting at the wall of boxes and gazing down at the numbers on the sheet in his hands. "You have your key?"

"Yes." She reached into her bag and grasped the gold key. "I'm ready when you are, Mr. Barnard."

Jock glanced at his watch — 5:20 P.M.

Jane and Caleb had been in the bank for over fifteen minutes.

Not a long time, but he still was experiencing the frisson of uneasiness that had

229

plagued him before Jane had gone into the bank.

He glanced down the street again. Just a typical urban rush hour, with all its attendant noise and bustle.

Not typical. His every instinct was telling them that there was something wrong, something that had nothing to do with Caleb's weird shenanigans in that bank.

5:22 P.M.

Come on, Jane. Let's get the hell out of here.

The large safety-deposit box was empty except for a fourteen-by-ten black container that was no more than four inches in depth.

"That's it?" Jane glanced down at it. "That's not a jewelry box. It looks too heavy-duty. Maybe you're right, and it's blackmail letters or something."

"Or something." He lifted the black container onto the table. "It has some weight to it."

She lifted the lid. "What the hell?" She frowned as she pushed aside the cotton padding. Inside was another box, but this one was gold and studded with blue lapis. "Wow. Now this is worthy of a Swiss bank deposit. But she'd have to have a lot of jewelry to fill this beauty." She lifted the thin, filigreed lid. More cotton padding. She impatiently pushed it aside. "A tablet?" A large stone tablet with script that was tiny, precise, and completely filled the tablet. She studied the script. "Arabic?"

"I don't think so. Maybe Aramaic . . ." His eyes were narrowed. "This is granite, and it looks old. Not that I'm an expert."

"Well, we're not going to be able to do anything with it here." She closed the lid and put the black box in her tote. "It *is* heavy. And it must have been important to Adah if she put this in a safety-deposit box."

"Maybe." Caleb shut the deposit box and locked it. "Let's get out of here."

"What do you mean? 'Maybe'?" She followed him into the vault room, where Barnard was waiting. She forced a smile as she handed him the metal box. "Thank you again, Mr. Barnard."

"It was my pleasure." He put the deposit box into the larger outer box and turned the key. "If you please?"

Jane inserted her key and turned it.

Caleb looked up at the video camera in a corner of the room. "It's a shame you're having trouble with those cameras, Barnard."

Jane's eyes widened. Count on Caleb to cover their tracks. She hadn't even thought beyond getting to the box.

Caleb was shaking his head. "Perhaps if you erased the video and started it over, it would reset them?"

Barnard frowned. "I suppose that's possible. Yes, I'll try it. It's a shame that you can't trust technology when you need it."

"I'm sure it will be fine once you reset it. You Swiss are the true masters of fine workmanship." He took Jane's elbow and urged her down the corridor toward the front door. "Good day, Mr. Barnard. I can't tell you how helpful you've been."

"Good day."

Jane glanced back to see Henrik Barnard standing where they'd left him, frowning up at the video camera.

"Will he erase them?" she asked in a low voice as Caleb opened the front door for her.

"Eighty-five percent probability. If he doesn't do it now, it will bother him enough to make him come back later and do it."

"It's scary that you have it down to percentages."

"I've been at this a long time. We didn't need a video record of our presence in the bank. It was only another little push for me."

"And what happens when he discovers that Adah Ziller is dead?"

232

"Nothing. After he erases the videos, he won't remember that you were ever here."

"What about the receptionist at the desk who announced you to him?"

He didn't reply. He didn't have to answer. "She won't remember either, will she?"

"Not if I did my job." He glanced at her as they reached the car. "It still bothers you, doesn't it?"

"Hell yes, it bothers me. I either have to doubt my sanity or accept the unacceptable. No one should have the ability to do that."

"But I do. I didn't ask for it, but it's part of me. I handle it the best way I can." He opened the passenger door for her. "And I'm going to use it to protect you whether you like it or not." He glanced at Jock behind the wheel. "Is everything okay?"

"No, I don't think so," Jock said curtly. "Get in the car."

"Right." Caleb jumped in the backseat and glanced at the rearview mirror. "What the hell is wrong?"

"I don't know." Jock started the car. "It just doesn't feel . . . I don't know. Are we going back to Lina's place now?"

"Yes." Jane was studying his face. She knew that expression. Tense, alert, on edge. "There was a gold box with a tablet in the deposit box. Very small script that might be Aramaic. We'll have to have Lina take a look at it."

"There wasn't anything else? Maybe some more of those coins you found in her bedroom?"

She shook her head and nodded at her handbag. "Nothing but the tablet. We'll have to see how important they are."

"They're important," Caleb said. "For one reason or another."

"Don't give me that enigmatic bullshit," Jane said. "I've had enough of your mysterious 'gift.' Just come through with good old down-to-earth answers."

"How boring," he murmured. "I'd much rather deal in enigmatic bullshit."

"Those tablets have to be important." Jock's gaze was on the rearview mirror. "Why else are we here?"

Jane's gaze followed his to the mirror. "Do you see someone?"

"No." He glanced at Caleb. "But I still don't feel right. Keep an eye on that rearview mirror."

"My pleasure," Caleb said. "Trust, at last."

"Not trust. Necessity. I'm driving, and I want a sharp eye on our backs. You might as well keep busy."

"By all means." He smiled. "If there's

anything to see, I'll see it. Now get us to Lina's cottage."

TEN

It was close to eleven when they drove up the road to Lina's cottage. The moon was bright overhead and illuminated the mountains and valley with almost surreal beauty.

"Peaceful," Jane said. "I can see why she's content to stay here."

"Yes, the light on the mountains is pretty spectacular." Caleb glanced casually back at the road through the mountains which they'd just traveled. "And she set herself up to ensure that she wouldn't have to move again. Let's just keep it peaceful." Caleb reached for his phone. "I'll tell Lina that it's us coming up her drive. We don't want to alarm her."

Or she might reach for that AK-47, Jane thought, as Caleb talked to Lina on the phone. It was difficult to accept that the woman who lived here gardening and working in seclusion could possibly be violent. But who could blame her for protecting herself after the life she had lived?

She could see the front door of the cottage open and Lina's slender figure silhouetted against the lamplight as they drew up before the cottage.

"I'm not quite finished," she said, as they got out of the car and walked toward her. "I'll give you what I have, but you'll have to wait for the rest."

"How long?" Jane asked.

Lina shrugged. "A few hours. It was more difficult than I thought it would be. Come in and have a cup of tea. Do you have the time?"

"We have the time," Caleb said. "We have no choice. Jane has something else for you to translate."

"Not tonight. I'll finish the first book that I promised you I'd do. But I need some time away from Adah Ziller." Her lips tightened. "I don't understand her. She liked it."

"What?"

"Pain." She turned and went back into the house. "She was twisted."

"S and M?"

"Oh, yes." She put on the kettle. "Some of the passages are very descriptive. Particularly the ones that have to do with Jack Millet. What he did to her was unbelievable."

"He was her lover?" Jane asked.

"That's not love," Lina said. "And she didn't care. She liked it." She got cups down. "You said that she'd been murdered? Maybe it was just that one of her lovers went too far. She said that Millet almost killed her several times while they were playing their games."

"No, that wasn't how it happened," Jane said. "And it's not another ledger we found in the safety-deposit box. There was a tablet that we need translated." She took the black container out of her tote and set it on the table. "As you can see, it's pretty large, and the script is very tiny. Caleb thinks that it may be very old."

"A tablet?" She looked suddenly thoughtful. Then she shrugged. "We'll see."

"It would help us," Jock said quietly. "I know you don't want us here, but we can't leave until we know."

"I don't mind you being here. I'm not that much of a hermit." She glanced at Caleb. "But don't bring me any more of this ugliness. It brought back too many memories."

"I didn't have any idea what I was bringing, or I would have warned you," Caleb said. "We know very little about Adah Ziller."

"Well, I know quite a bit." She poured tea over the leaves in the pot. "You can start with the printout on the table over there, but you'll have to plow through it. As I told you, it's disjointed."

"Can you summarize?"

"As long as you don't make me describe her sexual perversions."

"Sit down," Jock said as he crossed the room and nudged her away from the teapot. "Relax. I'll take care of this."

"I won't argue. I like to see a man do domestic chores." She dropped down in the easy chair. "It was strictly forbidden to let any male lift his hand in the house where I grew up."

"And my mother made sure that I helped out," Jock said. "Or I got boxed on the ears." He poured tea into cups. "So watch all you please. You won't see me shirk."

Lina gazed at him thoughtfully. "No, I don't think you would."

"Adah," Jane prompted.

Lina nodded. "The ledger begins when she's fourteen. She grew up in Syria. Her father was a merchant and was moderately well-to-do. She had a Western upbringing and was sent to England when she was sixteen to complete her education."

"Where did she meet Millet?"

"Before she left Syria. She met him at something called the Offering."

"What's that?"

"She doesn't elaborate much. A sort of meeting her family went to every year since she was a child. She always found it exciting, but when she met Millet there, that was the only thing she could think about. She called him the Guardian. He was older than she, in his early twenties, and she kept talking about his power and what she wanted to do with him. She seduced him."

"At sixteen?"

"She was no virgin. She had been experimenting since she was thirteen. But Millet was special to her. At last she'd found someone who had the same tastes. She was upset when she had to leave Syria." She took the cup Jock handed her. "But she replaced him quickly. She'd acquired a taste for power and knew that was the fast lane. She honed her sexual talents while she was at school and took a job with Med-Coast Oil. She climbed the ladder quickly there."

"What about Millet?"

"She still saw him occasionally. And they'd spend weekends together whenever she went back to Syria for this Offering meeting every year."

"She went back every year?"

"Sometimes she didn't want to go, but she said that she had to do it. It was her duty."

"Judging by what you've said, I wouldn't think she would pay much attention to duty."

"She paid attention to the Offering."

"And she never described exactly what kind of meeting it was?"

Lina shook her head. "No, but she usually liked the meetings once she was there. It was exciting. She said that she was able to make contacts she'd never have made otherwise. She said that rich and powerful people came who were completely out of her reach in everyday life."

"When she wasn't screwing Millet," Caleb said.

"He was entertainment. The other men she met there were business."

"Did she mention names?"

Lina nodded. "Two movie stars. A Wall Street financier. A fast-food chain CEO. She wasn't choosy as long as they could move her ahead." She paused. "But toward the end of the ledger, she talked about one man quite a bit. He was going to grease her way to the top. All she had to do was to do what he ordered, and he'd give her whatever she wanted."

"Who?"

"Alan Roland. She said he was a mover and shaker in the financial world. Very rich, tremendously powerful."

"I've never heard of him," Jane said. "And was he talking about sexual favors?"

"She went to bed with him, but that wasn't what she was talking about. She evidently found someone who was using her as much as she used everyone else."

"To do what?"

She glanced at the box on the table. "A tablet. Something called Hadar's Tablet. Roland wanted her to steal the tablet from Millet, who was evidently its custodian."

"Why?"

Lina shook her head. "She didn't go into reasons. But it was very valuable, and she knew it would be dangerous. It was kept in a special cabinet in the Offering Room, and she had access because of her affair with Millet. But if she were caught, he would kill her. She was going to make Roland pay."

"It seems that she did it." Jane's gaze was on the black container on the table. "That tablet we found in the safety-deposit box."

"Yes. She was to give it to Roland. That was part of their deal. He was to take possession, but Millet wasn't to know that she no longer had it. Which meant that she had to run the entire risk."

"Charming."

"She was willing to do it. He gave her two

hundred thousand dollars to steal the tablet and promised her another five if she kept her mouth shut about his involvement. But she double-crossed him. She kept the tablet herself and was trying to squeeze Millet for every dime she could get." Her lips twisted. "And she was getting hush money from Roland for not telling Millet that he'd paid her to steal the tablet. Money was rolling in from every direction."

"How could she get away with it? Millet would think nothing of grabbing her and torturing her until she told him where she'd hidden the tablet."

"She told Millet that she'd placed the tablet with a friend who would send it to the police if Adah didn't check in with her regularly."

Jock shook his head. "Big risk."

"And why would this tablet be important anyway?" Jane asked. "No hint?"

"I should know by the end of the ledger," Lina said. "I scanned it and saw several references to Hadar and a tablet."

"But if this tablet was her cash cow, why would she leave the information about the safety-deposit box lying around in the office, where anyone could find it?" Jane shook her head. "If Weismann and Adah were intimate, then she must have known that he'd have access to it. That gold key is very showy, and she left the information in the study where it would be seen. She was either careless or wanted someone to know about that Swiss account. She doesn't appear to have been careless."

"A puzzle," Caleb smiled at Lina. "So will you finish up this translation and let us get out of your hair?"

"Gladly," she said emphatically.

"Good." He moved toward the door. "I believe I'll wait outside. It's so beautiful looking down at your valley. Call me when you're ready."

Jane watched the door shut behind him and turned to Lina. "How can I help?"

"Be quiet and stay out of my way." Lina had picked up the ledger again. "Sit down over there, and I'll tell you when I'm finished."

"Another cup of tea?" Jock asked Lina. "I'll even make a fresh pot so that you can enjoy having me wait on you."

Lina didn't answer. She was already deep in her work.

Jock looked at Jane inquiringly.

She shook her head. She was still thinking about Adah Ziller and trying to put it together. "Weismann. We have to assume Millet sent him to Adah to get the tablet or find out where it was. But if she was as cynical as Lina says, I can't believe he fooled her for long. She was very sharp, and I can see her having a sexual fling, but she would have gotten around to checking him out. She had to be playing him along, and leaving that gold key and bank info was just too obvious."

"Makes sense," Jock said. "But the key was genuine and the tablet was in the bank. Why run a risk like that? Weismann was —"

"Get out," Lina said. "If you can't be still, go for a walk."

"Sorry." Jane headed for the door. "You're right."

Jock was at the door and opening it for her. "If you need anything just —"

"I need you out of here," Lina said flatly.

Jock chuckled as the door shut behind them. "She definitely makes her desires known. Interesting woman."

"Yes." Jane took a deep breath of the cool night air to clear her head. Her mind was full of deceptions and tablets and the twisted desires of Adah Ziller. She had been thinking of her as a victim, but that was far from the truth. She had been balancing Millet, Roland, and Weismann and trying to cheat all three men. But her clever machinations had been useless in the end. She had been caught off guard for one moment, and that had been enough to kill her. "Weismann bothers me. I can't see how he figured in —"

"Where's Caleb?" Jock interrupted. His gaze was darting over the garden and down the road. "Oh, *shit.*"

"Where the hell is he?" Jane asked. "What's wrong?"

"What's wrong is that I don't think Caleb just went for a stroll," Jock said. "I should have known I couldn't trust him." He went to the edge of the road and looked out at the foothills. "He must have noticed someone following us."

Jane remembered that instant when they'd gotten out of the car and Caleb's gaze had wandered casually back toward the curve of the road and commented on the light on the mountains. "And didn't tell us?"

"He's not into sharing. He left us on that damn doorstep at Adah Ziller's." His lips thinned. "I may break his neck."

Jane felt the same way. "Dammit, if we'd known we were being followed, we could have lost him."

"Yes."

She caught an undertone in his voice that caused her gaze to fly to his face. "You wouldn't have tried to lose him either."

"I don't know if I'd have led him here, but I would have tried to trap the bastard."

"Who is it? You said we weren't followed from Paris."

He nodded. "And because we weren't followed, that meant someone was at the bank waiting for us."

"Weismann."

"He didn't have time to go to the study and get the key after he killed Adah Ziller. He probably decided to camp out at the bank and see if we managed to get whatever was in that deposit box. He must have been parked around the corner and was in one of the buildings watching until we came out of the bank."

"And Caleb also figured it was Weismann when he saw we were being followed." Her hands clenched at her sides. "Damn him."

"Go inside." He started down the road. "I'm going after him."

"No! Do you think I don't want to do that, too?" she asked fiercely. "We can't leave here. We brought this on Lina. We have to make sure nothing happens to her."

He stopped and turned back. "And what happens to Seth Caleb? We don't know if Weismann picked up some help."

She had been thinking the same thing.

Anger and frustration and a deep underlying fear had been struggling within her. "It was Caleb's choice. He closed us out. He clearly thinks he doesn't need us."

He studied her expression. "You're sure?"

She nodded jerkily. "He made the choice. Lina is innocent. No one could ever call Caleb innocent. He'll have to fend for himself." She turned back toward the cottage. "We'll just have to wait until he comes back."

"He didn't take the car."

"We would have heard him leave. That's not what he wanted. I imagine he functions very well on foot." She could visualize him running over those hills, his dark eyes narrowed, his expression intent.

Darkness.

Power.

Blood.

She took a deep breath and reached for the doorknob. "He'll be fine. After all, he's a hunter."

Just ahead.

In the trees on the hill overlooking the cottage.

Caleb's pace lengthened, his gaze on the trees. Weismann had left the car he had parked a few hundred yards away and was moving up the hill. He was carrying an M-25. Otherwise known as a light sniper.

A sharpshooter weapon.

He was planning on picking them off as they left the cottage.

Caleb could feel the blood coursing through his veins as he began to run.

Exhilaration.

Heady joy.

Silence.

Wind.

The earth moving, giving, beneath his pounding feet.

His heart beating, beating, beating.

This was the way a hunt was meant to be. Not on city streets or a rolling sea. A hunt could take place anywhere, but this was the best, this was how it had been at the dawn of man.

Weismann had stopped and was lying down, positioning himself on a hillock.

Come in from behind?

No cover.

The trees. There was a huge oak tree near the spot where Weismann lay.

Four strides, and he was next to it. He shinnied up the oak tree and crawled out onto the branch.

Don't rustle a leaf.

Slide smoothly, like a python, without a sound.

He was directly over Weismann.

And Weismann knew he wasn't alone. Caleb could see it in the slight stiffening of his body. He knew he'd not made a mistake but there was no way to fight primitive instinct.

Then strike fast before instinct became thought.

He dove from the tree.

Weismann rolled away at the last moment and Caleb landed on his hands and knees beside him.

"Son of a bitch!" Weismann swung the barrel of the gun toward him.

Caleb rolled the few feet toward him, grabbing at the gun and jerking it away. In one motion he rose and swung the barrel at Weismann's head.

Weismann grunted and fell to the ground. Unconscious but still alive.

Caleb stared down at him in disappointment, his heart still racing.

Too easy. He wanted more.

He wanted a kill.

He reached down and gently pushed back the hair from Weismann's temple, where the blood was pouring from the cut made by the rifle barrel. What harm? Weismann was a murderer. Take what he wanted and walk away.

Not possible.

The realization caused a bolt of fury to sear through him.

Keep it under control. Anger was the enemy. It made every breach of the code seem valid.

But killing this scum wasn't a breach of his code. That was why he was a hunter.

Excuses. This was more complicated. Jane needed information from the bastard. She wanted him alive.

He had to let him live . . . for a while.

He reached down, picked Weismann up, and slung him over his shoulder. He was a big man but Caleb didn't mind the weight.

He needed to channel every bit of his mind and strength into trying to keep himself from making the kill.

"He's coming." Jock turned away from the window. "And he looks like paintings I've seen of frontiersmen carrying home the carcasses from a buffalo hunt."

"He's here?" Jane ran to the door and flung it open.

Caleb was coming up the road, and the carcass on his back was no animal. He was carrying the burden without effort, striding quickly. His hair was rumpled and his shirt stained with blood.

She stepped out on the doorstep. "Caleb?"

He stopped before her and threw the man on his back to the ground. "Weismann. As promised."

She gazed down at the man. Eyes closed, auburn hair now covered in blood. "Is he dead?"

"No. I hit him with a rifle butt. He'll probably have a concussion, but the chances are fair that he'll be able to talk. Let's get it over with."

The words were spoken with such leashed ferocity that her gaze flew to his face.

Caleb's dark eyes were glittering in his taut face, and his lips were full and sensual and slightly drawn back from his teeth. He looked wild, barbaric. No, he looked . . . hungry.

"Get what over with, Caleb?" Jock said softly as he shut the door and moved to stand beside her.

Caleb's glance at him was like a dagger thrust. "Don't mess with me, Gavin. This isn't the time."

"No, I can see that." Jock turned to Jane. "Why don't you go in and —"

"No," Caleb said sharply. "She wanted him. She's got him. I have to have it finished." He looked at Jane, and she unconsciously braced herself. She felt . . . scorched. "Do you want me to wake him so that you can talk to him?"

"He's unconscious. How can you —"

"If you want it, I can do it." He knelt beside Weismann and added recklessly, "What the hell. I'll do it anyway. It's just a question of adjusting the blood flow . . ."

"I'm not sure that —"

Weismann screamed in agony, and his lids flew open.

"What happened?" Jane asked, startled.

"I told you, blood flow. I didn't say it wouldn't hurt."

Weismann was cursing venomously, his eyes fixed balefully on Caleb.

Caleb bent closer to Weismann, and said softly, "Be polite. I'm holding on by a thread. The lady wants answers, give them to her." He looked at Jane. "Ask your questions."

"I will. Just don't hurt him again."

"Do you hear that, Weismann? She's feeling sorry for you. That weapon I took away from him was an M-25, very good for sharpshooting up to 980 yards, and he was getting set to pick us all off as we came out of the cottage."

"And I would have gotten you." Weismann's gaze went to Jock. "Stop him. You're not going to do anything to me. You're in Venable's pocket. The CIA needs the information I have. He's willing to pay."

"You killed Adah Ziller, and God knows what other deals you've been making on the side," Jock said. "Venable may not have any use for you any longer."

"You don't believe that. What's the death of one greedy bitch matter? Tell him to let me go. Who is he anyway?"

"Seth Caleb," Caleb said. "And no one tells me anything, Weismann. They ask politely. Or, in your case, they beg."

"Stop this," Jane said as she took a step nearer. She wanted to be done both with Weismann's ugliness and the wild recklessness she could sense in Caleb. "All I want is for you to tell me what you know about why I've been targeted, Weismann."

Weismann's lips curled. "Then tell Venable to pay me. Or you can spend the next few days trying to dodge Millet and hope he doesn't find you. Let me go, and we can negotiate."

"I think not," Caleb said. "I've lost patience. Talk."

"Caleb," Jane said.

He smiled. "I won't touch him."

That brilliant smile was terrifying. "Just

persuade him to change his mind. I don't care if he thinks you're his brother."

"I care." He leaned still closer to Weismann, and whispered, "You're not worth the extra effort I'd have to make. So tell Jane what she wants to know."

"Screw you."

"Screw. Interesting word. Painful word."

Weismann shrieked, his body convulsing, his spine trying to curve.

"Talk to Jane," Caleb said. "Don't be impolite. She asked you a question."

"Son of a bitch." Tears were running down Weismann's cheeks. "What's happening?"

"Caleb," Jane said sharply.

"Too late." Caleb said. "A little hemorrhage . . ."

Blood was pouring from Weismann's nose. "Convulsion."

Weismann howled and bent double in agony.

"Dammit, Caleb," Jane said.

"He can stop it. All he has to do is talk to you."

And Caleb wouldn't stop. He was enjoying it too much.

"Do it, Weismann," Jane said curtly. "For God's sake, answer."

Weismann was scrambling, desperately trying to scoot backward. "Get him away from me." He gazed frantically at Jock. "Gavin, do something."

"Why? I'm finding this very interesting. I'd guess you're the only who can end it."

"Cramps," Caleb said.

Weismann flinched back, his legs twitching. "Monster," he gasped. "You're — a — monster."

"Yes, tell her what she wants to know."

More pain.

Weismann howled.

"Why did they target her, Weismann?"

"Damn you." He could barely talk because of the blood running down into his mouth. "Stop it. How can I talk when you keep —"

"Two minutes. Then it starts again if you don't tell her everything that she needs to know. Why?"

He was silent. "It's that painting of the man. The one she called *Guilt*."

"That painting?" Jane repeated. "That doesn't make sense."

"Weismann is going to make sense out of it for you," Caleb said. "Go on, Weismann."

"I don't know everything," Weismann said sulkily. "Millet doesn't trust me as far as he could throw me. But I managed to slip around and listen to him rant to some of the others after I saw how angry he was when he received that clipping."

"You thought it would prove valuable," Gavin said.

Weismann ignored him. "It wasn't the painting as much as the title that bothered Millet and the others. He said by naming it *Guilt,* you'd committed blasphemy."

Blasphemy. That word again. "How could I do that when that painting was born purely from imagination?" Jane asked, in frustration.

Weismann shook his head. "That's not what Millet said. He said you must have seen it in the temple. He said that even if you weren't a blasphemer, they'd have to stop you before you could tell anyone about the temple."

"What temple?"

"I don't know." He groaned, twisted in a ball. "Stop him. Stop — Caleb. I don't *know.*"

Jane whirled on Caleb.

He shrugged. "Just a little nudge." His gaze shifted to Weismann. "The name of the man who sent Millet the photo?"

He didn't answer.

Then he screamed. "Alan — Roland."

"Ah, the man pulling strings behind the scenes," Gavin said. "What do you know about Hadar's Tablet?"

"I know that bitch Adah had it. I know

Millet wanted it."

"But what is it?" Jane asked.

"I don't know. Maybe some artifact Millet thought was valuable. He grew up in Syria and did a little smuggling before he formed the Sang Noir." He looked in panic at Caleb. "That's the truth. I swear that's the truth. Millet sent me to Adah and told me to pretend that I was a wealthy businessman and try to find out where she was keeping it. No problem. I'm good with women. She was easy. It was in the safe-deposit box, right?"

"Yes," Jane said. "But I can't believe she didn't realize what scum you were."

"I *had* her. The bitch was going to take me to get the tablet, and she thought we were going to go away together."

"And you were going to give the tablet to Millet."

"Maybe. I hadn't decided."

"Are you through with him?" Caleb asked.

"Don't be impatient," Gavin said. "I can understand your dislike for him, but I don't believe Jane is going to let you have your way."

"You don't understand anything about me," Caleb said curtly. "Neither does she. It's my nature to be impatient. He's no use to us."

"Back off. I can't let you murder him in cold blood," Jane said.

"Not cold blood, hot blood," Caleb said. "That's the problem."

"He's a freak." Weismann moistened his lips. "Don't let him near me."

"We'll do our best. Alan Roland," Jock said. "What do you know about him?"

"Not much. I overheard Millet talking to him on the phone a couple times. I got the impression they've known each other for a long time. I think he lives in London."

"More," Jane said.

"There isn't any more. Just something about an Offering." He shrugged. "They don't like each other. But I think Roland had something on him."

"And Jane was part of the deal?" Gavin asked.

Weismann nodded. "Roland threw her to Millet as a kind of appetizer, but she wasn't the main course."

"How humiliating," Jane said ironically. "My life isn't even that important in the scheme of things. Well, it's important to me, dammit."

"It's important to me, too," Caleb said roughly. "Or I wouldn't have brought this bastard here gift-wrapped. But he's told you all he can."

"How do you know?" Gavin asked.

"I don't. The only way to make sure is to go inside and take a look. But if I did that, I couldn't promise you that he'd come out of it intact. He'd probably be a vegetable. I don't have much control right now. Any resistance, and I'd burn him away." He glanced at Jane. "But I don't mind, if you don't."

The words are cool but they are the only thing cool about him, Jane thought. Kneeling there in the moonlight, she could almost feel the heat emitting from him. No, not heat, fire. His muscular body was taut, his eyes dark and glittering, and she somehow felt as if she could see him surrounded, enveloped, in flames. She couldn't look away from him. She felt as if he were drawing her close, closer, into the fire that he was generating. She was dizzy with it. She *wanted* it.

"He's just scum," Caleb said softly, coaxingly. "He was going to kill all of us. Let me go inside. Just say yes."

She could feel herself sway, yield. After all, he was right.

No, he was wrong. She finally managed to tear her gaze away from him. "I believe he's told us everything he knows." She turned to Jock. "Will you call Venable and have him send someone to pick Weismann up?"

Jock nodded. "And I'll take him to the toolshed and find some rope to tie him up." His lips lifted in a half smile as he glanced at Caleb. "You lose."

Caleb didn't look away from Jane. "I didn't expect to win. She's very strong. But I had to try." He got to his feet in one graceful motion and turned toward the door. "Be careful with him."

"You're worried about me? I can handle him."

"No, I meant don't let him get loose. It isn't over."

What isn't over? Jane wondered. His bloodlust, which was nearly visible in intensity? His attempt to persuade her that had been almost a seduction of the senses? She shook her head to clear it. "Lina. I need to get back and see if anything she's translated has any connection with what Weismann told us."

"We can make a deal," Weismann said jerkily. "I'll go back to Millet and find out whatever you need to know."

"No deal."

His lips curled. "Venable won't be so reluctant. Go ahead. Turn me over to him. I'll win anyway."

"I don't think so." Caleb opened the door

for Jane and stepped aside to let her precede him into the cottage. "You were very stupid with Adah Ziller. I can't see you coming out of this in one piece."

He closed the door behind them. "You're sure that you don't want me to take care of him now?" he asked Jane wistfully. "It would be no trouble."

"I'm quite sure." She looked away from him. She was still too aware of that disturbing aura of electricity that seemed to surround him. "He may be a murderer, but I don't have to be one."

"Very commendable. In the abstract. But there's a streak of savagery in you, too. Would you feel the same if he had killed your Eve?"

"No, I'd squash him without a qualm," she said bluntly. "But that's different."

"No, that's selective savagery," he said. "My selectivity range is just wider than yours."

"Much wider." She looked around the room. "Where's Lina?"

"Here." Lina Alsouk came out of the bedroom, an AK-47 cradled in her arm. "What have you been doing, Caleb? Did you think I wouldn't hear all that caterwauling out there?"

"I was hoping you wouldn't." Caleb

glanced at the AK-47. "And my second hope was that you wouldn't come out with that weapon blazing."

"It's not blazing." She gave him a cool look. "But I'm ready. I'm always ready these days. I don't intend ever to be caught with my guard down again. What's happening?"

"Nothing that concerns you. We have it under control."

"Everything that occurs here concerns me. You're in my space, Caleb."

"Of course, it concerns her," Jane said. "Stop being soothing. We were followed, Lina. Caleb caught him. We're calling someone to come to get him."

She was silent, then slowly lowered the weapon. "How soon?"

"Right away. Immediately."

"Then I suppose it will be all right." She paused. "But I want you off my property as soon as possible. You're as close to a friend as I have, Caleb, but you're not welcome here right now."

"We understand," Jane hesitated. "In the meantime, could you finish that translation?"

Lina studied her face. "You're pushing."

"I want to live. I want the people I love to live. I have to know what I'm up against. These people are crazy."

Lina nodded. "After translating the last of that ledger, I don't have any doubt of that." Her lips tightened. "I don't want to have anything to do with them. Which means anything to do with you. I know men who would kill their own families for the chance to get their hands on something this priceless. People would claw at each other, destroy everyone around them to touch it. I *won't* be caught in the middle of that madness. I want my peace."

Jane frowned, puzzled. "You're talking about the tablet?"

"No." She set the weapon on a chair by the door. "The tablet is valuable. It's not priceless." She moved toward her easy chair, sat down, and flipped open the computer. "And these fanatics are already destroying each other. They've been killing for centuries." She glanced up at them. "Adah Ziller became very precise, very explicit in the last section of this ledger. It wasn't disjointed or vague like the rest of the book. I think perhaps she may have known what thin ice she was skating and instinctively wanted to make sure someone would know what had happened if she didn't survive."

"How explicit?" Jane asked.

Lina smiled without mirth. "She talked about the Offering. Evidently, that's the height of betrayal. It's strictly forbidden to speak of it. Do you want to know what it is?"

A small boy screaming as the knife descended.

"Human sacrifice," Jane said.

"You knew?" Lina asked.

She moistened her lips. "Offering. The word is close enough in meaning."

"Not to *human* sacrifice." Caleb was gazing at Jane searchingly. "But you jumped at it." His glance shifted to Lina. "A cult of some sort?"

"A religion." Lina looked down at her computer screen. "They would be insulted to be called a cult. Though that's exactly what they are. It's very old and as powerful in its way as the Catholic Church. Not as well-known, of course. Particularly since they advocate sacrifice and have no problem with murder. It wouldn't do to let outsiders know they exist. The faith has been passed down through the centuries from father to son and has members all over the world. No new members are accepted unless they're connected by blood to a member. They regard themselves as the only true religion."

"A religion that makes human sacrifices," Jane said dryly.

"Abraham was asked to sacrifice his son," Lina said. "The Aztecs and Mayans used sacrifices as a regular course." She held up her hand. "I'm only saying that it's not that unusual except in present day."

"This is present day. And killing children isn't —"

"Children? I didn't mention children," Lina said, puzzled. "According to Adah, they rarely sacrifice children these days. They used to do it in early days because they were more easily obtained. Parents were pressured to offer their children to gain status and secure their place in paradise. Adah said sacrifices were chosen from lists of candidates submitted by members."

"Candidates?" Caleb asked.

"In the present day there's only one offering every year, and members of the faith were urged to submit a name of a person whom they wished sacrificed. It was a mark of respect if their submission was chosen for the kill."

"Who did they submit?"

"An enemy, a business rival, a member of the family," Lina said. "The family member was considered the purest of all the sacrifices. It gave instant status." She paused. "Millet submitted his mother as a candidate. Her death won him a position as Guardian of the Offering."

Shock upon shock. A man so callous he would put his mother on that altar and take her life. "Exactly what is a Guardian?"

"He heads up a sort of guard of honor at the Offerings. He's custodian of holy artifacts and presides at the sacrifices." Lina's lips twisted. "Adah admired his strength of will as well as his sexual techniques. She envied his star status in the Offerings. In short, he was her kind of man."

"You mean she watched him kill and got off on it."

"Power," Lina said. "Yes, but she might have been content to obey the rules if Roland hadn't offered her a new and golden ladder to climb."

"You said she met him at one of these Offerings? He's a member?"

"Oh, yes. Or he would have ended up as a sacrifice if he'd shown up there. The ceremony and religion itself are top secret."

"And I was supposed to be scheduled to be a sacrifice at this Offering?" Jane asked.

"I don't know," Lina said. "Adah didn't mention you. She was very self-absorbed and evidently you didn't enter into any of her plans."

"I can't think of any other reason why Millet would want to wait until April 1 to kill me."

"April 1?" Lina nodded. "Then you're probably right. April 1 is the traditional day of the Offering."

"And what is this Hadar's Tablet? You said it was one of the holy artifacts that Millet protected?"

"Yes, Hadar was the founder of the cult. He was a scribe and an artist. The tablet supposedly describes his journey from Jerusalem and his philosophies. He's looked upon as a great prophet."

" 'Supposedly'? Don't they know what's in the tablet?"

She shook her head. "There are rumors about it that have been handed down over the centuries, but Hadar commanded that no one open the gold box where he'd placed the tablet. It was forbidden to see the light of day after his death. It was placed in a special cabinet of honor near the altar in the Offering room."

Caleb gave a low whistle. "Then Millet's letting the tablet be stolen would have been regarded as a mega sin by the members."

"And so would Alan Roland's involvement. Adah had them both by the throat."

"According to Weismann, Millet thought I was guilty of blasphemy. It must have been against their great holy man." Jane looked at Caleb. "That's crazy. I tell you, any resemblance of anyone to my painting was purely coincidental."

"Blasphemy?" Lina repeated. She was silent a moment, then said thoughtfully, "I don't think that your crime was against Hadar."

"Who else? You said he was the founder of their blasted religion. And you said his tablet was priceless."

"No, I didn't say the tablet is priceless. I only told you that Hadar's Tablet is valuable and held in reverence by the members of this cult."

Caleb shook his head. "You referred to a priceless artifact."

"I wasn't talking about the tablet."

"Then what were you talking about?" Jane asked impatiently.

"I'm speaking about the rumors that have been handed down through the centuries about what was in Hadar's tablet. He was supposed to have knowledge about a very special treasure."

"What treasure?"

"A handful of ancient coins."

Jane stiffened, her gaze narrowed on Lina's face. "Go on."

"You didn't ask me to what deity they make their sacrifices," Lina said. "Aren't you curious?"

"Satan?"

"No."

"Tell me, dammit."

"Their religion is dedicated to the glorification and redemption of the man who they say sits at God's side, who is beloved by all the angels of heaven."

Jane looked at her in bewilderment. "Jesus?"

Lina shook her head. "No," she said quietly. "Judas Iscariot."

ELEVEN

"Judas," Jane whispered. "Incredible."

Or perhaps it wasn't, she thought. Why was she surprised that a religion that lauded death and murder would also worship the most treacherous betrayer the world had ever known.

"I thought you would be surprised," Lina said. "Of course, I was not raised in your religion, but I know what Judas stands for in your culture."

"Judas is almost a universal symbol," Caleb said. "But Lucifer would have been my guess. A religion that worships power would more likely choose the devil than a mere traitor."

"Not according to Hadar. Judas was not a traitor, he was a martyr."

Jane made an impatient gesture. "Whatever. At the moment, I don't care why he was elected to sainthood by those monsters. I need to know why Millet wants to kill me and how I can stop him."

Caleb shrugged. "If it was Judas, not Hadar, you supposedly painted, then you can see how fanatics would react. You painted Judas as tormented by guilt."

"According to their religion, Judas had no guilt in the crucifixion of Christ," Lina said. "He was just obeying the wishes of God in the betrayal. Jesus was destined to die on the cross, and someone had to hand him over to the soldiers to make that happen. So Judas sacrificed himself and his place among the disciples to further the will of God."

"That's what Hadar said in this tablet?" Jane asked.

"How do I know?" Lina said. "But Adah said there were other Hadar tablets and teachings handed down over the centuries that weren't on the forbidden list. That's their doctrine."

"Twisted," Jane said. "And this handful of coins that's so priceless that everyone is after them. Is it what I'm thinking it is?"

"Adah said that it was the pouch of coins that the priests paid Judas for betraying Jesus."

"Yes, I'd say that would be priceless," Caleb said. "It would electrify the Christian world. The ultimate symbol of the worst tragedy the world has ever known."

"Or the proof that the greatest miracle really happened," Jane said. The idea of those coins still existing stunned her. "Providing that there's proof and documentation."

"Adah said Alan Roland was too smart to follow a trail unless there was some proof that it was going to pay off. Roland had been searching for the coins for years. It had become an obsession. He not only had gone over all of Hadar's teachings but traveled the world investigating every bit of information that had anything to do with the Judas coins. If he was excited about the prospect of what was in Hadar's Tablet, then Adah thought it was worth latching on to a shooting star. She was willing to risk Millet killing her to find a way of negotiating a partnership with Roland."

"We found two coins in Adah's bedroom. Could they be part of the Judas coins?"

Lina shook her head. "Adah bought those coins on the Internet. They had no value. She deliberately left them around where Weismann would find them to lead him down the path she wanted him to go. She did the same thing with the bank keys. She knew that no one but her could access the box." She added, "It was a kind of test. She actually loved him. All the men in her life, and she had never loved any of them. But Weismann managed to touch something in her. She couldn't believe he would betray her."

Jane remembered the look of incredulous horror on Adah's face. "She believed it in that last moment."

"For the little good it did her," Caleb said. "Anything else, Lina?"

"No. That's all."

"I think that we have to find out a good deal more about Alan Roland," Jane said. "He seems to be the puppeteer pulling the strings behind the scenes."

"Do what you like." Lina snapped her computer shut. "Just do it somewhere else. I've given you what you asked. Get someone else to translate that tablet. Now get Weismann off my property, and all of you go with him."

"I'll go check to make sure that Jock was able to get through to Venable." Jane headed for the door. "I'm sorry we brought this down on you, Lina. We'll try to get out of your hair as soon as possible."

For an instant the hardness in her expression softened a trifle. "I'm sorry, too. But I'm not angry with you. You're a victim, and I've been in your place. I just have to protect myself." She added briskly, "I'll have the printouts ready to take with you in fifteen minutes so that you can examine them more carefully." She glanced at Caleb. "And you owe me. This was more than I bargained for."

"Name your price."

"I'll have to think about it." She got up from the chair. "Now get out. I have to get these translations printed. Then I'm going to blow away the file. I want my mind and my house clear of you."

"Understandable." Caleb followed Jane out of the cottage. "We'll try to oblige." He turned to Jane as he closed the door behind him. "Judas. You seemed to have stirred up a hornet's nest."

"I didn't stir up anything. Hadar is the crazy bastard who decided to found an equally crazy religion. I was only guilty of painting a face that resembled Judas." She shook her head in frustration. "And how do we know that it actually looked like Judas? That was almost two thousand years ago. And how could Judas's blood money have survived all these centuries?"

"Lots of questions. Shall we see if Weismann knows any of the answers?"

She stiffened as she glanced at him. She had been so absorbed in the information that Lina had been imparting that she had forgotten the wariness she had felt with Caleb's attitude toward Weismann. Perhaps she had hoped that it had been dispersed by the distraction.

It had not dispersed. The fire was not unleashed, but it was still there, smoldering.

"It's not that easy," Caleb said, as if reading her mind. "It doesn't go away. Let me have him."

"No." She looked away. "You did what you promised. You found Weismann for me. Now I think it's time we parted ways."

"Too late. I'm in too deep." He smiled faintly. "I scared you, didn't I? I knew I probably would before this was over. You had a glimmer of what I could be, but you hadn't actually seen it. I was hoping you might not have to see it." He shrugged. "But it may be a relief. I am what I am. I told you that you had to accept me."

"Do you really know what you are?" Jane asked.

"Oh, yes."

"I don't. Sometimes I think I do, then you change. You've shown me too many facets to your character for me to be sure."

"But you don't like this particular facet."

"Hell, no."

He turned away. "Then I'd better not accompany you to the toolshed to see Weismann and Gavin. I'm frustrated and edgy, and he's not technically mine. I know I don't have a good enough reason to override you since I promised you Weismann." He started down the road. "I'll see you in ten or fifteen minutes."

"Where are you going?"

"I'm going to try to find a good enough reason."

She watched him walk away. What kind of answer was that? The only kind of answer she could expect from him. She should have learned that by now. He walked his own path and was as uncommunicative as the Sphinx. He was right, he had frightened her tonight. Caleb had revealed a violence and bloodlust that had been shocking. She had instinctively tried to edge away from him.

And he had refused to let her go. When he had said those words, she had felt helpless. It had been ridiculous to feel that powerless. He could not dominate her. She had her own will. Yet for that moment, she had felt . . . caught.

She shook her head as she started across the garden toward the toolshed. The sooner she sent him away and out of her life, the better. Just keeping alive was difficult enough without having to worry about controlling Caleb.

Control wasn't even a concept he would deal with if tonight was any example. Yet he would argue that he'd shown the ultimate control. He'd been savage but not lethal. Was that control in his view?

She couldn't spend time trying to decipher the dark nuances of Seth Caleb. The revelations of the night had been too mind-boggling to comprehend, and she was still trying to put together the pieces Lina had thrown out to them.

"I finally reached Venable." Jock had opened the door of the toolshed and stepped outside. "He said he'd send someone to pick up Weismann, but it would take a few hours."

"That's not good. Lina wants us out of here."

"Who can blame her? She heard Weismann screaming?"

"Yes, he wasn't exactly quiet."

"He was hurting," Jock said. "I confess I didn't really believe what you told me about Caleb. I'm not even sure I believe what I saw him do tonight. He's a very dangerous man, Jane."

"Yes," she said. "I'm going to send him away."

"That might not be easy." He was silent a

moment. "Tonight, all the gloves were off. When he threw Weismann down before you in the dirt, he was pure, raw emotion. It was a gift that wasn't easy for him to give you. But he did it, and I think that he'll collect."

"Then it's not a gift."

Jock shrugged. "You're probably right. You know that I'd rather you send him packing. I'm just saying that we may have trouble doing it."

"Not you, Jock. I'm the one who asked him to come." She saw he was about to argue and changed the subject. "Lina translated the last of the ledger. Close the shed door. I don't want Weismann to hear this. He seems to think he can make a deal with Venable, and I don't want him to have any more information than he has already."

"That was the only reason I agreed with Caleb that it would be better to rid ourselves of him." Jock closed the door. "I take it that Adah had something interesting to tell us?"

"Yes, you could say that," she said grimly. "Judas."

Run fast, Caleb told himself.

Keep the hunger at bay.

His blood was pounding in his veins as he ran down the hill into the small glade beside the road.

Find a reason.

Not that Jane would forgive him for being what he was no matter what reason he'd give her. But he would forgive himself, and that was enough.

No time for regret. He had jettisoned that emotion decades ago when he had realized that he could not change. He couldn't live with regret. That was the way of hollowness and instability.

Yet he had felt a tingle of regret after he had met Jane MacGuire. Even though he had known that it would end as it had tonight.

She had looked away from him. She had not wanted him to see the dread and fear in her eyes. Fear that she refused to admit even to herself.

He had seen it, felt it.

And again, he had known regret.

Stop it. Crush it. There were ways to play the game with his own rules. He didn't have to obey hers.

He could see Weismann's car where he had left it in the glade. He ran toward it, the heat rising in him.

Search and find a reason.

If not a reason, an excuse, to take back the kill.

"Judas?" Jock repeated. "The whole thing is totally bizarre."

"I agree," Jane said. "And we don't know enough to make any sense of it. But we have to find out. Did you mention Alan Roland to Venable?"

He nodded. "Only that I wanted him to check into Roland. Nothing else."

"Good. If the CIA is suspecting leaks, we don't want to be too up-front with Venable."

He smiled. "That's what I thought. By the way, where is Caleb?"

"I have no idea. He stalked off without a word." She frowned. "That's not quite true. He wanted to question Weismann again, and I wouldn't listen to him. He said he was going to find a good reason to do it."

"Why?"

"How should I know? Because he's a damn sadist? I can't see any —"

A scream! Long. Shrill. Agonized.

From inside the toolshed!

"What the hell!" Jock turned and threw open the door.

Weismann was crumpled on the floor, his eyes bulging from their sockets, staring straight at them but not seeing them. His face twisted with unbearable pain.

"What happened to —"

"I found a good reason."

Jane whirled to face Caleb, who was only a few paces away, walking toward them across the garden. "*You* did this?"

"Yes."

Her hands clenched at her sides. "What you did to him before wasn't enough? You had to torture him?"

"No, it wasn't enough. He's stronger than I thought. He didn't tell us everything." He looked down at Weismann. "I had to go in and see if I could move him to tell me more."

"How do you know he didn't tell us everything? You *hurt* him, dammit."

"He's greedy. Sometimes greed overcomes everything." He turned to Jock. "We've got to get out of here. We may have company anytime."

"Who?" Jock asked. "You told us that you'd checked Weismann's past cell calls and there had been none made to anyone tonight. That he was probably acting alone."

"He didn't make any calls on his cell." He added grimly, "But he had a laptop computer in his car, and he had a remote setup there. He made a call an hour and thirty minutes ago to a number in London."

"Roland?"

"Yes, that's why I had to go into the slime in Weismann's head and verify. He wasn't only on Venable's payroll; Roland had him in his pocket. He was paying him to bypass Millet and give him information about Adah. Weismann had to call Roland and tell him where we were and get instructions. Roland told him that he'd tell Millet that Jane was here and to grab the tablet and get out before Millet got here." He glanced at Jane. "And maybe he wasn't going to kill all of us if he wasn't totally on his own. Roland probably told him to save you for the big show. You're a very special key piece in this scenario." He turned to face her. "You're angry with me. Get over it. We don't have time to do anything but damage control."

She wanted to sock him. But if he was right, then she couldn't afford to indulge in personal feelings. But there was one thing she had to know. "What about him?" She gestured to Weismann. She shuddered as she studied his pain-filled expression. "Is what you did to him permanent?"

He shrugged. "Sometimes. The brain is very delicate, and I wasn't gentle." He added, "Don't feel too sorry for him. I came across all kinds of filth when I went in to see what else he knew. Besides murder, he had a passion for little boys. He tortured and killed a twelve-year-old he picked up in Genoa last year." He turned away. "If he does survive, it will take him months to recover enough to cause us any trouble. It's safe for us to leave him for Millet. Not safe for him. He's just got to hope Venable gets here before Millet." He walked out of the toolshed.

Caleb had already dismissed Weismann from his mind, Jane realized in astonishment. He had done what he had chosen to do and was going on his way. How hard did you have to be to destroy a man's mind and just ignore the consequences? Even though she was disgusted and appalled by the evil Weismann generated, she would have found it impossible to be that cold. But he had said that it wasn't coldness, she remembered. Hot blood, he had told her. If it was hot, the flames were enveloped in ice. Yes, that image definitely came to mind when she thought of Caleb.

"We have to move, Jane," Jock said quietly. "Lina may be isolated here, but there's no such thing as total isolation in this day of supercommunication and helicopters. All we can hope is to see them coming."

"Lina." She turned on her heel. "We can't

leave her here. They'll kill her as they did Celine."

"My thought exactly," Jock said as he followed her from the toolshed. "Let's see what we can do about it."

"We're twenty minutes away from the Alsouk cottage, Roland." Millet raised his voice to be heard above the rotors of the helicopter. "I've checked out the info, and there should be no one in the vicinity to cause us any trouble. Lina Alsouk lives alone, and we should be able to zero in on Gavin and Jane MacGuire within a few minutes after we land."

"But I understand there's a man, Seth Caleb, who has joined the party," Roland said. "My informant with the CIA had no information on him. If I were you, I'd proceed with caution."

"You're not me. I run my own job, Roland. You did as I asked and tracked Weismann down. Now butt out."

"Don't be rude. I'm handing you Jane MacGuire and Weismann. But I have a few requirements. When you gather Weismann up, I want him eliminated at once. He obviously knows too much about your business, and I can't be sure that he hasn't picked up any hints about our relationship."

"I was careful."

"I want him dead on the spot," Roland said flatly. "Don't even let him open his mouth."

"No problem. But not because you want it. The son of a bitch betrayed me."

"Remember that when you see him." It was time to get off the phone and let Millet concentrate his venom on his prey. Roland wanted him to be primed for the kill by the time he reached that cottage. "Remember I expect my turn with the MacGuire woman. Let me know when you've secured her." He hung up the phone.

Everything was falling neatly into place. When Weismann had reported in that he had located Jane MacGuire and that she might have picked up the tablet at the bank, he had known it could be a bonanza. If Weismann managed to do as Roland ordered, then Millet would find nothing but a live Jane MacGuire and a few other dead bodies. Then Roland would be able to meet with Weismann and get the tablet.

But things didn't always go as they should, and a wise man always had to have insurance. If Weismann had failed, then he couldn't afford to have him use that lying viper's tongue to try to make a deal with Millet to save his neck.

He would have to die quickly . . . and in silence.

"I'm not going," Lina said flatly. "This is my home. Do you know how hard I've worked to say those words? *My home.* Not my father's, not my husband's. My home. I'm not giving it up."

"And I'm not letting you stay here and be butchered," Jane said fiercely. "I won't be responsible. You can come back when this is all over, but you can't stay now."

"You insult me. You're not responsible. I'm responsible for my life. No one else." Lina glared at her. "Now get out. Maybe these people will follow you and leave me alone."

"It's not likely, Lina," Jock said. "First, they'd torture you to find out if you know where we're going. Then they'd kill you because you translated Adah's ledger, and you know too much."

"Do you think this is the first time this has happened to me? People come to me when they want confidentiality. I give it to them. I run the risk."

"You've never run this high a risk," Jane said. "I won't have you join the body count." She added desperately, "Come with us. We can't leave without you."

"Then stay. I don't care. That's your prerogative," she said grimly. "But get your own AK-47. You can't have mine."

"I couldn't have gotten you a more desired present, could I?" Caleb had come into the cottage. "But you shouldn't be so selfish."

"It wasn't a present, it was payment," Lina said.

"And now you're causing me to rue the day. If you didn't have the weapon, this discussion wouldn't be taking place." He was walking toward her. "Because you're not stupid. You wouldn't try to defend your castle without that gun. So I guess all I can do is try to persuade you not to do it."

Jane stiffened. Persuade. She had a vision of Weismann lying in the toolshed, face contorted with pain.

"No, Caleb."

"Be quiet, Jane. This is between Lina and me. We've worked together for a long time." He stopped only two feet away from Lina. "I brought you and Gavin here. I took the chance of leading Weismann here so that I could gather him in. I'm the one who has to take care of the fallout." He stared into Lina's eyes. "What can I say to persuade you to go with us, Lina?"

"Nothing."

He sighed. "I was afraid you'd say that."

He was turning away, Jane saw with relief. Thank God. She had been so afraid that he would —

"Forgive me," he said softly.

No!

Jane took a step forward.

Too late.

Caleb had turned in one catlike motion and leaped toward Lina.

She had barely time to lift her arm before the edge of Caleb's hand came down on her neck.

Her eyes turned glassy, her knees gave way, and she started to slump.

He caught her as she started to fall to the floor. He glanced at Jock, who had leaped across the room toward him and was in attack mode. "She's okay. It was the quickest way to solve the problem."

Jock stopped, and said grimly, "You almost had a bigger problem."

"I took that into account. Grab the AK-47. Let's get her out of here. I want her in the car and out of the valley before she regains consciousness."

"Excellent idea." He turned and picked up the weapon. "I'll go start the car."

Jane was at the door, opening it for them. Gavin ran past her toward the road. "I thought you were —"

"I know what you thought." He passed her and carried Lina across the garden down the road. "I hate to be predictable. Come on."

"I'll be there in a minute." She turned back to the room. "I have to get Lina's computer and all the printouts."

"Hurry."

She grabbed the computer, pulled a garbage bag from beneath the sink and started throwing the ledger and printouts into it. She added the box with the tablet and even scraps of paper from her wastebasket.

What else? Dammit, they were taking away Lina's life. She didn't know what was important to her.

She opened the desk drawer and scooped the contents into the bag. Passport, some official-looking documents.

"Jane!"

"Coming!"

No photo albums in this room. That was what Jane would take first in the event of an emergency. She ran to the closet in the bedroom and threw clothes haphazardly into the bag.

She was out of time to search any longer.

She picked up the garbage bag and ran out of the cottage.

Caleb was in the backseat with Lina

slumped against him.

She jumped into the passenger seat beside Jock. "Is she okay?"

"At the moment," Caleb said. "If we can get the hell out of here. Drive, Gavin."

"I believe that's what I'm doing." The car was skidding on the rutted dirt road as Jock pressed hard on the accelerator. "Maybe we'll get lucky. It could be that we have a time margin that's not as —"

Rotors.

A roar of sound coming in fast from the south.

"Helicopter," Jock said. "On second thought, I don't think that we should count on luck."

The helicopter is almost on top of us, Jane thought in panic. The blue spears of light coming down from the aircraft were blindingly bright as it descended toward them.

"They've seen us. Turn off the headlights."

"It's a little late." He increased speed. 'Why don't you take care of turning off their headlights, Caleb? That AK-47 is on the floor back there. A well-placed shot should —"

A bullet splintered the corner of the windshield!

"Move." Caleb was rolling down the window. "It will take a couple minutes for

291

them to turn around and come back, but they'll line up for a clear shot at us." He had the AK-47. "Line me up for a shot at them, Gavin. I can't be accurate with this car moving like a bucking bronco. We're not going to have much time. If I don't get the gas tank the first shot, we're going to have to get out of this car before they blow us to kingdom come. Their firepower is probably a hell of a lot more sophisticated than this automatic weapon."

"Here they come," Jock murmured, his gaze on the sky. "Low and fast. Tell me when I should slow down."

"Not slow, stop." Caleb was sighting. "On three. One . . . two . . ."

The copter was so close the roar was drowning out Caleb's voice, Jane realized. But she could see his lips move.

"Three!"

Jock put on the brakes.

An instant later Caleb fired.

He must have missed, Jane thought. The copter was over them, passing them.

No, it was listing drunkenly to one side and dipping!

"I couldn't get the gas tank. I was in the wrong position. But I got the rotor engine. That should bring them down."

"Which means they'll be after us in a

heartbeat," Jock said dryly. "Lina's car is parked at the cottage. They'll have transport. We have another thirty miles before we get out of this valley."

Jane's grip tightened on the plastic bag. "Then let's get through that pass and on a decent highway before they catch up to us."

Millet cursed as he jumped out of the helicopter. "Medford, take the men up to that cottage and see if one of you can find a car."

"Right." Medford gestured to the four men jumping out of the aircraft. "Fan out and look sharp."

Look sharp for what? Millet thought bitterly. He gazed at the taillights of the BMW, and his fingers clenched into fists. He had been so close. "Son of a bitch!"

He still had a chance if they could get their hands on a decent car.

His phone rang two minutes later. Medford.

"We found a Volvo parked in back of the cottage. We're jumpstarting it now."

"Hurry. Is the place deserted?"

"Almost." Medford paused. "We found Weismann in the toolshed. He's tied up and he's . . . I don't know. Something."

"Bastard."

"What do you want us to do?"

"What do you think? I want you to get down here with that damn car."

"What about Weismann? Should I bring him along?"

Shoot him on sight, Roland had said.

But Millet didn't take orders from anyone. He'd do whatever he liked with Weismann.

But what he didn't like was having to drag a wounded man along with him while he went after Jane MacGuire. What he didn't like was leaving him to be picked up by his buddy, Venable. Roland was worried about his own ass, but the chances of Weismann's incriminating Millet were much greater. He should have known that Weismann would try to double-cross him when he sent him to get that tablet from Adah.

Two-faced prick. A bullet in the brain was too good for him.

"Hell, no," he said harshly. "Burn the bastard. Torch that toolshed. Torch the whole damn place."

TWELVE

"Lina's stirring," Caleb said. "Maybe you'd better take the AK-47 up there. It might be too accessible when she comes out of it."

"Take your chances," Jane said. "You're the one who knocked her out."

"You were being too polite. It wasn't going to work with Lina. She wasn't going anywhere."

"So you gave her a karate chop."

"It ended the discussion." He met her gaze. "And admit it, you were glad I didn't use more 'unusual' methods. You were ready to jump me."

"Hell yes. I'd just seen what your persuasion did to Weismann."

"I was in a hurry, and I didn't give a damn. I would have been careful with Lina. If I'd chosen to do it."

"Then why didn't you?"

"Because I didn't want to tamper with her. I know Lina. I like her. It wasn't fair to take the advantage. I don't intrude with personal relationships unless I can't do anything else."

"Your code again?"

He shrugged. "When I can go along with it. As you saw tonight, it's a very loose code."

"Exceptionally," Jock said. "Almost non-existent."

"And you didn't seem to be overly worried about it."

"I was too busy watching and sifting through your weird vibes."

"I'm glad you held your — Shit!"

His hand closed on Lina's wrist and jerked her hand away from between his legs. "Dammit, are you trying to tear off my balls?"

"Yes," Lina said fiercely. "You bastard. You *hit* me."

"And I guarantee that you hurt me just now more than I hurt you."

"Good." She straightened in the seat. "And I'll hurt you again. As soon as I get a chance." Her eyes were blazing in her white face. "I didn't think you'd — I don't trust many people, but I thought that you were —"

"I didn't have time to argue." He paused. "This seemed the least intrusive way to move you."

"Well, it won't do you any good. Let me out. I'm going back." She glanced out the window. "We haven't reached the pass yet. It will only take a couple hours to hike back home."

"And you'll be welcomed by Millet and his men," Jane said. "A few things happened while you were unconscious, Lina. They're not far behind us."

"Let — me — out."

"Okay." Jock stopped the car. "Get out, Lina."

"No," Jane said sharply.

"You can't convince her. She has to make the decision." His gaze was on the rearview mirror. "Or have it made for her."

"You've already tried that," Lina said as she opened the car door and got out. "And I don't appreciate it. This is my life. I don't want your protection or your pity. I take care of myself. I won't have — My God." She was staring at the southern sky, which was glowing orange-red in the darkness. "Fire."

That's what Jock was staring at in the rearview mirror, Jane thought as she got out of the car and joined Lina on the edge of the road. That's why he stopped the car and let Lina get out. The hillside was wreathed in smoke, and the cottage and outbuildings were being devoured by flames. "It's your place, Lina," she said gently.

"I know that," she whispered. "I've driven this road hundreds of times, and knew I was almost home when I reached this point."

Jane put her hand on Lina's arm. "I'm sorry. It's senseless destruction. There was no reason for them to do it." She added bitterly, "But that doesn't seem to matter."

"I could have stopped them."

"No." Jock got out of the car. "Those are trained killers, and there are too many of them. You might have slowed them down, but this wasn't the place to stand your ground. If it had been, we'd have stayed."

Her gaze never left the burning cottage. "I'd have found a way."

"Headlights." Caleb suddenly said, his gaze on the valley below. "Get going, Gavin."

Jock got back in the car. "And this isn't the place to stand our ground either, Lina. We can't risk Jane. Will you come with us?"

Lina didn't answer.

"I'm not going to knock you out again," Caleb said. "But Jane is wasting time she doesn't have on you. She's not going to leave you."

"That's her decision." Lina glanced at Jane, then turned on her heel. "Oh, hell, I'll go. For now. Get in that car. Let's get out of here." She jumped in the car. "But if that car has any speed, it could overtake us in ten minutes if you keep on this road."

"You should know. It's your car they stole."

"Then it has the speed. I made sure of that when I bought it."

"According to the map, there's no other road," Jock said.

"There's a road. Go straight ahead." She turned to Caleb in the seat beside her. "And you'll never be in the position to knock me out again. I trusted you enough to let you near me. I won't do that a second time."

"You never know," Caleb said. "Circumstances usually dictate response."

"I know." She leaned forward, and said to Jock, "Around the next curve is a little lay-by on the right that disappears into the brush and trees. Go off the road and into the brush. In about forty yards you'll see the road. It runs parallel to the main road. But go very slowly and be careful to stay on the road. Four feet on the other side is a three-hundred-foot drop to the valley below. You won't be able to see it because of the tree cover."

"How did you learn about the road?" Jane asked.

"I don't like not to have options. It makes me nervous. I went to the government highway planning office and did some research when I moved into the cottage. It was built by the Swiss government along with several other roads during World War II and leads directly to the highway. Switzerland was neutral but evidently they don't like not to have options either. They conveniently forgot to list the road when they put out the new maps the Germans requested. It stayed forgotten after the war." She pointed to the right. "There. Quick. I think I hear their car." Her lips tightened. "*My* car. Bastards."

Jane could hear it, too. Were they that close, or was the air so thin that sound traveled with extra clarity?

Then they were in the lay-by, pushing through the overgrown shrubbery. The BMW jounced wildly over the rocky ground, and branches hit the windshield.

"You're sure we're not heading for the cliff?" Jock said. "I can't see a thing."

"Cut the lights," Lina said. "They'll see us when they come around that curve."

"Great." Jock turned off the lights. "Now I'm sure that I won't know when we reach the edge of the cliff."

"I will. The road is gravel. As soon as you reach it and feel the crunch, turn left immediately and hug the left side of the road."

Darkness.

They were surrounded by trees and brush and couldn't see two feet in front of them.

Jane's heart was beating hard, her chest was tight.

They had to be heading straight for the cliff. How did they even know that the road still existed? Maybe it had washed away or something.

Crunch.

"Turn left." Lina said sharply. "Quick."

Jock jerked the wheel. Gravel flew as the BMW moved onto the gravel road.

"Now slow," Lina said. "Very slow. The cliff winds a bit here, and we're right on the edge."

A beam of light speared the darkness above them.

"They just turned the curve," Caleb murmured. "At least I think they did. All I can see is that blur of a headlight through the trees."

"Then they shouldn't be able to see us at all." Jane said. Lord, she wished they were off this road. It was like walking a tightrope blindfolded.

As long as she could hear the crunch of the gravel on all four tires, then they were safely on the road.

Just listen for the crunch of the gravel.

The lights above them had disappeared. They must have gone ahead. Perhaps it would be safe to go back on the main road.

"They could come back," Caleb said as if reading her thoughts. "When they find out they've lost us, they're going to wonder why."

"Or they might decide that we made it through the pass to the highway," Jock said. "But I'm going to give it five more minutes, then make an executive decision. I'm going to turn on the headlights. I don't like this option you found for us, Lina."

"It works," Lina said curtly. "Don't argue."

"If I can keep this car from going over the cliff," Jock murmured.

The BMW suddenly teetered uncertainly.

No crunch under the right-side tires.

Jock cursed and jerked the wheel to the left.

"I told you the cliff curved around," Lina said.

Gravel under all four tires again.

Jane breathed a sigh of relief and tried to catch her breath. "Jock, that executive decision? Implement it now, please."

"Right." Jock flicked on the headlights. "I'll keep them on dim."

Even with the lights on, there was little to see but brush, tall grass, and trees encroaching on the narrow road. But at least they could see the direction of the gravel stretching ahead.

"How much farther, Lina?" Caleb asked.

"Fifteen minutes. We would have been at the highway by now if we'd kept on the main road."

"Which means that Millet has already reached the highway," Jane said. "The question is whether he'll assume we're still ahead of him or cruise back to see if we're behind him?"

"We'll see in fifteen minutes, won't we?" Caleb said.

In sixteen minutes, they made the turn that left the edge of the cliff and wandered up through a forest of evergreens. Two minutes later they were gazing down at the traffic racing on the four-lane highway.

"Civilization," Caleb murmured. "Or what passes for it."

"There's nothing civilized about Millet," Jane said. "And we've got to hope that he's ahead of us still in chase mode and not waiting for us somewhere along the highway."

"We'll play it safe and get off at the first exit that has a good-sized town," Jock said. "Thanks to Weismann, Millet probably has a description of the car and license plates. We've got to get out of this BMW. Can you take care of that, Caleb?"

"Not right away. I'll have to work on it."

"I'm disappointed," Jock said as he entered the highway. "I was expecting you to meet our every need."

"I'll work on it," Caleb repeated. "First, let's get off the highway and find a hotel where we can stay for an hour or so and assess the situation. That will give me a chance to see what I can do about transportation."

"Studgard," Lina said. "Two exits down. There are three hotels in the town." It was the first time she had spoken in the last twenty minutes. "The Merrier is a lower-income motel and would probably be less public."

"Thank you," Jock said. "The Merrier. You haven't steered us wrong yet."

"I don't want to help you. I have to do it," Lina said coldly. "You're the lesser of two evils right now. And if I decide that I'd do better without you, then I'll walk away. I'm just a little confused right now, and I need time to clear my thinking."

Of course, she's confused, Jane thought sympathetically. She watched the life she had so painstakingly built from disaster destroyed in the space of less than an hour. "I tried to bring some of your personal things when we left the cottage, but I didn't know what you'd want. I cleaned out your desk drawers and grabbed some clothes. I looked for your photo albums, but I couldn't find them."

Lina frowned. "Photo albums?"

"It's what I'd want to take with me if I was ever forced to leave a place. Memories."

"I have no photo albums." Lina looked out the window at the stream of passing cars. "I prefer to live in the present."

Jane felt again that surge of pity. She had not lived an easy life, but she had good memories of good people. Lina had been brutalized and cut off from family and country. Jane could not imagine being stripped of her memories of Eve and Joe. "But the present is tomorrow's memory. I guess we just have to make it as good as possible."

"I did make it good," Lina said. "And it just blew up in my face."

"I'm sorry that we were involved. I can't blame you for resenting us."

Lina's gaze shifted back to her. "I don't know how I feel right now. I have to think about it. I know I resent you interfering with my free will. I do blame you for that." She glanced at Caleb. "Or rather, I blame him."

"No, blame me," Jane said. "I'm not sure if I would have been desperate enough to give you a karate chop, but I suspect it might have come to that. I couldn't have left you there. And when it all comes down to basics, I'm the one who this is all about. Jock and Caleb are only helping me, trying to keep me alive."

"What a splendid whitewash," Caleb said. "I feel like a knight in shining armor."

Lina ignored him. "You don't defend yourself?" She studied Jane's face. "Curious. Everyone is sure that what they do is right even when it isn't."

"Not in my world," Jane said. "You try to do what's right and hope. Life is too complex to be certain of anything."

"This Millet is certain that you should be killed."

"But he doesn't belong to my world. He's a monster who hovers in the shadows."

Lina closed her eyes for an instant. "He didn't hover tonight. He came out and destroyed my —" Her eyes opened. "I believe that's a sight that I will hold in my mind for a long time. I must erase it."

"How?"

"What's difficult to erase, I find a way to replace." Her lips tightened. "I don't like to remember failure. I refuse to do it." She leaned forward again to speak to Jock. "Next exit."

"Right."

She turned to Caleb. "Now. Where is my gun?"

"We're on Highway 6, but we've lost them," Millet said to Roland on his cell. "I don't know how. We were right behind them. Dammit, they just vanished."

"Weismann didn't take care of them?"

"I told you, we've lost them. The cottage was deserted . . . except for Weismann."

"And you took care of that problem?"

"I roasted the son of a bitch. Not for you, Roland. For me."

"I don't care why, just so it was done. Did you find any sign of the tablet?"

"Nothing. They must have taken it with them. If we find them, we find the tablet. You have the make and number of that BMW, find someone to locate it. We'll stay in the area and zero in as soon as I get a call from you."

"I can't create miracles, Millet."

"You can call Ned Simpson at NORAD and have them do a satellite scan of the area for the car. He'll do it. I saw him sucking up to you at the last Offering."

"It will mean putting his job in jeopardy. You're sure you can't find them without Simpson's help?"

"What does his job matter? We're on the side of the angels."

Millet always uses that religious bullshit when he wants to justify doing anything he wants to do, Roland thought. "His job matters because we can use him in little difficulties like this. But you're right, we should let him help us. Doing this job will cement him firmly under my influence."

"Then do it," Millet hung up.

Roland smothered the flare of anger. Things were not going well, and he needed that prick Millet right now. But at least Millet had killed Weismann before he could talk. Now if Millet could get his hands on the MacGuire woman, he'd work on manipulating both her and that tablet out of Millet's hands.

Roland reached for his phone and started to look up Col. Ned Simpson's number.

Now what was the best way to persuade him that it was really the angels and not Millet who wanted him to send that satellite over Switzerland in the next few hours?

The Merrier Inn was a modest one-story redwood structure, and Caleb had to wake the young desk clerk in the office to check them into the motel.

"Around the corner of the building." He got back into the driver's seat. "Two units side by side for Lina and Jane. One end unit that I'll take, and Jock has one a little farther down." He drove around the corner. "With any luck, we'll get a little rest before we have to check out."

"Is it safe? You had to show the clerk your passport, didn't you?"

"Yes, but I have a spare in a different name."

"Of course, you do," Jane said with irony. "Doesn't everyone?"

"It would be chaos if they did," Caleb said. "And I do like to be special." He handed out the keys. "It's the middle of the night, and the town seems to be locked up tight. But the clerk said there were kitchenettes in all the units. Gavin, will you call Venable back and see if he has any information we need to know? The team he sent to pick up Weismann must have gotten to the cottage by now."

Jock nodded as he headed for his end unit.

"Suppose we agree to meet in an hour in Jane's room? That will give us time to clean up and relax a little. I don't think we can spare more time than that."

He meant that Millet was still on the hunt, Jane realized. They had probably only evaded him for a brief time before he caught the scent again. She felt the tension tightening the muscles of her neck and lower back as she unlocked the room. It had been a wild, violent night, and she was still reeling from it.

She glanced at Lina, who had just gotten out of the car. Lina's night had been as devastating as the one Jane had undergone. No, probably more devastating. "I wish I could tell you that you're safe now, but that wouldn't be the truth. Millet knows that you probably learned more than he wants you to know while you were translating that ledger. If we can arrange for you to disappear somewhere, we'll try to do it. But please don't run away from us."

" 'Disappear'? I spent years of my life in hiding before I learned how to protect myself." Lina opened the door of her room. "I won't do it again." She slammed the door shut behind her, and Jane heard the slide of the bolt lock.

"She's not going to run," Caleb said.

She turned to look at him. "How can you be certain?"

"She's very intelligent. She's not pleased with us, but she can see that we're not the destroyers, Millet is the enemy. She'll just have to decide how to handle it."

"The last thing I wanted to do was to hurt her," she said wearily. "Millet would have killed her, wouldn't he?"

"Yes. But he didn't kill her. He destroyed her possessions, not her. Possessions can be replaced."

She knew that was true. "But I still don't like being responsible for their loss. She'd worked so hard to make a life for herself. I want to help her."

"May I suggest you worry about yourself at the moment? You're the one whose heart Millet wants to carve out of her chest. Everyone else is second in line." He turned away. "Lock your door. I'll see you in an hour."

Jane shot the bolt and leaned back against the door. She would take a moment to get her breath. The adrenaline that had kept her going was beginning to ebb out of her. She had to face the fear and tension again but not yet. For an instant, in this little box of a room, she felt like an animal who had found a cave in which to go to ground. She was safe. She could close everything out.

But she couldn't close out what Lina had told them of her translation. The information kept tumbling through her mind.

Hadar's Tablet.

Judas at the right hand of God.

Coins that could shake the Christian world.

Sacrifices to Judas that had taken place for centuries and were still taking place.

Guilt.

She shook her head and straightened away from the door. Try to make her mind go blank. Wash. Rest. Maybe make a cup of coffee.

And get ready to face the chase again.

Lina knocked on Jane's door thirty minutes later. "I need to talk to you." She came into the room and sat down. "Or rather I need you to talk to me."

"What is it?"

"You're the key. I want to know everything about you."

"Why?"

"Because I've decided that I need to kill this man, Millet." Her hands clenched together on her lap. "I'm very angry with him. And I would be safer with him dead." She smiled mirthlessly. "No Millet, no more disappearing. True?"

"If Millet were the only one to worry about. But you're the one who told us about that hideous cult."

"I'll worry about the rest of those maniacs later. Millet is the one who burned down my home." She sat down in the chair at the table. "I know only what was in Adah's ledger. I need to know everything I can about him. You have an important connection with him. Killer and victim. So you must tell me everything about yourself."

"Oh, must I?" She smiled faintly. "And are you going to tell me everything about yourself?"

She looked at her in surprise. "No, I did you no injury. You owe me. I do not owe you."

"You have a point." She was discovering that Lina had an almost childlike clarity of vision that was both innocent and brutal in scope. It was a strange facet of character in a woman who had gone through the hell she had experienced. "Very well, I have fifteen minutes before Jock and Caleb should be here. I hope that I'm not shallow enough to bare my entire soul in that time, but I can give you the broad strokes." She went into the kitchenette. "I've just put on a pot of coffee. Would you like a cup?"

"Not now. Talk to me."

Jane looked over her shoulder. "In a minute. I need the caffeine even if you don't."

"But I want you to —" She stopped. "I'm antagonizing you by being too demanding. It is a habit of mine. I will try to curb it."

Jane smiled. "And I will try to hurry through my cup of coffee. That's what compromise is about."

"I'm not good at that either."

"I've been known to have a few problems with it, too. We'll work on it together."

"Okay, Millet. Simpson's zeroed in on the BMW," Roland said. "And it's stationary at the moment. They're sitting ducks. I'm sending you the coordinates on your phone."

"How close?"

"In the general area where you are. I went to a great deal of trouble convincing Simpson to do this. I'm going to owe him, and that pisses me off. You'd better make it worth my while. Don't bungle it."

"Don't threaten me. Simpson should be doing this for the glory of the Offering. So should you, Roland."

"How pure. May I remind you that you're the one who lost the tablet because you couldn't keep your hands off Adah Ziller?"

"I'm the Guardian. It is my privilege to take any woman I wish in any way I wish. Just as it is my privilege to cut her heart out if she betrayed me."

"Then you should have done it in a way that didn't get in the way of our arrangement. Get the tablet and Jane MacGuire."

Millet glanced at his phone screen and he forget anger as satisfaction surged through him as he saw the blip. "I'm on my way."

Jock's brows rose as he gazed at Lina sitting relaxed at Jane's small table. "I wasn't sure that you'd be here. I was prepared to have to chase you down."

"You wouldn't have found me. But I decided that it would be more efficient to have Millet come to me than go after him." She glanced at Jane. "Or to come to Jane. From what she tells me, he will do a great deal to try to find her. That is good."

"I don't believe I'd describe it quite that way," Jane said dryly.

She smiled faintly. "I'm very good at languages. Not so good at tactfulness."

"We've found that out," Jane said.

Jock looked from Jane to Lina. "I detect a slight lessening of abrasiveness between you. Or am I mistaken?"

"With knowledge comes understanding," Jane said. "We had a talk. But knowledge only goes one way at the moment. So understanding is tentative at best."

"And I don't know what the hell you're talking about." He paused. "Have you heard from Caleb?"

She stiffened. "No, he should be here any minute."

"I knocked on his door, and there was no answer."

"What?"

He shrugged. "Maybe he was in the shower."

Or maybe he was doing something that he didn't want them to know about. It wouldn't surprise Jane. Secretive bastard.

Or maybe something had happened to him.

The thought brought a rush of panic. She had been worried about everyone else, but Caleb always seemed to be invulnerable. Perhaps because she didn't understand those psychic gifts that were such a disturbing part of him.

No one was invulnerable. Not with Millet on the loose.

There was a knock on the door before Caleb walked into the room. "Sorry I'm late. I had a few things to tidy up."

She wanted to hit him. Of course, nothing had happened to him. And of course he wasn't going to be explicit about those few things he had to "tidy." "It doesn't matter," she said curtly. "We didn't miss you."

Caleb's brows rose. "I'm crushed." He went to the bar in the kitchenette and poured himself a cup of coffee. "But that will only make me work harder to please."

Her displeasure had been obvious but had rolled off him like water off a duck. "You haven't tried to please anyone but yourself lately."

"That's not true. I made a real effort to please you when I went after Weismann, but it didn't work out." He glanced at Lina. "And I had to balance keeping you alive or doing what you wanted, and I chose to keep you alive. Sorry."

Lina said, "Screw you."

"Then I'll forget about offering apologies." He paused. "Offering. That word brings to mind a few more current matters. Have you found out anything about Alan Roland from Venable, Gavin?"

"Wait a minute," Jock turned to Lina. "Venable's team arrived at your place thirty minutes ago. I'm sorry, there wasn't anything left but ashes."

Lina flinched. "I was expecting it."

He glanced back at Caleb. "And there were some human remains in the toolshed. I guess Millet didn't like Weismann any more than you did."

"What about Roland?" Caleb asked again.

"Venable hasn't had a chance to compile an in-depth dossier, but he gave me a brief sketch." Jock said. "Alan Roland. Very important man. British. Mid-forties. Inherited wealth but he's managed to triple it since he took control of the family fortune. Banking background. His father was reputed to be a mover and a shaker, and Alan has stepped into his shoes. In earlier centuries he would have been called a kingmaker. He has a passion for power and indulges it."

"Any criminal record?" Jane asked.

Jock shook his head. "No record, not even a speeding ticket. And no obvious connection with Millet. He's absolutely clean."

"What about Syria? If he goes yearly to those Offerings at the temple, there has to be a record of it."

"No, as a financier he's out of London a good deal, but according to immigration, he's never been to Syria."

"I'd guess Roland may have a few passports, too," Caleb said. "And handles those visits with great discretion."

318

Jane frowned. "Very smart."

"But you already knew that from Adah's ledger," Lina said. "He would have to be clever to be able to control Millet. From what you've told me, Millet is very volatile."

Like a nuclear explosion, Jane thought.

"I don't care about this Roland," Lina said. "I want the man who burned my home to the ground. Tell me about Millet."

"Well, I do care about Roland," Jane said coldly. "Be quiet, Lina. Millet may have done the killings, but Roland is the one who pointed the way. No one is safe as long as Roland is out there. I won't let them have any more of the people I care about. I want both of them. I'll *have* both of them."

Lina blinked. "Very well." She didn't speak for a moment. "You're not what I thought. There were moments when I was feeling sorry for you. I'm glad I don't have to worry about doing that any longer."

"No, that's not something for you to bother about," Jane said. She didn't know why that single-minded comment of Lina's had caused her to suddenly explode, but now that she had started, she couldn't stop. All the frustration and threat of the day had overflowed like a raging river over a dam. "Shall I tell you what we're going to do? We're going to find that temple where they kill children and anyone else who gets in their way. We're going to stop them from ever doing that again. We're going to find that pouch of Judas coins so that Roland won't get his dirty hands on them. Then we're going to trap Roland and Millet and send them straight to hell." She got up, went to the closet, and pulled out the green garbage bag she'd stuffed at Lina's cottage. "And right now I'd like you to concentrate on something besides what you'd like to do to Millet." She pulled out Lina's computer and tossed it on the bed. Then she took out the box containing the tablet and set it on top of the computer. "Earn your keep. We need to know exactly what's in that tablet. Give me a translation."

Lina didn't move for a moment. Then she reached out and took both the box and the computer. "It will take time. I glanced at it at the cottage. The script is incredibly tiny, and I'll have to be extremely careful with it. It's more like a book than a tablet. And since it's ancient Aramaic, I'll need some reference books that I might not be able to find online."

"Then we'll get them for you," Caleb said. "But you'll need a place to work, and this isn't it." He glanced at Jane. "In spite of Jane's hurry to push you forward, I'd prefer you be out of Millet's path before you start."

Lina gave him a cool look. "I don't care what you prefer. Go to hell, Caleb."

"No, that would only be an interesting diversion." He lifted his coffee to his lips. "And Jane doesn't want any detours. I realize you're still angry with me, but you're sensible enough to realize that I could be valuable to you."

"I don't need you." She looked at Jane. "Do you need him?"

"No. I don't need him." She was still as shocked and wary of Caleb as she had been when he had thrown Weismann down at her feet. Yet she was feeling a curious reluctance to reject him that had something to do with the panic she had felt for him before he walked through her door tonight. "But this isn't the time to send anyone away. We should stay together." Jock was studying her with narrowed eyes, and she added quickly, "It's safer for everyone."

"Maybe." Jock gazed at Caleb. "Tell me, is it safer for you?"

"Of course, I feel very secure with you keeping an eye on me." He added, "And such a close eye." He finished his coffee and checked his watch. "And now I think we'd better get out of here. We should be picked up in about five minutes at the front of the motel."

Jane's eyes widened. "And just who is to pick us up?"

"His name is Hans Wolfe. He works at the local gas station about two miles from here. A very pleasant fellow."

"And how did you meet this pleasant fellow?"

"I was running an errand and asked him to help me out. He was very cooperative."

"I imagine he was. What errand?"

"I'll tell you all about it. But we should get moving." He headed for the door. "Hans is going to take us to a small private airport about forty miles from here. I've called and arranged for a charter pilot, Marc Lestall, to pick us up there. He's flying in from Paris. I've used him before, and he's reliable and exceptionally discreet. He should be arriving shortly after we reach the airport."

"All of this in one hour," Jane said. "And without consulting us."

"It didn't hurt to set it up. I figured you could always refuse."

She didn't move. "Yes, we can. Where is this plane supposed to take us?"

"Anywhere you want to go. I suspect you might want to go to London first to pay a

322

visit to Alan Roland. Or perhaps MacDuff's Run to drop off Lina and Gavin. She'd be safe there while she's translating the tablet." He repeated softly, "Anywhere you want to go."

She looked at Jock.

He shrugged. "It's true that Lina would be safer at MacDuff's Run."

"Then let's get to that plane. Get anything out of the rooms you need." She turned and grabbed her jacket and bag. "By all means, we mustn't keep Hans waiting."

They had just left the room when the shock wave came. The earth shifted slightly beneath Jane's feet, and she instinctively reached out to clutch Caleb's arm. "What on earth was —"

Caleb's gaze was on the trees in the distance that were glowing orange. "I believe that might be Millet exercising his venom and frustration."

Jane's gaze followed his to the trees. "What are you talking about?"

"That's the general direction where I abandoned the BMW. Millet must have found it and got a little irritated that we were nowhere near it."

"Millet?" Her gaze flew to his face. "How far?"

"Over thirty miles away. And not in the

direction we're going. He used quite some firepower to cause that kind of vibration." He took her elbow. "But I do think we should accelerate our departure, don't you?"

THIRTEEN

Hans Wolfe dropped them off at the small private airport thirty-five minutes later.

"Is there anything else I can do?" His square, blunt face was eager. "I could go back and get you food at that bakery we passed."

"The bakery was closed," Caleb said.

"But I know the owner. I know everyone in this town. He'd open up the shop for me."

"Thank you, but I believe we'll be fine," Caleb said. "Our plane should be arriving any minute."

Hans's face fell. "Then what else may I do for you?"

Caleb smiled gently. "Nothing more. You've been a good friend to me, Hans."

"Yes, we're very good friends. It's good that you were able to stop by after all these years."

"But it's time for you to go home now. I think it's best that you forget us."

He nodded. "Because of that trouble you said you were in. I understand. You'll come and see me again?"

"Yes, someday." He shook his hand. "I think I hear the plane. Now go home and don't let anyone see you on the way. Good-bye, Hans."

"Yes, I hear it, too," Hans said as he turned away. "Good-bye, Seth. I'll see you next time."

Lina turned to Caleb as Hans drove away. "He's very accommodating. How long have you known him?"

"Long enough." He turned and watched the Gulfstream jet coming in for a landing. "I think I'm going to be his silent partner. He's always wanted to own his own gas station."

"Providing he could trust you," Lina said, as she and Jock moved toward the Gulf-stream.

Caleb made a face. "It's going to take quite a while to get her to think kindly of me, isn't it?"

"You could use the same voodoo you did on Hans Wolfe," Jane said.

"No, I couldn't. I told you that I have a few rules I don't break."

She was silent a moment. "It's very gener-ous of you to give Hans his dream."

He shrugged. "I put him at risk. He may still be at risk."

"Will he forget everything just as that bank manager did?"

"Yes. It's safer for him as well as us." He walked toward the tall, sandy-haired man who was getting out of the plane. "Thanks for coming on short notice, Marc. We need to move quickly." He gestured to the pilot. "This is Marc Lestall. Get on the plane. I'll make formal introductions later."

"Where are we going?" Lestall asked. "It would be a good idea if I knew. Right?"

Caleb looked at Jane. "MacDuff's Run?"

She nodded. "But I want to go see Alan Roland first."

He was silent for a moment. "It might be dangerous."

"Not if we go to his office. He's not going to make a move surrounded by all his office staff."

"And it might not accomplish anything. He's not going to admit anything."

"I don't care. I don't want him to think that he's safe because he's hiding behind all that money and power. I want him to be aware that we *know* what a bastard he is."

"Then we'll go to Edinburgh and split up. You and I will go to London to see Roland and send Lina and Gavin to MacDuff's

Run. We'll join them later." Caleb followed her up the steps and said over his shoulder to Lestall. "Scotland."

They were in the air within a few minutes, and Jane gazed down at the ground disappearing from view. Millet might be down there, but he couldn't touch them. Not now.

Relief. Intense relief.

"Blanket?" Caleb was standing beside her with a navy blue blanket in his hands. "We have a few hours, and you might be able to catch a few winks on the trip. We haven't had a chance to get much rest since this began."

"That's an understatement." She started to take the blanket, but he was already tucking it around her. His hand brushed her throat, and she inhaled sharply. It was only the lightest touch but her skin tingled, burned.

And he knew it. His gaze was on her face, and there was a stillness, a watchfulness, that made her chest tighten and her heart start to pound. It was like that primitive moment at the cottage when he'd thrown Weismann down before her. He was wrapped, surrounded in heat, but now it had nothing to do with violence and everything to do with sexuality.

328

She jerked her own eyes away and moved back away from him. She huddled under the blanket and tried desperately to think of something that would break that intimacy. "It's soft . . ."

"Cashmere." His gaze never left her face. "Marc has a lot of business executives who hire him to fly them around. They appreciate the finer things."

She looked around the luxuriously appointed cabin. Thick, gray carpet, twelve plush seats in burgundy suede framed in polished mahogany. Lina and Jock were sitting near the back of the plane, and Lina's eyes were already closed.

"I appreciate the finer things, too." She stroked the feather-soft wool. "Particularly when they have to do with comfort. Celine and I never agreed about designer luxuries. She thought a little discomfort was worth the —" She stopped as her eyes started to sting. They had been so frantically busy that Celine's death had faded from the forefront of her mind. Now the memory was back and all the more poignant for the suddenness of its coming. She blinked fast, hard. "Damn. Sneak attack."

"The worst kind of ambush." That almost primitive sensuality was gone though the electricity still lingered between them. Ca-

329

leb handed her his handkerchief as he sat down in the seat across the aisle from her.

She dabbed at her eyes. "I want to go back. I want her alive. I want to change things. If I hadn't agreed to that damn art show and gone to Paris, then she wouldn't be dead."

"That's true. Unless you believe in destiny. You could also say that if you'd never painted *Guilt,* none of this would have happened. Maybe changing one piece of the puzzle wouldn't make a difference."

"It's all crazy. I told you, it was pure chance that *Guilt* looks like their idea of Judas. He's a figment of my imagination. A dream."

His brows rose. "Dream?"

She hadn't meant to blurt that out. Certainly not to him. "Maybe I did see his face in a few dreams, but that doesn't mean anything."

He was smiling. "Oh, Jane. You do protest too much."

"Bullshit."

"I realize that admitting that you may have a tinge of weirdness yourself is against your every instinct. You're such a wonderfully grounded, practical woman. It took all your tolerance just to accept that I'm a freak."

"I'm not that closed-minded. I've come to

330

realize that there are some people with legitimate psychic gifts. I'm just not one of them."

"Then why did I immediately feel a closeness to you the moment we met? I knew you'd understand whatever I —"

"I don't know why you would feel like that," she interrupted.

"And you don't want to hear it. I scared you tonight. You don't want to claim any similarity with me. You're shying away from everything about me that you don't understand."

"You didn't scare me. But you're right, there are too many things about you that I don't understand."

"Then ask me. I don't promise to answer everything, but I'll be honest with what I do tell you."

She wasn't sure she wanted him to be honest when she remembered the brutality of the night. And when she was still overpoweringly aware of how he had aroused her only a moment ago.

Yes, she did. He had fascinated and intrigued her since the moment he had come into her life. Admit it, she thought. I want those answers. "You seem to go into people's minds and mold them and pull out whatever you need so easily. Yet you told me that you wanted to be careful with Adah so that it would be smoother. Is it harder to do than it appears?"

"Sometimes. It depends on the mind. Most of the time it's like skating on firm, fresh ice. Sometimes it's a fight to get in, and that can cause serious damage unless I take my time. But I can overcome it."

"But you didn't take your time with Weismann."

"No, I didn't give a damn. He was already a dead man as far as I was concerned."

The blunt ruthlessness of the statement shocked her. He had promised to be honest with her, and he was keeping to his word.

He smiled crookedly. "Was that a little too much information for you? Is that all you wanted to know?"

She was silent a moment. "No, one more question. You said it was very rare that you ran up against someone you couldn't manipulate. Even if you try all your bag of tricks?"

"After all these years of practice, I'm close to perfect." He shrugged. "But yes, there are a few people out there who I can't touch. Very strong minds. And then there are the quagmires. Whenever I hit one of those, I pull out and run like hell."

"Quagmires? What's that?"

"I call it the quagmire effect. There are some people whose minds are constructed oddly. They don't necessarily even have to be strong. They're just . . . different. It's like being caught in quicksand. Intense pain and sensation of smothering. If it went on too long, I think it would kill me."

"How do you know?"

"I've only had it happen twice. The first time I didn't know what was happening, and I backed out right away. But I was still dizzy and sick for a day afterward. The second time, I couldn't get out of his mind and I blacked out. I didn't wake up for two days. I was very careful after that. I've learned to recognize the signs." He smiled. "You see, I trust you. I'm letting you know all my vulnerabilities."

"Perhaps a tiny percentage of your vulnerabilities. You're as heavily armored as a tank."

He chuckled. "Next time I'll reveal another Achilles' heel. I'll be like Scheherazade telling you a tale a night to keep you interested."

"More like a narrator from the *Twilight Zone*." She pulled the blanket higher around her. "I'm going to take that nap now."

"Do that. I didn't mean to disturb you." He was silent a moment. "Have there been other dreams, Jane?"

She tensed. "Everyone has dreams."

"Like that one?"

She didn't want to answer. Why was she feeling compelled to do it? "Sort of. Maybe."

"What's it like when you dream? Disjointed?"

"No."

"Then what?"

"I don't know. Clear. Very clear. As if I'm there, part of it. It's as if a story is . . . unfolding."

"Interesting. Will you tell me more about them?"

"No."

"If you change your mind . . ."

"No."

"Dreams don't make you weird. Or at least only in the most minor category on the scale. Believe me, I know about weird."

"I do believe you," she said emphatically.

He chuckled. "I know you do. Tell me, where is *Guilt* right now."

"MacDuff's Run. MacDuff took it for safekeeping. Why?"

"I want to see it. I want to see your dream, Jane," he added thoughtfully. "It must have been a very powerful dream. Do you believe that it could have been brought on by the thoughts and vibes of all those thousands of worshipers in Judas's temple?"

Shock jolted through her. "No, I do not."

"Just a thought."

A very disturbing thought. But then Caleb was a very disturbing man. She wished she'd never made that verbal slip about the dream of *Guilt.* He would probe and gnaw at it until he was satisfied or had it in pieces and devoured.

Caleb tilted his head. "Or it might have been a case of remote viewing."

"Remote viewing? What on earth is that?"

"It's a technique that the CIA has been experimenting with though they don't admit to it. It's rather like astral projection or out-of-body experience where their psychic agent actually can mentally go to a place or situation and view it. I guess you could call it a form of psychic espionage."

She frowned. "In dreams?"

"Or deep hypnosis, or, if they're gifted enough, they merely concentrate and pull it off. If that mosaic of Judas is that close in resemblance to your painting, then maybe you did a little mental visiting."

"The CIA? That's absolutely absurd. They wouldn't be doing experiments like that."

"No? As I said, they're very careful of their credibility, but the intelligence community will do anything to keep the advantage. When they learned the Chinese and Russians were ahead of them in experimentation they jumped on the bandwagon in 1972. There was even a multimillion-dollar research program called the Stargate Project, which came to light in the nineties, that probed military applications of psychic phenomena."

"And they claimed it worked?"

"Of course not. That would be giving away a valuable asset and endanger their psychic operatives."

"Or they were embarrassed to admit that they'd even entertained the idea of anything so crazy." She added curtly, "If remote viewing even exists, I have nothing to do with it. That's even more bizarre than thinking I'm attuned to those idiots' vibes."

"I'm just exploring possibilities. I'm finding that one very promising. It would explain why you —"

"And I'm finding it total bullshit."

He held up his hand. "No need to become upset. I'll keep my thoughts to myself for the present."

"Good idea."

"Go to sleep," Caleb said. "I'll try to stop asking questions. I'm not trying to catch you at a weak moment. It's just my nature."

"I don't have to answer your questions."

He was silent a moment. "I might have nudged a little."

"What?"

"Just a little. Then I backed away. And I'm admitting it, aren't I?"

She stared at him in disbelief. "And that makes everything all right?"

"No, but it makes it a little less threatening. And I took 'no' for an answer."

"I don't want to talk to you anymore, Caleb."

"I know. I had to tell you. You'd have wondered later, and it might have damaged our relationship."

He was totally impossible. One moment she was chilled and terrified by him. The next he was showing her a side that was almost vulnerable. "We have no relationship."

"Yes, we do." His eyes were holding her own, and she was aware that the sensuality she had thought gone was still there, waiting. "I don't know what it's going to turn out to be. It's tentative, but I'm working on it." His voice was velvet soft. "Sleep well, Jane."

"Take it." Judas threw the pouch on the ground at the feet of the high priest, Caiaphas. "I don't

337

want it. I never wanted it. You made me take it."

"You wanted it." The high priest's lips curled. "Don't lie. But now you're having second thoughts. I don't know why. Everything is working out quite well."

"I didn't think it would be like this." Tears were running down his face. "They all think I'm Satan. I tell you, he wanted to die. I only helped him."

"So it didn't hurt to take a few pieces of silver?" Caiaphas said sarcastically. "I understand. I would have done the same."

"I don't want your understanding." Judas's hands clenched at his sides. "I want you to take the money and tell everyone I gave it back."

The high priest stared down at the pouch on the floor. "There are difficulties. It's blood money. I'm not sure it should return to our coffers. No, you'll have to keep it."

"I can't keep it," Judas said hoarsely. "It's dirty. Every time I touch it, I feel the filth enter my soul."

"Oh, it's the money that's dirty?" The high priest's brows rose. "One would think that the act, not the payment, would be dirty. Betrayal is so very ugly, Judas."

"Take it," Judas said. "It's all there. Pick up the pouch."

Caiaphas slowly shook his head. "You say to touch it makes you feel the filth. I cannot take a chance of destroying the purity of my calling."

"Pick it up!" Judas screamed. "Take it. Tell them I didn't mean to —"

"Leave the temple. You're beginning to annoy me. Your task is done." He turned away. "Tell your friend, Jesus, that you meant no harm. I doubt if he will believe you either. As far as I'm concerned, the matter is closed."

"Take back your money! Please." He gazed in agony as the high priest walked away from him. It was not going to happen. He was forever going to be damned in the eyes of the world.

Not in the eyes of God. Surely God would realize he meant only to help perform His will.

Or had that really been his intention?

Was he lying to himself as the priest had said?

He had been disappointed when they had arrived in Jerusalem and there had been no magical coming of the kingdom as he had interpreted should happen from Jesus's teaching. Had he meant to force that coming by betraying Jesus?

What was truth or lies?

Doubt was twisting, sickening him, darkening the world.

Answer.

He had to find the answer.

He turned and stumbled out of the temple.

"They would not take it?" Hadar asked. The young scribe rose to his feet as Judas appeared in the street. "They did not believe you?"

Judas shook his head. "He left the pouch lying on the floor of the temple. The high priest, Caiaphas, wouldn't risk soiling himself by touching it."

"I'll go get it and bring it back to you."

"No!" He started down the street. "Don't you realize that would damn me forever?" He was sobbing. "As if I was not damned already."

"But you are innocent."

"Am I?" He had convinced Hadar, but how was he to make himself believe when his heart was shriveling within him with doubt. Hadar had been one of the faithful who had followed the disciples from town to town, and he had attached himself to Judas with a tenacity that had first flattered him, then brought him comfort. He could neither read nor write, and yet this scribe looked upon him with adoration. Hadar had clung to him even after everyone else had turned their backs in horror. "The priests say that I wanted the money. That it's blood money. His blood."

"All lies. You'll be a prince in God's heaven.

We'll both be there together just as you promised me." Hadar's lips thinned, his eyes blazing with rage. "I could kill them all. I will kill them."

A young boy willing to bathe in blood for Judas's sake.

Blood. Crucifix. Jesus.

Dear God in heaven. What have I done?

He started to run through the streets, pushing through the crowds.

"Judas!" He heard Hadar calling from behind him. "Wait!"

He could not wait. He could not face Hadar again. He could not face the world again.

Betrayal.

Eternal damnation.

Guilt.

"Jane. Wake up."

She was being shaken.

Her lids flew open.

Caleb's face was only inches from her own.

"What is it?" she gasped.

"You tell me." He was in the aisle squatting beside her chair. "You were muttering and moaning. Nightmare?"

Judas. Hadar. The high priest.

She sat up straight in the chair and pushed her hair back from her face. "Sort of."

"My fault?"

She frowned. "What?"

"One of the words you were muttering was Guilt. I asked you about the painting right before you went to sleep."

"No." She moistened her lips. "I wasn't dreaming about the painting."

"The Judas face again?"

Raw despair. Betrayal. Eternal damnation. "Partly."

"But you're not going to talk about it."

"It was just a dream."

His gaze narrowed on her face. "Someday you'll trust me enough to talk to me." He rose to his feet. "Or maybe not. Other things can replace trust that may be just as binding." He sat down in his seat across from her again. "We should be arriving in Edinburgh within the next thirty minutes."

"Already?" Her gaze flew to the window. "I must have slept longer than I thought."

"You got a few good hours of sleep before the demons began to plague you."

"What demons?" she asked warily.

"How do I know? Any demon that's particular to you. We all have them."

"What's your demon, Caleb?"

"If I told you that, then I'd have to share. You don't want to share my demons, Jane."

She remembered that moment when he'd

thrown Weismann down in front of Lina's door. "No, you can have them all to yourself."

He smiled. "But I'll be willing to share your demons. I know most demons by name, and others are bosom friends. If I can't fight them, I'll persuade them to come visit me instead."

She shook her head. "You're impossible."

"In more ways than one." He paused. "Will you tell me one thing about your dream?"

"It's just a dream."

"Then you shouldn't mind discussing it. Was Hadar in it?"

She looked at him in surprise. "How did you guess?"

"If they play out like a story unfolding, then Hadar would be a central character, wouldn't he?"

"Or I might be influenced by all the talk about Hadar to have had him creep into my subconscious."

"Yes, that's a possibility. Was there anything that we can grab on to about Hadar?"

"Don't be ridiculous," she said impatiently. "You can't grab on to a dream."

He was silent, waiting.

"Even if you were to put any weight in what I dreamed, Hadar was only a young scribe." She made a face. "Who was willing to kill for Judas."

"Where?"

"Jerusalem. Outside the temple. Judas had just tried to give the pouch of coins back to the high priest."

"A very crucial time."

She looked back at the red-tipped clouds outside the window. "A dream."

"Or a story beginning to unfold," Caleb said quietly. "And a demon being born."

London
Day Five
Roland Enterprises.

The name engraved in gold on the black granite gave the impression of being discreet, important, and affluent, Jane thought. But then so did the skyscraper that occupied a piece of London's prime real estate.

"Into the lion's den?" Caleb said as he opened the glass door for her. "Unless you've changed your mind?"

She shook her head. "No way." She moved toward the elevator. "But I expected you to try to talk me out of it. Jock certainly did."

"I agree with you that there's a risk, but it's not major. A man who has tried so hard to keep in the shadows isn't going to take a chance unless he's sure that it's not going

344

to damage his reputation."

"That's what I thought."

He smiled. "And you've got me. I'd probably be able to sense any impending danger. I've got pretty good instincts."

Hunter's instincts. "You said the executive offices were on the top floor?"

He nodded. "Twelve." He got into the elevator and punched the button. "And, according to the receptionist, Roland is in London at the moment."

"Why not? He sends Millet to do his dirty work while he cools his heels in this granite mausoleum." She got off on the twelfth floor and strode toward the receptionist's desk. There were executive offices on both sides of the hall and at least a dozen secretaries in cubicles down the hall.

The secretary was blond, sleek, and attractive. SHEILA CARMODY was the name on the bronze plate on her desk. "May I help you?"

"I need to see Alan Roland," Jane said.

"Do you have an appointment?"

"No, tell him that Jane MacGuire wants to see him."

"I'm afraid that he never sees anyone without an appointment."

"Except Jane MacGuire," Caleb said. "She's always the exception, isn't she?"

Sheila Carmody frowned. "I believe you're right. I'll see if he's busy." She got up and disappeared through the heavy oak doors.

"Just a nudge?" Jane murmured.

"Only a fraction of a nudge."

The secretary returned. "He'll see you, Ms. MacGuire." She shook her head at Caleb, who had started for the door. "I'm sorry. Only Ms. MacGuire."

"No," Jane said, as Caleb opened his lips to protest. "I'll handle it, Caleb." She opened the door and went into the office. Strong light streamed through huge rectangular windows and burnished the rich mahogany desk and glass doors of the bookcases with a soft glow.

There was nothing soft about the man sitting at that desk. Her first impression was of confidence born of years of meeting and attaining goals. He looked to be in his mid-forties and very fit. He was big, broad-shouldered, with a ruddy complexion, piercing blue eyes, and dark hair barbered to perfection.

"Ms. MacGuire." His smile was charismatic. "Or may I call you Jane? I feel as if I know you well." He paused. "And you must feel the same, or you wouldn't be here. I suppose that Adah left a trail that led you to me? I was hoping to close that avenue, but you and your friends were a bit too quick."

Her eyes widened in surprise. "You're not denying that you're working with Millet, that you belong to this cult?"

"Did you expect me to deny it? It would be useless. I'll just have to deal with your knowing about it. Actually, I look forward to dealing directly with you."

"Instead of having Millet go after me. You're the one who started all this. You sent that photo to Millet."

He nodded. "I wanted to make sure that he saw it. Millet isn't the type who would be interested in the art section of a newspaper. He's a little crude. You might have noticed."

"Oh, I noticed. Why did you send it?"

"I needed attention paid to you. I don't do that kind of thing myself. I have an image to maintain." He was studying her. "You're a beautiful woman. That photo didn't do you justice."

"It served its purpose for you. It started a killing spree. Millet butchered my friend."

"That was only a necessary side effect. Millet had to be given something since he couldn't have immediate satisfaction in your case."

"Why?" Her hands clenched. "I didn't know anything about your damn Hadar.

347

And that painting was pure coincidence."

He shook his head. "Not possible. The resemblance is too close. You must have found a way to get into the temple. I'd judge it had to have occurred several years ago. About the time you had your run-in with Thomas Reilly."

She stiffened in shock. "What do you know about Thomas Reilly?"

"If Adah led you to me, then you probably know that I've been searching for years for the Judas coins. I've scoured the world and dug in the background of everyone I ran across who was also on the hunt for them. Thomas Reilly was a criminal but an avid collector and I took a particular interest in him. Not easy since I had to bribe my way into several CIA files after Reilly's death." He smiled. "But it was worth it. Because I discovered that Reilly was convinced that you knew where those Judas coins could be found. He thought that they'd been thrown into a chest of gold coins that came from Herculaneum to Scotland." He paused. "And that you knew where that chest had been hidden."

"If you know about this mythical chest, then you know that I've never tried to find it. And I certainly had no idea whether the Judas coins were in it or not. I don't *care*."

"I think you do. I've kept my eye on you over the years, and it's true you haven't initiated any search. But that could be because you're very clever, very patient. Then I saw the photo of *Guilt*. Big mistake. Did you feel safe because of the years that had passed?"

"I don't know what you're talking about."

He leaned back in his chair. "After I saw the photo, I decided that Reilly was wrong about that gold treasure chest. Maybe it was a red herring you tossed out. You knew the Judas coins were somewhere else entirely. I think when you were hunting for those coins, you found your way into the temple and saw the mosaic. It's not beyond the realm of possibility that you also saw Hadar's Tablet. But I don't think you'd risk taking it. It was enough that you knew that it was there and could reach out and grab it when you could figure a way to do it."

"That's insane. I don't give a damn about the Judas coins." But he isn't going to believe me, she realized. He's obsessed and thinks everyone would be equally obsessed. "And I never saw that mosaic in your temple."

He shook his head. "You want the coins." He added softly, "And now you have the tablet. But you're afraid that we're going to stop you from getting what you want, so you come and try to convince me that it's all a mistake. Are things getting a little hot for you, Jane? You're not playing with amateurs now."

"No, I'm dealing with thieves and murderers. And I came here to let you know that I know who you are and what you are. You can't hide from me. I'm going find a way to bust you and all those monsters who think they can torture and kill and —" She stopped. He was smiling. Her words weren't making any impact on him. "You don't believe me."

"Tell me where the Judas coins are," he said. "We can make a deal. It won't be easy, but I can get Millet to forget about you. I'll give you a fat share, and you'll be safe."

"I'll be safe anyway. You won't be able to touch me or the people I love."

"Tell me where they are."

"Is that why you let me come in here to see you? I was surprised it was so easy. You wanted to make a deal?"

"I thought I'd try. It would have made life simpler."

"How did you know I wouldn't bug our conversation?"

"I do business of all kinds in this office. I have electronic monitors. If you were wired,

I would have known within the first fifteen seconds. I knew we could have an intimate conversation that wouldn't hurt me and might further my aims. Besides, I was curious about you." His smile faded. "You can't hurt me, Jane. I own judges, members of Parliament, even senators in your Congress. If Millet doesn't get you, then I'll call on someone else. Do you feel secure with the little circle you've managed to gather around you? Try to fight me, and I'll turn the big guns on them."

"I don't think they'd worry too much."

"But you'd worry. You've already demonstrated that, haven't you? You're a strange mixture of greed and sentiment. You were very transparent when Millet killed Celine Denarve."

Yes, she'd worry.

"Make a deal, Jane."

She turned on her heel. "Go to hell." She walked out of the office and slammed the door. The secretary looked up, startled.

"Problems?" Caleb asked.

"No, he's exactly what we thought he was. Maybe a little more obsessive." She headed for the elevator. "And stronger."

"Yes."

She glanced at him.

"I was doing a little probing."

"And?"

"He wouldn't be impossible to manipulate, but it would take a good deal of time at close quarters."

"No! Stay away from him."

His brows rose. "It could be valuable."

Close quarters with a man who had killers, judges, and senators on tap? "We'll go another route. Roland is totally obsessive. Let's go find out where those Judas coins are and let him come to us."

"Lina and MacDuff's Run?"

She nodded. "MacDuff's Run. I'll call Eve and fill her in before we get there." The thought of Eve was like a warm, soothing breeze after that disturbing conversation with Roland. "And I'll call Jock and ask him to send someone to get several versions of the Bible and any reference books they can find about Judas and have them waiting for me. I don't want to have to rely solely on Lina."

"What are you going to be looking for?"

"I don't know. Anything I can find out about Judas, Hadar, or Caiaphas."

"Caiaphas?" Caleb repeated. "Who the hell is Caiaphas? I've never heard of him."

"He's the high priest who paid Judas for the betrayal." She wearily shook her head. "Or maybe he's not." The name had just tumbled out. "I don't think I've ever heard of him either."

"No?" Caleb was smiling curiously. "Let's just see what we can find out about him, shall we?"

"Whatever. We're going to have to move quickly. Roland didn't believe a word I was saying. He has his mind made up, and he's blind to anything that contradicts it." It was incredible that Roland had interpreted and twisted Thomas Reilly's belief that Jane had found those coins to apply to his own driving fixation.

Two men with an obsession about the Judas coins that had hopelessly lured and held them captive. It couldn't be just the money. What force would cause that kind of — ?

She had a sudden memory of the face of *Guilt.*

Judas.

"Jane?" Caleb was gazing curiously at her.

She shook her head to clear it. She didn't know where her mind had been wandering, but it was time she stopped thinking about mystical concepts and got down to trying to bring this nightmare to a close. "Nothing. I was just thinking. We should be at MacDuff's Run by late afternoon, shouldn't we?"

FOURTEEN

"Jane MacGuire was just here, Millet," Roland said. "She knows about me. And she probably knows a hell of a lot more. You should have gotten to Adah before it ever came to this."

"Tough. It's too bad you can't hide away like you usually do. But at least we know where she is right now. My man, Nelson, who's set up a camp in the hills above MacDuff's Run, said that Gavin and Lina Alsouk arrived there earlier today. What are the chances the MacGuire woman will go there, too?"

"Good. She'll feel safe there, and she may need some time to examine that tablet. Can we take her before she reaches the castle?"

"No, security is too tight. But we're working on a way to get access."

"Do it. No more excuses. Get her."

"I told you, we're working on it. I'm on

my way to join Nelson right now." He hung up.

Roland pressed the disconnect and leaned back in his chair.

He should be angrier. It was serious that Jane MacGuire had found out that he was involved. Yet he was experiencing more excitement and anticipation than rage. Some of it was sexual. Their encounter had been challenging, and the woman turned him on. Conflict and the desire to break and conquer was always intriguing. But the greater excitement came from the feeling that he was close, closer than he had ever been to the Judas coins. She had them or would have them. Every instinct was telling him that he had been right about Jane MacGuire being the road to the coins.

And he would run roughshod over that path, and her along with it.

I've called in the wolves, Jane.

You should have made a deal before I set them to devour you.

Eve was waiting at the helipad at MacDuff's Run when their helicopter landed at sunset. The wind was blowing her red-brown hair back from her face and her fine white shirt against her body. Her feet were spread slightly apart, bracing against the tornado caused by the rotors.

She looked fragile and strong at the same time, Jane thought as she opened the door. And totally indomitable, like a tree that could bend but never break. A rock in the middle of chaos.

"Eve!" She jumped out of the aircraft and ran toward her.

"It's about time." Eve hugged her close, then pushed her back to look at her. "You're tired."

"It's been a rough few days. Is everything okay with you?"

"As well as could be expected."

"Is Joe still here?"

She shook her head. "In Rome with Venable. Discovering all kinds of nasty things about Millet. The more I heard, the happier I was to hear that you were coming here." She looked beyond Jane. "Hello, Caleb. Should I thank you for taking care of Jane? Or do you have an agenda?"

"Maybe my agenda is taking care of Jane." He smiled and took Eve's hand. "How suspicious you are. But always interesting and a delight." His gaze went over the massive castle perched above the stormy sea. "It's quite a place. A fortress."

"Yes, MacDuff's family has a history of needing fortresses." She gazed at MacDuff, who was striding toward them. "But he couldn't have been kinder or more protective of me."

"It was my pleasure." MacDuff was scowling at Jane. "You're not forgiven, you know."

"I don't ask for your forgiveness, MacDuff. I did what I thought best." She looked at Eve. "But I thank you for keeping Eve and Joe safe."

"There was no question about that." His gaze was focused on Caleb. "You're Seth Caleb? Jock told me some rather bizarre things about you. But I have an idea he still skated over a good many details. Jane thought you would prove valuable to her. Have you?"

"Yes and no." He smiled. "But at any rate, I account only to her. Ask Jane."

"I prefer to find out on my own."

"There are a few things I'd like to find out myself. I've been told how secure you are here. Have you seen any signs of Millet?"

"Possible surveillance in the hills." His gaze went to the rolling hills in the distance. "More than possible. We're keeping our eyes open."

"You haven't sent anyone up there to scout?"

"Of course I have. Signs but no sightings."

"Who have you got to check it out? What kind of experience?"

"Tim Mactaggert. Royal Marines veteran. Special Forces." His gaze narrowed. "And I'm the one who is supposed to be questioning you. I believe that we should have a chat." He gestured for Caleb to precede him. He glanced at Jane. "Will I see you at dinner?"

"Probably not. If Jock managed to get the reference books I needed."

"You'll have to ask him. He's been running around getting Lina Alsouk settled. You'd think I didn't have a housekeeper."

"How is Mrs. Dalbrey?"

"The same. A little older, like the rest of us. But that young scamp of a son keeps her bustling. I'll tell her to serve you in your room." He turned away. "Coming?"

"Not yet," Eve said. "We're going to walk down to the Run. It's become one of my favorite places since I came here. I want some time with Jane."

"Is it safe?" Jane asked MacDuff.

"Would I have let her go, if it wasn't? You'll be watched from the gates. I'll see you when you get back to the castle."

"You're very careful about my safety," Eve said dryly, as they started for the path that led around the castle. "But going to see Roland today wasn't very safe."

"It was a calculated risk, but meeting with him wasn't all that dangerous considering that he's so careful of his image." She made a face. "It's not as if he'd rig a trapdoor in his office to spring when an enemy walked through the door. I guarantee that he's no comic-book-type character."

"Ugly?"

"In his way as ugly as Millet. But it's all inside. Neither one of them looks like what he is. I meant to send you a photo of Millet."

"Joe sent me one when he got Rome, along with photos of a few of Millet's men in the Sang Noir."

"You said Joe has been finding out unsavory details about Millet. Anything that I should know about?"

Eve shook her head. "Nothing that has a connection with you."

"What about Alan Roland? We've heard about his public image. We don't know anything about his personal life."

Eve frowned, trying to remember. "He's in his forties. He owns two race horses. He likes women. He's been divorced three times. None of his wives appears to have been heavy in the IQ department. No children. He wields a lot of influence. He dabbles in politics, but he's never run for any office. It's all behind the scenes." She shrugged. "But he doesn't seem as much of a threat as Millet."

"You're discounting him. You're saying he doesn't give the impression of being a force to reckon with. That's an asset in itself."

Eve nodded slowly. "Yes, I guess it is." She looked at Jane. "This is the bastard who sent your photo to Millet? He just threw you to that maniac like a fish to a shark?"

"You could choose a kinder comparison," Jane said. "Millet may be a shark, but I'm no helpless, flopping fish. But, yes, Roland sent my photo to Millet."

Eve's lips tightened. "Then the bastard is totally without a conscience." They had reached the edge of the steep cliff that bordered the back of the castle, and she was gazing thoughtfully down at the waves crashing against the limestone over a hundred feet below them. "It always surprises me when I run into people like Roland. It shouldn't, I suppose. It's not that I haven't dealt with my share of monsters."

"I know." Jane had watched her battle against those monsters while searching for the killer of her child, Bonnie. She'd had to stand by, wanting desperately to help and not being able to do anything. "But you've always had hope. You want people to be good, to do the right thing."

"Yes, I do. And I have to believe that most people are good. Life wouldn't be worth living if I didn't." She changed the subject. "I do like this place. I never realized why they called this place the Run." Her gaze wandered around the rough rocks that formed a theaterlike circle around a stretch of green grass. "MacDuff told me that once a year his ancestors hosted games here and invited all the warriors in Scotland to participate. I can almost see those strong, bare-chested lads in kilts running across the green."

"So can I." Jane sat down on one of the rocks. "It was my first thought when I saw it a few years ago." She smiled. "I should have known you'd feel the same way."

"Yes, we generally have the same response." Eve sat down beside her and linked her hand with Jane's. "From the time you were a kid fighting everyone on your block. But I'm surprised that the MacDuffs built this castle on the edge of the cliff. It's a beautiful view, but you'd think that they'd want an escape route since they were a warrior clan."

"You're right, the MacDuffs always thought about the safety of the clan first.

But they managed to get around the problem of this cliff. They wouldn't have built the castle here if they hadn't worked out an escape route. But I'm sure they were relieved they could have their fortress here and enjoy having this to look at every evening."

The rays of the setting sun were burnishing the waves far below them, and Jane could feel the cool breeze touch her cheeks. Peace was flowing over her, and she was aware that all the tension and desperation of the last days was beginning to ebb away. How many times had she sat on the porch at the lake with Eve, enveloped in this same sense of peace and contentment?

And love. Whenever she was with Eve, there was always love and the belief that as long as they were together, everything would be all right.

They were silent, enjoying the sound of the surf and the wind. No need to talk. Being with someone you cared about was like being by yourself, with no stress, no need to force the words.

It was minutes later before Jane asked, "How is your reconstruction going?"

"Slowly. Maybe he doesn't want to be found."

Jane's brows rose. "That's the first time

I've heard you say that."

"Just because I want to bring him home is no sign that his parents would welcome him." She wearily shook her head. "Hell, maybe they're the reason he ended up in that hole in the ground. Sometimes the parents are responsible either directly or indirectly."

"But you've always told me they're in the minority."

"And they are. I suppose I'm just being negative." She smiled. "By tomorrow, I'll be back to normal and working my butt off to finish and ship him home."

"But why are you being this discouraged now?" She gazed at her searchingly. "Is it my fault? I've disrupted your life and torn you away from Atlanta."

"You did no such thing," Eve said brusquely. "And you know it. It wasn't your fault that there are crazies out there." She was silent. "But maybe it has something to do with you. I'm afraid for you. I guess I'm wondering why I'm trying to bring home this poor dead child when I can't bring you home safe and sound. It's not a great exchange." She shrugged. "But we'll work it out."

"You're right, we will." Her hand tightened on Eve's. "And you're not really wondering. You've spent years giving solace to hundreds of families of lost children. What you do is damn wonderful."

Eve gazed out at the horizon. "Wonderful or not, I have to do it. It's what I am." She fell silent again. "Now we'll stop talking about me. We have to go back to the castle soon, but I want you to fill me in on every single detail of what's been happening to you."

"I haven't been keeping anything from you. I tried to be honest with you all the way, Eve."

"But you were in a hurry, you were in shock, things were happening too fast. Little things get lost when you're traveling at light speed." She smiled. "But now you're slowing down. You can take a deep breath and let yourself remember all those little things. I hate it that I wasn't there to help you. Maybe if we share, it will make it less painful for both of us." She urged softly, "Take that breath, Jane."

"There you are." Jock was coming down the staircase when Jane and Eve entered the castle. "I was just coming after you. MacDuff said you were watching the sunset at the Run." He looked at Jane quizzically. "I thought it a bit odd. You haven't been in

364

the mood for staring at scenery lately."

But she was still feeling that inner peace and serenity that had surrounded her while she was sitting with Eve on the cliff. "I was in the mood today."

"I can see that." His gaze shifted to Eve. "Your influence? Good for you. She looks as if she's been on vacation."

"We needed a little downtime. We're both better now."

"How is Lina?" Jane asked.

"She couldn't wait to settle in her room and start to work." His lips quirked mischievously. "I put her in the Laird's suite. MacDuff doesn't use it any longer. It's too formal for his liking. I wanted her to get a taste of grandeur."

"Why? She made it plain that she likes to live simply."

"I couldn't resist. She informed me very curtly that she didn't like castles, but she'd put up with it until she finished the translations."

"I like her," Eve said. "She has thorns, but you'd always know where you were with her."

"No doubt about that," Jane said. "Did you get my books, Jock?"

He nodded. "They're in your room. Two boxes of Bibles and reference books as requested."

"Good." She started for the grand staircase. "I'll shower and hit the Internet first, then dive into the books."

"You're in a great hurry," Eve said quietly. "You're safe here. Why the frantic pace?"

She grimaced. "I guess I'm still operating under Millet's countdown. I can't believe those bastards are going to let me live past April 1. I feel as if the only way to stop it is to stop them."

"I wish I could disagree with you," Eve said soberly. "I'd like to tell you to stay here and let Venable and Joe hunt down Millet and Roland."

Jane shook her head. "And let those murderers go after everyone I care about? Joe would be a target. Anyone I love will be a target. I can't hide away."

Eve nodded. "That's why I'm not arguing with you. They have to be stopped." She stopped as she saw the housekeeper coming down the steps. "I was just going to call you, Mrs. Dalbrey. I'm hoping you can persuade Jane to eat something before she starts to work. You know each other, don't you?"

"Of course, we do." Nora Dalbrey's smile lit her plump face. She was dressed in a black skirt, sensible shoes, and a white blouse that should have made her appear serious and practical but somehow didn't. Her light brown hair was pulled back from her face, but rebellious frizzy ringlets had come loose and hung about her temples. "We met the last time she came to the Run. It's good to see you again, Ms. MacGuire."

"You're looking well. How is your son?"

She made a face. "Sixteen and won't leave those Nintendo games alone." Then her face softened. "But my Ian's a good boy and doesn't give me any trouble." She turned to Eve. "I'll take her a tray with that stew I made for dinner. Don't worry. I'll make sure she doesn't starve herself. I remember the last time she was here, she didn't eat as well as she should." She started down the hall. "You have the same room you had before, Ms. MacGuire. I'll be up there with your dinner quick as the shake of a lamb's tail."

"It seems I'm having dinner," Jane said as she gazed after the housekeeper. "How quick *is* the shake of a lamb's tail?"

"Evidently pretty quick," Eve said. "I'd hurry with that shower if I were you."

The Laird's suite was three doors down from the room Jane had been assigned.

Jane hesitated as she went past it, then stopped and knocked on the door.

"Come."

Jane opened the door. "I just wanted to make sure that you were comfortable."

Lina looked up from her pad. "I'm not comfortable. This place is splendid, and splendid is cold. But I'll be fine. You don't have to worry about me."

"I'm not worrying." She looked around the room. The huge four-poster bed and other massive furniture dominated the room. "It's just that this room is a little overpowering. I could have Mrs. Dalbrey switch you."

"No, thank you." There was the slightest glimmer of humor in her expression. "That would disappoint Jock. I'm sure he's enjoying thinking of me here."

"His mother was housekeeper before Mrs. Dalbrey. He lived in the village, but he practically grew up here. He can't understand anyone not loving it."

"I know he can't." She looked back down at her pad. "But I think he tries. Now, please leave. I have to get back to work."

"How is it going?"

"Well," she said absently.

Lina had already closed her out, Jane realized.

"I'm three doors down, and Eve is in the tower room. If you need us, just call."

Lina nodded impatiently, not looking up.

Jane shook her head as she quietly left the room. Lina might be prickly as Eve said, but she was displaying signs of vulnerability. Lina had been married to a wealthy man, and she had experienced all the splendor connected with it. She had been a frightened child, and that splendor must have seemed like an ice palace. No wonder she wanted nothing to do with it.

Yet there had been that slight flash of humor when she had been talking about Jock.

Jane opened her door and looked around her high-ceilinged chamber. It looked the same as the last time she had stayed here. Ancient tapestries, large-scaled, comfortable furniture. Lina was wrong. Rich, yes, but there was nothing cold about this room or any other room at MacDuff's Run.

Cold was generated by the people who lived in a place. The MacDuffs who had lived and loved in this castle had never been cold. Lina would just have to learn that truth.

And Jane would have to stop fretting over Lina and take her shower before Mrs. Dalbrey got here with her meal. As she headed for the bathroom, she noticed the two boxes of books that Jock had mentioned against the far wall. She felt a surge of anticipation.

She had work to do.

Caleb knocked on Eve's door a little over an hour later.

Her brows lifted when she opened the door. "To what do I owe this pleasure, Caleb? I thought you were busy sparring with MacDuff over security arrangements."

"It didn't take that long. MacDuff isn't going to listen to anyone's opinion or suggestions about his castle and his people. I knew that the minute I met him. But I had to know what the setup was, and it was a way we could take each other's measure." He shrugged. "But his security appears to be top-notch. You don't have to be concerned. May I come in?"

She hesitated. "Why? I'm working."

"I want to talk to you. I thought it was a good opportunity. Jane is busy on the Internet and Lina is barricaded in that Laird's chamber, translating." He smiled. "And it doesn't surprise me that she doesn't appreciate castle life."

"It's really not my cup of tea either." Eve hesitated, then stepped aside and gestured for him to enter. "But MacDuff has been very gracious . . . in his way."

"You bring that quality out in most people," Caleb said as he came into the room. "Even I feel the stirrings when I'm with you. Amazing."

"Bullshit. You're a chameleon. You're what you want to be. And I don't mean that freakish gift of yours. You study the situation and adapt. Now sit down and tell me why you're here."

"Blunt and insightful." He grinned as he dropped into a chair. "I've missed you, Eve."

"You barely knew me. We were only together for the short time we were forced to work at finding that serial killer that we were both after. And it was Jane who drew you like a moth to a flame. It worried me." She stared directly into his eyes. "It still does."

"Do you want me to reassure you?" He thought about it. "No, I won't lie. You should be worried. If it's any comfort, I'm worried about it, too. I don't like the thought of destroying her, even hurting her."

"Go away, Caleb. You've done what you promised Jane you'd do. Now leave her alone."

"I can't," he said simply. "The moth to the flame. You're right, she draws me. I don't know why. Or maybe I do, and I don't want to admit it."

"Hurt her, and I'll kill you," she said quietly.

"I know."

"Why are you here, Caleb?"

"The dreams."

"What?"

"She has dreams, not the usual dreams. She dreamed about the man in the *Guilt* painting. I need to know everything there is to know about those dreams."

"Then go ask Jane."

"She won't talk to me about them." He smiled sardonically. "You'd think that she didn't have complete trust in me, wouldn't you? I don't see why. Do you suppose it's because she can see more than I want anyone to see? No, she's not going to tell me anything. She thinks I'm weird, and she doesn't want to be grouped under the same umbrella. She's fighting admitting that those dreams are a little on the fey side."

"Yes, she would. Jane has problems accepting anything that's not solid and completely no-nonsense."

"But you have no such problem," he said softly. "That's why I came to you."

"And why should I tell you something that Jane wouldn't?"

"Because I believe the dreams are the key. I can't help her until I can unlock the puzzle."

Eve was silent, gazing at him. "Jane is right, you *are* weird, and I'm not sure that I should give you any keys. You find out entirely too much on your own."

"But I haven't broken the code and gone in and made Jane tell me. That should count for something."

"Since I have an idea that your code is superflexible, I haven't got much faith in it."

"I didn't yield to temptation. I was tempted, Eve."

"And I should give you a reward?"

He smiled. "Please."

She shook her head. "You're a formidable man, Caleb."

"But you're going to help me. For Jane's sake."

"Is it for Jane's sake?"

"Yes," he said quietly. "That I can promise you. It's all for Jane, Eve."

She believed him. He was complex, convoluted, and the chameleon she had called him; but he was telling the truth about wanting to help Jane.

And Lord knows she wanted Jane to have all the help that she could get, no matter where it came from.

She turned away and looked out the window. "I don't know a lot about the dreams. You're talking about those special dreams. Right? Jane didn't confide much, and I didn't push her. Some of it I found out later, and some I'm sure she's never told me."

"When did they start?"

Eve had no trouble remembering when she'd first become aware of them. "She was seventeen. She began to have dreams that were different from the usual run that most of us experience."

"Like a story unfolding."

She glanced at him. "It seems she did tell you a little about them. I'm surprised."

"And suspicious. I did push a little, but I backed away. And I told her I'd done it."

"How admirable," she said ironically.

"I thought so. What were the dreams about?"

"Cira, an actress who lived in ancient Herculaneum. The dreams were so real that Jane started to investigate the possibility that Cira had actually existed. She thought that she might have run across something in a book or the Internet that could have triggered the dreams. She was a student, and that made the idea at least plausible."

"That sounds like Jane. Explore every possibility based in reality before even considering anything psychic."

"It's what I would have done. Jane and I are a lot alike."

"Yes, but there are differences that make

both of you fascinating. Was there a Cira?"

"Oh, yes. She was quite famous in her day. There were even statues sculpted of her." She paused. "And she looked remarkably like Jane."

"Really? That must have shaken her."

Eve smiled. "Not Jane. Or at least she wouldn't admit it. She says everyone has a double somewhere."

"But she was interested enough to search out everything she could find about this Cira?"

"She had no choice. She'd opened a can of worms when she started probing. Cira had possessed a chest of ancient gold coins that would have been worth millions, perhaps billions. When Jane started the search, it attracted the attention of a criminal, Thomas Reilly, who went on the attack. Jane had to dig in and find out everything she could just to survive."

"Billions?" Caleb repeated thoughtfully. "Millions I can understand for ancient gold coins. But not billions. Why?"

"There were certain rumors." She met his gaze. "That there were other coins in the chest. Coins brought by Cira's slave when he came from Jerusalem."

Caleb stiffened. "Jerusalem."

She nodded. "The Judas coins."

"Shit."

"It was my first thought when Jane told me what Roland was after. Strange co-incidence."

"Even stranger that Jane didn't make the connection."

"When the dreams stopped, she went into denial about those dreams of Cira. It's more comfortable for her that way. She prefers to block them out."

"The chest was never found?"

She shook her head. "Cira ran away from Herculaneum during the eruption of Vesuvius and traveled here to Scotland. She and her husband took on new identities and moved to the Highlands."

"What new identities?"

She smiled. "MacDuff."

He nodded. "Of course. It's rather annoying that everyone here at the Run must know about it but me. Sometimes being the outsider is an uphill struggle. But it's all coming together now. Except for that chest of coins. Are you sure that MacDuff hasn't found it?"

"I'm sure. It's driving him crazy that he can't convince Jane to help him search for it."

"Too bad." He was frowning. "The Judas coins. If they're in a chest somewhere in

Scotland, then Hadar's Tablet isn't going to help us much."

"Or maybe it will," Eve said. "I told you, it's only a rumor that the coins are in that chest."

"Connections. Jane dreams about a chest that may contain the Judas coins. Years later she starts to dream about the face of a man who could be Judas. Then she's hunted by members of a cult who worship Judas. It's all bound together."

"Perhaps. Perhaps not."

"I choose to believe that there's a connection." He rose to his feet. "It pleases my analytical soul."

"It won't please Jane's pragmatic approach on life."

"Then one of us will have to bend." He started for the door. "And I may have an advantage. Every time she closes her eyes, I may have an ally come out and whisper in her ear."

"Judas?"

"I don't know. Judas, the devil, an angel trying to set things right? It's a mystery." He glanced back at her as he opened the door. "Thank you for helping me. I know you have some serious doubts."

She nodded. "And I don't want you messing with Jane's mind or will. I only trust you so far."

"But I trust you to Hell and back. It's nice being able to feel like that about someone. Good-night, Eve."

She stood there as the door closed behind him. Those last words had been oddly touching and unexpected. Caleb was always surprising, but she was usually aware of mockery running beneath his words. There had been no mockery tonight.

Particularly when he spoke about Jane. He had been unsure, bewildered about his own emotions toward her, and that had made him seem more vulnerable. His willingness to admit that vulnerability to her had drawn her inexplicably closer to him.

Of course, that could have been pure sham.

But she didn't believe that was the case. Which made her shifting relationship with Caleb all the more disturbing. She was aware of the ephemeral beginnings of a tentative alliance.

And who in hell wanted to have a vampire for an ally?

It was close to nine that night when Jock knocked on Jane's door. "Coffee."

Jane pushed back away from the computer and rubbed her eyes before she got up and crossed the room to open the door.

Jock stood there with a tray. "Coffee and a sandwich. Mrs. Dalbrey said you didn't eat much of her stew. She's very disapproving. But even if you don't want to eat, I figured you'd still need the coffee."

"You didn't have to do this." She stood aside to let him into the room. "But coffee sounds good."

"I thought it would." He set the tray on the small table by the window. "You're sure you won't have the sandwich? I'm not going to let you get ill. That would cause me all kinds of trouble."

"I wouldn't want that." She sat down in the chair. "I'll have the coffee. I had enough of that stew to satisfy me. You eat the sandwich."

He shook his head. "I had a fine meal at dinner. Mrs. Dalbrey's stew was magnificent, wasn't it? Though MacDuff would have preferred I eat crow. He's still not pleased with me."

"Did he give you a hard time?"

"Moderate. He felt better after I let him interrogate me for a while. He always feels more in control once he knows all there is to know about everything. To be out of control is MacDuff's prime bugaboo."

"You told him everything?"

He shrugged. "Why not? We may need him soon." He paused. "You mean did I tell him what a strange bedfellow you have in Caleb?"

"Strange bedfellow." The common slang phrase applied to Caleb caused a ripple of shock to go through her. "Yes."

He nodded. "I decided it was time to break it to MacDuff gently before we ran into a situation where Caleb was slinging bodies down in front of him and making people scream with agony. It might come as a slight surprise."

"I was a bit surprised," she said dryly. "To put it mildly."

"But you haven't sent him on his way."

"No." She had tried, but somehow she hadn't been able to get him to go. Maybe she hadn't tried hard enough. Maybe she hadn't really wanted him to go. "No, I haven't done that yet. When MacDuff met him, he didn't give any indication that he thought Caleb was . . . unusual."

"I'm not sure if he really believed everything. He's probably taking everything I said with a grain of salt and making his own judgment."

"That sounds like him. He and Caleb were definitely searching for flaws and weaknesses."

"Well, MacDuff won't find that a lack of determination is one of Caleb's weaknesses." He looked at the pile of Bibles that were strewn on the bed. "I see you're going through all your holy books. Do you have enough?"

"More than I need." She took a sip of coffee. "You believe in overkill."

"Have they helped?"

"I haven't started to go through them yet. I've been too busy searching the Internet for information. It's mostly repetitive, but some sites have more than others do." She finished her sandwich. "But I'm almost ready to start on the Bibles."

"Do you need any help?"

She shook her head. "Not unless you're an expert and can fill in some of missing chinks in these passages."

"No, my mother always saw that I went to church, but I don't remember a lot of biblical details."

"Neither do I." She swallowed the last of her coffee. "Sorry to kick you out. But if you can't help, then all you can do is leave me alone so that I can get back to work."

"I was going anyway." He turned to the door. "I have to get a tray and take it to Lina. It seems my present duty is just to be a waiter."

"You do it very well. You're taking care of everyone."

He smiled as he opened the door. "Not Caleb. He can get his own tray. I have to draw the line somewhere."

"I'm glad you didn't draw it before you brought mine. That caffeine is making my brain start to function again."

He studied her face. "I don't think that your mind is too dull at the moment. You're excited."

She nodded. "I'm learning things. That's always exciting." She got to her feet and started toward the computer. "Thank you, Jock. I'm glad you're checking on Lina. Though she may kick you out."

"I'll risk it. I'll see you in the morning."

"Yes, good-night."

The door closed softly behind him, but she wouldn't have heard it anyway. She was already absorbed in the theories surrounding the man whose face had haunted her until she'd been forced to put it on canvas.

Thirty shekels of silver.

Judas hanging from the willow tree.

The field of blood . . .

FIFTEEN

It was after midnight, but there was no way she was going to be able to go to sleep, Jane realized. She was too wired. Too much coffee. Too much adrenaline.

And she didn't want to be alone. She wanted to talk, to discuss, pour out all she had learned and brainstorm. She started to reach for her phone to call Eve or Jock, then stopped. She should be considerate and let anyone who could sleep do so.

To hell with it. She quickly dialed a number.

"Trouble?" Caleb asked.

"No, I can't sleep, and I want to talk to someone, anyone."

"And I take it I've been chosen."

"I didn't want to wake Eve or Jock."

He chuckled. "And I don't matter."

"Yes or no?"

"Where? Your room or mine?"

Too intimate. "Neither. I'll meet you in

the courtyard in five minutes."

"I'll be there." He hung up.

She went to the bathroom, washed her face, and ran a comb through her hair. Then she was out the door and running down the grand staircase.

Caleb was standing by the fountain in the middle of the stone-paved courtyard. He was dressed in dark trousers and a white shirt open at the throat. The bright moonlight caught glints of the silver threading his temples.

She stopped short as she came out the front door.

He was waiting for her.

Of course, he's waiting for me, she thought impatiently. Why had the sight of him brought that sense of alarm?

Because she had the strange feeling that the waiting was not just for this night, this moment.

Nonsense. Her head was still swimming from hours spent on the computer.

"You can't change your mind," Caleb said. "You dragged me from my bed and didn't even flatter me that you did it because I'm special." He smiled. "In fact, I got the opposite impression just as you wanted." He sat down on the edge of the fountain and patted the stone rim beside him. "Now come and talk to me. After all, I did risk my life wandering around this courtyard in the dead of night. MacDuff's guards don't like midnight callers."

She hadn't thought about the security guards. She had only wanted to avoid the intimacy with Caleb that always disturbed her. "They challenged you?"

"It doesn't matter. I handled it."

She started across the courtyard. "I didn't mean to cause a problem. I just thought it would be best if —"

"I know why you wanted to meet me here. It's all right, Jane. I take what I can get."

"And most of the time you take more than is offered," she said tartly.

"Not from you." He suddenly chuckled. "Well, not usually. For instance, you see me patiently waiting for you to tell me what you learned from those dozens of Bibles Jock brought you."

Waiting. Again that word brought a frisson of uneasiness.

She instinctively lifted her shoulders as if to shrug it off. "Actually, I found out more from the Internet. April first is supposed to be Judas's birthday, hence the Offering." She sat down beside him on the fountain's rim. "And you'd be surprised how many scholars have been intrigued by Judas over the centuries."

"No, I wouldn't. The greatest betrayal of all time. Greed. The struggle of evil and good. It would fascinate most sinners and angels alike. For a scholar, it would prove irresistible."

"But most of them ended up with suppositions and theories. There's just not enough written about Judas. In Mark, Judas is an enigma. His entire purpose in Mark's writings is to hand over Jesus to the authorities. He has no character beyond the act itself and no clear motives."

"Thirty pieces of silver."

"That wasn't mentioned in the Gospel of Mark. It was all very vague. It's Matthew who talks about the money Judas received for the betrayal . . . and the field of blood."

"Field of blood?"

"After Judas returned the money he'd received from the priests, they decided they couldn't put it into the treasury. It was blood money. So they decided to buy a potter's field in which to bury strangers. They gave the silver to the owner of the field."

"Then that's the end of the story of the Judas coins. The chances of the pouch of coins still being kept intact is practically nil."

"It would seem that's true." She frowned. "But Roland must have known all this. And he's certain those coins weren't scattered to the four winds. Part of it is because of all the research he's done over the years, but it's mostly the rumors and stories handed down through the centuries in Hadar's cult." She nibbled at her lower lip. "Is he right?"

He was studying her expression. "You tell me."

She shook her head. "I don't know."

"Perhaps there was no field of blood. Maybe Matthew just wanted everyone to think that the priests had realized what a sin they had committed. After all, those disciples were only men, and memory fails. I understand that many times their stories didn't agree."

She nodded. "Luke wrote in his Gospel and the Book of Acts that it was Judas who bought the field with money he'd received as reward for his wickedness." She made a face. "And according to him, Judas didn't hang himself, he fell headlong in the field and his middle burst open and all his bowels gushed out. When the people of Jerusalem heard of it, they began to call the field *Akeldama* or Field of Blood."

"Very different."

"Yes, even the terms for the field aren't the same. Matthew referred to it as *agros* of blood because it was bought with the price of the blood of Jesus. In Acts it was referred to as *chorin* of blood because Judas supposedly committed suicide there. But they both talked about a field of blood. And a couple generations later, Papias wrote still another version. According to him, Judas died of a painful, shameful disease on his own property. The stench of him still lingers over the land to this day." She looked at him. "Another field."

"What are you saying?"

"I'm saying that no matter how the stories change, there's always a field of blood."

"But no other mention of the coins."

"They could still be there."

His brows rose skeptically.

"It's possible."

"If it even exists."

"The tour guides in Jerusalem say it exists. It's on their regular tour."

"What?"

"Or what they claim is the Field of Blood. It's a field south of the city. But there appears to be some doubt among the scholars that their potter's field is the actual place mentioned in Matthew."

"Since there's controversy about the

field's existence, that doesn't surprise me."

"And if it did happen, we don't actually know what happened to the coins after they were given to the owner of the field."

"I doubt if he'd treasure a traitor's ill-gotten gains."

"But we don't *know*. Unless Hadar's tablet can tell us something."

"Or Caiaphas," he said quietly. "There's always that possibility, isn't there?"

She stiffened. "What?"

"Who would know better than the high priest?"

"I told you that it was all guesswork. There wasn't any more mention in the testaments about Caiaphas's disbursement of the thirty shekels of silver."

"Not in the testaments. By the way, did you verify that Caiaphas was the high priest's name?"

She didn't speak for a moment. "Yes."

"And it didn't strike you as curious that you already knew his name?"

"I'm not a heathen. I could have run across it somewhere."

"Stop fighting, Jane. You know where you ran 'across' it. Eve said you went into denial after your experience with dreams of Cira years ago, but it's too dangerous to do that now."

"Eve?" Her eyes widened with shock. "Eve told you about those dreams? No, she wouldn't do that."

"Because you wouldn't tell me? It wasn't a breach of faith. She's ready to try anything to keep you safe, and she trusted me." He grimaced. "In this single instance. I didn't let it go to my head."

She was silent a moment. "I'm not in denial. I just have to believe that what appears extraordinary may be ordinary if we knew everything behind it. That's how I have to think. That's who I am."

"And I believe that what appears extraordinary may well be only the tip of the iceberg and entirely out of the realm of the ordinary." He smiled. "And that's how I have to think. That's who I am."

Yes, that's how Caleb would have to think since he dealt with the extraordinary and bizarre every minute of his life. "Then we'll have to disagree. I couldn't live like that."

His smile faded. "Yes, you could. I can teach you." He looked away. "But we won't go into that. You've got to accept the dreams and use them. It's a valuable weapon, and you shouldn't ignore it."

"Even if I did accept that there was some validity to what you're saying, it's not something I can control. It's smarter to rely on what's real and predictable."

"Think about it. You're a very strong woman. There's not much you can't control if you put your mind to it."

"I don't want to put my mind to anything but what I've learned about the Field of Blood. I want to do something about it."

"What? You said yourself that you'd read that the field in Jerusalem where they take all the tourists isn't necessarily the real place."

"That's what I read." She paused. "I want to go there. I want to see for myself."

His gaze narrowed on her face, but his tone was light. "Why not? But could we wait until Millet isn't on our heels trying to crucify you?"

"Maybe. But it might be a way to draw Roland if he thinks I know something he doesn't. He wants those Judas coins."

"True." He tilted his head. "Then by all means let's stake you out. What's a little risk? Millet *might* not cut off your head as he did Celine's sister."

"Don't be ridiculous. There has to be a way. I thought you'd be more reasonable."

"More reasonable than Eve or Jock? Yes, they might object to you going to the Field of Blood and trying to add a little of your own to the mix." He paused. "While I have an affinity for blood, don't I?"

His voice was without inflection yet she was aware of a tension and something else. Anger? "It's very reasonable that I'd expect you to be objective. You have less personal involvement."

"Not less personal, just different." He added, "You should understand that about me. You think everything about me is different, don't you?"

She gazed at him in helpless frustration. What was she supposed to say? Caleb wasn't like anyone else. She wasn't sure at any given moment what he was feeling. Yet in this moment she thought she was seeing a flash of vulnerability. Dammit, she didn't want to acknowledge that vulnerability. It was safer for her not to see anything in him that would make her respond emotionally. "Perhaps. At any rate, it seems you're not going to help me think of something that will bring an end to this any quicker." She started to get to her feet. "Good night, Caleb. Thank you for listening if not for —" She inhaled sharply as his hand closed on her wrist.

Heat. Tingling. Sexuality.

"Not yet," Caleb said. "Don't walk away from me."

Her chest was suddenly tight. She was

having trouble breathing. "Let me go, Caleb."

"In a minute." His thumb was slowly rubbing up and down along the sensitive inner flesh of her wrist. With every movement she felt a jolt of sheer primitive sensuality. "I want you to realize I'm not all that different. I have needs. I may even have a few other sentimental similarities to your other lovers."

She stiffened. "Lovers?"

"Did I forget to tell you that I did a little research on you when I left the lake cottage all those weeks ago? You're very discriminating. Your relationships are rare, and they have to involve something besides sex. You had one long-standing affair with a Mark Trevor, but you backed away before you committed. I was very happy that you did, but it didn't surprise me. You're afraid of commitment. I won't ask for a commitment. I won't ask anything from you that you don't want to give."

She stared at him in angry disbelief. "Why the hell would you pry into my business?"

"Because I knew that I wanted to be with you," he said simply. "I was just waiting for the right time. And then you called me."

Waiting.

She tried to pull away, but his grasp on

her wrist tightened. "Let me go, or I'll clobber you," she said between her teeth.

He chuckled. "Delicate and ladylike as usual. Just give me one more minute."

"Screw you."

"I only wanted to say that the reason I'm telling you is that I want to be honest with you." His lips twisted. "Which isn't precisely true. I was planning on making a move, but you managed to goad me into doing it too soon. You have an unusual way of upsetting my control." He released his grasp on her wrist. "Besides, I wanted to touch you. I've been wanting that for a long time."

The wrist that he had released was throbbing, the pulse pounding, the skin exquisitely sensitive. She was shaking. Lord, he had only touched her for a moment, and she felt as if she'd gone up in flames. She had a sudden thought. "Did you —"

He smiled. "No, it's just chemistry. I think we both knew it would be like this."

She started to turn away. "Just stay away from me."

"I can't," he said simply. "But I won't touch you again until you're ready for me."

"That's not good enough."

"It will have to be. I can't keep my distance when I know that Millet may be around the next corner. Think. You're going after Millet and Roland, and I'll be valuable to you." His voice was soft. "What difference does it make in the scheme of things if we want to go to bed with each other? We'll just ignore it until the time is right."

Ignore it? She was still feeling that deep throbbing sensuality, and just looking at him was causing her heart to pound, hard, harder. The sensation was more powerful than anything she had ever experienced, and it was frightening her. "It's not going to happen."

"No." He smiled. "Not until you're ready." He reached down and let the water in the fountain slowly trickle through his fingers. The movement was inexpressibly sensual. "You'd better go to bed now. You're tired. And you're going to want to start planning and moving as soon as Lina gets done with the translation." His dark eyes were glittering as he looked up from the water. "But I'm going to have to keep busy. I think I'll go back to London and pay a visit to Roland. I thought I'd ask you what you want me to accomplish with the visit so that I can prepare. Just a conversation or something more final?"

"You mean you want to know if I want you to kill him. No, I'm not turning you loose to go hunting."

"You don't have to shoulder the responsibility. Just tell me what you need from Roland."

How simplistic could you get? Of course, she would be responsible. "No, Caleb. Nothing has changed since we left him yesterday."

"Yes, something has changed. I need distraction. Roland thinks he's a hunter, but he only points the way. I could teach him what hunting is all about."

Yes, Caleb knew every nuance of that skill. But what he proposed was incredibly dangerous for him. "You said it would be difficult and take a long time. Forget it."

"But I can't forget it. I'm a primitive soul, and I have to satisfy that side of me in some way. But I'll put it off for a little while until you become used to the idea." He got to his feet. "I've arranged for the helicopter to be on standby a short distance from here. He can be at the helipad in twenty minutes." He passed her as he moved toward the front door of the castle. "I'll let you know what I decide."

She watched in helpless frustration as he disappeared into the castle. Dammit, he had told her to go to bed and get some sleep, but she didn't see how she was going to do it. If she'd been wired before she phoned

Caleb, she was doubly hyper now. Not only had she been caught up in an emotional upset when Caleb had mentioned talking to Eve about the dreams, but that upset had been followed by the sexual explosion that had rocked her to her core. Anger and resentment had been overshadowed by a physical response that had left her hot and weak and breathless. She was still experiencing the same sexual tornado even though he was no longer with her.

It was too strong. She had wanted to run as far as she could to get away from the bond that was tightening around her.

And he had known it and thrown her the one distraction that she couldn't ignore. He had realized that she had been worried about his trying to manipulate Roland and had decided to use it. She should ignore that threat. There was more than one way to manipulate, and he was clever and perceptive enough for any sort of deviousness.

Why was she standing here in the middle of the courtyard and trying to decipher his motives? As long as she wasn't deceived by anything he did, she didn't have to understand him. As long as she wasn't foolish enough to go to bed with him, that attraction might be strong but not overpowering.

He was right. He was a valuable commodity and might prove particularly valuable if she decided on going after the Judas coins. She would be stupid to send him away.

She started quickly for the front door. And, of course, she would sleep. She had told Caleb she could not control her dreams, but she had the will to block all the emotional upheaval and get some much-needed rest. She was beginning to feel the excitement stirring.

Steps. If she took the right steps, she'd be able to keep her head above water and survive.

The way to capture Millet was to use Roland to set the trap. To be sure of Roland, she had to get her hands on the Judas coins. To find the Judas coins, she had to locate the Field of Blood.

Field of Blood. She was suddenly shivering at the words. Foolish. It hadn't bothered her at all when she had been researching. Yet now it seemed to cast a shadow of malevolence and evil.

Field of Blood . . .

Someone was in the room.

Jane's eyes flew open, jarred wide-awake.

Caleb?

"I'm sorry." Lina was sitting in the tufted red velvet chair across the room. "I didn't mean to startle you. It's still early. I was going to wait until you woke."

It wasn't yet dawn, judging by the pale light streaming in the window, Jane noticed. She raised herself on her elbow. "Is anything wrong?"

Lina shook her head. "Something is right. I finished the translation on the tablet." She nodded at the papers on the table beside her. "I worked all night, and I didn't want to go to bed until I went over it with you."

Jane swung her legs to the floor. "Give me a few minutes to splash some water on my face, and I'll be right with you. I'm still drowsy."

"I thought you would be. You got to bed late yourself."

She glanced over her shoulder as she started for the bathroom. "How do you know?"

"I was taking a break and opened the shutters to get some air. You were down in the courtyard with Caleb."

Jane glanced over her shoulder. "You were watching us?"

"Don't be silly," Lina said. "Why would I waste my time? I just saw you before I closed the shutters again. I don't care if you have a hundred rendezvous with Caleb. It's your bad luck if you let him seduce you."

"He wasn't seducing me."

Lina smiled crookedly. "He was coming close. He never tried it with me, but I always knew that he was capable of spinning a web to get what he wants. My husband never bothered to try persuasion, he always demanded and coerced. But when it comes down to the end, it's all the same. Taking."

"There are some big differences." But Lina probably can't see them, Jane thought. Almost from childhood, she had been abused and sexually exploited. "You can tear the web and get out." She opened the bathroom door. "I'll be with you in a few minutes."

Lina nodded. "I'll pull up the text on the computer and get these papers in order."

Lina was still frowning down at the computer when Jane came out of the bathroom. "I think I have every nuance right. I had to call the language institute in Tel Aviv."

"In the middle of the night?"

"I've dealt with them before. We have a relationship." She gestured to the chair on the other side of the table. "Sit down. I'll pull up the translation on the computer."

Jane dropped down in the chair. "I fully intend to read all of it, but set it up for me. Is it what we need?"

Lina nodded. "I think it may be. No, I'm

almost sure that it's what you want, providing Hadar wasn't a liar. Why do you think that I was sitting here waiting for you to wake up?"

Because she was excited, Jane realized. Lina kept her emotions so well concealed that she hadn't realized it until this moment. "Tell me."

"First, it was written years after he reached Syria and had founded his religion glorifying Judas. It was a sort of a justification of all the atrocities he committed in the name of Judas. The first paragraph is just a sort of discourse on the injustices that had been inflicted on him as a boy and how Judas had come into his life and he had seen the light."

"Not Jesus, Judas?"

"He mentions Jesus only fleetingly; it was Judas who was the center of his life. He rants and raves about the priests and the disciples who didn't understand that Judas was only doing what God wanted in betraying Jesus. That Judas was only a divine tool to bring about the salvation of the world. That the condemnation that led to the suicide of Judas was an act against all the angels of heaven and should be revenged." She looked up at Jane. "And the suggested methods of that revenge are pretty bloodthirsty. Crucifixion figured prominently. Boiling in oil was another. I don't think there's much doubt that Hadar was psychotic. He might have had a genuine affection for Judas, but it became a destructive obsession after his death."

"He got all of that venom into one tablet?"

She nodded. "As you saw, the tablet was fourteen by ten, and the script was very tiny. I almost went blind trying to decipher it. And after those first paragraphs, it was all about why and how he fled Jerusalem."

"The coins," Jane prompted.

"He said that Judas tried to give them back to the high priest, but he was refused. The priest wouldn't pick them up from the floor of the temple. Hadar offered to go back and get the pouch for Judas, but he wouldn't let him. Judas ran away from the temple, and later Hadar heard that he had hanged himself. Hadar went crazy. He wanted to kill all the priests. He wanted to kill all the disciples. He was in a fury. He said that it was Judas who was the martyr and should be worshipped."

"And so a cult was born."

"At least the seeds were planted. But he got it into his head that the thirty pieces of silver were a symbol of that martyrdom. That Judas's returning the coins to the temple had some sort of divine significance. Hadar was enraged that the priests were going to spend the money buying a field to bury strangers instead of preserving it as a holy relic."

"So there was a Field of Blood?"

Lina nodded. "If you choose to believe Hadar. He was definitely unstable."

"Did the priests actually buy the field?"

"Yes, but it wasn't the field that they first intended to buy. It was some distance from the city. Hadar had evidently caused a huge scene in the temple, and the priests decided to keep a low profile among the citizens of Jerusalem. There was already too much uproar in the city about the crucifixion of Jesus. They decided to not let anyone know where the field was located."

"But Hadar found out?"

Lina nodded. "The second day after Caiaphas purchased the field from Ezra, a potter, to the far north of the city. Hadar went there that night after the money had been exchanged."

"And?"

Lina handed her the computer. "Read the translation for yourself. It will give you an idea what kind of man the founder of that cult really was. I pulled it up to the point where he's approaching the hut."

She already had an idea of Hadar's character, Jane thought. It wasn't pretty. She began to read the translation.

The night was dark. My master, Judas, must have interceded to make sure that no one would see me punish those greedy sinners. I stared in the window at Ezra, the potter, sitting at the table with his wife and two sons. They were laughing, joking, happy at their good fortune.

Blasphemers.

I knocked on the door and asked them to share their bread with a poor traveler. They gave me food and a blanket on the floor to rest for the night.

After they slept, I did my master's will and slew them all. I left Ezra alive until I'd forced him to give me the pouch of coins. There were only twenty-eight. He had given two to his slave, Dominic, when he'd freed him and sent him on his way earlier in the day.

Gave those precious coins to a slave as if they were nothing? I could not bear it. I struck him in the heart with my dagger over and over until the blood ran red on the dirt floor. Then I dragged him out into the field along with his accursed family. It took several hours, but I mounted them all on crosses I'd made from tearing down the fencing. Then I lit the crosses and watched the crucifixes burn through the night.

Burn Blasphemers. Glory unto Judas.

But I could not risk returning to Jerusalem. The soldiers would be after me as soon as the potter and his family were found. I had let my anger be known by the priests. I could not even risk taking the coins in case they were found on me if I was captured. I sealed the coins along with Ezra's copy of the writ of sale for that cursed Field of Blood in a fine alabaster bottle I had brought to hold the sacred coins. Then I fled north to leave all those hypocrites and liars behind me so that I could start a new life serving my holy master.

"He sealed the coins in a bottle?" Jane shook her head as she looked up from the laptop at Lina. "Then we're out of luck. Too fragile. The coins wouldn't stand a chance of surviving since that time." She frowned. "Or maybe they would. Some vases and dishes survived in the ruins of Pompeii and Herculaneum. I remember seeing them while I was on digs when I was in college."

"It depends on where he put the bottle." Lina was smiling faintly. "And I think that there is a chance. Later in the document he talks of planning to go back and retrieve his holy coins. He gives exact directions to where he placed the bottle."

Jane's eyes widened. "Exact?"

Lina nodded. "Yes. This field he's talking about isn't the one where they take tourists. It's too far north. And he buried the bottle deep in the clay in a cave on the south perimeter bordering the property. That was probably why it was forbidden for anyone to break the seal on his holy tablet. He didn't want anyone else to know how to find the Judas coins. He never got around to going back for the pouch himself, but he wasn't going to let any of his followers go after them and get all the glory."

"He mentioned a writ of sale. If it specifically refers to them as the coins given to Judas, that would document the coins." She grimaced. "But that would be expecting too much."

"Not necessarily. Documents during that period could be very explicit. If the priests had refused the return of the Judas money, I'd think they'd be even more certain to have the writ very clear about whose money was being used for this purchase. It would be a form of self-justification. We'll have to see." She got to her feet. "But right now I'm going to go to bed and get some sleep. I feel so tired, I'm numb. Read the rest of the translation, and we'll discuss it later."

"It shouldn't take me long." She was scrolling down the pages on the computer. "It's very clean. You've done a great job."

"I know. I always do." She was opening the door. "Which proves I'm not a sex toy who is only good for having babies. Imagine that. I will call you when I wake."

"Yes," she said absently as she scanned the text before her. "Sleep well."

She was barely aware of the door's closing as she continued reading. The contents of the tablet were ugly, disjointed, and definitely unbalanced. It gave the general rules of Hadar's Church of Judas, including the yearly sacrifices to be offered to honor him. He had set himself up as a high priest, and evidently the first sacrifices were people in the village who opposed or suspected him. Later, during Hadar's control of the religion, the sacrifices were chosen by Hadar and his acolytes for their worthiness to ascend to Judas.

She shivered as she remembered her dream of the young boy being sacrificed in the temple. Hadar was a terrible man who had spawned an even-more-terrible cult.

She quickly skimmed through the sacrifices to the section where Hadar was considering going back for the Judas coins. She felt excitement stirring. Exact directions, indeed . . .

Why was she getting excited? Hell, for all she knew that cave could have been bulldozed to the ground and become a major highway. Yet what if that cave was still there?

Her gaze lifted and she stared out at the pink and lavender clouds clustered in the sky outside the window signaling the coming dawn.

What if?

Opportunity. Far-fetched but not totally impossible.

And she'd never know unless she went to see for herself.

She reached for her phone and dialed Caleb. "That helicopter you told me you could have here in fifteen minutes? Call him and tell him to come."

Jock was standing in the foyer when Jane came down the stairs fifteen minutes later. "I know there's no use trying to talk you out of this. But this isn't going to be a walk in the park."

"No, hopefully it's going to be a walk in a

field." She smiled as she headed for the door. "I'm glad to see you. I told Caleb we needed you, but I wasn't sure he'd ask you to come with us."

"I may object to his methods, but not his intelligence. He said that he'd have no problem coming to an understanding with MacDuff's security guards, but he was concerned about interference on a higher level. To leave here, he knew that he would have to deal with me or MacDuff since this castle is an armed camp. He prefers the devil he knows." He shrugged as he opened the door for her. "And it only means that I'll have to do the dealing with MacDuff when we get back." He glanced at her. "But I'd rather deal with MacDuff than Eve. Did you tell her?"

"She knew I'd probably be leaving today. Not that we were going to Jerusalem."

"You're quibbling."

"Yes, I am. I'll tell her once we're under way." She moved past the fountain toward the courtyard gates. "Okay, so I'm a coward. I didn't want her trying to go with us. I didn't want to worry her until I had to do it."

"Because you knew this is a crazy idea."

"It's actually less dangerous going after the coins than it would be directly confronting Roland or Millet."

"As long as they don't manage to follow us." His gaze went to the hills. "They're out there. They'll know we're leaving."

"We change to a private jet in Edinburgh, and you call Venable and make sure that the pilot doesn't have to file a flight plan to Tel Aviv. Make certain the only person Venable tells anything about this trip is Joe. We won't even tell the pilot the destination until we're in the air."

"And once we're in Tel Aviv? The Israelis are tough customers, and they're not going to let us stroll around the area without keeping an eye on us. There are checkpoints and unbelievable security. And what about the Palestinians? They're likely to blow us up just on general principles. Even taking Millet and Roland out of the equation, it's still crazy."

"If we didn't have Caleb, it would be crazy. With Caleb, it's marginally possible."

"If he doesn't lose it and start a blood binge." He shook his head. "Even you don't trust him."

"I trust him . . . sometimes."

"That's not reassuring."

"He won't do anything to get us killed. He'll help us to the best of his ability to get Millet and Roland. That has to be enough for me right now." She could see Caleb standing at the helipad, and her pace quickened. "Come on. Let's get out of here before everyone in the castle wakes up. We've got to be on that helicopter and away within a few minutes. The noise is bound to wake the household." Her mind was working at top speed. "And I'll need to type those directions in Hadar's tablet into the Internet and Google it. I have to pull up a map of the area as it was during the time of Christ, then superimpose a current map on top of it. It was a clay potter's field, so the topography might be a help. No, that's only contour. I'll have to find something else. I want to see if I can bring up a match anywhere around Jerusalem."

"It's possible," Jock said thoughtfully. "The Internet satellites have amazing map capability."

"That's what I'm hoping. Once we've zeroed in on a site, we can get Venable to scope out the area and find a way to get us to that field. Tell him we want to be met in Tel Aviv and that I want a .38 Special revolver."

"To go treasure hunting?"

"No, I'm just tired of not having a weapon with these scumbags after us. I was beginning to envy Lina her AK-47. I'll also need a backpack, some kind of heavy protective wrapping, magnifying glass, a small sifter shovel, a brush, and tweezers. Maybe a spoon."

"A spoon?"

"That's what I used when I went on archaeological digs when I was in college. A spoon is gentle and controllable and less likely to do damage."

"All these preparations. It may all be for nothing, you know."

"And we may hit the jackpot. If we get our hands on those Judas coins, we'll have a lure that Roland won't be able to resist."

"That's all it means to you?" Jock asked curiously. "Those coins are a treasure that will be worth billions if there's any authentication at all."

"What would I do with billions? I don't need it. Would it make me a better artist? It would just get in the way. I could give it to Eve and Joe, but they get along just fine." She shook her head. "MacDuff is the only one interested in treasure or anything else that would preserve his precious castle."

He nodded. "MacDuff would definitely make use of any spare billions that he could beg, borrow, or steal."

"Then he can work on finding his family

treasure." Her lips tightened grimly. "I have a use for the Judas coins."

SIXTEEN

"She left MacDuff's Run by helicopter fifteen minutes ago," Millet said when Roland picked up the phone. "She was with Jock Gavin and Caleb."

"What direction? Edinburgh?"

"Yes. But they might change directions," Millet said. "She only took a small duffel. She may come back."

"And she may not. She's had time to have that tablet translated. She could be going after the coins. You've lost her again, dammit."

"What could I do? There were all kinds of security guards watching from the castle, and they know we're here in the hills. We might have been able to take her down, but I won't do that. I have to have her for the Offering."

"Then you'd better find a way to get hold of her damn quick. We're running out of time."

"Go screw yourself. I'll get her. I've called my man in Edinburgh and told him to get out to the airport and locate that helicopter and find out if they're changing to another flight. And I haven't been sitting here just twiddling my thumbs looking at that castle. There are still ways to pull her into the net. Eve Duncan is still there at the castle, and I think I know a way to get beyond those security guards all around her."

"Then wouldn't it be wise to stop thinking and start acting?" Millet hung up on him.

Bastard. Roland pressed the disconnect and stuffed his phone into his jacket pocket. He should have handled Millet better, but his anger had erupted, and he hadn't been able to control it. It would be easier trying to reason with an orangutan. And the primate would probably have been more intelligent in getting his hands on Jane MacGuire.

Forget him. He was expecting an important OPEC oilman to come to see him today, but he'd call and cancel. It was time he stopped relying on Millet and started to take all the reins in his own hands. This sudden move on Jane MacGuire's part was making him nervous. His every instinct was screaming that she was going after the coins.

His coins. All the years of searching, bribing, manipulating, and he might lose them to that bitch.

No! He would not let her have them. They belonged to him, and he would slice her to pieces himself if she tried to take them.

But first he had to find her. What are you up to, bitch?

Day Six

Jane called Eve after they landed in Edinburgh. Eve listened quietly, then said, "You could have awakened me. We both know why you didn't."

"Yes, I knew you'd be upset." She paused. "But it's not as if I'm going after Millet or Roland. This is much safer."

"Tell that to the Israelis and Palestinians," she said dryly. "That area is so volatile that it changes from minute to minute."

"I'll call you as often as I can." She was silent a moment. "I wanted you to be safe. That's the only thing that's important to me, Eve."

"If I didn't know that, I'd be much more pissed than I am right now." She added thoughtfully, "Twenty-eight pieces of silver instead of thirty. And the potter's slave's name was Dominic. Didn't you tell me that in your dreams of Cira years ago, her servant's name was Dominic?"

"Yes."

"Stop closing up on me. I can feel it even over this phone. All I'm saying is that it's odd that this servant, Dominic, appears in Hadar's Tablet as having received two of the Judas coins. And that a Dominic appears a little later in Herculaneum as Cira's servant. Those two Judas coins could well have been added to the treasure chest Cira brought with her when she fled Herculaneum. Interesting connection."

"Connection. You sound like Caleb. He's been probing and searching *ad nauseam*. Do you know he even thinks there's a possibility I do some kind of weird remote viewing and can actually mentally go to a place like that temple? Crazy."

"I can see how he'd be looking for the way the puzzle is fitting together."

"You told him about the Cira dreams."

"And you resent it. Tough. I've been tiptoeing around the subject for a long time. Those dreams are too closely founded on historical fact not to be accepted on some level. It's time you came to terms with them." She paused. "And I don't know what's happening, but I'm finding it curious that both the Cira dreams and the ones you've had recently have a bond with these

417

Judas coins. It's as if there's a kind of reaching out . . . Oh, I don't know. Just think about it. Don't reject it because you don't want to believe that you could be a little less than totally grounded in reality. What the hell is reality anyway?"

"You're real. Joe is real. I'm real. I'm working on accepting all this other eerie crap, but I have trouble when it applies to me."

"Keep working on it."

"I will. I promise." She changed the subject. "Will you take care of Lina? She's going to be as upset as you when she finds out we left her. I don't want her leaving the Run and setting off on her own toting that AK-47. By now Millet and Roland know she's been doing the translation for us. They mustn't get their hands on her."

"I'll see what I can do. But she seems to be very determined." She added ruefully, "If I stand in her way, she may turn that AK-47 on me."

"She won't do that." Jane hesitated. "She's . . . solid, Eve. She's abrupt and sometimes rude, but I feel as if she's —" She tried to put her thoughts into words. "She's a survivor, but she doesn't know how to enjoy that survival. She hardly ever smiles. I want to —"

"Help her," Eve finished. "Another lost puppy, Jane?"

"Tiger, maybe."

"Good comparison. Tigers are beautiful, and Lina is exceptional." She added, "I like survivors. I feel a kinship for them. I'll see that your Lina doesn't run afoul of Millet."

"Thank you. I have to board the plane now. I'll call you from Israel." She hung up.

Eve slowly turned away as she pressed the disconnect. Jane had better call me from Israel, she thought grimly. She was getting tired of staying behind and watching Joe and now Jane go off into heaven knew what danger. She wasn't going to put up with it for much longer.

"They've gone." Lina stood in the doorway, her hands clenched at her sides. "Jock just called me. I told Jane what she needed, then she left me."

"We seem to be in the same boat," Eve said. "I just spoke to Jane, and she was all apologies, but it all came down to the fact that I wasn't wanted."

"She had no *right.* They burned my home. I had the right to go after them."

"She was very clear that wasn't the purpose of the trip."

"Purpose? It doesn't matter. One thing will lead to another. Millet and Roland will

419

go after them."

That was what Eve feared. "Then we have to hope we'll be able to join her before it's over."

" 'Hope'?" Lina's eyes were blazing. "I'm not going to wait here and hope. I'm going to go after those bastards. I don't need anyone to help me."

This was just what Jane was afraid would happen, Eve thought. And she had left Eve with the task of dissuading this angry woman from doing what she thought was her right.

And it was her right. She was protecting her way of life and avenging the loss of her home. Eve was in perfect agreement with her. She would have felt the same.

"Jane was mistaken. She took it upon herself to try to protect both of us." She stared Lina in the eye. "That's Jane's way. She can't help herself, but it was wrong of her arbitrarily to try to run your life." She shook her head. "And mine. But we'll have to reclaim them. Together."

"You have nothing to do with my life." Lina was gazing at her warily. "And you mean nothing to me."

"But you came here with Jane and the others because you could see that you'd be more effective if you had a backup. Isn't that true?"

"Partly."

"I'm a very good backup, Lina. Suppose we team up and see what we can do about getting Millet?"

"I don't need you. You'd get in my way."

She shook her head. "You've heard Jane talk about Joe Quinn. He's with the CIA in Rome right now. We could join him there."

"The CIA," Lina repeated. "I knew someone once who worked with them. He got me out of Afghanistan. They can help . . . if they want to do it."

"Joe will make sure that they want to do it."

"When would we go?"

"As soon as I contact Joe and make arrangements. Perhaps tomorrow morning?"

Lina thought about it. "I guess I can wait until then." Her gaze narrowed on Eve's face. "You're not fooling me? You're being honest?"

"I'm being honest. I admit I'm like Jane in that I tend to be overprotective, and I understand her reasons. But it's time I stopped letting her run the show." She was feeling an overpowering relief at the decision. It had been completely uncharacteristic of her to have been so patient when she had only wanted to dive in and help Jane.

"Yes, I think going to Joe would definitely be for the best." She smiled. "You help me. I'll help you. And Joe will help both of us. We can't lose." She got to her feet. "Now let me go and call Joe. It will take a little persuading to make him see we should leave here. Joe is very protective, too."

"But it will happen?" Lina asked. "Men like to have it all their own way."

"So do we. It's all a balance, Lina." But that had never been Lina's experience, Eve realized. "Joe is very special. It will be fine."

"If you say so." Lina turned away. "But I trust you to tell me if you have a problem with him."

She chuckled. "I always have problems with him. But I wouldn't have it any other way. That's what makes our life together a challenge."

Lina shook her head. "I don't understand."

"I hope you will someday. Now go away, and I'll make the arrangements. Then I have to do some work on my reconstruction and go and talk to MacDuff about our plans. He'll probably be as dead set against them as Jane would be. Too bad. Will you join me for dinner later?"

Lina hesitated, then slowly nodded. "Yes. I think I'd like that very much."

"Good." She pulled out her phone. "It will probably be just the two of us. MacDuff isn't going to be in a sociable mood. He likes control and he's lost Jane and is about to lose both of us. There's not much left to protect but this grand pile of boulders he calls a castle."

"How did she take it?" Caleb asked, as Jane got on the plane. "Or need I ask?"

"She resented my leaving her behind." Jane sat down and opened her laptop. "I don't blame her. I'd feel the same way. She did say she'd take care of Lina." Her voice was absent as she gazed down at the screen. "I think I've found the map I need. Oxford University did a study in 1997 for the Church of England. They did all kinds of topography and historical data searches to create a map that would show Israel and Syria as they were at the time of Christ." She pointed to two areas north of Jerusalem. "Both these areas have low hills, and the one closer to Jerusalem looks like it might possibly have a flatter sunken field adjoining it. The fields from which potters took their clay were basically rock and silt with high iron content that were windblown or brought in and deposited by rivers or glaciers. I don't see any riverbed, but it could still be Hadar's Field of Blood."

"It's pretty flimsy."

"Do you think I don't know that?" She pointed to a wall that enclosed the south-west side of Jerusalem. "But look at this." She did an overlay of ancient Jerusalem with a modern-day map. "This is a thematic soil content map of the area that Oxford did at the same time. Do you see that heavy clay content in the valley of Hamman? That's the supposed Field of Blood, where the tour guides take the tourists. The clay content looks the same in that area north of the city."

"Does the Oxford study mention any historical information about another potter's field being north of Jerusalem?"

She shook her head. "But that doesn't mean it didn't exist. For Pete's sake, it was almost two thousand years ago." She gazed down at the map. "We have a chance. Soil content doesn't change that much unless there's some gigantic natural event like an ice age. Will you call Oxford Mideast Studies and see if you can find out if that clay content could have been heavy enough to be a potter's field?" She was flipping through other maps and superimposing them. "I'd do it, but I need to get as much information as I can about the area before we get airborne and I lose the Net."

"I'll see what I can do." He turned away and pulled out his phone.

It *could* be the field.

Excitement was slowly taking hold as she gazed down at the map. Keep it under control. It's a long shot, she said to herself.

Long shots weren't based on scientific maps and university studies.

She was lying to herself. She wanted it too much.

The plane was taxiing down the runway.

One more map . . .

"Bingo," Caleb said as he hung up the phone. "That area definitely had the potential for heavy clay content in biblical times. And they did a current day scan two years ago, and the potential still exists. Very high iron content." He smiled. "Which means we still have a chance that your potter's field isn't under a freeway."

"No." She was looking down at the map she'd just superimposed on the ancient map. It wasn't a thematic but a political map. Her forefinger touched the field. Did she feel the slightest tingle? Imagination. "I think it's farmland. In Palestinian territory."

Tel Aviv, Israel

"I do believe we're being welcomed," Jock murmured as he gazed out of the window of the jet as it taxied toward the private hangars at the far end of the runway.

A sleek black car was parked at the hangar, and a slender, dark-skinned man in a navy blue suit was getting out of the car.

"Looks like CIA issue to me," Caleb said. He got to his feet as the jet came to a halt. "But let me go ahead and make sure. Stay in the plane until I tell you to come."

Jane nodded as she unbuckled her seat belt. She was stiff from sitting for so many hours but eager to get out and get going.

The man to whom Caleb was talking did not look like a threat. He reminded her of some kind of diplomatic bureaucrat.

"Let's go," Jock said, as Caleb turned and waved to them.

"Jane, Gavin, this is Bill Gillem," Caleb said, as they approached. "Venable asked him to take us to the general location where you think the field is located."

Gillem shrugged. " 'General' is right. I think you're barking up the wrong tree. It's only a barren piece of land surrounded by farmland."

"Barren?" Jane asked. "Because there's too much clay in the soil?"

"Maybe. But it hasn't been used to extract clay since the 1930s. There was some bullshit rumor about the place being cursed.

The Palestinians tried to reclaim it and use it as farmland, but it didn't work out."

"Surrounded by farmland," Jock repeated. "No hills or plateaus where there could be a cave? It showed something on the topographical map on the Net."

"Not much. Maybe a few shallow hills on the edge of the field. You'll have to check that out for yourself." He opened the back door of the car. "If you want to go, let's get on the road. I've called in all kinds of favors with the guards at the checkpoints, but it's a whole new ball game after the shifts change. We've got three hours to get in and get out."

"Then go back and get us more time. Bribe them."

"What are you talking about? This is Israel. These people have seen their friends blown up by suicide bombers. They wouldn't risk taking a bribe. If they didn't trust me, you'd be shit out of luck." He shook his head. "And I'm not ruining contacts I've spent ten years in this country building because you want to take your time. It's going to be rough enough to have you tramping over that field without getting shot. There are rumors that several farmhouses near the field are being used by drug dealers who furnish money to the PLO."

"What if that three hours isn't enough?" Jane got into the car, followed by Caleb. Jock got into the passenger seat. "What do we do then?"

"You're on your own. Venable only gave me orders to get you in and out in a timely manner. Three hours is plenty of time considering that there's nothing much to see." He got into the driver's seat. "I brought that .38 Special and some additional fire-power, your backpack, and that equipment you requested. They're all in the trunk. I don't know what you're searching for, but I think you're going to come up with zilch."

"Very negative," Caleb murmured to Jane as Gillem started the car and drove away from the hangar. "Do you want me to adjust his attitude?"

"No. It sounds as if this trip is damn risky. He has a right to his feelings."

"As long as they don't get in the way." His glance shifted out the window to the lights of Tel Aviv. "I'll check back when we reach the field."

Or he'll use his own judgment and do as he pleases, Jane thought.

He glanced at her and smiled. "Probably," he said as if reading her thoughts. "But I did want to involve you in the decision."

"As long as I don't get in the way," she

paraphrased his own words.

"Sometimes there isn't time to consult and discuss."

"There may not be any urgency connected to this trip at all. Maybe Gillem is right, and this is a wild-goose chase."

"It could be. But it's worth a shot. Don't let him bring you down."

"He's not. I'm just trying not to get my hopes up." But that wasn't going to happen. She was charged with excitement. That breathless moment on the plane when she'd seen that tiny square superimposed on the computer map was still with her. She wanted to be there, see for herself. "It's hard to be cool and analytical when I want to move, to fly."

"Cool, you're not," he said. "I've never seen you anything but intense and charged with emotion even when you're trying to hide it. And I like the idea of your flying." He added softly, "So screw anyone who wants to keep you grounded."

She felt warmth surge through her. She had to tear her gaze away from his. She said lightly, "That's what I say. Screw them."

MacDuff's Run
"Will there be anything else?" Mrs. Dalbrey asked as she set the tray down on the table

in Eve's room. "It's soup and sandwiches as you asked. I made lemon pudding for a sweet. Would you like me to take off the covers and set the table?"

"No, Ms. Alsouk will be here any moment." Eve closed her suitcase and fastened it. "I'll do it then. Thank you, Mrs. Dalbrey."

"You're very welcome." The housekeeper hesitated. "I'll be back to pick up the tray when you call me. If that will suit you."

Eve smiled. "That will be fine."

Mrs. Dalbrey still stood at the door. "I understand you're leaving us. I want to say that I've enjoyed serving you, Ms. Duncan." She paused. "I hope all goes well with you. Oh, I do hope that." She turned, and her voice was muffled as she went out the door. "Good luck and God bless."

"Thank you. You've been very —" But the housekeeper was gone.

Eve frowned, puzzled. The woman had always been pleasant, but they hadn't done more than exchange a few words in the time she'd been here. Yet those last words had been tinged with emotion. It struck her as odd that —

A knock on the door.

MacDuff stood there when she opened it. "I wish you to stay," he said curtly. "Change your mind. Nothing has changed because Jane has taken it into her head to go on this wild-goose chase. You're still in just as much danger. Maybe more. Millet's men are still moving about the hills above the castle waiting to pounce. Leave here, and you give them their chance at you."

She shook her head. "I can't hide away here forever while Jane goes trekking about the world. I have to be out and doing something. Joe and I have taken care of ourselves for a long time. We'll be all right, MacDuff."

"You're making a mistake."

"Perhaps. I've made them before." She smiled. "And so have you. It's what makes us what we are. Thank you for mounting guard and keeping me safe, MacDuff. I know it was for Jane's sake, but it was kind nevertheless."

He didn't speak for a moment. "It wasn't entirely for Jane's sake. I have a liking for you, Eve Duncan." He started to turn away. "Enjoy your dinner. I'll see you in the morning before you leave. I'm going to the hills to check with my men there to make sure Millet's men aren't moving closer. There have been some signs that may be happening. It wouldn't do to have your helicopter blown out of the sky, would it?"

"What a pleasant thought."

"I'm not feeling pleasant. I'm frustrated and angry and dour." He strode down the hall. "I'll take you to your helicopter tomorrow and see you safely off my land."

So much the Laird. In this moment, she could clearly see in him the Robber Barons who had been his ancestors.

And she had a liking for MacDuff, too.

"He's angry," Lina said as she came down the hall from her own room. Her gaze was on MacDuff's straight back and the barely contained tension of his carriage as he started down the staircase. "What did you do to him?"

"I said no." She stepped aside to let Lina enter. "He doesn't like the word." She gestured to the table. "Mrs. Dalbrey already brought our meal. She wished us good luck."

"That was kind." She looked at Eve. "You made the arrangements?"

Eve nodded. "Joe is coming himself. He'll be arranging for the helicopter and will be on the helipad at eight tomorrow morning."

"He didn't argue?"

"Yes, I told you that Joe is never easy. But I think you'll like him." She moved toward the table. "Now help me set out our meal, then we'll talk. I'll tell you about my work and Joe, and you can tell me whatever you feel safe sharing with me."

"Safe?"

She removed the silver covers from the dishes. "I imagine you're not accustomed to feeling safe in confiding many experiences. I'm the same way. Perhaps we can work our way through to some kind of understanding."

Lina stared at her for a moment, then moved across the room to help her set out the plates. She said quietly, "Perhaps we can."

"It's over there beyond that farmhouse," Gillem said as he parked the car beneath a tree. "I'll wait for you here." He checked his watch. "You have less than two hours now. I won't be here if you come back later."

Caleb glanced at Jane as he got out and held the door open for her. "Attitude adjustment?"

"No." She was barely aware of what he had said. Her gaze was fixed on the farmhouse, and she began moving toward it. Her excitement was growing by the moment, and she could feel her heart start to pound. It was *there*. She knew it was there.

Beyond that house she'd be able to see the field.

"Suppose I scout around a little." Jock had caught up with her, and his gaze was raking the farmhouse. "This place doesn't seem to have had very good upkeep. Gillem mentioned terrorist activity and possible drug dealers. I think it would be a good idea to see if he's right."

Jane nodded. "Do what you like." Her pace quickened. "I'm going to find that field."

"I'll go with her," Caleb said. "Catch up with us, Gavin."

"Right." Jock faded away toward the rear of the farmhouse.

Jane moved down the dirt road bordering the farmyard. The moon was behind a cloud, and she could barely see her hand in front of her face. Damn, she hoped she didn't run into anything.

Oh good, the clouds were starting to drift away, and there was bright moonlight. Just in time she skirted a rake in the middle of the path. She had seen a few tools scattered in the farmyard before she had started down this path. Again, not a good sign. Good farmers took care of their equipment. Perhaps Jock was right to check up on —

She stopped, her gaze going to the earth that stretched before her. "Good Lord."

Caleb gave a low whistle. "Yes, I could see

this land being cursed."

The field was large, perhaps eight or ten acres and stretched out flat and puckered like the bottom of a riverbed. In places it appeared scored by some kind of sharp tool that had formed wavy, snakelike indentations that seemed to writhe as the light changed. Even in the dim illumination cast by the moonlight, she could see the dark earth that must have been rusty-red. Surrounded by the lush crop planting of the farmlands, the solitary field appeared stark and barren, yet teeming with eerie life.

She could almost see Hadar standing beside her watching those four crucifixes burning in the darkness.

She shuddered.

"Those rolling hills bordering the field to the south are our only hope for a cave," Caleb said. "Let's get moving."

"Right." She braced herself and started toward the field.

The red earth was quicksand soft, squishy, yielding beneath her feet, and she tried to ignore the feeling that any moment it would pull her down and suffocate her. She found she was even trying to avoid stepping on the scored snakelike indentations.

Ridiculous. Imagination.

Yet there was no question that her pace

435

was quickening as she was halfway across the field.

"I don't see any openings in the face of the hill," Caleb said.

"Even if the cave was once there, it might have collapsed over the centuries." Her gaze was raking the hill. "Or it might be completely covered by shrubbery. According to Hadar's directions, the cave entrance was several yards away from the field, but the earth in the cave was also clay. He dug down and buried the sealed bottle deep in the ground."

"We can only hope the clay remained moist and didn't crack the bottle. You go to the left, I'll take the right. Don't use the flashlight unless you need to do it. I'm not sure that —"

"Good advice," Jock said from behind them. "There are two guards outside that farmhouse, and I don't think they like strangers."

"PLO?" Caleb asked.

"No, I'd bet on drug traffickers. They probably have pot stashed all over this property and make periodic rounds. If we're going to search, let's do it and get the hell out. I'll take the area straight ahead." He strode past them up the hill.

Jane moved swiftly toward the left.

An hour later, they were still searching.

"We have a choice," Caleb said as he joined her. "Either you let me go back and persuade Gillem that it's the sensible thing for him to wait for us, or we give it up and come back tomorrow night."

"We still have time." She pushed her hair back from her face. She was hot and tired and had a painful scratch on her arm from pushing through the thorny bushes. "Keep looking."

He shook his head. "Stubborn." He turned and disappeared into the shrubs.

It wasn't only stubbornness. It was *here*, dammit. She was feeling a desperation that wouldn't go away. She couldn't wait for tomorrow night. It would be too late.

Crazy. Too late when those coins had been lost for two thousand years? One more day would make a difference?

Yes.

Okay, then go with it. Unreasonable and completely insane though that instinct might be she couldn't ignore it.

She had searched this area thoroughly. She'd have to go farther up the —

"I've found something."

Jock!

She whirled and ran toward the slope where Jock had been searching, her feet slipping on the uneven dirt. He was on his hands and knees, tearing at rocks and shrubs.

"What is it?"

"An opening of some kind behind these bushes. Not very big . . . Give me a hand."

"I'll do it." Caleb was beside him, pulling at a huge rock. "You're right. This entrance isn't over four feet. I don't know. This may not even be —" The rock came away, revealing a dark cavity, "Or then again it might."

Yes.

Jane dropped to her knees and started to crawl toward it.

"No." Jock's hand was on her shoulder. "We don't know how unstable the ground is here. The entire hill could collapse on you. Or it could be infested with snakes. It seems an ideal habitat for them. You can't go in there without turning on your flashlight. And we can't be sure that those guards back at the farmhouse won't see it."

She knew everything that he'd said was true. It didn't matter. "I have to go in." She was wriggling forward on her hands and knees. "Do whatever you have to do."

"Then let me go in first," Jock said.

"No." She was already crawling through the opening. "My job."

Caleb muttered a curse, turned on his

flashlight, and pressed it into her hand. "Stop and look around, dammit."

She lifted the flashlight and cast the beam around the cave. Small, so small. The interior was no more than five feet high by eight feet in length and jutted up a rocky wall. The ceiling of the cave wasn't stone but earth.

"Snakes?" Jock called.

"No snakes." But Jock's other concern about the cave's collapsing was definitely valid. It was a wonder that the dirt ceiling hadn't fallen in over the years. "The ground in here has high clay content, so that part of Hadar's writings could be correct."

"Move to the side," Caleb said. "I'm coming in."

"No, there's barely enough room for me, and I have to maneuver around in here and see if I can find the place where Hadar buried the bottle." Her gaze shifted around the small area. "He said it was close to a stone wall. This is basically a dirt cave. The only stone wall I can see is the one at the far end of the cave." She was wriggling toward it. "Let's hope that he didn't bury that bottle too deep. You'd think that Hadar would want to get rid of the coins and be on his way fast."

"Hadar had just crucified and burned four

people. And he stayed there to watch them burn," Jock said. "That doesn't indicate a man who was in any great hurry." He added, "But could you hurry a little? I'm trying to block the glimmers of light coming out of the cave from your flashlight, but all it would take is one glance from the guards at the wrong time."

"I am hurrying." She had her small pick out of the backpack and was gently digging into the clay. "I don't want to break the bottle."

"What difference does it make? Why worry about the bottle. It's the coins that matter."

"If there's any documentation with the coins, I don't want to destroy it. Just exposing it to air could cause serious damage." She adjusted the flashlight and went back to carefully scratching in the dirt. "The ground is moist, at least on the area nearest the surface. It's a good thing that the bottle was alabaster and not clay." But the ceiling of the cave was dry, and her movements had caused dirt particles to begin falling.

Not good. Best not to mention that to Jock.

He couldn't just stand here, dammit.

Caleb glanced back at the farmhouse. No lights yet, but that didn't meant they might not pop on at any minute.

"Go on," Jock said quietly.

Caleb's gaze flew to Jock's face.

"We're sitting ducks out here," Jock said. "Time to alter the situation. Go do it. I'll stay here and stand guard over her."

Jock didn't have to tell Caleb twice. He whirled and started down the hill. "Take care of her."

And he'd take care of clearing the path. First, get back to the car and make sure that Gillem didn't take it into his head to leave no matter how hot the situation became.

Then locate the two guards Jock had mentioned and remove them from the equation.

He could feel his blood start to pump hot and heady as he ran across the field. He felt strong enough to take on the whole damn world.

Alter the situation, Jock had said.

Consider it done.

The air was suffocatingly hot in the cave, and Jane could feel the sweat beading her nape.

Ignore it.

Go slowly, carefully.

She was going slowly, dammit. It had been over fifteen minutes since she had started digging, and she had gotten only a foot or so down into the earth.

Be patient.

Go slowly.

Go slowly, Caleb told himself.

The guard was leaning against the tree, a cigarette hanging from his lips and gazing moodily at the farmhouse a few yards away.

Evidently he doesn't like sentry duty, Caleb thought, as he moved silently behind him. It was clearly his duty to save the bastard from his boredom. He'd already liberated the first sentry a few minutes ago at the back of the house.

Now he had only to make sure that this morose fellow was sent to the happy hunting grounds.

No problem.

Seventeen

A gleam of metal.

Jane inhaled sharply, her gaze fixed on the small, corroded bronze object she'd uncovered.

A stopper?

She carefully cleared more earth away from the object.

Yes, a stopper.

She cleared away more earth.

A bronze stopper sealing a bottle.

She sat back on her heels and drew a deep breath.

"Hadar, you bastard. I think I've found it," she whispered. "Now to get it out of the ground and we'll see what we —"

"Jane, get out of there," Jock's voice was sharp. "Lights in that farmhouse."

Shit.

"I can't go yet." She was digging frantically around the bottle. "A few more minutes."

"You don't have a few minutes." Jock was cursing. "Caleb must have blown it."

"What the hell are you talking about?" She was digging the earth away from around the bottom of the bottle. "Never mind. I don't give a damn. Just keep them off me for one more minute. I'm almost there."

"Two men are running out of the farmhouse. Get out of that gopher hole, and let's get away from here."

Careful . . .

She cautiously, slowly pulled the smooth, opaque bottle from the earth. It was over eighteen inches high; the width varied from seven inches at the bottom to about four inches at the top, and it was sealed by a bronze stopper. And it's heavier than I expected, she thought as she lifted it.

"Jane."

"I'm coming." She carefully wrapped the bottle in several rolls of protective plastic and put it in her backpack. She started wriggling through the cave toward the entrance. "I found it, Jock."

"Great." He reached down as her upper body emerged from the cave, grabbed her hand, and pulled her to her feet. He took her flashlight and dropped it fully lit to the ground in front of the cave. "We'll leave it here to light their way. Now let's *move,* Jane."

She could see the lights of several flash-lights bobbing across farmyard toward the Field of Blood as Jock half pulled, half dragged her down the hill.

"Where's Caleb?"

"I don't know. I don't care." He dragged her behind a hillock and pushed her to the ground. "We'll wait until they get to the cave, then start across the field."

Four running men were only yards from the hills now.

Dammit, where's Caleb? What happened to him?

Guns. The men were carrying guns.

They were almost upon them.

Then they were climbing past them up the hill toward the cave, where Jock had dropped her flashlight.

"Just a little longer," Jock whispered. "Get ready."

Her muscles tensed.

"Now!"

She leaped to her feet and streaked after him down the few yards to the field.

She heard a shout from up the hill.

The clay sank deep beneath her feet as she ran.

Another shout.

She glanced over her shoulder. The four

445

men were bolting full speed down the hill.

She stumbled, caught her balance, and kept running.

"Okay?" Jock asked.

"Yes, but where's Caleb? We shouldn't leave him."

"He may have left us. Keep running."

She wasn't about to slow down. Their pursuers had reached the field and were gaining on them.

A bullet whistled by her ear.

Shit. They're firing on us, she thought.

"Zag to the left!"

Caleb's voice. Caleb himself in the stable yard, kneeling on one knee, leveling a rifle.

"Left!" Jock said. "He needs a clear shot."

She zagged left.

Another shot. But this one was from Caleb's rifle.

A scream from behind her, and she looked back. The leader of the pack had fallen to the ground, and the other three men were splitting to either side. They were hesitating, their attention fixed on Caleb.

The next moment, Jane and Jock reached the farmyard.

"Get to the car." Caleb was sighting again. "One more down should distract them enough to hold them."

She slowed, hesitating.

"Come on," Jock grabbed her arm. "He'll take care of it. He doesn't need us. You'll get in his way."

Caleb pressed the trigger, and another man fell to the red clay.

Field of Blood.

And no one knew more about blood than Caleb.

No, he didn't need her.

She ran with Jock toward the car.

Gillem was standing beside the car. "Get in. What were those shots? I was supposed to get you in and out with no trouble. I don't like this."

"Neither do we," Jock said. "So get in that driver's seat and get us out of here."

"Wait," Jane said. "Caleb."

"I wasn't going to leave him." He was watching out the window. "Here he comes."

"Go!" Caleb dove into the passenger seat. "We have maybe two minutes before they reach the cars parked in the driveway."

Gillem pressed the accelerator, and the car jumped forward. "I don't like this," he repeated.

"But you'll do what you're supposed to do, what we want you to do," Caleb said. "Won't you, Gillem? Whatever it takes."

Gillem muttered a curse as he raced away

from the farmhouse. "I'll do whatever it takes."

"Attitude adjustment," Jane murmured.

Caleb met her eyes in the rearview mirror. "I had to keep busy. You had both Jock and me twiddling our thumbs. Did you find it?"

"I found a bottle. I think it may be alabaster. I'll have to see if there's anything in it. I didn't want to risk opening it."

"You blew it, Caleb," Jock said. "You were supposed to keep those two guards from giving an alarm."

"I took care of the guards. Someone from the house must have spotted the light." He glanced back over his shoulder and stiffened. "I see headlights. Lose them, Gillem."

Gillem stomped on the accelerator, and the tires screeched as he tore down the road.

MacDuff's Run

Lord, she was sick.

Eve barely made it to the bathroom before she threw up.

And again. And again.

She sank to her knees on the floor beside the toilet.

Nausea and pain.

Flu?

Food poisoning?

But she had felt fine earlier in the evening.

She threw up again.

But she didn't feel fine now.

Her cell phone was ringing. She didn't want to move.

She had to move. She had to get help. She crawled to the bedside table. "Hello."

"I'm sick," Lina said. "I keep throwing up."

"Me, too," Eve said. Lord, she was dizzy. "Food poisoning?"

"I don't know. I feel like the time the midwives gave me some powerful herbs to make me fertile, and they only made me sick."

"I'm calling MacDuff to get a doctor."

"I'm coming to your room. I don't want to be alone." She was retching. "Dammit. If I can stop throwing up."

Eve had to wait a moment before she was able to dial MacDuff's number.

"Sick. Both Lina and me. Throwing up. Maybe food poisoning . . . I don't know," she said when he picked up. "We need a doctor."

MacDuff muttered a curse. "I'll call Dr. Kelsey in the village and tell him to get up there. I'm phoning Mrs. Dalbrey to go to your room and see if she can help. I'm on my way back from the hills. I should be there in twenty minutes." He hung up.

If I didn't feel so rotten, I'd be relieved, Eve thought hazily. MacDuff was on the job doing what he did best. Taking care and bossing everyone around.

Her door opened and Lina came into the room. She was white as a sheet, her eyes rimmed and dark.

"Do I look as bad as you?" Eve asked. "Don't answer. I don't give a damn." She curled up on the floor. "I called MacDuff. He's getting help."

"So sick." Lina sank to the floor beside her and leaned against the nightstand. "Like those herbs . . ."

Herbs.

I hope all goes well with you.

There's sighting in the hills. I have to check on it.

The MacDuffs wouldn't have built their castle here if they hadn't worked out an escape route.

But an escape route could also be an entry.

Wrong. Something was very wrong.

Eve's lids flicked open. "We have to get to the guards at the gates. It's not . . . safe here."

"What?"

Eve was struggling to her feet. "It's all

450

wrong. Mrs. Dalbrey . . . acting . . . strange."

Eve tried to help Lina up, but she was weak as a kitten. "They drew MacDuff . . . away from the castle. And if there's a way to escape, there's a way to . . . get in."

Lina staggered to her feet. "But you said . . . they can't get to us here."

"Not from outside. But there's a way. Jane told me that there's a way." She slipped her arm around Lina's waist. "Come on. We'll help each other." She was staggering toward the door. "We have to — get to the gates."

The staircase seemed a hundred yards from her bedroom door. They paused at the top of the stairs. How were they going to get down without falling in a heap at the bottom?

"Let me go. We'll go tumbling. I'll hold on to the banister." Lina broke away from her and grabbed the banister.

Eve slowly followed Lina down the steps.

Lina was panting by the time she reached the landing. "It's too far. Maybe if we shouted for the housekeeper."

"No. Keep going."

Lina started down the last flight. "Why?"

Eve didn't have the strength for explanations. "Herbs."

It was enough. Lina's lips tightened. "We'll make it to the gates."

But it took another five minutes for them to reach the bottom of the stairs.

They started for the front door.

It was thrown open before they reached it.

Mrs. Dalbrey stood in the doorway. Her hair was pulled from its smooth knot and her face was haggard. Tears were running down her cheeks. "You've got to get out of here. Come with me."

Eve shook her head.

"Don't argue. They'll kill you." She was sobbing. "They kill everybody. They killed my boy." Her hand grasped Eve's arm, and she pulled her out into the courtyard. "Get out the gates and run."

"Can't run — sick."

She flinched. "I know. I had to do it. They had my son. They said the only way I could save him was to do what they said. They lied." She put her arm beneath Eve's shoulders. "I'll help you." She glanced at Lina. "Can you walk?"

Lina nodded.

"Come. Hurry. They're going to —" The housekeeper arched, her eyes widening with shock. Blood was staining her white blouse. She fell to the stones of the courtyard.

Dead. She'd been shot, Eve realized.

But she hadn't heard the sound of the bullet.

A silencer.

Men were pouring out of the stable. Some were heading for the gates carrying automatic weapons.

Rotors. A helicopter was overhead . . .

Two men were coming toward them. One was tall, burley, dark. Thick lips, hook nose. She recognized that face from the photo. Millet.

A low ping of sound.

Lina gave a low cry.

Eve turned and saw Lina staggering backward, clutching her upper arm.

She was shot, Eve realized. Lina was falling to her knees.

"Finish her, Medford," Millet said as he came toward them. "She's no use to us."

The other man lifted his gun.

"Stop!" Eve turned, dove in front of Lina, and took her down.

Pain exploded in her upper body.

"You fool," Millet shouted. "Not her. You killed Eve Duncan."

Death?

Darkness.

Tel Aviv, Israel

"What next?" Gillem asked as he pulled up in front of the hangar. "Do you need me for anything else?"

453

"No," Jane said as she got out of the car. "We'll handle it from here." She turned to Jock. "I want you to call Venable and tell him to get an expert out here to find a way to X-ray this bottle so that it won't damage anything inside."

"Providing there is anything inside," Caleb said. "Why don't we take it back to MacDuff's Run and have it done there?"

"Because if we don't come up with the jackpot, I'm going to go back to that field and try again."

"I was afraid you'd say that." He turned to Gillem. "It seems there is something you can do. Arrange someplace safe for us to stay until we get some answers."

"That won't be easy on short notice. Venable didn't tell me I was supposed to do anything but get you in and get you out."

"But a good agent always reacts to the situation," Caleb said. "Isn't that right?"

Gillem reached for his phone. "I'll find a place."

Jane was unfastening her backpack and gently taking out the bottle she'd swathed in heavy plastic. It appeared to be intact, she realized with relief. Amazing after that headlong race across the field.

"Curious? Not even a peek inside?" Caleb asked.

Curious? She was practically biting her nails. "I can't risk it. It has to be incredibly fragile. We've just got to hope that Venable can get that expert here in a hurry." She glanced at Jock, who was still on the phone. "And that the expert won't be tempted to call the local authorities when we try to take a priceless artifact out of the country."

"That depends on whether there's a document in the bottle that would authenticate. Otherwise, he would have no idea that he was looking at anything other than a couple of ancient Aramaic items."

"In that case I might be tempted to invent a document of my own if it will lure Roland to take the bait." She grimaced. "You seem to know a lot of people who aren't exactly lily-white. You could probably point —" Her cell phone rang, and she glanced at the ID. "MacDuff?" Her heart stopped, then went into high gear. She punched the answer button. "What's wrong, MacDuff?"

"God, I wish I could tell you that there was nothing wrong."

Her hand clenched on the phone. "Answer me. What's wrong? Is Eve okay?"

"I'm not sure. I'll tell you what I know."

"Is Eve —" She closed her eyes. Let him talk. Don't jump to conclusions. Never that conclusion. She opened her eyes. "Tell me."

"I know she was shot. I don't know how bad or if she was killed. They took her with them." He paused. "I promised she'd be safe. I lied. I failed. There was activity in the hills, and I went up to check it out. Dammit, it was a red herring. I thought the castle was secure. I left good people in charge. Millet was more clever than I thought."

"What do you mean?"

"Do you remember the inner staircase from the stable that leads down to sea?"

She had used that passage herself years ago. She had just spoken of that escape route to Eve yesterday. "Of course, I do. But no one knew about that entrance but your most trusted people."

"My housekeeper knew about it."

"Mrs. Dalbrey? She betrayed you? Millet bribed her?"

"No, she would never have done it for money. I'm guessing Millet kidnapped her son and told her that he would kill him unless she let him through that stable door that led to the sea entrance and did whatever else he told her to do. She gave Eve and Lina the sedative he provided her, but evidently not enough. It made them sick but didn't knock them out. They tried to get to the gates but only managed to get down to the courtyard before Millet showed up."

The thought of Eve sick and helpless, struggling to get away, made Jane go cold. "And Millet shot her?"

"Not intentionally. Lina said they were trying to kill her, and Eve stepped in front of the bullet."

"And Lina doesn't know how badly Eve was hurt? Why the hell not?"

"Lina was shot too. Upper arm. We believe she's going to be okay but she was barely conscious when they took Eve away in the helicopter. She thinks that she saw Eve move, but she can't be sure."

Celine pinned to the oak door.

Blood flowing in a stream from a white flower box.

"If Eve's not dead now, he'll kill her."

"No, if she's not dead, we'll get her back," MacDuff said. "I promise you."

"You promised to keep her safe."

He was silent a moment. "You have a right not to believe in me, but I'll move heaven and earth and I *will* get her back. I won't let Millet beat me. He killed two of my men at the gates and one guarding the stable exit down to the sea. We found my housekeeper's son in the stable with his throat cut. They only waited until they managed to get through that stable door before they killed the hostage. Mrs. Dalbrey was shot trying to help Eve and Lina get to the gates. Those were *my* people. That's a big score for me to settle even without Eve."

"I don't care about your big score." Her voice was shaking. "All I care about right now is Eve. If she's alive, I have to keep her that way."

Brilliant butterfly pinned to the door.

But now she kept seeing Eve instead of Celine on that door.

"I can't talk right now. I'm going to give the phone to Jock. You tell him how you're going to bring Eve back to me." She had another thought. "Have you called Joe?"

"No, I'll do that next."

"Yes, right away." No one was smarter than Joe or loved Eve more. "I'll talk to him later." She handed the phone to Jock. "You heard me. Millet's got Eve."

"Lord, I'm sorry, Jane."

"Don't be sorry. Just find a way to get her back."

Jock nodded and turned away as he spoke into the phone. "What the hell happened, MacDuff?"

Jane walked away from him. She was shaking, and the muscles of her stomach were clenching with fear. She took a deep breath, then another.

"Jane." Caleb's hand was on her shoulder.

She stepped away from him. "Don't touch me. I'm trying to keep from breaking apart."

"I know." His hand dropped away from her. "And I know you'll be okay once you get over the shock. Just take a few minutes, then we'll start planning what we're going to do."

How had he known that those were the words she needed? Not sympathy, just acceptance and understanding, and a plan to make things right. "She stepped in front of Lina to keep them from killing her. I won't believe Eve's dead. I'd *know.*"

"I don't believe it either. They might have wanted to do a revenge killing earlier in the game, but now she'd be more valuable to them alive. If she was wounded, it was accidental and they took her with them because they're hoping to use her."

"Or convince me she's still alive."

"You said you'd know," Caleb said quietly. "I have faith in your instincts. You have to have faith in them, too."

Her faith was ebbing and flowing from minute to minute through this crippling terror. But she had to get a grip on herself. She tried to smile. "Maybe I need an attitude adjustment."

459

"Anytime. Anything you want." He said quietly. "Now?"

Her eyes widened in shock. "No! I wasn't serious. I don't want anesthesia. I want a solution." And he had known that and had given her that emotional jolt to counteract the one she was experiencing. "Everything I've ever felt for Eve has been honest. I wouldn't exchange even the pain for anything counterfeit."

He nodded. "Then let's start preparing." He turned to Gillem. "Have you found us a place to stay?"

Gillem nodded. "A house on the outskirts of town that we use to hold political prisoners for the Israelis is available. The prisoners whose existence the government denies any knowledge of."

"Then let's go and set up shop." He turned to Jane. "Unless you'd rather go back to Scotland?"

She shook her head. "Why? Millet wouldn't keep Eve anywhere near MacDuff's Run. She's probably out of the country by now. We'll stay here until we have an idea where Millet has her hidden." She was able to think again, thank God. Maybe that cold numbness was wearing away. She climbed into the rear seat of Gillem's car.

Jock had finished his call and was coming toward them. "I've never seen MacDuff this angry," he said as he got into the passenger seat. "He's feeling guilty and outraged and maybe even a little helpless. He doesn't like any of those feelings. I wouldn't want to be Millet when he catches up with him."

"He'll have to stand in line," Jane said. "When you got through to Venable, did he promise to send someone to examine that bottle?"

"Right away. He didn't think there would be any problem. There are a good many historical artifact experts in the area. It's the Mideast, after all." He paused. "You're not thinking of putting it on the back burner?"

"No, I want to speed it up. I may need a negotiating tool." She leaned back in the seat as Gillem started the car. "One that won't involve me being tied to a slab with that mosaic of Judas staring down at me."

"You think that's what Millet and Roland will demand?" Caleb asked.

"Don't you? That's what this has always been about. Millet wants a sacrifice, and I'm the Offering of choice." Her lips twisted. "My time is almost up. April 1 is right around the corner."

"That's what Millet wants, but Roland

may be tempted by the Judas coins."

She nodded. "That's what I'm hoping. But I've got to have proof I have something to trade." She paused. "And it's Millet who has Eve, and I don't have much faith that he'll be willing to give up Eve for the coins. He wants his blood Offering."

Caleb smiled. "Then we'll have to find a way to make sure he has all the blood he's craving."

That smile was cold and deadly, but it didn't bring the usual chill. Not when it concerned Millet. Not when Millet had Eve. "Not until I have Eve safe. Then you can do anything you want to the bastard."

"Ah, isn't it strange that my savagery doesn't seem nearly as wicked when it concerns the people you care about?" He didn't wait for her to answer but turned to Jock. "Did you call Venable back after you talked to MacDuff?"

"Yes, he said that he'd tap every source he knew to see if he could get a lead on where Millet took her." He added, "He has motivation. Joe Quinn is working with him, and he knows Joe will murder him if he doesn't come up with something."

She had to call Joe, Jane thought. But not right now. He wouldn't want talk to her until he got over the shock and started moving on trying to find Eve. Maybe not even then. Eve was everything to Joe, and in situations like this, he would be blind to anything but her. "When did it happen, Jock?"

"Over an hour ago."

Over an hour ago. While she had been running across that Field of Blood, they had shot Eve, taken Eve. "That's not long. We probably won't hear from Millet for a little while."

"No, he'll want to have her safely stashed in a secure place before he calls you," Jock said. "The Sang Noir has their main headquarters in Rome."

"I wish I could believe it would be Rome. Venable and Joe are right there."

"But you don't think he's heading for Rome," Caleb said. "Do you?"

Guilt.

A mosaic face staring down in torment.

Jane slowly shook her head. "No, he won't take her to Rome."

The small stucco house where Gillem took them was on the outskirts of Tel Aviv and was set back among the cedar trees away from the main road.

"It has two bedrooms, a bath, a kitchenette, and a living room," Gillem said as he pulled up in front of the house. "The freezer is always stocked. So you should have food. Is there anything else I should do?"

"No, I'll call you if we need you. Just bring that expert here as quick as you can," Caleb said, as they got out of the car. "Thanks. You did your job, Gillem."

Gillem gave him a sour smile. "Of course, I did my job. I always do my job." He waited until they had unlocked the door before he drove off.

"His change of attitude may be effective, but not particularly pleasant," Jane said.

"Some people can't accept pleasant. I have to work with what I have," Caleb said as he turned on the lights. "He's become very cynical over the years. I had to settle for reviving an almost extinct sense of duty."

The room they had entered was basic in every detail. Navy blue couch and matching easy chair, a metal stand and small TV, an oak table, a kitchenette on one side of the room.

"I'll take your bags into the bedroom," Jock said as he took her backpack and duffel. "And then I think I'll call and see if I can talk to Lina. She may need someone. She's probably blaming herself for Eve's being shot."

"That's nonsense," Jane said curtly. "It was all Millet. Being Eve, she had no choice but to try to save Lina from the bastard. It would be as natural as breathing to her. Lina just had the bad luck to be in Millet's way."

Jock smiled faintly. "I know that. But if you don't mind, I'll let Lina know that's how you feel."

Jane nodded. "I'll tell her myself later. I just have to deal with one thing at a time right now."

"I can see that." He disappeared into the bedroom.

"I should have thought of Lina," Jane said wearily. "She's another victim in this nightmare. We've taken away her home and almost her life. I'll have to try to make it up to her."

"Stop blaming yourself," Caleb said. "To repeat your words. It's all Millet." He added, "And Roland."

"Yes, and Roland," she said. "And we have to hope that Roland will want those coins enough to help me break Eve away from Millet."

"Help us," Caleb said. "You're not alone in this, Jane."

She felt alone. Alone and frightened and sick with apprehension. "In the end, I'm always alone. Except for Eve. It's always been that way since I was a kid. I was ten years old when she came into my life. I'd battled my way through a dozen foster-care homes, then she was there." Her voice was uneven. "And everything changed. I knew I'd never have to be really alone again as long as we were together. We could take care of each other. Always."

He nodded. "And you don't really trust anyone but Eve. That's why you have problems committing."

She had to pull herself together. "I'm not in the mood to listen to your analyzing me. I have a few other things to think about."

"Just a comment. Not a criticism. I have no right since I suffer from the same difficulty." He moved toward the tiny kitchenette. "Suppose I go through those cabinets and see if I can find some coffee or tea to make. I don't think the caffeine will bother any of us since there won't be any way any of us can sleep."

"That would be good." She moved toward the bathroom. "I'll go and wash some of this dirt and clay off me. Then I think I'll call Venable myself and nag him about getting that expert out here."

"If it would make you feel better," Caleb said. "But I imagine that between Jock and Joe Quinn, he has plenty of pressure on him."

"It will make me feel better." She closed the bathroom door and leaned back against it in the darkness. Alone. No one to pity her. No need to be brave and capable. Not for this moment. Let the pain come.

She drew a deep, shaky breath, feeling the tears sting her eyes.

Eve.

It will be all right, Eve. I promise you that it will be all right. I'll use everything I know and feel, and maybe some things that I don't know at all about. I'll reach out and grab anything I can to find you. I know you're not afraid of dying. But we're afraid of losing you. We *can't* lose you.

One more minute. It was dangerous to indulge this wrenching sorrow. It could weaken her, and she had to be strong.

Eve . . .

She braced herself and reached out and turned on the light.

She was only a few feet from a basin and mirrored medicine cabinet.

Her face was pasty white, and she looked as if she had been through a war.

She straightened and crossed to the basin and started to run the water.

She hadn't been through a war.

The war was yet to come.

EIGHTEEN

"You look better." Caleb looked up as she came out of the bathroom fifteen minutes later. "I found some tea bags. No coffee." He was pouring hot water from a kettle into the cups. "Not classy but adequate."

"Where's Jock? Still on the phone?"

"No, he went out to reconnoiter the area and make sure the house is secure. But he said to tell you that Venable should have that artifacts expert out within two hours. His name is Professor Joseph Tischler, and he's highly qualified."

"Good. I wish it was sooner."

"He had to get his equipment from the university lab." He handed her a cup. "Venable told him that preservation was essential, and Tischler was arguing that he didn't want to do the inspection on site. He wanted to take the bottle to the university and take his time."

"There is no time." She took a sip of the

tea. It was bitter but hot. She needed the heat. "Two hours?"

"And then the time it will take to X-ray and give us his findings." He lifted his cup. "We'll hurry him along, Jane."

But in the meantime she was going to have to sit here and do nothing but wait for him, wait for a call from Millet.

No, there was something she could do.

"I can't waste the time." She gazed directly into his eyes. "I have to go to sleep, Caleb."

He went still. "Yes?"

"I'm so wired that I won't be able to do that." She paused. "Not without help."

His eyes narrowed on her face. "Why do you want to sleep, Jane?"

" 'To sleep, perchance to dream,' " she quoted. "I have to dream, Caleb."

He didn't speak for a moment. "But aren't you the woman who is too grounded in reality to accept that dreams are anything but bullshit?"

"Eve told me that I had to stop hiding and accept the dreams. She said my dreams had to do with the Judas coins years ago, and when they started again, it had the same connection. She said that maybe there was some kind of reason for it all. And you told me that I could be doing some kind of remote viewing. I've no idea if any of that is true." She wearily shook her head. "I just don't know. I don't know if there's some mysterious reason. I sure don't know if I can do any of that CIA viewing bullshit. I don't even know if I can reach Eve. All my dreams have been of past events. But if there's a reason I'm having these dreams, then I've never had a greater reason than now. I'm going to try because they could be a weapon. I need weapons. Lord, do I need weapons." She looked down into the amber tea in her cup. "I saw the sacrifice of a little boy in a dream. I saw the mosaic of Judas on the wall. I followed the boy and his mother from outside the temple to the sacrificial chamber. I've been trying to remember all the twists and turns they took as they went down that corridor. But it's not enough. Eve may not even be in that temple. I have to find out where she is." She looked up at him again. "I have to dream about Eve."

He stared at her thoughtfully. "You want me to go in and give you a suggestion to sleep?"

"A damn strong suggestion. I feel as if I'll never be able to sleep again."

"Oh, I can make you sleep." His brow knitted in a frown. "But I can't control the dream process. That's out of my area of capability. Dreams are will-o'-the-wisps and can disappear as soon as they drift by."

"My dreams aren't will-o'-the-wisps."

He smiled. "And that's why we know that perhaps there's a way to use them. But you're the one who will have to do all the work. I'll give you a suggestion about Eve, but you'll have to run with it."

"I don't know how to do that." Her lips tightened. "But I'll learn. I'll make it work."

"I know you will." He took the cup from her hand and put it on the bar. "Go lie down on the couch."

"I thought I'd go to the bedroom . . . by myself."

He smiled. "And close me out." He shook his head. "I'm in this, Jane. I won't do anything to you that I can't monitor and make sure that you're safe."

"It's just sleep."

"And what do they call death? The long sleep. I won't leave you. But you won't even know I'm here."

She hesitated, then went to the couch and sat down. "Very well. It's not important."

"No, it's just your nature." He pushed her down and tucked the couch cushion beneath her head. He went over to the easy chair and sat down. "I won't leave you," he repeated. "Whatever happens, you don't have to be afraid. It might help if you think about Eve. I don't know. It's alien territory to me."

"It's alien territory to me, too," she said. "I keep wondering what if I'm wrong? What if Eve was killed at MacDuff's Run. What if she's dead?"

"Then if you do find her, this search may have an ending that's both unusual and mind-blowing. Are you afraid?"

"No, not for her. She's never been afraid of death. She's gone through so much since she lost her daughter, Bonnie, that she came to terms with it. She might even look upon it as a wonderful adventure." She whispered, "But I'm afraid for me. I don't know what I'd do without her."

"You won't have to worry about that. Remember, you said you'd know."

"That's right, and I have to stop having second thoughts." She closed her eyes. "Do something. I don't feel sleepy."

He chuckled. "What a demanding woman. It will come. Gently. I have an aversion to any roughness connected to you, Jane. Which is pretty astonishing when you consider that gentleness isn't my forte."

"I've noticed." She moistened her lips. "I didn't thank you for doing this."

"I accepted it as a given," Caleb said.

"And you'd have trouble not being a little resentful at giving up your will to anyone."

"I'm not giving up anything. This *is* my will."

"You see? You're going down deeper. It's time to start thinking about Eve."

She had never stopped thinking about her. Not really. Deeper? She didn't feel as if she was drifting off into . . .

Darkness.

No, misty grayness.

Sleep, but not sleep.

Eve.

She wasn't here.

Bring her. Get past the darkness. Get to her.

But perhaps she was lost in that darkness. Maybe she was lost forever.

No, keep searching.

Eve!

Vibration. A familiar hum of sound. Stale air.

I'm on an airplane, Eve thought hazily. Her second thought was of the throbbing pain in her right shoulder. Why . . .

The courtyard at MacDuff's Run.

Millet.

Her eyes flew open.

"Are you comfortable?" Millet was standing

over her, gazing down at her. "Medford told me that you'd regained consciousness. He was eager to make sure I knew that he hadn't killed you. I was a little upset with him."

"I can't imagine your being upset about any kind of brutality," Eve said. "You told him to kill Lina."

"She wasn't important."

"She's a human being, young, smart, with her whole life ahead of her."

"And totally unimportant. She was helping Jane MacGuire, and that is a sin."

She gazed at him in disbelief. "And what you do isn't a sin?"

"I'm one of the chosen. I can do as I please as long as I serve the Master."

"You're certifiable." She gazed around the interior of the plane. It appeared to be more of a cargo than a passenger aircraft. There were several wood boxes stamped with a crescent surrounded by a circle. Seven or eight men sitting on long hard benches on either side of the plane. She was lying on a stretcher close to the door that must lead to the cockpit. "How many people did you shoot back at the castle."

"I didn't count. Whatever was necessary."

"Shooting Lina wasn't necessary."

"It was a way to get you into the helicopter faster. Then you stepped in front of that bullet and spoiled everything. I thought Medford had killed you."

She looked down at her shoulder that had been roughly bandaged. "How bad is it?"

"Not too bad at all. You lost some blood, but you'll survive to be useful." He smiled. "And I may be able to play with you a little if I have time. I understand that Jane MacGuire cares a good deal about you. It would make her suffer to know that you're in pain."

She gazed at him coldly. "Don't bullshit me. I've known men like you before. You don't have to have an excuse to hurt and maim." She paused. "Though it's curious that you think that your master is going to protect you from every consequence when he's probably in hell."

"Liar!"

Her head snapped back as he slapped her with all his strength.

The plane whirled around her, and it was a moment before it steadied enough so that she could focus on his face again.

Ugliness. Pleasure. Eagerness. What a sicko, she thought dizzily. He was a crazy fanatic with his sadistic soul in overdrive. "Where are you taking me, Millet?"

"The temple. We should be landing fairly shortly."

"Syria?"

"Yes. The situation may become tense, and I need to be on my own territory." He smiled. "And I would have had to come anyway. The Offering is day after tomorrow."

"And you're hoping to have Jane as that Offering."

"Not 'hoping.' I will have her. Roland has done extensive research on your relationship. I don't think there's any doubt that she'll be ready to make a trade when I give her the opportunity."

No, Eve didn't have a doubt either, and it was scaring her to death. "Why bother with her? You have me."

His brows rose. "You surprise me. You've already suffered a great deal, and now you wish to give your life for her? You're very strong. You're going to prove entertaining."

"What difference does it really make? You and your scumbag cohorts won't care who dies under the knife."

"Oh, but we will. Jane MacGuire has to be made an example. More than one of the members has seen that photo of the painting and called me. She's the Blasphemer, and it will please the members that she's punished. Besides, I have to determine how she was able to duplicate the mosaic. I have to have my time with her."

Torture. The bastard was practically salivating. "It was purely coincidental."

"Perhaps. Since she hasn't revealed the location of the temple in the time since she did the painting, there is that possibility. Or perhaps she was just afraid of my retribution." His smile deepened. "I'll enjoy the process of discovering the truth."

And she couldn't even give him an explanation more substantial than coincidence. He'd laugh if she told him that Guilt was born of dreams. It wouldn't do any good anyway. He wanted his pound of flesh and would fight anyone who tried to cheat him of it. What was important was that she couldn't convince him not to try to trade for Jane.

So she had to find a way to get away from him.

"You're very thoughtful." Millet's gaze was on her face. "You're a scheming bitch, just like her. I hear you work on skulls. Maybe I'll give you MacGuire's head to play with. Yes, I believe I'd enjoy having you do that."

Keep cool. He was only trying intimidation, to play on her fear, to hurt her. But she was almost certain he'd follow through on any threat. "I'd rather work on yours. I think that possibility is considerably more likely."

His smile faded. "I'm growing tired of your —"

"Captain Faruk said that we're on the ap-

477

proach." A dark, thin, man was at Millet's elbow. "He asked if you'll need him after we land or if he can return to Damascus. He's received several requests from other members wanting to hire him to take them to the Offering."

"You remember Medford, Eve," Millet said. "He's the fool who almost killed you."

Medford cheeks flushed. "I didn't expect her to jump in front of —"

"You made a mistake," Millet said. "It's beginning to be a habit."

"Faruk," Medford repeated.

"I won't need him. I expect to be busy until the Offering. If I do, I'll call."

Medford turned and strode back toward the cockpit.

"You see, everyone is excited to come to this Offering," Millet said to Eve. "How could I disappoint them?" He turned and sat down in a seat across from her stretcher. "I'll permit you to rest for a little while before we land. I've decided that I'll let you walk to the temple. We have plenty of time. I'm going to let your Jane worry about you for a while. It will make her more amenable when I do call her." His tone became mocking. "A strong woman like you would be insulted to be carried on a stretcher."

Eve closed her eyes. Think. Is there a way

of escaping after we land or would it be better to wait? Lord knows, I'm weak right now, and they will be more alert during a transfer. It would probably be smarter to be patient until they reached this temple and I can access the situation.

It was going to be hard to wait . . .

Drifting . . .

Darkness.

Gray mist . . .

No! Jane struggled desperately. She couldn't leave Eve. She had to stay with her, help her.

But the grayness was now disappearing, too.

"Stop fighting it," Caleb said softly. "You're back, Jane."

Her lids slowly lifted. It took a moment for her to focus. "I have to go back. I have to help her."

"Not now. You were going too deep. I had to pull you back."

"Help me."

"I won't help you. Not that way."

"Dammit, she's alone."

"But not dead evidently. That's a good thing."

"Yes." She sat up and brushed her hair away from her face. "It's her right shoulder.

It was throbbing. It looked as if it had been bandaged very clumsily. She'll be lucky if it doesn't get infected."

"If we get her away from him quickly enough, we won't have to worry about that." He handed her a glass of water. "Now clear your head and let's see if we can find a way to do it. You definitely made it through? You were dreaming about Eve?"

"Yes. And I think it was that remote viewing you told me about. It was too real to be anything else." She drank a few sips of water and handed the glass back to him. "How long was I asleep?"

"Over an hour."

Her eyes widened. "That's odd. Dreams are supposed to last only minutes, seconds."

"But then your dreams aren't exactly run-of-the-mill, are they?"

She shook her head. That was an understatement if she'd ever heard one. "He told Eve he wants a trade. He's not going to kill her just as a way to punish me the way he did with Celine." Her lips twisted. "There's not enough time to waste when he needs me for the Offering."

"Do you know where she is?"

"She was on a plane on her way to the temple in Syria. They were almost there when I had to leave her."

"And where is this temple located?"

"I told you, Syria. I don't know anything else." She gazed at him accusingly. "They hadn't landed yet when you made me leave her."

"It was necessary."

She knew it was probably true, but it didn't lessen her disappointment. "Okay, it's done. There has to be something else I can use to find her." Her brow knitted as she tried to sift through that ugly conversation Eve had had with Millet. "A man named Medford shot her. Millet wasn't pleased with him. The plane they were on was some kind of a cargo aircraft. A few seats but mostly benches on either side of the plane. There were huge boxes that —"

"Any writing on the boxes?"

"Yes, but it was in Arabic." She made a face. "There was no way I could decipher that script. But there was some kind of symbol under the writing. A crescent in a circle."

He reached in his jacket pocket and pulled out a small notebook and pen and handed it to her. "Draw it for me."

As she began to draw the symbol, she suddenly stiffened, her gaze flying to meet his own. "I just remembered something else. Why the hell didn't I zero in on it immediately? The pilot was a Captain Faruk," she said. "He was going to return to Damascus to bring back other members to the Offering."

"Jackpot!" he said softly. "Any description?"

She shook her head. "Eve never saw him. Medford was only talking about him."

"Never mind. The name may be enough." He got to his feet. "I'm going to go outside and get Gavin. I need to fill him in and have him stir Venable into getting us information about Faruk." He opened the door. "Damn fast. You try to think of anything else we can use."

As if she weren't doing that already. But searching her memory word by word, the pilot's name had been the only thing that even had a chance of being helpful. Excitement was beginning to build within her the more she thought about it. Faruk could be a major help to them. He wasn't just a hired pilot. He knew about the Offering. Therefore, he must know the location of the temple.

And, in Damascus, he was relatively vulnerable and isolated from Millet's gang of thugs.

As Caleb had said.

Jackpot.

■ ■ ■ ■

"Faruk, Ahmed," Jock said as he came into the house fifteen minutes later. "Formerly a copilot with Alitalia Airlines. He moved to Damascus four years ago and opened his own cargo line. He makes regular runs between Damascus and cities in Italy and does a bustling cargo and charter business out of Rome." His brows lifted. "Now I wonder where he got the money to start his own business?"

"Does Venable show any connection with Millet?"

He shook his head. "And no criminal record. He's clean." He turned to Caleb, who had come in behind him. "Did you find anything else about him on the Net?"

"Only his home address in Damascus," he said. "But that was really all I was interested in." He inclined his head to Jane. "I believe I should take a run to Damascus and pay Faruk a visit."

"No, Millet hasn't even contacted me yet. What if something went wrong, and it got back to Millet? I don't want to rush in and risk Eve unless we have a sure thing."

"That's not going to happen, Jane," Jock said gently.

"As close to a sure thing as we can make it." It was hard to be patient when all she wanted to do was rush forward as much as Caleb did. "Millet is letting me stew, so that he can have a maximum effect when he does contact me. We've got to take that time and try to turn it against him." She turned to Caleb. "Look, find Faruk, zero in on him. Get ready to pounce. But hold off."

He just looked at her.

The hunter, again.

Not now. She didn't want to have to deal with that savage side of him. Dammit, he was such a complex blend of lethal aggression and sophisticated persuasiveness that she could never know which one was going to surface. It made her feel angry and helpless and she wanted to strike out.

She couldn't strike out. The last thing she wanted was for him to strike back. She had enough battles looming on the horizon.

She drew a deep breath. "Please."

He gazed at her for another moment. "That was extremely hard for you." He shrugged. "If you like." He turned and headed for the door. "I'll head for the airport. I should be in Damascus within an hour or so, and I'll locate Faruk. But keep in touch with me. I have to know that we're moving or it becomes . . . difficult."

"It may be difficult anyway," Jock said as the door closed behind him. "What Venable knows, Joe Quinn will know. How are you going to keep Joe from going after Faruk? That would be the first thing I'd do. Caleb won't let anyone else take his prey while you keep his hands tied. It could be major mayhem."

Dammit, she hadn't thought that far ahead. She seemed to be operating purely on instinct, and that wasn't going to work. "I'll have to call Joe." She took out her phone. "In the meantime, can't you see if you can get that artifacts professor here any sooner?"

He nodded. "I'll call Gillem and check on his progress."

She went into the bedroom and quickly dialed Joe's number.

"Are you all right?" Joe asked curtly when he picked up. "I meant to call you, but I've been scrambling."

"I know." It was what she had expected. "I'm scared. Frantic. But working through it. You got Jock's report?"

"Yes, I'm heading for the airport now. I'll be in Damascus in a few hours."

"No!"

"Jane, don't tell me no."

"I don't have any choice. Do you think I

don't know how you feel?" she asked fiercely. "I'm not letting there be even the smallest chance of anything going wrong until we have some kind of trap in place. I'm not going to let either you or Caleb run your own show. We have to work together, dammit."

"What the hell are you thinking? I won't do anything to risk Eve."

"Listen to me. Millet took Eve because of me. All of this is because of me. He knows about you and Venable and that he has to walk very carefully. But that's not going to stop him from trying for a trade." She paused. "If I feel as if I've lost control, and there's a risk, he'll get his trade."

Joe was cursing. "That's crazy. He won't let her live regardless."

"Then stop and clear your head and help me get a plan together. I won't have you rushing to Damascus and grabbing Faruk and trying to force him. I gave you and Venable this lead to Faruk. He's *mine*."

He was silent. "God, I'm scared, Jane," he said hoarsely. "She's . . . everything."

"I know. Me too." She couldn't speak for a moment. "It's going to be okay," she said unevenly. "I know it will." She steadied her voice. "The temple is definitely in Syria. We don't know where yet. You and Venable go on to Damascus, but leave Faruk alone. That's as good a jumping-off place as you can get. I'm going to call MacDuff and tell him to join you there. You're going to have your hands full just keeping him in line." She paused. "I'm not trying to close you out of this, Joe. If you or anyone else can come up with a foolproof plan that's safe for Eve, then I'll grab it."

"I *hate* this. I don't know enough to have a plan. But I'm not going to sit in Damascus and twiddle my thumbs for very long."

"You shouldn't have to worry about that," she said dryly. "Millet's not going to give me very long. Day after tomorrow is the day of offering." She added, "I'll let you know what's happening as soon as I do."

"You'd better," he said. "And don't do anything stupid. Eve isn't the only one I care about." He hung up.

But Eve is the only one who makes his world worthwhile, Jane thought. She knew Joe loved her, but Eve was the center of his universe. It was amazing that he'd let her talk him into restraining that explosive anger and fear that was tearing at him. But the situation was still volatile, and keeping Caleb and Joe in check was going to be a delicate balance.

Well, she'd just have to do it. But one

thing at a time. First, she had to see if that bottle possessed the genie that would make all this terror go away.

She opened the door and went to see if Jock had any news about the professor who was going to free that genie.

"He's still calibrating his equipment," Jock said as he walked out of the bedroom where Professor Tischler had set up shop over an hour ago. "He doesn't seem to be in any hurry. I've never seen anyone this painstaking."

Jane leaned back against the couch. "Good. Then he won't damage anything."

"That backpack was heavier than I thought it would be when I took it into the bedroom. How much does thirty pieces of silver weigh?"

"It's actually shekels of silver. Each shekel is about twenty-nine millimeters in diameter and thirteen grams in weight. It's a little smaller than a half-dollar. Then you take into consideration the alabaster bottle. It's not really heavy, but it's substantial." She shook her head. "That's why Adah Ziller's red herring of those two little ancient coins she left around for Weismann to find was so pitiful. I don't think she did her research. They weren't even Shekels of Tyre. Though it might have just been a teaser. Or maybe she thought that Weismann wouldn't have done his research."

"What's a Shekel of Tyre?"

"It's the only coin that the priests of the temple would use or accept. That was why Judas would have had to be paid in Shekels of Tyre. They were minted in Phoenicia, but were in common usage in Jerusalem."

"Evidently you did your research."

"Part of that bundle of books you got for me. But Professor Tischler will know a hell of a lot more." She glanced at the door again. "He has to be close to getting answers. I don't need museum-type authenticity. All I need is to know that it's a possible."

"Which may take a while. You could take a nap. I'll wake you."

She shook her head. "I've already had a nap."

"So Caleb told me." He looked down into the tea in his cup. "Dreams. Strange."

"You mean I'm strange," she said.

He shook his head. "I don't have as much problem accepting dreams as I do the weird stuff Caleb does. Dreams happen to everyone. I can see how a dream might wander off into the deep end."

"That's an odd way to put it."

He smiled. "Is it? I know a lot about getting lost in the deep ends. You just have to hold on and keep going until you see a break ahead."

"That's what I'm doing." She added quietly, "With a little help from my friends. Thank you for being my friend, Jock."

He inclined his head. "It's my pleasure."

"Not at the moment. Right now being my friend is a pain in the ass."

"Well, I'm not bored. There's something to say —"

"I've finished," Joseph Tischler stood in the bedroom doorway. He was a small, wiry man in his early fifties whose rust red hair was streaked with gray and whose dark brown eyes glittered with vitality. "As much as I can complete without actually breaking the seal and opening the bottle. I refuse to do that. The scroll could disintegrate."

"You X-rayed it?"

"In a manner of speaking. I've developed my own digital-process X-ray-based CT scans of rolled papyrus and carbon-based ink samples. It's been done before, but I've combined it with some rather sophisticated imaging. I used it extensively in Cairo when they discovered several scrolls that would have been destroyed or remained unopened for the foreseeable future. It lets you slice through an object and develop a three-dimensional data set without having to open it. Then you can digitally unroll the scrolls on a computer screen. It was the only possible solution with that bottle."

Jane sat up straight on the couch. "And?"

His lips tightened. "Come and see for yourself." He turned on his heel and went back into the bedroom.

"Very curt," Jock said. "Too bad Caleb isn't here to give him an attitude adjustment."

"I don't care how polite he is," Jane said as she got to her feet. "As long as he did his job." She moved toward the bedroom. "Let's go see what he came up with."

"I'll have a picture for you in a minute." Tischler was arranging one of three cameras he had surrounding the small pedestal on which the bottle sat. "The interior of the bottle will be projected on the computer monitor over there on the wall. It's probably not exactly what you want, but I won't expose the contents in the bottle to air without proper precautions. The writ is probably goatskin leather instead of papyrus, or it wouldn't have survived. If it had been plant-based papyrus, it would have disintegrated already. I'm not risking it."

"You said that before," Jane said. "I never asked you to open the bottle. That's why you're here."

He gave her a cool glance. "No, you didn't ask, but I know with whom I'm dealing. I had no idea what was in that bottle when they told me to come here. I was only pressed by the prime minister to cooperate with the CIA because Israel needs United States goodwill. We need everyone's goodwill if we're going to survive the next decade."

She ignored the coldness and leaped on the inference in that second sentence. Excitement was zinging through her. "But now you're able to tell what it is?"

He didn't answer directly. "You and your CIA really care nothing about history or religion. This discovery is probably going to end up as just another chess piece. It doesn't matter that this find could prove of gigantic importance to the religions of the world."

"It matters." Jane stared him in the eye. "But life means more to me. If this chess piece will save a life I value, I'm not about to let you take it to your lab to study and publish all your erudite findings in journals. Can you guarantee that if you take this back to your university, it won't become just another reason for your government and the Palestinians to try to blow each other up?

We took that bottle from Palestinian-held territory."

"Which should have been our territory." He looked at her defiantly for an instant, then his gaze wearily shifted back to the monitor. "There are no guarantees. Not in this world. The deaths never seem to stop."

"Then tell me what's in that bottle."

"I'll let you see it." He turned on the machine and adjusted the focus. "The difficulty was fine-tuning so that I could see both outside and inside the pouch with the flick of the button."

A grayish haze appeared on the wall.

He sharpened and zoomed in, and the haze began to take a defined shape. A crumpled cloth container at the bottom of the bottle.

The pouch?

"There's a document of some sort on the other side of the pouch." Tischler revolved the picture and focused on what appeared to be a piece of rolled leather. "As you can see, it was apparently crammed carelessly into the bottle. It wasn't even rolled properly, the writing is on the outside instead of protected on the inside of the scroll."

Jane could see that, but the leather was cracked, the writing was smeared and almost indistinguishable. She couldn't make out anything. Not that I would have been able to decipher it anyway, she thought ruefully. "It's ancient Aramaic?"

"Yes, the temple priests were practically the only ones who used Hebrew, but they often were forced to use Aramaic when dealing with commoners like the potter, who couldn't read Hebrew." He made another adjustment. "It's damaged, but the protection of the bottle itself and being buried in the clay kept it in better shape than I would have thought. But it would take months to be able to decipher the entire document."

Her gaze flew to his face. "You'd be able to do it?"

"With time and care and the right technology. Yes, I could do it." He looked at her. "But you're not interested in a complete translation, are you? That's not what you want."

"And what do you think I want, Professor?"

He zeroed the camera in on a wrinkled upper corner of the document. "I think this is why you brought me here."

She looked at him in bewilderment. "If this is supposed to be some great dramatic revelation, it's not working. I can't read the damn thing."

He zeroed in a little more toward the edge of the folded scroll and hit the laser. "This word is a name." He paused. "Judas."

She inhaled sharply. *"Yes."*

"Of course, it could be another Judas. It's not as if there weren't other men named Judas during that time period." He pointed the laser again. "But we can see two other Aramaic equilvalent letters before it reaches the fold. "I and S."

Judas Iscariot.

"Interesting, isn't it?" Tischler asked sarcastically. "You can see how it caught my attention."

"And made you angry."

He shrugged. "I always seem to be angry these days. Angry and sad." He added, "If you'll give me a minute, I'll increase the depth of field so that you can look in the pouch."

"You've already seen what's inside?" Jock asked.

He nodded as he pressed the button to show them the interior of the pouch. "Coins."

Jane stared at the coins. They were discolored, oxidized, with just a hint of the original silver, none of them impressive. No one would guess that there was anything unusual or valuable about them.

"Are they Shekels of Tyre?"

"Oh, yes."

"How can you tell?" Jock asked.

"They're very identifiable," Jane said. "One side has a laureate head of a man with a lion skin around his neck. The reverse side has an eagle with a palm-frond background." She glanced at Tischler. "But they're so discolored, I'm asking the same question. How can you tell?"

"It's not as bad as it could have been. The brass stopper and being buried kept it almost airtight." Tischler pointed his laser light at the coins. "First we select, magnify, then we zero in." The image gradually grew larger and larger until it filled the wall. It was dark but distinguishable. "The noble laureate head of Melquart."

Jane inhaled sharply.

He switched to another coin. "This one is turned on its side in the bottle."

The eagle.

"The palm is partially blackened on it, but there's a plus. See the two symbols to the left of the eagle? That indicates the year 130 in the Phoenician calendar, the Era of Tyre. That's four or five A.D., squarely in the right time period." He ran the laser over the stack of coins. "As you can see, they're jumbled up, some on their sides. It took me a while to count them. But evidently Matthew was wrong. There were only twenty-eight shekels of silver."

"He wasn't wrong. The potter, Ezra, gave two to his slave, Dominic, after he freed him."

Tischler's brows rose. "You wouldn't care to tell me how you know that?"

"Not now. But I will," Jane said. "If you'll do one more thing for me."

"What is that?"

"Is it possible for you take photos of both the document and the coins?"

He nodded. "Of course, it's possible. I brought the equipment to do it. I fully intended to make records." He paused, "Whether or not you or the CIA liked it."

"I do like it. Take all the photos you like for your own files," Jane said. "I want photos of the coins, and I need shots as clear as you can make it of that text."

"Very well." He hesitated, then said belligerently, "It won't only be for my own files. I'm going to go to the prime minister and report to him."

"We can't let you do that," Jock said.

"You can't stop me."

"Oh, but I can," Jock said softly.

"But he won't," Jane said hurriedly. "All

we want is your promise to wait until after the first of April. After that, we don't care who you talk to about the Judas bottle."

He didn't answer.

Lord, he was stubborn, she thought. Give him something else. "And I swear that I'll come back and tell you what this is all about when I can do it safely for everyone concerned. If I can, I'll even let you publish your findings."

Tischler frowned, then finally said, "You're only asking me to wait one day. I suppose it wouldn't be irresponsible to wait."

"No, not at all. When can I have the photos? And could you put them on my phone camera?"

He nodded. "I believe I could. Leave your phone and give me forty-five minutes."

She put her phone down on the bedside table and turned toward the door. "Thank you, Professor Tischler."

He didn't answer, his gaze narrowed on the screen.

"Do you think he'll keep his word?" Jock asked as he closed the door behind them.

"I don't know. I hope he will. If he doesn't, we'll cope with the fallout later. I won't have him hurt or even intimidated. There have been too many innocent people who have suffered because of those coins."

Jock nodded. "I'm not arguing. It's your call."

And the decisions were becoming more and more terrifying. "Do you know, I don't believe I actually thought the coins would be in that bottle. I followed the directions. I dug in that damn clay. And yet part of my mind wouldn't accept that . . ." She shook her head. "I'm still not accepting that we found Hadar's bottle. It seems impossible."

"There are many stories in the Bible that seem impossible. The Bible is founded on wonder and miracles. Actually, everything in Hadar's Tablet is fairly believable. Ugly, but that adds to the veracity. And, after all this trouble we've gone through, you'd better accept it."

"I'm working on it." She grimaced. "But the important thing is to make Roland accept it."

NINETEEN

Tischler came out of the bedroom fifty minutes later and handed her phone back to her. "It came out fairly clear. I was surprised it was that good." He paused. "I'll pack up my equipment and get out of here. You're sure you wouldn't consider letting me take the bottle back to the university?"

She shook her head. "But I promise I won't damage it by opening the bottle and exposing it to air."

"I won't risk it. I'm going to leave a small portable metal container with you. It's got an oxygen gauge. I'll put the bottle in the container. All you have to do is press the button and it will take out the oxygen and keep the container airtight."

"Thank you."

"I'm not doing it for you. I'm trying to preserve a precious historical artifact from being destroyed." He turned and started back toward the bedroom. "Besides the fact that you appealed to my curiosity, and I'm taking a chance that you'll keep your word."

"I'll keep it," she said absently, already accessing the photo on her cell phone.

He was right. The photos were amazingly clear. He had given her two of the script on the scroll and one of the coins themselves.

She handed the phone to Jock. "We got lucky. They're astonishing."

His lips curved in a faint smile as she gazed at the photos. "You might say almost miraculous, wouldn't you?"

"I'll take a miracle or two." She took the phone back. "Now all I have to do is convince Roland that he should —"

Her cell phone rang.

Private number.

She tensed, then punched the button.

"I've been very eager to talk to you, bitch." The man's voice was mocking. "And I'm sure you've been waiting for my call with bated breath."

"Millet?"

"You guessed. I thought you would. I had to keep myself from calling you before this. You've caused me a good deal of trouble, and I wanted to vent. But then I told myself wait, anticipate, let the bitch suffer. I took a great deal of pleasure thinking how frantic you must be about your Eve Duncan."

"How is she? How badly is she hurt?"

"Not too badly. Yet. But I plan on entertaining myself with her after I hang up. She may be in considerably worse shape by the time the two of you are reunited."

"Don't hurt her."

"But I must. Still, there's a possibility that she could live if we could come to an agreement."

"You're talking about a trade."

"Consider the situation. Look at all the innocent people that you've forced me to kill just so that you could keep on living. Do you want me to have to kill Eve Duncan? You know you've sinned. You may even be forgiven if you give yourself as the Offering."

"I haven't forced you to do anything. If you weren't totally unbalanced, you'd realize that you're the sinner. Murder is the ultimate sin, Millet."

"I'm beginning to tire of talking to you. I think I'll seek other amusement. Do you wish to speak to your Eve before I take her away?"

And she knew what that amusement would be. "Don't hurt her. I'll consider a trade. You can't expect me to jump at the chance of having you stick your knife in me."

"That's not good enough. I don't have time to let you hem and haw before you give in to the inevitable. The members mustn't have a major disappointment at the last moment. I have to make preparations. Six hours from now, I'm going to send out a message to them either confirming that you'll be the Offering or announcing a new sacrifice. I'll give you those six hours, and no more, for you to tell me that you're going to pay for your sins. After that, I'll announce to the members that Eve Duncan will be the Offering." He added, "They won't be as pleased as having you, but she has a certain notoriety that will make the sacrifice titillating. It's always exciting to bring down a star in any field. The most popular Offerings are always the rich, the famous, the brightest. You didn't answer me. Do you wish to speak to Eve Duncan?"

"Of course, I do."

"I'm turning up the volume so that you can share every precious word with me," Millet said.

The next moment, Eve came on the line. "You know that I don't want you to give in to this monster. I'll work it out."

"No, we'll work it out. How is your wound? Did they change the bandage?"

"No, but I'll survive. Stop fretting, Jane."

"Fretting? I'm not *fretting.* I'm scared to death. I never dreamed that I'd get you into this mess." She paused. "Though even if I *had* dreamed it, I wouldn't know enough to get you out. I don't know where you are, how to get to you. I feel helpless, Eve. Like I did when I was a kid, and I'd come running to you to make everything all right."

Eve was silent. "I'll try to do that now, Jane. But I imagine that in the end, it will be up to you."

"Very touching." Millet was back on the line. "But she's right, it's up to you. I'll call you in six hours. I hope she'll still be able to speak coherently." He hung up.

That last threat was meant to drive me to panic, Jane thought as she hung up. It came close to succeeding.

"Did she understand what you were saying?" Jock asked. "It was pretty obscure."

"It was the best I could do. He was listening to the conversation. I think she understood that she wasn't alone, and I wanted her to find a way to let us know where she was in the temple." She shook her head. "But I can't be sure. I'm not going to rely on it." She got to her feet and moved to the window and stood staring out into the darkness. She had to take a moment to steady her nerves before she dove into what she knew must be done. Professor Tischler was loading his equipment into his car, she noticed. He must have left the house while she was on the phone talking to Millet. She hadn't even realized that he had passed through the room. "Eve called Millet a monster, and that's what he is. He wants to hurt her, Jock. I can't let him do it."

He crossed the room to stand beside her at the window. "He won't do anything critical. She's important to him."

"Critical? I don't want him to touch her. But I can't stop it. I'm not there. He won't listen to me. And he believes anything he does to her will help bring me down."

"Then what are you going to do?"

She reached for her phone. "I think it's time that I brought someone on board who he will listen to." She looked up the number in her directory and dialed.

"How delightful to hear from you," Roland said. "Though I admit I expected it. My friend, Millet, said he was going to phone you and make you an offer you couldn't refuse."

"It wasn't an offer, it was a threat. You knew it would be."

"Millet is a little on edge. Time's running out for him. If he doesn't produce you after he promised the members, then he'll lose prestige. He's seen other Guardians start that slide, and it scares him. He doesn't want someone to suggest that he'd make an excellent Offering."

"I can't imagine a more fitting ending for the bastard."

"Neither can I. But he has his uses, and he's not sharp enough to cause me any real problems." He paused. "But you didn't call me to listen to my assessment of Millet. You have your own by now. What is it? Begging? Pleading? Tears?"

"He's going to hurt Eve. He may be doing it now. I want you to stop him."

"Do you? But you have to understand that Millet derives a monumental amount of pleasure out of exercising that side of his character. It's one of the ways I have of controlling him. So it wouldn't do for me to attempt to curb him." He chuckled. "As a matter of fact, I recall I once suggested that Eve Duncan would be a wonderful candidate for his games."

"You bastard."

"You'd do better with pleading than name-calling. Though neither is going to do you any good. I'll have to let Millet run his course unless you can persuade me that it would be to my advantage to stop him." He added softly, "You know what I want, Jane.

I think you're on the trail and may be very close. If you're close enough, then we may have something to talk about. I do hope that's the case because otherwise Eve Duncan doesn't stand a chance. I won't lift a finger."

"I didn't expect anything else of you."

"Then tell me what I want to know. Are you going to be able to find the coins?"

"No." She paused. "I've already found them."

He inhaled sharply. "The hell you have." Then he said, "You wouldn't be trying any desperation tactics, would you?"

"I am desperate, or I wouldn't have called you. That doesn't mean that I'm not telling the truth. I'm going to send you three photos." She pressed the button on her phone to make the transfer. "Look at them, then we'll talk."

"Oh, I intend to look at them . . ."

She waited.

He came back on the line. "Interesting," he said cautiously. "But that doesn't mean I can be sure they're authentic. And I can't decipher the script on that scroll."

"I couldn't either. But I've been informed that in the upper right-hand corner is the name Judas followed by the letters I and S. You're a powerful man who has been hunting for the Judas coins for years. You have to have contacts who can look at these pictures and tell you whether or not they're counterfeit. Call them and tell them to get the hell over there right away."

"I'll consider it."

"Don't consider it, do it," she said fiercely. "I'll not have that son of a bitch torturing Eve because you can't get your act together. And if he kills her, there won't be a chance in hell of your getting your hands on the Judas coins. I'll throw it into the ocean before I let you have that pouch."

"No reason to become so upset. I believe I can accommodate you."

"No more than an hour, Roland. And while you're checking up on me, find a way to keep Millet busy and away from Eve."

"Don't give me orders, Jane."

"One hour, Roland." She hung up.

"You were very tough." Jock handed her a cup of tea. "I was impressed. Now sit down and relax for a little while. It's been a roller-coaster night for you. But I think that Roland knows that he's been in a battle."

"Only a skirmish." She sipped the tea and dropped down on the couch. Yes, she would try to relax. It was the intelligent thing to do. Certainly not the easiest thing when her nerves were strung this tight. "But the war

508

has officially begun."

Roland called her fifty-five minutes later. His voice vibrated with excitement. "Where are they?"

"You got a confirmation on the coins?"

"I got a highly probable. The expert I called in said the script appeared to be carbon-based as was common during that period. But it's not the correct number of coins."

"Don't be greedy. I could tell you where the other two coins went."

"Where?"

"I *could* tell you. I won't do it without a cast-iron deal."

"Where is that pouch?" he asked. "And I've been told that writ of sale could disintegrate if care isn't taken."

"Safe. Hadar stuffed it in a bottle near the Field of Blood. I couldn't chance opening it, so I had someone do opaque digital X-rays. It's now protected in an airtight container. If you want to verify, you'll have to have your expert do a digital scan when I hand it over. I guarantee it will remain intact if you agree to my terms."

"You're not in a position to dictate terms. You're too vulnerable. Millet has Eve Duncan, which means I have Eve Duncan."

"Those are my terms. I want Eve freed, and I want both of us to walk away from this nightmare. If you can find a way to rid the earth of Millet, I'd consider it a bonus."

He was silent for a moment. "And I get the coins and the scroll with no conditions?"

"With no conditions."

He suddenly chuckled. "Good God, I wonder if Eve Duncan will ever appreciate how valuable her life has turned out to be. You're willing to give up billions."

"Her life has a value you can't even imagine, Roland."

"I couldn't be happier that you feel that way. In fact, I'm positively giddy. Do you know how long I've searched for those coins?"

"You told me it was years. I don't give a damn. When can we arrange a trade that doesn't involve either Eve or me ending up on that slab in the temple?"

"I'll have to think about ways and means. You may well get your bonus if I can't figure a way to pluck Eve out of Millet's hands."

"You'd better think fast. Millet gave me six hours to agree to his terms. I only have a little over four hours left." She paused. "Did you call Millet and tell him that Eve's not to be touched?"

"If I gave him orders, then he'd be certain to do the opposite. I phoned and let him brag a little, then said that you're obviously an overemotional woman, and if you saw signs of mistreatment, you might blow up and ruin the trade. He can't afford to have that happen. He'll back off."

"You told the truth. I'm very emotional, and I'll react accordingly. You might remember that when you make your plans on getting Eve out of Millet's hands."

"I remember everything about you." His voice lowered silkily. "You're an unusual woman. I enjoy emotion. I was disappointed that I had to throw you to Millet to butcher. I much prefer the prospect of getting together with you at some future date. I could show you a few very exciting games."

"In your dreams." She hung up before she realized what she had said. Dreams, again. That response had come out of nowhere.

"He's going to cooperate?" Jock asked.

"He's telling me that he is. He could go either way. He wants the coins so bad that he can taste it. But if he thinks he can get the pouch without endangering his position within that cult, then he'll have no compunction about serving me up to Millet." She added wearily, "I realize we can't trust him. I just had to have his help with Millet

511

to keep Eve safe while we scramble to help her."

He smiled. "And are we prepared to scramble?"

"Yes, call Gillem and tell him that I'll need a helicopter to take me to Damascus."

His smile faded. "You're going to Caleb?"

She nodded. "That pilot, Faruk, is the key. I have to make sure that Caleb doesn't break the man before he can unlock the doors to the temple."

"I'd prefer to go with you."

"Why? To protect me from Caleb? I thought you were over that."

"I don't believe he'd hurt you intentionally. But he's volatile, and it might happen. I can't predict what he's going to do. It makes me uneasy."

She couldn't predict Caleb either. "He can get Faruk to tell us about the location and layout of the temple. He may be able to use him to take us in with some of those members he's supposed to be flying in. That's worth being a little uneasy."

"But you don't want me with you."

"We'll need what amounts to an army if we have to attack that temple. Wait until you hear from Venable that they've arrived in Damascus, then join them. Millet will have all his top goons there for the Offering." She smiled. "You'd make a fantastic general, Jock."

He shook his head. "That's MacDuff. I'm better at guerrilla tactics. You're sure?"

"I'm sure." She did not want to have to referee any conflict between Caleb and Jock. She could handle Caleb better on her own. The intimacy that was growing between them wasn't easily understood. Not even by me, she thought. She couldn't afford any interference. Every moment was a challenge. He held a power she had to learn to wield if she was to get through this nightmare.

And, together, they could find a way for her to dream again.

Day Seven

Caleb strolled up to her helicopter as it came into the small airport on the outskirts of Damascus, where he'd told her to land. "I'm flattered." He helped her out of the aircraft. "I only left you a matter of hours ago. You obviously couldn't wait to be with me again."

"You're right," Jane said dryly. "Waiting for anything isn't on my agenda at the moment."

"And you wanted to be here to remind me that I mustn't follow my natural instincts. You didn't trust me." He reached out and gently touched her cheek. "How wise you are, Jane."

Her skin was warm, tingling beneath his fingers. She wanted to step closer . . .

She shook her head to clear it and stepped back. "I thought I could be more useful here than waiting in Tel Aviv. As I told you on the phone, everything is in motion now."

He glanced at his watch. "And in an hour you should be receiving your call from Millet."

She nodded. "He's not going to allow me much time. I'm not going to be able to stall him. We have to find a way to get Eve out before whatever time he gives me runs out."

"That's why I'm here, isn't it? Faruk? It shouldn't be a problem."

"Can you get him to actually take us to the temple?"

"As I said, no problem."

Hope suddenly surged through her. It was the first bright beacon in all the hours since she'd found the coins. "Then we'd better go find him. Did you check his home address on the Net?"

He nodded. "But we won't bother to go there. After all, you're pressed for time."

"What do you —" Her gaze narrowed on

his face. "This airport. Faruk uses this airport?"

He nodded. "He has two cargo planes parked in that hangar over there."

"You couldn't have just told me that's why you wanted me to come here?"

"It was convenient. You had to land somewhere." He glanced away from her. "And maybe I was a little irritated that you tied my hands. I didn't feel like sharing." He smiled. "Not that way."

Intimacy.

Push it away.

"Too bad. This isn't about you . . . or me. It's about Eve. Have you contacted Faruk yet?"

He shook his head. "He's not here. He went to downtown Damascus after he came back from dropping off Millet and Eve. He should be back soon. I spent the last hour or so talking to mechanics and Nasra, the receptionist at the office, gathering information. Faruk seems to be pretty ordinary. Early forties, unmarried, quiet, doesn't talk much to the other pilots or mechanics. He's considered a good pilot. Definitely not a troublemaker."

"Just a good-old-boy cult member who likes to watch people stabbed to death."

"How often have you read stories about

serial killers whose neighbors say they can't believe their friend is the same man who did those killings?"

"Point taken. Where do we wait for Faruk to appear?"

"Definitely out of sight." He drew her into a hangar a few yards from the small brightly lit main office. "If your picture was circulated among the cult members, Faruk has probably seen it." He leaned back against the metal wall. "We don't want to put him on his guard. It will make things difficult." He saw her expression and smiled. "No, I'm not on the attack. I'll handle him gently. You've slapped my hands. How could I do otherwise?"

"Let me count the ways. You let me come blindly on his turf. You weren't worried about his recognizing me then."

"I was on watch. And I knew he wasn't due back yet. I took a chance." He made a face. "Though maybe I wanted an excuse to go after him. Who knows?"

"All I want from him is information. Faruk's a pilot, not one of Millet's killers. He's no real danger."

"We'll see." He was studying her. "You look as if you've been stretched on a rack. One touch, and you'd break. How long do you think you can go on?"

"Until we get Eve back." She gazed out at the tarmac. "And I won't break."

His intent gaze remained on her face. "It makes me angry seeing you like this, you know."

Her gaze shifted back to his face. "Why?"

He shrugged. "I've been wondering that myself. I thought I'd left all that protective bullshit behind me. But it appears that there are some tendrils of emotion that can't be uprooted. You . . . stir me."

She stared at him, speechless.

"I just thought you should know." His lips twisted. "You're always saying you don't understand me. Now you can see in what direction I'm heading. I don't think it's just the sex. I wouldn't have let you take me off the hunt for Faruk if it was only that." He held her gaze. "Though I could be wrong. I keep thinking of all the ways I want to have you."

She was suddenly vibrantly, physically, aware of everything about him. His hand resting on the doorjamb, the muscles of his chest and shoulders relaxed but possessing a catlike readiness, his eyes . . . Her chest was so tight that she couldn't breathe. "And that's supposed to make me understand you?"

"Maybe not. I thought I'd try. Sometimes,

I think, I get lonely. Though I thought I'd put that behind me, too." He suddenly chuckled. "But understanding me might cause you to shun me even more. Maybe I should count my blessings."

She was feeling an aching, almost tender, impulse to reach out, to comfort. It bewildered her. Surely no one on earth had less need for either of those emotions. He had even laughed at himself as he had said those words. Somehow that only made them more poignant. "I . . . don't shun you."

"Because I keep coming at you. It's easier for you to come to terms than push me away."

Damn, he could read her. "Right now I can't deal —"

"He's here." Caleb straightened, his gaze on the hangar across the tarmac. "Tall, a little plump, mustache. That's the description I got from Nasra, the receptionist."

Jane's gaze focused on the man in neat gray trousers and brown leather flight jacket who was unlocking the door of the hangar. As Caleb had said, Faruk looked very ordinary.

If anything about this nightmare was ordinary. "What happens now?"

"Nothing radical. I do a little tentative probing, then I go talk to him. You don't have to —" He stiffened, staring at Faruk.

Her gaze flew to his face. "What's wrong?"

"Nothing." He left the hangar. "Stay here. I should be back in a few minutes." He strolled across the tarmac. "Captain Faruk, may I have a word with you? I spoke to the receptionist at the front office, and she said that you might be just the man I need to fly a very valuable shipment of rugs to Rome."

Faruk turned and smiled. "Nasra is a smart woman. I'm the best, and I could give you a good price."

"I'm sure we'll be able to come to an agreement. I already feel a closeness that you —" Caleb bent double, his face contorted with pain. "No!"

Jane stiffened. What on earth was —

Faruk was staring at Caleb in bewilderment. "What's wrong? Are you ill?"

"Stomach." Caleb was stumbling back, his face white as a tombstone. He gasped, "Later." He turned and half ran, half reeled across the tarmac. The next moment he lurched into the hangar and fell against the wall where Jane was standing.

"Make sure — he's not following. Mustn't — see you." His face was beaded with sweat.

Jane tore her gaze away from Caleb to glance quickly across the tarmac. "Faruk's just standing there, looking confused. What the hell is wrong?"

"Can't talk — give — me a minute." He slid down the metal wall and leaned back, breathing hard.

Agony. The muscles of his neck were distended, his teeth clenched.

She grabbed his hand. "Shall I find a doctor?"

He shook his head.

"Dammit, what can I do?" She started to get to her feet, but his grasp held her locked to his side. "Let me go. I've got to —"

He shook his head. "No good."

"There has to be some —"

"Be quiet." He was shaking. "Quagmire."

"What? I don't —" Then she remembered what he had told her on the plane when she'd asked him if he ever ran across anyone he couldn't mentally manipulate.

Quagmire. Intense pain. Smothering.

I went too deep and was unconscious for two days.

"Quagmire," she repeated. "Faruk?"

He nodded jerkily.

"Dear God."

"A minute. Give — me a minute."

She didn't know if he could stand another minute of that pain, she thought desperately. The skin was drawn tight over his cheekbones as he fought the spasms. She had never felt so helpless.

She couldn't help him.

She had to help him.

She had to *do* something.

She slid her arms around him and drew him close. "I'm sorry," she whispered. "I'm so sorry." She stroked his hair back from his face. "I can't take this. Tell me what to do."

He didn't answer. Lord, he was cold. She held him closer and tried to share her warmth. "Relax. We'll stay like this for a while and you'll be okay." She prayed she was telling the truth. "Just relax . . ."

Five minutes passed.

Fifteen minutes.

He was no longer shaking.

Thank God.

Twenty minutes.

He lifted his head and looked down at her. "Hello."

"Hi." She drew a relieved breath that came from the depths of her being. "You scared me."

"I can tell." The corners of his lips quirked. "At the moment I don't feel in the least bit shunned. But I don't believe I want to go through that again. We'll have to work on some other kind of solution."

She rolled away from him, sat up, and gazed at him searchingly. He might be joking, but he was still very pale. "I didn't know what to do. Are you better?"

He nodded. "It wasn't bad. I got out soon enough."

"That wasn't bad?" She shook her head. "It seemed damn bad to me."

"Maybe I was just making a bid for sympathy," he said lightly as he slowly sat up. "You know you can't trust me."

He still wasn't entirely normal. She wanted to touch him, stroke him, make all the pain go away. "Stop joking. This isn't funny."

"No, part of it was hell but the last part was kind of nice. There's always a balance." He put his hand out to the metal wall and levered himself up. "But I think I need a drink. Let's go find a bar."

"We don't have a car."

"Of course we do." He took her elbow and headed for the entrance. "One of the mechanics I talked to insisted that he lend me his car while I was in the city."

"How convenient. Another long-lost best friend?"

"You've got it. I think I saw a little coffee bar about two miles down the road. Let's see if they have anything stronger under the counter for the Westerners."

■ ■ ■ ■

The coffee bar was small, with only a few tables and almost empty except for four Arabs who stared at Jane coldly when they walked through the door.

"Prejudice seems to be raising its ugly head," she murmured. "The locals don't approve of women outside their homes. So much for freeing the masses."

"Do you want me to have a talk with them?"

"No!" She sat down at a corner table. "I don't want you to hunt, and I don't want you to manipulate. I just want you to rest and have your drink."

"How protective you sound." He motioned for a swarthy, young waiter, who was glaring at Jane. "It wouldn't hurt me. Faruk was one of those freakish exceptions. What do you want?"

"Just a coffee."

A few minutes later the waiter set a whiskey in front of Caleb and a tiny glass brimming with steaming black coffee before Jane.

"That looks stronger than my whiskey," Caleb said. "Want to switch?"

"No."

He downed the whiskey. "You're smart. Foul stuff." He motioned the waiter for another one. "But it keeps the blood going."

"Is whiskey a cure-all for this . . ." She searched for the word again. "This quagmire."

"No, it just causes the chill to go away." He looked down into his whiskey. "I'm sorry, Jane. I told you it would be no problem. It was a big problem."

"You're sorry? How could you help it? You're the one who went through more pain than a victim of the Spanish Inquisition. What if you'd gone into shock?"

"I didn't." He frowned. "And there has to be a way to control it and do the job. I've just been too wary to play around with it. It's so rare, and it was easier to walk away." He grimaced. "Or crawl away. I wasn't a very admirable specimen, was I?"

"Play around with it? That's like playing Russian roulette with every chamber filled with bullets. You just have to wonder which one is going to kill you."

"There has to be a way."

Dear God, he was actually serious. "The way is to use Faruk like a normal person would do it. Maybe we can bug his plane when he takes those other members to the temple."

"Millet will kill Eve as soon as he knows the temple is under attack. We'll still need the layout of the temple if we're to get to Eve before he knows we're there."

She knew that he was right, and the alternative of blundering around searching for her was terrifying. "I thought about trying to get Roland to give me the information as part of the deal, but I couldn't trust him." She paused. "But there's something else that could work."

He studied her, then smiled faintly. "The other reason why you came to Damascus after me. You need me to help you dream."

"I can't take a chance on doing it on my own. What if my sleep isn't deep enough to dream? You kept me asleep for a long time. We have to do it together."

He shook his head, still smiling. "And is this your idea of how a normal person would handle the situation? My, how your viewpoint has changed."

She couldn't argue. "Everything is different now. I'm just trying to keep everyone alive."

"So am I," Caleb said quietly. "That's why I think I should work on overcoming this —"

"No!" She finished her coffee. "Let's get

out of here. It's almost time for Millet to call me, and I don't want to take it here with all these men in the bar looking daggers at me." She stood up. "One bastard at a time."

Jane and Caleb had been sitting in the car outside the bar for only fifteen minutes when Jane's phone rang.

"Have you been waiting for me?" Millet asked. "I imagine you're very torn. It's not every day that anyone is given the opportunity to make the ultimate sacrifice to save another. You're very special."

"And you're very nuts."

"Ugly."

"Did you hurt Eve?"

"I'd like to say yes, but I decided that I should save myself for you, Jane."

Relief surged through her. Roland must know Millet very well to be able to manipulate him to this extent. "May I talk to Eve again?"

"No, I'm not feeling generous. No contact until the exchange." He paused. "If there is to be an exchange. Is Eve going to live, Jane?"

"Yes." She moistened her lips. "But I don't trust you. You'll kill Eve, too, if you get the chance. I'm not going to walk into your trap until I'm sure Eve is out of it."

"I have no use for Eve Duncan."

"That doesn't mean you wouldn't enjoy tearing her limb from limb. I've seen your work, Millet."

He chuckled. "Yes, you did. I was exceptionally artistic when I was working on Celine Denarve. I did enjoy that evening enormously."

Poor butterfly, caught, pierced, pinned.

"It's not going to happen to Eve. What are your plans?"

"I'm going to have you flown here to the temple and send Eve Duncan out on the same plane."

"Good God, do you think I'm that gullible?"

"No, but I thought I'd try. Sometimes desperation robs one of common sense. Suppose we meet somewhere in the desert and do the exchange. That should be safer for both of you."

"I'll consider it."

"Arrogant bitch." His voice had harshened. "If I weren't short on time, you'd have no choice at all. I'd kill Duncan, then go after you. It wouldn't be long before I'd have it all."

"But I do have a choice. Not much of one, but I'm not giving it up."

"I need you at the temple by seven tomorrow night for the Offering. The exchange has to take place in time for me to get back to the temple before that. Five, six, at the latest. Do you understand? I *need* an Offering and I won't quibble about taking Eve Duncan if I can't have you."

"I know you won't."

"I'll call you in four hours, and you'd better have set a place for the transfer. I'll need to send my men ahead to make sure you're not setting a trap. That wouldn't be wise, Jane. One sign, and I slice your Eve's throat." He hung up.

Her hand was shaking as she pressed the disconnect. It was what she had been expecting, but the violence and ugliness was striking hard at her. Millet's vicious intensity had been like an exploding bullet. Everything had been leading up to this time and she had a crazy feeling that it was inevitable that Millet would triumph no matter what she did.

Tomorrow was the first of April.

Judas's birthday.

The day of her death.

"Jane?"

She turned to look at Caleb in the seat next to her. "Four hours. I have to tell him where we'll meet in the desert. He wants the exchange by five tomorrow evening." She tried to keep her voice even. "He doesn't want me to be late for the Offering. That wouldn't be polite."

Caleb muttered a curse. "He got to you."

"No . . . Yes." Her lips were trembling. "He's such a monster. They're all such monsters. Sometimes I can't believe it. *Blasphemer.* They keep using that word. Cults and sacrifices and archaic words that shouldn't even exist any longer. They should all be in the Dark Ages. It doesn't seem real. I thought it was bad the night that Celine died, but it's been going on so long. Tomorrow will be eight days, Caleb. Every minute has been like a dagger stabbing at me." She tried to keep her voice steady. "I'm ready for it to be over."

"And it will be." His hands were gently cupping her face. "You'll go through it all and come out clean and bright. It will be fine. I promise you."

"I'll be better soon." She should move away from him, but she felt warm and treasured with his hands cupping her cheeks. She needed to feel as if she was more than the pawn in Millet's dirty game. "I have to think how we'll be able to handle this. I should call Roland, but nothing is clear right now."

"It will be clear soon." He was looking down into her eyes. His own eyes were dark and soft, and she couldn't look away from them. So much gentleness, so much sensuality, so much intensity, that she was caught, held. It was flowing over her, around her, within her.

His hands left her face and moved to her shoulders. "Stop fighting. You don't have to be strong right now. It's not going to make any difference. I'm the only one here, and I'll never judge you." He was pulling her close. "You helped me. Now let me help you."

She could hear his heart beneath her ear, and she didn't move. She was safe, wonderfully content, enfolded in velvet darkness.

"That's right, Jane," he whispered. "Come dream with me . . ."

TWENTY

Millet is coming, Eve thought hazily. She could hear his footsteps on the marble tiles in the hall. Concentrate. She had to focus. It was difficult with her shoulder throbbing with hot pain. Fever. It must be getting infected.

Ignore it. She had to concentrate on doing what Jane needed from her.

"You and your dear Jane are going to be reunited," Millet said mockingly as he unlocked the door and entered the room. "She's going to do the right thing and save you from the knife like a good daughter. I couldn't wait to rush here and tell you."

"Because you knew it would hurt me." She slowly sat up on the cot. "You're chock-full of malice and satisfaction and who better to share it with than a victim?"

His smile faded. "But you're not giving me all the satisfaction that I hoped. Where is your fear? I thought that if I gave you time alone, you'd have to time to think and anticipate."

"And dread?" She met his gaze. "Because it doesn't matter what deal you struck with Jane. You're not going to let me go. You'll kill me the minute you get your hands on Jane."

"That's not true," he said softly. "I won't have time to toy with her before the Offering. I feel cheated. It's only right that I keep you alive for a short while to amuse me."

"And then I'll end up on the altar, too?"

"A private Offering. It will be convenient. You're here. Your death might as well be dedicated to the Master. His light will shine brighter on me."

"How can you believe that?"

"How can I not? Look how far I've climbed. In the village, I lived with a father and mother who beat me and told me that I would never climb out of that dungheap. Now I'm the Guardian. I can have anything or anyone that pleases me. It had to be Judas showing his pleasure in everything I do."

She shook her head. "You just changed dungheaps."

His lips tightened. "Arrogant bitch. You're just like Jane MacGuire."

"Thank you." She had to curb her tongue. This wasn't the way to find out anything but what a degenerate scumbag he was. She was silent a moment. "You think you're king of this pile of crap you call a temple. When you brought me here, I didn't see anything impressive about it. It's small, not much ornamentation, a copy of a dozen other temples I saw in Greece. That makes you king of nothing."

His cheeks flushed. "It's magnificent. Hadar said we had no need of pomp. We have the Offering Room, and that's all that's important to Judas."

"And your glorious Offering Room is probably as unimpressive as the rest of this place. You made sure I didn't see it when we came here." She added deliberately, "As unimpressive as you must be when you make your so-called Offering. Do they laugh at you, Millet?"

He was cursing beneath his breath. She had thought that last taunt would tip the balance.

He strode toward her and jerked her off the cot to her feet. "They worship me. They know how important I am. You don't know what you're talking about." His eyes were glittering, and his grip on her arm was bruising. "But I'll show you. You'll see where your Jane MacGuire is going to die. You'll see where you're going to die." He was pulling her toward the door. "You'll see all the power and feel the souls who have gone before you."

Good. He was taking her from the room. For a moment she had been afraid she would only loose that sadistic streak. It had been a precarious balance. "You don't have to pull me. I'm not fighting you."

He released her, then frowned as he saw her sway. "You're weak. Can you walk?"

"I can walk." She got her balance and headed for the door. She was weak. Ignore it, she said to herself. "I have a little fever."

"What? Not as strong as you thought you were?" He opened the door. "Come along. I can't wait to see a little more of that strength crumble."

The corridor was straight, with no doors on either side. High ceilings, with a coffered stone inset. Guards. They turned left at the end of the corridor and went a hundred yards, then faced a huge arched doorway guarded by another two men dressed in black leather.

How many other guards had they passed? Two at her door. Four on the long corridor. I'm trying, Jane.

Millet gestured mockingly for her to precede him through the arched doorway. "The Offering Room."

She went through the doorway and stopped in shock. It looked like a small stadium, with at least forty rows of stone benches. In the center was a black granite altar facing a wall on which the Judas mosaic hovered like a dark vulture.

"I told you. It's magnificent, isn't it?" Millet asked. He pointed to a spot on the left side of the altar. "That's where I stand. Where all the audience can see me." He smiled. "And the Offering can see me. In that moment, they know I'm a god. Able to take their life or give it. I can see it in their eyes." He held Eve's gaze. "I'll see that look in her eyes."

She tore her eyes away from him to the far left, where a ramp led into the stadium. "Where does that go?"

"Outside. No member is permitted in the temple until the time of the Offering. Then they can only come to the stadium. They have to understand that they may have power in their own world, but here I'm the only power."

"As long as you stay Guardian. What if they boot you out?"

"That won't happen. I keep my eye on anyone who seems unstable. They have accidents. Or become candidates for the Offering."

"But you were afraid of the consequences if they found out you'd lost Hadar's Tablet."

He scowled. "I wasn't afraid. It was a matter that had to be addressed. The tablet is considered holy. I'll find a way to get it back after I get rid of the MacGuire woman."

"How many members will be here tomorrow night?"

"Between nine hundred and a thousand. There are a few thousand more around the world, but if they have an adequate excuse, they're permitted to excuse themselves once every five years. It's important that they attend frequently, not only to do homage but to witness. Witnesses can be declared accomplices in a court of law. Guilt is the strongest bond in the world. I have photos taken of everyone who attends the Offering and make sure they know that the pictures are kept in a safe place."

"Blackmail? Charming. And you decide what excuse is adequate?"

"Of course, I'm the Guardian. I rule the Offering." He turned to her. "I've decided I'll let you see the MacGuire Offering tomorrow night. It will be thrilling for you. The roar of the crowd, the chanting. I'm the king. I'm death. They all fear me. It will be a preview of your own private ceremony."

"I can hardly wait."

His exhilaration faded. "You're not as nervous as I hoped." He studied her. "Perhaps it's because you're ill. Your cheeks are flushed, and your lips are so dry, they're cracked. I may have to have Faruk fly you in some antibiotics. I don't want your reactions to be dulled."

"Perish the thought." She had obviously seen all she was going to see. Guards. Corridors. Main ramp to the stadium. Now, give him something to make him think he'd won. "You've proved your point. This Offering Room is . . . a little frightening. I'm ready to go back to my room."

"It's my decision whether you go or stay." Then he slowly nodded. "But maybe you did have a jolt. Now you know that the Offering is actually going to happen. It can't be stopped. For two thousand years, the Master has taken his vengeance."

"And how many times have you presided?"

"Seventeen at the Offerings themselves."

"And I'd bet hundreds more on the side."

He smiled. "But experience is a fine teacher. The members don't like a quick cut. They want a scream or two, and I know just how to please them." He gestured. "Now we'll go back and let you rest and absorb. I want you fresh for tomorrow night."

She headed for the arch. She was dizzier than she had been when they started. She was glad that she'd been able to concentrate on the way to the Offering Room.

Did you get it, Jane?

I'll try again later, but this may have been my best chance.

I hope you were with me. . . .

Got it!

Darkness lessening, Jane realized.

Gray.

Lighter.

Lighter still.

Fast. So fast.

Much faster than the last time.

Caleb!

Her lids flew open.

No Caleb.

She was no longer in his arms as she had been when she had gone to sleep. She was still in the car but leaning against the passenger door.

She sat up groggily and pushed her hair back from her face. Where was Caleb? Had he gone back into the bar? She had to tell him about the temple. She had to tell him that Eve —

They weren't in the bar parking lot any longer.

Her heart was pounding with panic as she realized where the car was parked now.

It was a few yards from the door of Faruk's hangar.

There should be a way I can work it out, Caleb had said.

No!

She opened the passenger door and was out of the car in seconds.

No. No. No.

She threw open the door of the hangar.

538

The harsh overhead lights were blazing.

And Caleb was crumpled on the floor across the room.

She ran toward him.

White. So white.

Blood trickling from the corner of his mouth.

Dead?

Please God. Don't let him be dead.

She fell to her knees on the concrete. Was he breathing? "Why?" Tears were pouring down her cheeks. "Dammit, why would you do this? Don't you die. Do you hear me? Don't you die, Caleb."

"I . . . hear you." His eyes were still closed. "I'm . . . not dying. I need to rest. It was . . . not fun."

Relief, then anger. "Stupid. Incredibly stupid." She couldn't stop the tears. "After what happened to you before, you went right back for an encore?"

"We needed to know where the temple is located." His eyes opened. "Faruk . . . knew." He smiled. "Tears?" He reached up and touched her damp cheek. "Nice . . ."

"You don't deserve them."

"Of course I do. I'm a hero. I saved the day."

She wiped her cheeks on the back of her hand. "There's blood coming out of your mouth. Do you have internal injuries?"

"Nothing so dramatic. I bit my tongue when I was trying to persuade Faruk." He struggled up on one elbow. "I think I was clenching my teeth. I don't remember."

"Where is Faruk?"

"Over there, behind the plane. He's fast asleep. He'll stay that way for the next two hours. When he wakes, he'll think he was just exhausted and curled up for a nap."

She stared at him in bewilderment. "How? I *saw* you. He nearly put you into shock before. And you said that you got out before he caused any real damage."

"I had to find a way to go in without being pulled deep." The color was coming back into his cheeks and he sat up. "I told you, it was like sinking into a quagmire. You either walk carefully, lightly, over a marsh, or you skirt around it. I've been diving in and backing out." He added, "The problem is that I'm very strong. And the only way I could walk lightly was to divide my attention."

"When you put me to sleep," she said.

"And kept you asleep. It worked . . . sort of. Even then, it was difficult as hell." He added soberly, "I was able to get Faruk to give me coordinates and draw a rough map of the area around the temple. But there's no way I'd be able to keep him under control if I tried to make him take us there." He frowned. "Unless I can think of a —"

"We don't need him," she interrupted quickly. "You found out everything we have to know. We can send the coordinates to Joe. You're sure Faruk is just sleeping?"

"See for yourself." He got to his feet. "Maybe I'd better check. You were coming back out of the dream stage when I was putting him under. I was distracted."

Faruk was slumbering peacefully, curled on his side.

"He won't remember?"

"No, he won't remember anything but talking to me about a rug shipment and deciding the money wasn't good enough." He took her elbow. "Eve?"

"She has a fever. That bastard hasn't given her any antibiotics." She smiled grimly. "But she made sure I can draw a map of the interior of the temple and that I know the number of guards in each corridor."

"What a unique woman." He moved toward the door. "Then let's get out of here and find a place where we can send the info to Joe Quinn and Venable. We've still got a long way to go, but now we've got a start."

Long way? They had to juggle Roland and Millet and some thousand or so cult members and try to keep Eve alive. Damn right, they had a hell of a long way to go.

"Then by all means, save the day, Caleb," she said dryly. "You do it so well."

"I do, don't I?" he said cheerfully. "I'll work on it."

Roland phoned Jane two hours later. "I can't find a way to get Millet away from your Eve. He doesn't want to leave the temple on the day of the Offering. That's his big day. He's in his glory."

"I'm sure you can arrange something. I meant it. I'll make sure you never get those coins."

"I realize that you'd do it. We all have our weaknesses, and yours is Eve Duncan." He paused. "So I've got to find a way to give her to you. But you're the one who has to make sure Millet is far enough away from her to make it work. He's given you the option of choosing the transfer point. I want him at least forty minutes away from the temple."

"But I don't know where this temple is," Jane said. "And he's supposed to bring Eve for the transfer, remember?"

"But you don't really think that's going to happen? He knows that he has you. He'll scout out the area and set up an ambush.

He's not a great brain, but he's very clever at what he does."

"He won't bring Eve?"

"No way on earth. He'll hold her in case something goes wrong."

"At the temple."

"Yes."

"Then how do we get her out of that temple?"

"We send Millet after you, and we go in and get her."

"How?"

"There's a secret tunnel that leads from outside to the corridor going to the Offering Room. Only the Guardian was supposed to know that it exists, but Adah Ziller was very persuasive. She told me that she and Millet used to play some of their erotic games in the passage. It was a kick for her. Later, she used the passage to sneak into the Offering Room and steal the tablet."

"Why do I have to go? Why can't you bring her out that way yourself?"

"Because we have to go past Millet's guards to get to her. They know your face. They probably know that an exchange is going to take place. I've made sure that Millet's men don't know me. I couldn't get to the room where Millet is keeping Eve without an okay from Millet." He paused.

"Unless it seemed I had a purpose in those corridors. What better purpose than bringing the sacrifice for the Offering? I get you and Eve out of the room with some pushing and shoving and general rough handling, and we go back down through the passage."

Jane was silent a moment. "It's too much of a risk. I couldn't trust you."

"But you'll still have the coins. We'll meet at a designated spot a few miles from the temple, and I'll have your bottle examined by my expert. You can bring one man, Gavin or MacDuff or anyone else you choose, and have him stay with the coins until we bring Eve out of the temple. Of course, I'll also have someone there to guard the coins on my behalf. Unfortunately, I have as little trust as you, Jane. The moment that I take possession of the coins, you're free to go. I'm quite certain you'll protect your right to do that."

"But then I'll know where your temple is located."

"But will I care? The Judas coins are all I ever wanted. I'm afraid I'm not truly a religious man. It was useful to me on occasion. On the offering table, I disposed of two business associates who got in my way. But I'm careful. No one can prove I'm one of the chosen. Money blurs the memory and twists truth. I'll let you and Millet battle. I don't give a damn who kills whom after I get the coins." He said softly, "I'll be the only one who really wins. So what about it, Jane? It's the best deal I can give you."

"Where should I meet you?"

He chuckled. "So that you can figure out the location of the temple? No, I'll tell you the meeting place after you're in the air and five minutes from the destination."

She hesitated. "Then how can I tell Millet where we should arrange the exchange?"

"I'll give you the coordinates for that." He paused. "Agree, Jane. It's your best shot."

"I'll think about it."

"Don't think too long. I want those coins. I might have to have a talk with Millet about enjoying his time with Eve to a greater extent." He hung up.

She turned down the volume and glanced at Caleb. "You heard? He wants me to walk into the lion's mouth."

Caleb's gaze was on her face. "And you're thinking about doing it."

"We can make it safer. We can make sure that Millet is a good distance away from the temple. We were going to bring Jock and the others into it anyway. He told me that he was good at guerrilla tactics."

"There's no way it can be safe," he said flatly.

"Safer," she repeated. "And we knew that Millet wouldn't give up Eve if he could prevent it. She's a witness against him. So Roland is right. Millet would set a trap for me."

"That doesn't mean that Roland isn't going to do the same thing."

"You're not telling me anything I don't know." She stared thoughtfully down at the phone. "But we might work out a way to use this ploy of Roland's when there wouldn't be a chance if I dealt strictly with Millet. And I'd be with Eve. I'd be able to help her more if we're in the same place."

"And you wouldn't trust anyone else to be there for her," he said roughly. "Only you. Okay, I know you wouldn't trust me, but what about Jock Gavin. What about Joe Quinn? Let someone else take the risk."

She raised her gaze. "You know that I'd have a better chance to get to Eve. And you know that Millet will kill her if he thinks he's going down. She's hurt, Caleb. Someone's got to be there if she needs help."

He muttered a curse. "And who's going to be there if you need help?"

"Who do you think?" She smiled faintly. "Eve."

"A united front," he said curtly. "And you think that's all you need. But this time, you may find it's not quite enough."

"Then we have to do whatever is necessary to make up the difference." She added, "I'm not fool enough to think that I can do this alone. That would be crazy. All I'm saying is that we've got to have a plan that will give us a chance."

"And still lets you go into that damn temple with Eve."

"Yes." He wasn't going to like this. "And I want you to be the one to stay with the coins and guard them."

"Hell, no. Don't try to stick me with that kind of bullshit milk-toast job."

"Milk toast? As soon as Roland takes me away from those Judas coins, whoever he leaves with you is going to have orders to take off with them." She paused. "And that means that you're going to be in the way."

He thought about it. "If I protect your coins and get rid of Roland's man, who's going to try to cut my throat, am I on my own?"

He was always on his own. He meant he wanted her blessing to turn hunter.

Why not? she thought recklessly. He would probably do it anyway no matter what she said. He had told her that savagery could be selective, and if it concerned Eve, she would have no qualms about it.

It did concern Eve. Tomorrow, Eve could live or die depending on what they all did or didn't do to save her. It was time to forget about anything but getting her away from Millet alive.

"Do what you like." She lifted her phone again to call Jock. "As long as it doesn't interfere with any plan we can put in place to get Eve out."

"I won't interfere." His lips twisted. "And I'd be touched that you trusted me enough to give me carte blanche if I didn't realize that this time you really didn't give a damn. You wouldn't care if I brought that temple down like the biblical Samson did."

Is he right? Jane wondered wearily. The answer came back clear and direct as an arrow. Of course he's right.

Stop the killing. Let their damn Judas temple collapse on the heads of those bastards.

5:05 p.m.
Day Eight

"There it is." Caleb nodded down at the knoll they were flying over. "And I believe that's our Mr. Roland and party." He glanced at Jane. "Last chance to change

548

your mind."

She shook her head and turned to Marc Lestall, the pilot. "But fly around that knoll and make sure there's no one else there but them."

"Right." Marc banked to the left.

Three men as Roland had promised, Jane thought. The expert to examine the bottle, Roland himself, and the third man, who was probably fairly lethal. A jeep and a motor-cycle parked in the trees.

"Clear," Marc said. "Should I land?"

"Just a minute." Caleb dialed Jock. "Millet?" He hung up and turned to Jane. "Ten minutes south of here heading toward the place you agreed on with a jeep full of men and firepower." He paused. "And no Eve."

It was what they had expected.

"Then we'll have to go find her. Remember, try to delay any move you make against Roland's man in case Roland checks back with him. I want to keep from bringing the situation to a head before we have to do it." She nodded at Marc. "Let's go down."

Three minutes later, the helicopter was on the ground, and Jane jumped out of the aircraft.

"You're late," Roland said. "But considering that your nerves are probably coming into play, I'll forgive you. You've been dread-ing this day for some time, haven't you?" He smiled. "And Millet has been looking forward to it with anticipation."

"It's just another day. It's you ghouls who have made it into something horrible." She called to Marc, who was still at the controls. "Get out of here, Marc."

The pilot's gaze was on Roland. "You're certain?"

"Go," Caleb said.

A moment later, Marc was lifting off.

Jane handed Roland the portable container. "You turn the switch to open the case. Where's your expert?"

He turned to a thin, tall man wearing glasses. "George Kandor. George, take the case and run a check on it."

"Be careful," Jane said. "And don't remove the stopper."

"I know my business." Kandor took the case and turned back to his equipment beside the tree. "I won't be able to tell much, Roland."

"I just want to make sure that bottle contains the same objects that were in the photo." Roland turned to Jane. "This won't take long. I know you're eager to be on your way." His gaze shifted to Caleb. "You must be Seth Caleb. You're something of an unknown factor to both Millet and me.

We've been able to access your CIA and Interpol records, and they've come back with very little information. Which means that you've been exceptionally law-abiding or that you're very clever."

"Guess," Caleb said.

"It doesn't matter. I've got both possibilities covered. Though I really expected Jane to bring Jock Gavin. Gavin has the reputation of being lethal." He gestured to the fair-haired man, who had been silent throughout the exchange. "Carl Trobell. Naturally, I can't tap Millet's resources, but Trobell comes with excellent references." He smiled. "He has almost as much experience as Jock Gavin, and he's fully capable of protecting my coins."

Trobell nodded, but didn't speak.

Dead eyes, Jane thought. Like the photos of killers you see in the newspapers who had committed hideous crimes, and you realized that there was nothing behind those eyes that had anything to do with humanity. She quickly glanced away from him. "They're not yours yet."

"Soon." Roland paused. "I'm sure you have a weapon. Give it to me."

"Go to hell."

He shrugged. "I can understand your concern. I'll let it pass as a gesture of good faith." He turned to Kandor, who was replacing the bottle in the case. "Well?"

"It appears to be the same as the photo you showed me."

"I thought it would be." He turned back to Jane. "You wouldn't take a chance on cheating me. You have too much at stake. Shall we go? I have a jeep parked in the trees, as I'm sure you verified on that pass."

She nodded and started to turn away but suddenly whirled back to face Caleb.

"It's all right," he said quietly. "Stop worrying, Jane." He smiled. "I'm Samson, remember."

But he hadn't been Samson when he'd faced Faruk yesterday. He'd been tragically, almost fatally weak. What if Trobell was like Faruk? Or even if he wasn't, every instinct was telling her that Trobell was every bit as deadly as Roland claimed.

"Eve," Caleb reminded her.

Yes, Eve. Eve needed her, and she couldn't change her mind now.

She whirled and headed for the trees.

"What is it?" Jane got out of the jeep and gazed at the sign that was posted on the barbed-wire fence. "What does it say?"

"Contaminated. Deadly." He swung open the gate. "Words to that effect, I believe. I don't speak Russian."

"Russian? In the middle of Syria?"

"Yes, the Russians did some bacteria experiments here during the Cold War." He got back in the jeep. "Do you see that huge building over there? It was the main lab before the accident. One day there was an unfortunate leak in one of the tanks, which killed several scientists and about two hundred workers. They examined the ground surrounding the lab and decided that it was going to be deadly for the next century. The installation has been deserted ever since then."

" 'Unfortunate leak,' " she repeated.

"Unfortunate for them. Fortunate for the chosen. The temple is in the mountains directly behind the lab. Hadar made sure that it was well hidden in the rocks, and it was safe for centuries as long as it was guarded. But modern-day technology made it more difficult to conceal." He smiled. "So we decided to take advantage of the lab. After the accident, the Syrian government was only anxious to conceal the deal they'd made with the Russians. The Russians discreetly pulled out of the area."

"And you falsified reports that the land was contaminated."

"We have friends in high places. No one

dares come near the lab now. So our members are entirely safe from discovery when they come to the Offering." He parked in front of the rear door of the installation. "And Millet was able to build his secret tunnel from the lab to the temple." He pointed to a bluff some distance away. "The temple is behind those massive boulders. The main entrance of the temple faces the other way." He took out a flashlight from the glove box. "We'll go in the back door." He started to laugh. "It just reminded me of Adah. She was always fond of using the back door."

Twenty-One

The passageway was long, dark, and winding, the ceiling barely seven feet high. It's like the tunnels in tombs I visited in Egypt, Jane thought.

"Keep up," Roland said, beaming his light on her face. "Mustn't hang back. I'm judging that we may have another forty minutes at most before Millet comes roaring back. We have to be on our way before he gets here. Only a little farther to go. We should be under the Offering Room now."

Under the Offering Room.

She deliberately slowed.

"Frightened?" Roland asked softly. "It's easy to be brave and self-sacrificing when you're not this close to the end."

She stopped. "But you said that it wasn't the end. We made a deal."

"And of course, I'll keep it."

She didn't move.

He pushed her forward. "Go!"

She staggered, lost her balance, and stretched out her hand to the wall of the passage to catch herself. "Don't touch me. I can't see anything. Shine that beam ahead of us."

The beam focused on the dark corridor, and Jane strode forward. "Let's get out of here. I hate close places."

Trobell was going to make a move, Caleb thought. But he couldn't tell when or how.

The bastard was hard to read and when Caleb went in and tried to manipulate him it was like wading through tar. He was blank yet focused. Caleb had run across an occasional schizophrenic who had that same mental profile. Trobell was very likely genuinely insane.

He glanced at his watch — 5:50. He'd been waiting until six to move, as he'd promised Jane, but Trobell seemed to be on his own schedule.

"You're watching me," Trobell said. "You want to kill me."

"Do I?"

"Roland said whoever she brought would want to kill me."

"And what are you going to do about it?"

"I'm not going to kill you." He turned away and pulled out his gun. "Yet."

The next moment he was gone, running for the trees. No, running toward one particular tree where Kandor, Roland's coin expert, sat.

Kandor's eyes widened as he saw the gun. "What are —"

Trobell shot the man in the chest.

Then he was whirling on Caleb.

But Caleb was gone, drawing his own gun as he streaked toward the trees, zigzagging in and out as Trobell got off two more shots.

Get to cover, then go on the offensive, he told himself. Too early, but he'd done his best to delay.

Sorry, Jane.

No, that was a lie. He wasn't sorry that he had an excuse to break free and go on the hunt. He was never sorry about that. He was just sorry that he'd have to struggle to strike a balance that would please both him and Jane.

He'd reached the trees and glanced over his shoulder.

Trobell was starting after him.

"Come on," Caleb murmured. "I have time. I'll wait for you. Let's see how good you are . . ."

"The door that leads to the corridor by the Offering Room is just ahead," Roland said.

"It took longer than I thought to get through the tunnel. We'll have to hurry."

Jane's pace quickened. "Then stop talking and let's go."

"One more thing." He pushed her against the door. "I'm sure you have a weapon, and gestures of good faith can only go so far. If one of those guards searched you, it would be all over." He reached into her windbreaker pocket and pulled out the 38 Special. "Nice efficient weapon. I'm sure you're very competent with it." He slipped the gun in the pocket of his own jacket. "You're very competent at most things, aren't you?"

"Let's go," she said through her teeth.

"But I have to add one more touch of authenticity." He slapped her with such force her head snapped to one side. "That does it. Your lip is even bleeding a little." He tore the front of her shirt open. "Now you look like a suitably abused prisoner."

Her lip was stinging, and she wanted to punch him in the gut. Don't fight back. Not until I get to Eve. "And you enjoyed it."

"I believe I did." He reached behind her to open the door. "I'm not generally a brutal man, but you've caused me a great deal of trouble." He pushed her forward. "You'll forgive the roughness, but the first guard is right down the corridor. We have

558

to impress him."

"No!" Eve sat bolt upright on the cot as Roland pushed Jane into the room. "Dammit, Jane, why? It's not going to do any good. He won't let me go."

"I know." Jane moved across the room. "You look terrible." Eve's eyes were sunk and dark-rimmed. She touched her forehead. "And you're burning up."

"You shouldn't have listened to them."

"Can you walk?"

"Of course I can walk." She looked at Roland. "Who are you?"

"Roland," Jane said. "He tells me that he's going to get us out of here. Isn't that right, Roland?"

"You sound skeptical. And after all I've done." His phone rang, and he glanced at the ID. "My friend, Trobell." He answered. "Roland."

He listened, then said, "Yes, you've done everything right. I'll be there to pick you up shortly." He hung up. "It seems that your friend, Caleb, had a fatal accident. His neck is broken."

She stiffened with shock. He was lying. He had to be lying.

Dead eyes. She could see Trobell's face before her.

No, there had to be a mistake.

But Trobell had been on the phone with Roland.

"I'm sorry." Roland's mocking gaze was on her face. "You appear to be upset. Was Caleb more than a business acquaintance?"

She wouldn't believe it. Caleb might have left Trobell alive, but that didn't mean he couldn't control him. But what if that hadn't happened?

Dear God.

"Jane." Eve reached out and touched her arm.

"Yes, definitely upset." Roland pulled out the gun from his jacket pocket. "But you'll be happy to know that you'll be able to join him soon."

She shouldn't have let him know that his words had cut deep. She had to get a grip. She looked him in the eye. "You told Trobell to kill Caleb."

"Oh yes, that's why I got the very best."

"And now you have the coins, and you have no need to keep us alive. What about Kandor?"

"He was a witness. Trobell was to take him out first." He glanced at his watch. "It's fifteen to seven. Now we can all settle down for an evening of fun entertainment. Millet should be back any minute."

"It was a setup."

"You're a clever woman. You suspected that could be the case. But you were desperate enough to take the chance." He nodded at Eve. "I always thought you might be the way we could trap her. You've been a valuable asset. I think I'm going to truly regret having to let Millet have his way with you."

"Let her go," Jane said. "Take her out of here after this damn ceremony starts. I'll do anything. What do you want?"

"I'm afraid you no longer have any bargaining power. I have the coins." He added, "And I have to stay with Millet for a little while longer. He has something I need."

"If you have those coins, you'll have all the power you'll ever want. And you told me you didn't care about this damn cult."

"Did I fail to mention that Millet has photos of me as well as the other members at the Offerings? It would be so much easier to deny any connection without that bit of proof. No, I have to have those photos." He turned to the door. "Now I have to leave you and go meet Millet in the Offering Room. For once, he'll be very pleased with me." He glanced back at Jane. "I wish you hadn't gotten in my way. I'm really not going to enjoy the Offering tonight."

"You're lying," she said. "You'll love every

minute of it. You like to pretend that you're different from Millet, but you're both savages, just like Hadar, who built this temple."

His smile faded. "Perhaps you're right. I'll see when I watch Millet tear into you with his dagger." He opened the door, and they were suddenly bombarded by a roar of sound; laughter, excited chatter.

"They've just let the members into the Offering Room," Roland paused, listening. "All that excitement is for you, Jane."

"Blasphemer. Blasphemer. Blasphemer."

Jane's hands clenched into fists. That horrible, archaic word again.

"Yes, all for you," Roland said. "I believe I'll join them for the next chorus. I'll see you when the guards bring you to —" He was suddenly thrown back into the room. "What the —"

"Out!" Caleb was in the room. "Jane, Eve. Get out in the corridor. It's almost time."

Alive. He was alive. Relief soared through Jane as she helped Eve get to her feet. "The guards?"

"One down, I couldn't take time to break him. The other three are sure they're doing what Millet would want them to do." He whirled toward Roland. "Trobell wants to see you."

Roland's eyes were wide with shock. "Trobell killed — He called me."

"He lied. But then he has no conscience. That's why you chose him."

"My coins. Where are —"

"With Trobell." He started toward him. "He's protecting them with his body. Of course, it's his dead body. I think it —"

Roland raised his gun.

"No!" Eve grabbed his arm.

Roland backhanded her and she fell to the floor. He pointed the gun at her.

But Caleb had reached Roland, and his hand closed like a vise on the man's wrist.

Roland screamed as the gun fell from his hand.

Jane could see the dark blood spread under the skin of his wrist and lower arm as the blood vessels ruptured.

"Get in the corridor," Caleb said between his teeth. "Don't wait. He's . . . strong."

"You get out." Jane snatched up the gun that had fallen from Roland's hand. "This is no time to rely on all that damn blood stuff." She pointed the gun at Roland. Monster puppeteer. Send a photo, make a phone call, and destroy the lives of innocent people. Celine, Yvette, Mrs. Dalbrey. He would have shot Eve just now if Caleb hadn't stopped him. Millet would never have entered any of their lives if Roland hadn't been there pushing and prodding and destroying. "I think Caleb is right. I think you should join Trobell."

She shot him in the heart.

"That's the first time that you've totally agreed with me in this kind of circumstance," Caleb said as he reached down and helped Eve to her feet. "Eve, you really shouldn't make a habit of this. You can't protect the entire world."

"Shut up." She was swaying as she headed for the door. "Get Jane out of here. The shot . . . would someone hear it?"

"Not with that hysteria going on in the Offering Room. Come on, Jane." He supported Eve as he started down the corridor. They passed two guards who merely nodded at Caleb and ignored Eve and Jane. "Three more minutes," Caleb said.

"Three . . ." Eve moistened her cracked lips. "What are you talking about?"

He glanced at Jane. "You managed to do it?"

"Yes, when I braced myself against the wall of the tunnel." Her gaze was fixed in fascination on the arched door ahead of them.

The chanting was like nothing she had ever heard. It was hideous, rhythmic, and full of excitement.

Blasphemer.
Take her.
Kill her.
Tear her.

"One minute," he murmured as he stopped to the left of the arched opening. "We stay back here until the stampede starts, then we let them take us out of the temple."

The screaming rose in intensity, and Jane could see why. Millet was striding up the ramp into the Offering Room. He was dressed in black leather jeans and jacket, and he was arrogance personified.

How he loves it, Jane thought. His cheeks were flushed, his eyes shining, and every muscle in his body seemed electrified, fed by the screaming horde.

He had reached the altar.

He bowed to the mosaic of Judas, then turned to the crowd and raised his arms. "You want the Blasphemer. I heard you shouting your will. How much do you want her?"

The screams shook the room.

"Then I'll give her to you. I'll show her how you punish Blasphemers."

Another shout.

"You want her blood? I'll make her scream as I take her blood for you."

"Blood? I'm beginning to take this personally," Caleb murmured. "It brings back too many memories. I'm not sure I can wait for —"

The floor of the temple exploded, the stones heaved upward!

Millet was thrown to the ground.

The altar cracked and shifted to one side.

The audience was screaming but in terror now. Jumping from their seats, they bolted toward the ramp that led outside.

"Now!" Caleb pushed Jane and Eve through the archway into the midst of the panicky crowd. "Get Eve outside before the next explosion goes off. It's due in about six minutes."

Jane was already pulling Eve through the mob. "Just keep on your feet," she told her. "If we go down, we'll be trampled."

"You planted explosives?"

"Plastic. Small but powerful. In the passage beneath this Offering Room." She was fighting, shoving her way. Where was Caleb? She couldn't see him in this mob. Hell, she couldn't see anything but wild-eyed, panicky people on every side. "Joe planted another set on the outside near the front entrance to go off seven minutes later. We figured that we'd be out of the temple by that time."

"We hope," Eve said. "This crowd isn't

moving at top speed."

But Jane could see the entrance just ahead. "We'll make it."

Where was Caleb?

"Blood? I'm beginning to take this personally."

Shit.

They had reached the entrance.

"Eve!"

Thank God. It was Joe running toward them. He grabbed Eve's arm and was pulling her away from the temple. She was looking over her shoulder at Jane. "I'm fine. Get Caleb before the idiot blows himself up."

Jane turned and ran back into the temple. Two minutes.

It was easier going back. The crowd had thinned as the bulk of the people had reached the entrance. She reached the top of the ramp.

The Offering Room was deserted.

Except for Caleb.

Except for the man lying on the shattered altar.

"You shouldn't be here," Caleb said, without looking at her. "It's going to blow."

She came slowly toward him. "Eve called you an idiot. She's right." She looked down at Millet. His face was a mask of agony.

Blood was pouring out of his eyes and mouth. "Why?"

"I told you, I didn't like his talking about what he was going to do to you. I'm very fond of every drop of your blood. It bothered me that he was planning to be so careless with it." He bent over him, and said softly, "But now you know how much it hurts to misuse blood, don't you? The flow can twist and sting like a dagger. You like to use daggers, I understand,"

Millet's body arched. He screamed.

"We have to get out of here, Caleb," Jane said.

"I know. Pity. I only had a few minutes with him. But I made them count." He held out his hand. "Come here. I want him to see you."

She came to stand beside him.

"Look at her, Millet," Caleb said. "She beat you. You wanted to take her down. But she took away your power and all the glory you lived for," he added softly, "and she took away your life. You have heavy internal bleeding. You can't last for more than five minutes tops. You've lost everything."

She could see that Millet knew that he'd lost. But he was staring at her with desperation and hatred that would go with him to the end. "You didn't . . . beat me. I'm the chosen. Hadar will keep me alive. Judas will . . . triumph."

"Then let them do it. I think they've reached the end of their trail, too." She turned away. "Let's get out of here, Caleb. I won't be buried in here with this bastard."

"You won't. We have forty seconds." He took her hand and was running with her away from the altar and down the ramp. "Providing my watch is right."

"Now you worry about it."

"Dammit, get her out of here." Jock was running toward them up the ramp. "What the hell do you think you're doing? I couldn't believe it when Eve said Jane had gone back in. Run!"

"We *are* running."

The next instant they were out of the temple. Ten seconds later the ground shook as the wood and mortar of the temple blew.

"Down!" Caleb pushed her to the ground as concrete chips and slabs blasted through the air.

She couldn't breathe through the thick layer of dust and smoke from the blast. She was still coughing as she sat up a few minutes later.

"All right?" Caleb asked.

She nodded and gazed at the remains of the temple, which was now a mass of brown stone and broken pillars. "I don't know what it looked like before, but there's not much left now."

"When Joe and I planted the charge last night, it reminded both of us of a small acropolis," Jock said. "Hadar didn't have much originality." He stood up and held out his hand to her. "Let's go. Eve and Joe are with MacDuff and his men up in the mountains. I promised I'd bring you to her as soon as I found you. It's not safe down here. No one knows what's happened, and Millet's men are still a threat."

Jane could see what he meant. Men and women were milling about, dazed and disbelieving. It was hard to connect them with the screaming vultures who had been thirsting for her blood only minutes before.

"Give them a chance, and they'd still cut your heart out," Caleb said. "Go on with Gavin."

She nodded. "I have to see Eve. She wasn't good."

"She'll survive," Caleb said. "She was burning with fever but still on the attack." He turned away. "I'll see you later."

"Where are you going?"

"I have to make sure."

"Millet?" She looked at the mass of rubble that had been the temple. "How? And you said he'd be dead in five minutes."

"I have to be sure. I won't have him come back to haunt you." He smiled. "I'll find a way."

She watched him walk away before she turned back to Jock. "He probably will. Though he'd have to be a snake to wriggle through all that wreckage." But all she wanted was to be done with the place and the people who had screamed for her blood. "Let's go. I want to be with Eve."

"He's dead."

Jane looked up to see Caleb standing beside her. She had been at MacDuff's encampment for hours, and there had been no sign or call from Caleb. He was dirty and covered with dust and mortar, but he didn't look tired. His eyes glittered in the lanternlight and he had never appeared more strong and vibrantly alive.

"You found Millet? He bled to death?"

"I'm not sure." He smiled. "I hope he didn't. The explosion dislodged the Judas mosaic and it fell on the altar. I'd like him to know that his Judas crushed him."

However it had happened, Millet was dead. She had not realized that she would feel so relieved at the certainty. But Caleb had realized that she needed that final resolution and had given it to her. "Thank you."

He inclined his head. "I had to be sure, too. Are you okay?"

She nodded. "I'm fine." She got to her feet. "Maybe a little shell-shocked. Or maybe just plain shocked that it's all over."

"It is over." He checked his watch. "It's after midnight. April second."

"That's right, it is." Eight long, agonizing days that had seemed to go on forever. She ran her hand through her hair. "I've got to go check on Eve. Joe brought a doctor with them, and he gave her a shot, but they've been waiting for the air ambulance."

His gaze went to the west, where blue lights were piercing the darkness. "It's coming in now."

They watched the helicopter land.

"Gavin said Joe's taking her to a hospital in Damascus?"

"Yes, he doesn't want to take her home until he's sure she's stable. The doctor didn't like that fever."

Joe had Eve in his arms and was carefully lifting her into the aircraft. Strength. Gentleness. Tenderness. He had Eve back, and nothing else mattered.

"I believe he likes her a little." Caleb took Jane's elbow and led her toward the helicopter. "You'll want to go with her to the hospital. I'll call Venable and tell him to have someone get you hotel reservations near there in case they don't release her right away." He gave her a lift into the copter and stepped back. "Take care."

"You're not going?"

He shook his head. "Some of Millet's men took off into the desert after the big boom. I'm going after them." He smiled faintly. "It's going to be good hunting tonight." He saw the expression that flickered over her face. "You'll never like it, and you may never get used to it, but I can't change."

"I've never asked you to change. It's not my business."

"I don't agree. But right now, you're tired, upset, and on edge. You can't decide if I'm worth your time trying to decipher. So I think it's best that I leave you alone for a while. If I don't, you'll start pushing me away, and I'll react. Sometimes, as you might have noticed, my reactions aren't very civilized." He started to turn away. "Tell Eve that I hope she recovers quickly."

"Wait." She moistened her lips. There was no way of appealing to him on anything but practical reasons but she didn't want him walking away. "This isn't smart. Your damn hunting may be good tonight, but you're bound to be outnumbered."

"Oh, I won't be alone." He started across the rocky ground toward the encampment. "Jock Gavin and MacDuff are going hunting, too."

Eve didn't open her eyes until late the next afternoon.

"Hi," Jane said softly. "How do you feel?"

Eve smiled. "I don't know. How should I feel?"

"Groggy. The doctors here at the hospital gave you massive antibiotics and put you under to do a little repair work on your shoulder. It's going to be fine. Joe was here with you up until ten minutes ago. He went outside to take a call from Venable."

"Groggy sounds about right." Her hand tightened on Jane's. "What happened to Millet? I was pretty out of it last night."

"Millet and Roland are dead. The temple was blown to the stratosphere. A number of Millet's men managed to get away, but Caleb, Jock, and MacDuff went after them."

"Caleb found a few soul mates?" A faint smile touched Eve's lips. "I imagine Joe would have been right there with them if this wound of mine hadn't put a crimp in his plans."

"You're probably right. But Caleb doesn't

574

know the meaning of soul mate. He's out there all alone."

"Alone? I never thought about Caleb like that. But I guess you're right."

"Don't start feeling sorry for him. It's his choice." She changed the subject. "I'm not sure what happened to all those people who were clawing to get out of the temple before it blew. Some of them were probably able to get away if they had immediate transport. Some of them were rounded up by MacDuff's men and Venable's agents. As far as I'm concerned, they can rot in the desert." She paused. "But Venable thinks he managed to snag all the photos that Millet had taken at the Offerings from the wreckage. So they might get a surprise when they manage to get home. There are going to be some very unhappy people."

"And how do you feel?"

"Tired, grateful." She said, "Oh, yes, very grateful. I was scared up to the very end. I was afraid I'd lose you."

"You shouldn't have been afraid. You'll never lose me. Love doesn't work that way. It goes on forever."

"I understand the concept. I'm not at a stage right now where I can believe that. I'll have to work on it. I had enough trouble just with all this dream stuff."

"But you made it happen for us."

"Did I?" She leaned back in her chair. "I've been sitting here thinking about that. Did I do it, or did Caleb help it along? He said he couldn't influence dreams, but should I believe him?"

"What do you think?"

"He's an enigma. But I think I do believe him . . . tentatively." She gazed thoughtfully down at their joined hands. "But that leaves me with another puzzle."

"The Judas coins."

She nodded. "You told me you thought that the dreams all those years ago about the treasure that had the Judas coins had something to do with the recent dreams I had of Judas and those sacrifices."

"I said I didn't know but that it was possible."

"And I remember you said when you came to MacDuff's Run that you felt that it was right, and you had an odd feeling you were going to be part of what was happening there." She looked up at Eve's face. "You were part of it, a big part, Eve."

"Yes." She wrinkled her nose. "But I'd rather have had a more passive role."

"I don't think so. You were about to go out and search for trouble when Millet appeared on the scene."

"What are you getting at?"

"Caleb once asked me if I thought the reason I was having the Judas dreams had anything to do with those people at the Offerings. That I was being influenced by their vibes. I told him no way."

"You've changed your mind?"

She shrugged. "Those Offerings have been going on for centuries. Then out of the blue one person is influenced by them?"

Eve shrugged. "I don't know. So much sin, so much wickedness."

"But maybe it was time for them to end. Evil can't go on forever. Yet it seemed to be doing that. Judas's guilt spawned two thousand years of horror. I wish we knew more about him. Why? He must have loved Jesus at one time. How did it all go wrong? I know people can convince themselves of anything, but what would trigger that betrayal? And all those other deaths committed in the name of Judas . . ."

"And you were an instrument to stop them?"

"Who, me?" She shook her head. "I wouldn't presume. I was just there at the right place and the right time."

"And the right dream."

She chuckled. "Okay, the right dream. But I probably won't have any other dreams like those again. I hope I don't."

"But MacDuff hopes that you do."

"Too bad." She squeezed Eve's hand and stood up. "Now I've got to go find Joe and tell him that you're awake. My cell doesn't work in this hospital."

"Joe . . ." Eve was already closing her eyes. "Yes, I'm tired but I want to see Joe."

And Jane was already fading out of the picture as she usually did when Eve and Joe came together. That was okay. It was good that Eve had a rock like Joe in her life. Jane wouldn't have it any other way.

"Jane."

She looked back over her shoulder to see that Eve's eyes were open. "Do you need something?"

"The coins. What are you going to do with the coins?"

"I have no idea right now. First, I'm going to call Tischler and have him meet me in Atlanta and let him examine the coins as I promised. Providing he doesn't feel he has to get permission from the Israeli government."

"And if he does?"

"If he doesn't promise to keep it confidential, he'll never see those coins again. No more deaths. I'm not going to let this become a bone for everyone to fight over.

Even if I have to bury them in a cave as Hadar did."

"There's always the Vatican."

"They're having their own problems. But they may have the power we need. Though they may choose not to believe the coins are authentic. I don't know. I'll worry about that later." She opened the door. "All I want to do now is to go to the lake cottage with you and Joe and forget that any of this happened."

"You won't forget."

"I know," she said soberly. "Not ever. But maybe after a while it won't hurt as much. Being with you and Joe at the lake always makes all the bad things seem to go away."

"For me, too." Eve smiled. "Let's go home, Jane."

Jane got a call two minutes after she stepped out of the hospital. Lina Alsouk.

"I've been trying to reach you," Lina said impatiently. "The call didn't go through."

"I was at the hospital with Eve."

"How is she? The head nurse said she was doing well when I called an hour ago."

"She's awake now. Joe is with her." She paused. "I meant to phone and check on you, Lina. Things just seemed to get out of hand."

"So Jock told me. I'm fine, better all the time. MacDuff wouldn't let them take me to the hospital. I'm being coddled and nursed by MacDuff's people." She hesitated before adding grudgingly, "It's not too bad."

"I'm sure it's not. MacDuff is probably feeling guilty about your injury."

"He should feel guilty. He let them take Eve. Where is she going after she leaves the hospital?"

"Home to Atlanta."

There was a silence. "Then I'm going, too."

"What?"

"Oh, I won't get in her way. I'll just be around when she needs me."

"What are you talking about? Eve can take care of herself."

"She saved my life."

"She won't want you to feel obligated."

"She saved my life. I have to repay her."

"Lina, she won't want —"

"I don't care. I'm going to hang up now. I want you to call that Venable person and tell him that he has to ease my way into going to the U.S. And I thought perhaps you should tell Eve that she won't be alone." She hung up.

Jane shook her head as she hung up. This was a development she'd never thought would come to pass. What was Lina going to do? Camp out by the cottage with her AK-47? No, Lina was neither intrusive nor stupid. She'd keep a low profile whatever she did. Eve had evidently won Lina's affection as well as her passionate gratitude, and she would express it in her own time and her own way.

It wasn't really Jane's business. Since she felt she still owed Lina a debt, she would give Venable a call. Then she would deliver Lina's message to Eve and leave it at that.

Eve would be able to handle her . . . and the AK-47.

TWENTY-TWO

Lake Cottage
Atlanta, Georgia
Three weeks later

"I've invited Lina to dinner tomorrow night," Eve said. "I thought she'd like to try Joe's barbecue."

"I'm sure she will." Jane's pencil raced over the pad, sketching Eve's hand resting on the porch rail. Eve had wonderful hands, strong, beautifully shaped . . . "She's being surprisingly sociable."

Eve chuckled. "She's trying to be good, but she's hovering."

"She cares about you. I thought she was being pretty subtle . . . for Lina. At first, I thought she was going to ascribe to that old Chinese philosophy that because you saved her life, it belonged to you. But it's not that bad. She's even keeping herself busy helping Tischler with his work on the coins at Georgia Tech." She sighed in frustration as

582

she tossed the pencil down on the porch swing. "I can't do any more on this sketch. It's getting too dark. I'll have to finish tomorrow."

"No loss. For heaven's sake, you've done four sketches of me since you got home. And two of Joe."

"You're both good subjects." She flipped the sketchbook closed. "Character. Lots of character."

"And you're getting restless and bored." Eve smiled. "You were fine for the first week, but you're beginning to need more now."

"I'm not bored." She looked out at the lake that was dark ink instead of brilliant blue now that the sun was down. "But I bounced back quicker than I thought I would. I suppose I should get serious about going back to work. But I'm feeling lazy."

"No hurry. It's good to have you home." She yawned. "I think I'll turn in. I was up most of last night finishing the reconstruction on Ronnie. Joe's going to be late. He had some paperwork to do at the precinct. If you're still up, tell him about Lina and the barbecue."

"Okay." Jane frowned. "The doctor said you should take it easy for a few weeks."

"I'll take it easy tonight. Last night I had

something to do." She moved toward the door. "It will all come out the same in the end."

Jane shook her head as Eve disappeared into the house. Eve and Joe were both back at work and on their usual intense schedule, while she was only playing at a few sketches.

But Eve was right, there was no hurry. She was enjoying this lazy cocoon, which demanded nothing and made her feel as if she was more asleep than awake . . .

"But you're not enjoying it. You're just not ready to face the real world yet," Caleb said.

Caleb?

She glanced up at him. She should have been surprised to see him, but somehow she wasn't. It was absolutely right that he was with her in this place. The sky was so blue, it made her throat tighten with the sheer beauty of it, the earth smelled of grass and fresh rain and felt soft and cushiony against her naked body.

But the sky shouldn't be blue, the sun had gone down, and it was night now.

"It's all right," Caleb said softly. "Everything is as it should be. It's my place in Lucerne. I wanted you to see it."

He was naked, too, and beautiful. From wide muscular shoulders to slim hips and tight buttocks, he was all sleek sexual power. She had

584

never seen Caleb naked, so this couldn't be real. "A dream . . ."

"Whatever." He moved over her. "I want you. Hell, I'm going crazy. Is it okay with you?"

"I don't —" He entered her, and her nails bit into his naked shoulders. Okay? This was what she had wanted since she first met him. "Yes!"

Driving heat. Total madness.

His lips covered her own, smothering her scream as his hips moved and plunged. She could feel his heart pounding against her.

She had never felt this complete —

"Now!" he whispered.

She arched as the wild explosion of pleasure tore through her.

She couldn't breathe.

She wanted it to go on and on.

"It can you know," Caleb said. "Anytime, any way you want."

"Again . . ."

He cupped her face in his hands and looked down at her. "It's good, isn't it?" he asked hoarsely. "I knew it would be like this for us. And it's going to be so much better when it's the real thing. I can't wait to have my hands on you."

But his hands are on me, she thought in bewilderment. He was inside her, moving, causing this inferno of feeling.

"No." He kissed her gently. "Not yet. But won't it be fantastic?"

"Not yet? What was —"

"I hate to leave you. Damn, you feel so good around me."

But he was leaving her, and she was terribly lonely.

"I'm lonely, too. I've never felt like that before. Do you think it will always be like that for us now?" He smiled. "We'll have to see, won't we?"

"Why am I feeling like this? I don't want it. It scares me, Caleb."

"I didn't do it. I just set the scene. The emotion is all yours . . . and mine."

Set the scene . . .

She stiffened.

Not a dream!

Her eyes flew open and she sat bolt upright on the porch swing.

Full darkness, with no moonlight on the lake.

She was alone, and Eve had just gone into the house to go to bed.

She was alone.

It had to have been a dream.

A dream even though her breasts were swollen and her body was still aching and tingling? Hell, she still felt as if she were still having sex. Great, wonderful sex . . .

Dammit, no *way!*

She was *not* alone.

She jumped to her feet and strode over to the top of the porch steps. Her hands were clenched as she glared out into the woods and lakeside. No more cocoon. That was all ripped aside. This was stark, raw reality, where every day was a challenge and the greatest challenge of all might have just come back to torment her.

She had never felt more alive or wide-awake in her life. She felt as if her mind as well as her body had suddenly been jump-started. She wanted to murder him. Yet she was filled with a wild mixture of anger, excitement, eagerness, and anticipation.

"Caleb," she shouted into the night darkness. "Damn you, I know you're out there. How could you *do* that? You come here, or I'll come and get you!"

ABOUT THE AUTHOR

Iris Johansen is the *New York Times* best-selling author of *Blood Game, Deadlock, Quicksand, Pandora's Daughter, Dark Summer,* and more. She lives near Atlanta, Georgia.